THE DEVIL'S STAIN

Pamela Gordon Hoad

Mauve
Square
Publishing

*For my husband, Peter Hoad,
with thanks for his patience
and support*

Acknowledgements

I should like to record thanks to the friends who have encouraged and supported me during the process of writing and preparing *The Devil's Stain* for publication. I owe a particular debt of gratitude to Iona McGregor and Oliver Eade, who both read the draft and advised on innumerable matters – editorial, technical and computer wisdom. They introduced me to Mauve Square Publishing and I am pleased to join the authors whose writing has been supported through this facility. In particular Annaliese Matheron gave me enormous technological assistance in preparing for publication. I am also grateful to my son, Francis Gordon, for solving an annoying technical problem which I had defeated me.

Any errors are of course my own.

CONTENTS

Prologue:
November 1441: page 1

Part I: Chapters 1 – 9:
1422 – 39: page 3

Part II: Chapters 10 – 24:
1439-41 – page 99

Part III: Chapters 25 – 26:
November 1441: page 273

Prologue – November 1441

There is no window in my cell, only a high slit through which I can see a thread of sky no broader than a strand of my mother's embroidery wool, but I can hear the roar of the crowd and know the spectacle is nearly over. That ambitious man has been taken down from the gallows, still twitching with the last spasms of life while his body is hacked into pieces. I have been present on such an occasion; I recognise the sound of the mob's bloodlust, rising to a climax as the victim's belly is ripped open and his guts splatter the executioner's boots. They say the ecstasy enjoyed by on-lookers at such events fires their senses and they surge away from the scene avid for their own violent satisfaction. Wives and maidens alike will be taken this night and next summer babies will be born who were conceived in frenzy after the death of a misguided and terrified wretch.

The woman is to be burned at the stake, so once again the ignorant will celebrate and feel the frisson of righteous superiority over evil. They know no better. They have not felt the joy of encountering brilliant minds as they respond to new ideas; they have not lived amongst beauty and learned to appreciate, even if hazily, the cultured glories of artists and scholars. I should have been as they are, un-lettered, uninformed, modestly plying my trade, a humble archer or stonemason. Misfortune robbed me of that destiny but great good fortune brought me a different future – a future I embraced, over-confident in my paltry skill, and now have squandered.

My fate has still to be decided by the court but for one of my origins the common gibbet looms. I looked for straightforward answers to a conundrum beyond my imagining and became trammelled in a dark web of intrigue. If I pass sentence on myself, I have merited the harshest recompense for my foolishness. Two years ago I had achieved a reputation for integrity, the upholder of honesty

1

and justice, solver of mysteries, but I could not live up to the expectations others had of me and, worst of all, I betrayed what I hold dear. My ability to divine the truth has been shown to be feeble, my past success a matter of chance. Perhaps those neighbours, who thought I should be drowned, new-born, like an unwanted puppy, were right to pronounce me cursed and the attempts of kind-hearted patrons to free me from my destiny were doomed to prove futile. Often random circumstances have shaped my life but there have been occasions for choice, where the responsibility was wholly mine. The indictment makes no mention of my foulest sin, yet in the labyrinth of my tortured mind it is guilt for this which plagues me and I recognise the impossibility of atoning for it.

Something in my heart cries out defiance to this miserable conclusion but defiance is untimely. In the hours which I have left, before I am taken from this cell to view a sadly bizarre pageant and face my judges, it would be better for me to mull over all that has happened and ready myself to make full confession to the priest. Where should I begin? The chain of events which led me here did not start with that battered body on the ridge. It stretches back through the defining moments of boyhood to my unpropitious birth.

May God have mercy on those others who are suffering and protect all whom I have loved and failed.

Part I – 1422-1439

Chapter 1

It did not begin well. On the day that I was born news was brought to the Palace of Westminster that our well-loved King Harry, victor of Agincourt, had died in France of the flux. England's bold champion had been felled by an ignoble disease and a nine month old infant was his successor. If my mother screamed with her birth-pangs in the servants' garret, the sound would have been lost in the wailing that filled every nook of the rambling building. Years later she told me how she was left alone by her distracted companions and she was already weeping when she lifted me into her arms, grieving that I had come on so unlucky a day. Then she looked at my dappled face and began to keen more desperately – on her own account as well as mine.

I have grown so used to it that nowadays I am surprised when people stare at the first sight of that blotch which disfigures the left side of my face from forehead to chin. On a new-born baby's flushed features it must have looked frightening, a patch of rough, angrily purple skin standing out from the soft flesh around it. My mother has never admitted that she was tempted to throttle me then and there but she must have wondered how she could endure a lifetime of taunts from busybodies who saw my affliction as a sign of Heaven's disapproval – or worse. The pantryman's wife threatened to have me exposed on the banks of the Thames for gulls to peck my eyes and rats to gnaw my bones. According to the goodwife I had come on a day of mourning and I bore the Devil's stain to make clear there was evil incarnate in my puny existence. 'Satan stroked the brat in your womb,' she said to my mother, 'and left the imprint of his burning hand to remind you he has marked the boy as his own.'

My father dismissed such prophecies and sent the old wives packing. He knew he had the favour of his overlord, Humphrey, Duke of Gloucester, and others knew it too, so he could speak with authority. He had returned to England ten months before I was born and he was one of the Duke's personal guards. Several times he had fought in France with the King's army and my sister, Alys, had been born six years earlier after his triumphal return from the victory at Agincourt. Her face was free from any imperfection and her birth had been celebrated as if she was a symbol of all the glory King Harry and his stalwart archers had brought to his kingdom.

Despite the wretched coincidence of my natal day and the hideous blot I bore, I was baptised Henry in honour of England's lost warrior and was known forever as Harry. Thereafter, protected and nurtured by my parents and adored big sister, I lived the first years of my childhood in careless innocence, unaware of my unsightly blemish or the malice which could be hidden in baleful hearts. I have an early memory of my mother stroking my face and looking anxiously at my father while he put his arm round us both. I remember the gist of his words to this day. 'Neither Duke nor King will care a groat what he looks like if he can pull a bowstring and race across the battlefield like his Dad. He's spry and sturdy and he'll do us proud. He bears a king's name and will serve his lord well.' From then on I made that ambition my own.

When I was five or six the Duke decided to establish his household in a newly acquired manor at Greenwich and my mother and I moved from Westminster, downstream to the rackety old house beside the river. For a lively small boy who loved to run, this brought with it the attraction of open country spreading up the hill and along the ridge, from which you could see the crowded roofs and spires of the City of London in the distance. Later, when the Duke replaced the house he had inherited with his dazzling palace, the park

4

was enclosed with a wall but in my childhood most of the land was covered in scrub or wooded. It was a paradise where small boys could play at killing dragons or fighting the French, as many of our fathers were doing in earnest.

My mother was a seamstress, trained by my grandmother who had served the house of Lancaster before King Harry's father took the throne from the tyrant Richard. Mother became attached to the Duke Humphrey's entourage when she wed my father and her fine needlework was widely praised, not least, it seems, by the Duchess Jacqueline who arrived upon the scene shortly after my birth. Of course I knew nothing of the Duke's unsuccessful attempt to be named as Regent for his infant nephew after King Harry's death, or the controversy surrounding his marriage, but I was aware later that he took an army across the Narrow Sea to assert his new wife's claim to the County of Hainault. My father went with the troop but returned home after only six months from what had proved an abortive expedition.

My memories of my father and the encouragement he gave me must derive from that time, up to my seventh birthday, before he returned to France to fight with Duke John of Bedford. He had no doubts that I would follow in his footsteps and had me practising with a little bow, even at that age, proud that I had a true eye to hit the target. In competition I could beat boys older than me, which must have caused some annoyance, but I took my skill for granted and it did not give me particular pleasure. What I enjoyed was my ability to run, fast and sure-footed, up and down hill, over rough ground and, more heavily, through the marshy swamps that bordered the river. Long afterwards, in dreams I found myself running, the breeze lifting my untidy hair, before my feet started to clomp uselessly and I was mired, unable to advance further, when my nightmares began.

After my father's return from Hainault my mother was often ill and lost two babies, so it was Alys who had charge of me in the house. I had no understanding that my sister was a pretty maiden, of interest to older lads, but I worshipped her for the love she gave me and the merriness of her laugh. She devised games to amuse and instruct me, counting the nests in the rookery, identifying the types of ship which sailed past Greenwich on their way to the City or out to sea, sniffing the air to see if the fox had come near the chickens in the night. I owe whatever talent for observation I have to those childish games. Alys's competence was appreciated by others in the Duke's household and soon after a new chamberlain came to Greenwich, his wife, Dame Margery, took my sister to serve her daughters who were much the same age as my sister. This was an honour for a girl from so humble a background but at the time I resented the fact that she had less time to spend with me. Meanwhile I began to carry messages around the demesne, haul bundles of fresh rushes into the hall and glean in the fields at harvest time.

I realise now that the changes at Greenwich were linked to alterations in the Duke's personal life but that meant nothing to me then. He had spent little enough time at the manor since he owned it and, even when he was in England, affairs of state kept him mainly at Westminster or travelling the country. The first I heard of Lady Eleanor was from the grooms while I helped fork hay into the horses' troughs and I was agog at their sniggering remarks. I cannot swear to their exact words but can imagine how they went.

'She was one of Duchess Jacqueline's ladies, I've heard. Went to Hainault with her and the Duke but he was soon undressing Eleanor Cobham rather than her dressing his wife.'

'She's a dainty piece right enough. I'd unlace her stomacher if I got the chance. Have you seen the swell of her orbs above her bodice?'

'You filthy slob! It's not for you to think such things of a lady. She's daughter to a baron.'

6

'I'd fuck her, mate, if I had the chance. She's a whore just as much as the trollops in the bawdy house. Besides old Humphrey's got a stable of mares, if you get my meaning.'

'Best hold your tongue if you know what's good for you. I've heard the Duke's to marry her.'

'That'd be bigamy!'

'All you know! He's getting an annulment with the Pope's blessing. Duchess Jacqueline wasn't free to wed the Duke lawfully, it seems. It'll be Duchess Eleanor before too long, mark my words.'

'That's not fitting. She's got no royal blood. Duke Humphrey's uncle to the King.'

'Christ, you're a good one! Lusting after the Duke's doxy one minute and upholder of moral standards the next.'

Then they would have guffawed and made vulgar gestures.

If my mother and Alys heard similar comments they made no reference to them and were soon making their curtsies to the new Duchess, accepting her rule in the household without question. She brought some of her own followers with her to Greenwich and among that company was one who opened my mind and taught me understanding I would never otherwise have possessed. Another was a fellow I came to loathe.

*****

Thomas Chope was nearer my sister's age than mine but he attached himself to the gaggle of us younger boys and set himself to be our leader. My companions had learned to ignore my disfigurement and when they teasingly called me, 'Fiery Face', I didn't object because it sounded rather grand; but, when Thomas saw that I commanded some respect for my fleetness of foot and skill with the bow, he set himself to humble me and mocked my most obvious weakness.

'That the mark of Satan, you've got then, young'un?

7

I stared in surprise. 'Other people have birthmarks,' one of my friends said.

'Not like that, they don't. Only one way that got there. Old Nick put you in your ma's belly and left the stain of his red juices on your face.'

The full horror of what he was suggesting did not register at first and I must have gawped stupidly at him.

'Your ma lay with the Devil, that's what. While your dad was away, I expect. He's a soldier, isn't he?'

'He's back home now and he'll wallop you if he hears what you said.'

It was not me who threw down the challenge but one of my supporters. Thomas simply shrugged and moved aside.

I was deeply shaken by this incident but embarrassed too and I did not dare tell my father. It wasn't that I believed the vile falsehood but perhaps for the first time I realised how complicated life could be when foul accusations were made without foundation, sowing a seed of doubt where before there was absolute trust.

Thomas was cautious after that encounter and set about belittling me by more honest means, shooting his arrow further than my shorter stature would allow and trying to out-run me in our races. This he found more difficult and after puffing at my shoulder once or twice, unable to overtake, he tried to trip me with his foot but I guessed his intention and leapt clear. Then, seeing I was gullible, he began to frighten me by spinning yarns of wicked magicians and he forced me to stand on the stump of a felled oak tree, saying a wizard had poured poison onto the lichen growing on the bark. 'It'll seep through the soles of your boots and up your legs until it curdles your guts and you scream in agony.'

I was innocent enough to find this credible until my father found me shaking with terror and persuaded me to tell him what was so alarming. 'It's just a silly boy's joke,' he said and supressed a smile. 'You must ignore it. You'll get worse teasing than that before you're much older. You're a good lad, Harry, but you need to toughen up a bit. Give as much as you get given.' I snuggled against him and hoped his strength would feed into me.

*****

A few months later Duke Humphrey's older brother, John of Bedford, who was Protector of our child-king's interests in France, sent for reinforcements and, in response, a troop set out from Greenwich to journey once more across the Narrow Sea. Among them was my father. From then on Thomas Chope's bullying became more brazen and, although I struggled to be brave and developed some skill in repartee, I was frightened of his burgeoning muscles and the malice in his eyes. What made it worse was that I knew he sensed my fear. Thomas's scornful hounding gained him adherents who joined in baiting me, as if I was a chained and toothless bear who could growl but do no damage. I tried to avoid them but when we were sent to carry out some task together, it was misery to suffer their taunts. I longed to be old enough to be taken as an archer in the King's army and leave Greenwich but that could not happen for several years.

One day we boys were summoned to carry stores to a ship which was due to leave the wharf before the tide turned. While we were under the eye of the storekeeper there was no opportunity for mischief but I knew that when the task was done I would be wise to take to my heels if I was to avoid a ducking in the river. Another barge was drawing alongside and, realising it was the Duke's personal vessel, I lingered a moment to admire the fluttering pennants and sweeping oars. Its arrival may have prevented me receiving rougher treatment but the push on my back sent me sprawling in the mud by the gangplank and I raised my slime-caked face to look straight at the Duke himself as he came ashore. It was the nearest I had ever come to the King's first councillor and Protector of the Realm of England and he raised his eyebrows in amusement.

'I rarely receive such an obeisance,' he said, 'although I understand it is the custom for some Eastern people to lie prone before their rulers. Who are you, boy?'

'Harry Somers, your Grace.' Mud spluttered from my mouth as I spoke.

'Will Somers' son. You are fortunate in your father. He is one of my most trusted guards.' I bowed my head and muck slithered down my cheek but at his next question my chin shot up and I trembled. 'Who was it pushed you?'

'I slipped, your Grace,' I lied.

'No, Harry, you did not and you know it. I saw it all. Will you name your attacker?'

I shook my head.

'That is honourable but unnecessary. Guards, take that tall youth with the smirk on his face and give him a thrashing he will remember.'

The Duke moved on and I started to shiver, fearful of the revenge Thomas Chope would wreak after his beating, but a man in a long black robe, who disembarked behind his lord, came forward and put his hand on my filthy shoulder. 'Come with me, boy, and we'll clean you up before your mother has a fit at the sight of her son turned merman.' He took me by the hand and led me to one of the outhouses.

The servant charged with removing the worst of the mud did not look pleased but he was respectful towards the priest, as I took him to be, and my rescuer watched while my features were restored to their natural hues. I heard his intake of breath when he saw the purple crust emerge from its miring. 'Do they tease you, Harry, because of that mark?'

'Some call it the Devil's stain, father,' I said.

'They are ignorant,' he said and he touched the flaw on my face, which few were brave enough to do. 'But I have no claim to the designation you give me. It's true I took minor orders in my youth but I have never been ordained priest. I am a physician. My name is Doctor Swanwych.' As I stared at him uncertainly he laughed. 'Duke Humphrey is a man of learning and wide interests. He has invited a group of physicians to stay in his house to pursue our studies, men from Italy and well as England, under the leadership of his physician-in-chief, the eminent Gilbert Kymer.' He stood back to appraise my improved but still grimy person. 'You look a strong, bright boy and I have seen proof of your honesty. Would you like to help me set up my chamber? I could put a few coins in your pocket.'

I nodded in a mixture of awe and excitement and from then on I helped Doctor Swanwych with simple tasks of fetching and carrying two or three times a week. This did not endear me to Thomas Chope and his friends but, since he had attracted the Duke's unwelcome attention, they were cautious about showing open ill feeling towards me, although I knew they would store up their anger until they had an opportunity to vent it safely. The doctor told me a little about his studies, in words I could understand, and he read to me from a great book which he said contained the wisdom of past ages. I learned to recognise some of the symbols on the page as he pointed them out and he offered to teach me to read them but I saw no value in such instruction. Clerks and great men had need of literacy, not a common archer.

*****

The year of my tenth birthday began happily. Thomas had been sent with some other boys to serve in the Duke's house in the City, so I was free from the plague of anxiety which his presence brought me, and the stonemasons arrived at Greenwich to start building the great palace destined to replace the crumbling old house. This was a thrilling enterprise and I was soon helping to carry stones and hand up tools to the craftsmen as they erected wooden scaffolds from which to build the walls. I tried my hand with a chisel and hammer and found it satisfying to make rough patterns on a broken block which I was given for practice. For the first time I discovered a pastime that seemed as worthwhile as archery but I did not waver from my ambition to follow my father's occupation.

My mother was in better health but she began to fret about Alys who was now a well-developed maid of fifteen and needed to be married. There was no shortage of aspiring suitors, that was the trouble, but my sister was not disposed to make a choice and seemed to enjoy receiving the attentions of many rather than committing herself to one. Besides, Dame Margery was anxious to retain her services until her daughters were wed and only the eldest, Anne, was yet betrothed. In this situation my mother reluctantly conceded that the matter of Alys's future should await my father's return from across the Narrow Sea. We believed this might not be long delayed for we heard talk of negotiations for a truce and understood only occasional skirmishes were now taking place between the opposing forces – albeit a chance arrow in a skirmish can pierce a jerkin as effectively as one shot in a pitched battle.

Two days after Thomas and his cronies returned to Greenwich, grown taller and glowering with hostility, Duke Humphrey's messenger came to the chamberlain bearing news sent from France by John of Bedford. The Greenwich troop had been caught in an ambush by some discontented mercenaries and they had suffered many casualties: among the list of the Duke's men who had been killed in this futile encounter was that of William Somers.

My mother's grief was raw and I sobbed privately, away from the eyes of mocking onlookers, frustrated that I was too young to go to France to avenge his death. I see now that, however hard I tried to disguise my distress, my persecutors understood that I was vulnerable as never before, bereft of my father's protection and full of misery for my loss, but my pain was so great I was off my guard and Thomas Chope knew this.

He was crafty in his approach; no longer the crass tormenter, he had matured into a more skilled enemy. He offered sympathy and admired my rough attempts to carve, inviting me to show him what the builders were working on and, deceived by his friendliness, I was enthusiastic to oblige. One evening, after the workmen had left the site to visit the alehouse, we scrambled about on their scaffolds, inspecting the half-built architraves above doorways, fingering the jagged edges of unfinished capitals and swinging on beams which held the platforms on which the masons stood. I knew such behaviour was forbidden but my relief at finding Thomas so agreeable overcame my usual obedience to authority. Shouting with delight we climbed higher, catching hold of each other as we tried to gain the highest position, merrily wriggling free and trying to impede the pursuer. For those brief moments I forgot my desolation and gloried in this new companionship.

Suddenly I was ahead and out of reach. I glanced back and saw Thomas bent over and puffing. There was no way he could come near me as I soared towards the topmost rung of the scaffolding. At every level, horizontal bars bearing the platforms were secured by knotted ropes to vertical struts, which held the edifice upright, although on the highest bar there was only a single plank. I clambered up but the board was not firmly fixed and it shifted as I landed and slid sideways. At the same time the cord holding the framework on which my weight now rested creaked and slipped and, as I clutched vainly to steady myself, I was flung into the air. I give thanks to the Virgin that, as I tumbled, I bounced against the lower platforms which broke my fall and doubtless saved my life but I could find no hand-hold, no way of stopping my descent. As I landed among the

13

debris below the half-built wall, I heard the crack as my leg buckled under me and, before I lost consciousness I glimpsed the bizarre angle at which my foot was lying.

Chapter 2

The fall changed my life. Without the injury and its consequences I would have followed my father's footsteps to France as an archer and, like him, I might have found a nameless grave there. I could not have dreamed of the joyful opportunities which would be opened up for me by that misadventure – nor would I be imprisoned here awaiting a cruel death. That fall led me to mix with those far above my station and to tangle with affairs I would have done well to shun. Of course I could not know that then and at the time I refused to acknowledge the severity of my disablement. Timid as I was, taken into Doctor Swanwych's care, I shouted defiance at him when he first hinted at the consequences for my future.

'No! I can't be crippled! I can't.'

He crouched beside my pallet. 'You won't be, Harry. Listen to me. You will walk again but your leg has taken a bad battering. It is shattered in more than one place and it will not mend as perfectly as it was before. The bone-setter has done his best but he cannot work miracles.'

'What do you mean?'

'It's likely your left leg will be somewhat shorter than your right so your stride will not be as even as you'd wish but you'll manage well enough. Believe me.'

I understood. 'I will not run as I did.'

'I'm afraid not. You will learn to move about at speed, in your own way, but you will not run as you did.'

'What use is that? They'll never take me as a soldier!' My self-control gave way and I sobbed with fury. 'Why did you help me? I wish I had died.'

'It will take time to convince you, Harry, but you are a sensible lad and will rise above it. There's many a man who's had to change his plans against his will and overcome misfortune.'

15

I turned my face away from him, rejecting the comfort he offered, and thanked God that at least my father would not see my shame. I could think of nothing worse that could happen.

*****

My mother must have been half demented by my accident, following so soon after her widowhood, and she was in awe of the doctor. She agreed readily that I should remain in his chamber, where I had been carried with my broken bones and a lump the size of a duck's egg on my head. I do not think she could comprehend at all when he suggested that I fill the time of my enforced inaction by studying how to read those manuscripts which filled his shelves, amazed that he should think me capable of such a thing. I railed against the idea, unwilling to contemplate performing clerkly duties as an alternative to a life of action but it was several weeks before I gained reasonable mobility and, after a few days of enforced idleness, I grudgingly acquiesced in attempting to learn my letters.

The chaplain, who taught a handful of well-born boys at the manor, came in to help me and he was delighted by my progress but it gave me no pleasure at first, because it seemed an insidious device to reconcile me to my lot. To my surprise he was sensitive to my discomfort and asked me what I feared from gaining literacy and, although it was awkward, I felt I owed him an explanation.

'If I cannot be an archer, perhaps I could become a stonemason, shaping the blocks on the ground for those who could climb the ladders better than me. I think I could do that. I would not need to read.'

'You are afraid of learning your letters? Doctor Swanwych says you are bright and could do well for yourself.'

'I know there are boys from humble homes who study and go on to hold good positions but they become churchmen and I don't think...' I faltered and he laughed.

'You don't see your future in the priesthood?' I shook my head. 'There's no harm in that. I wish all clergy considered their suitability before they were ordained. But things are changing. There are many learned men who have not taken holy orders – like Doctor Swanwych himself. Our Duke is a great patron of learning and certainly does not expect all those who visit him to possess a tonsure. Have you not noticed the colourful gentlemen who come to Greenwich from foreign parts with books they have written or transcribed from the writers of antiquity?'

'But they are gentlemen, not low-born.'

'I assure you some of the fellows from Italy are of the basest origins but their minds are sharp and the Duke revels in their conversation. Carry on with your studies, Harry, and when you have learned all you can, then decide whether it is worthwhile'

It was cleverly contrived by Doctor Swanwych and the chaplain and their ploy succeeded. After several months, when I had gained skill with the pen, I was asked to help the physician with simple scribing and he began to refer to me as his assistant. About a year later the priest made even more extraordinary arrangements, obtaining consent for me to sit in on the lessons he gave to his distinguished pupils. These lads were older than me but because they were reluctant students I quickly levelled with them in understanding, although I said little in front of them due to my inferior position. The chaplain told me Humphrey of Gloucester himself had given permission for my attendance because he hoped the presence of an uneducated lad anxious to learn might act as a spur to his own natural son, Arthur, who was pre-eminent among the other boys. Despite my initial terror I found Arthur pleasant and unpretentious so I warmed to him while not daring to address him directly. As time went on I found pleasure in what I did and this studious guise began to fit me comfortably.

At the beginning of my new life I dreaded encountering Thomas Chope for I thought my injured leg was bound to be the butt of mockery. I knew he had been given a beating for his part in our exploit but he had in no way been blamed for my accident. How could he be? I knew with certainty that he had been out of reach on the rung below me when I fell and no one but me could be blamed for my over-confident ascent. Even so, at times when I was most morose and discontented, I found myself wondering whether he might not have prepared a trap for me, climbing the scaffold to loosen the rope ties before he suggested our prank. It would explain his unusual failure to keep pace with me as we reached the upper levels, held back by unprecedented breathlessness. I forced myself to set such useless thoughts aside, for the truth could not be known and to indulge aching suspicions would hurt me more than him.

Inevitably, in time, I did come face to face with Thomas and his supporters as I crossed the courtyard carrying an armful of scrolls for the doctor. I had dispensed with the use of a stick to aid my progress and was managing to cover the ground fairly rapidly with my uneven gait but when I saw them coming I muttered to myself that I must not be browbeaten. One of Thomas's underlings stepped in front of me and made the sign of the cross.

'Why it's Harry Somers. Christ have mercy! The devil's put his mark on you more strongly than before. He's warped your whole left side with his evil touch.'

'Stop your stupid wittering. It could as easily been me that fell.'

The younger boy kicked the ground awkwardly at this rebuff and I stared speechlessly at Thomas Chope who looked more nearly shame-faced than I had ever seen him. He nodded to me and led his acolytes away in silence, leaving me to berate myself for the unworthy mistrust I had entertained. Even so I remained wary and uncomfortable because the sympathy of one's enemy can be a humiliation worse than open hostility.

*****

Over the next two years, while I gained in knowledge and maturity, I knew my mother was pre-occupied with worries about my sister. It was galling to overhear a scullion chuckling about her as 'a flighty piece' and I clenched my fists in readiness to thump him before remembering that the strapping youth would soon get the better of me and he had no inkling I was within earshot. Besides, I had reason to fear that his description of Alys was well deserved and I was troubled by my own doubts about her behaviour. The first time she came to the doctor's chamber, with a message for me from my mother, I thought it simple ignorance on her part when she spoke to my master with doe-eyed impudence. I was relieved, although surprised, that he did not seem offended by her familiarity and on future occasions when she called on me he seemed happy to join us and parry her cheeky gibes with good humour. There were aspects of Doctor Swanwych's character I had not suspected and levity in front of a pretty face was one of them. His colleague physician in the household, Giovanni dei Signorelli, was more open in admiration for Alys's sprightly figure and comely face, praising her lavishly behind her back, but I concluded that, as an Italian, he knew no better.

More distressing for me was to catch sight of Alys walking at twilight across the courtyard with Thomas Chope and turning her head provocatively to give him a sideways glance which I feared held a wealth of undesirable meaning. At least it seemed likely that he had no particular hold on her affections, for she was seen to keep company with other young fellows, but that was two-edged consolation. I was embarrassed for my own sake as much as for hers and puzzled how Dame Margery could consider her a suitable tiring-maid for her younger daughter, Blanche, now the eldest was wed and gone from Greenwich. Before long, however, my mother and I were relieved of immediate concern for Alys's well-being for in my fourteenth year Blanche's betrothal was announced and she married soon thereafter. It was a prestigious marriage, to a young knight, Sir Hugh de Grey, whose lands lay not far away, at Danson. He was interested in the new learning, which the Duke patronised, and had come frequently to listen to visiting scholars but it seems his concentration was disturbed when he set eyes on the chamberlain's daughter. In midsummer the wedding took place with much ceremonious ribaldry and the bride insisted on taking her trusted maid with her to her new home. Alys was removed from our oversight and, I thought maliciously, we could not be blamed if she came to no good.

The following year I received momentous news when I was required, along with Doctor Swanwych, to attend the Duke in person. The doctor clearly knew the reason for our summons, and was grinning like the witless boy who sat on the church steps with his begging bowl, but he would tell me nothing while we waited in the ante-chamber. When we were admitted to the private audience I bowed as best I could and raised my head, full of embarrassment, to meet my overlord's impassive gaze.

'I recall meeting you, Harry Somers, when you assumed the role of mudlark in front of my barge.' I was astonished he could recall so trivial an incident and dared not reply but I had no need as he continued speaking. 'I understand you are proving a worthy scholar now you have become Doctor Swanwych's assistant and the chaplain says you have brought welcome solemnity to the studies of my son and his companions.'

I lowered my head, aware of the flush which must be disfiguring my features even more than usual. 'That is kind, my lord Duke,' I managed to say.

'In view of these good reports I have prevailed upon the doctor to borrow your services for a year or two. My son is to study at the University of Oxford, at Balliol College, where I myself attended. Arthur needs a trustworthy and intelligent companion to accompany him – not just a body-servant – one who will be free to attend the lectures at his side and worthy to imbibe the learning they will offer. I am satisfied, Harry Somers, that you are fit for this charge. Do you agree?'

Somehow I overcame my tongue-tied amazement and stuttered my gratitude, keeping tight hold on my emotions. It was not until we had been ushered from the chamber and I faced Doctor Swanwych alone that I burst into tears. He put his hand on my shoulder. 'What is it, Harry? Are you not pleased?'

'Overwhelmed, sir,' I said. 'It is your doing, isn't it?'

'I had little to do with it but give consent. Faced with the necessity of continuing his studies, young Arthur asked for you go with him. I suspect he hopes to pick your brains and ensure you do the more tedious work for him. But I am overjoyed for you. With the experience of Oxford behind you, nothing will impede your progress towards becoming a physician. If you so choose.'

My weeping began again as I nodded in dumbfounded silence.

In the weeks before I was due to leave Greenwich the chamberlain and his wife received a visit from Lady Blanche and her husband and my mother was overjoyed that Alys came with them. My mind was full of other thoughts and I had little interest in meeting my sister so I was annoyed rather than gratified when she asked to meet me privately. The building of the new palace was nearing completion, with most of it already occupied, so I suggested I show her some of the outworks still under construction in the park. She paid scant attention to my description of the work in hand, not even when I mentioned that Thomas Chope was now apprenticed as a carpenter and engaged in panelling doors and wainscots inside the palace. Her disinterest was reassuring but she seemed preoccupied and after I had prattled for some time she pulled me round to face her.

'Harry,' she said. 'Mother says you must act in our father's place and I must speak to you, though it seems foolish to trouble you with such worldly matters when your head is full of book learning. She says I must seek your consent to my marriage even though I am already hand-fasted.'

I stared at her stupidly, confirming all her doubts about the limits of my practical capacity. 'Who has asked for you? Is it someone at Danson?'

She looked tiresomely coy as she replied. 'Yes. I am greatly honoured. It is Sir Hugh's marshal who seeks my hand. He was widowed last year.'

'He is an older man?'

I must have sounded surprised and she giggled. 'Oh, indeed, but he's still hardy and hopes to breed with me. His late wife was barren. Master Gregory offers a comfortable home and a position of respect. You should offer congratulations not stand like a ninny staring. Mother is ecstatic. You do agree?'

'If mother is happy, certainly. But you do like this man, Alys, enough... enough...?'

She shook with laughter. 'What a prissy boy you are! Enough to lie with him, you mean? Have no fear about that.'

I felt myself blushing and quickly gave my consent, secretly welcoming the fact that Master Gregory's new bride would henceforth be entirely his responsibility. Then we were interrupted by the ebullient Dottore Giovanni dei Signorelli, who bowed low before my sister and kissed her hand in a most inappropriate manner, whereupon she became all simpering modesty and fluttering eyelashes. I may have been somewhat slow in coming to appreciate womankind on my own account but I knew what I considered unseemly.

*****

My studies at the university gave me a wealth of new understanding but I had learned from Doctor Swanwych that the schoolmen who taught there were not likely to embrace knowledge of the ancient classics, such as the Duke encouraged through his contacts in Italy. Perhaps the other experiences I gathered were more valuable, particularly the skill I gained in handling my engaging but wayward master. There were many occasions when my ingenuity was needed to extricate Arthur from ill-advised escapades, keeping watch for him when he visited places where he should not have been and diverting the attention of the proctors while he made good his escape. I became expert at detecting the approach of these guardians of the university's rules, noting the determined footfall of their boots on the cobbles, and I was acquainted with every back-alley and scalable fence in the city. The merry excitement I enjoyed at Oxford made my time there a happy one. Now I ponder the past, in this place of despair, I recall it was from Arthur that I first learned of his father's serious disagreements with the King's other principal adviser, Cardinal Beaufort.

At the end of the university terms I travelled on horseback – for I had learned to ride, after a fashion – with Arthur to other parts of England where his father owned houses and only once during the two years did we return to Greenwich. I was pleased to find my mother pretty well on that occasion and heard from her that Lady Blanche had been delivered safely of a son. As yet my sister had not obliged Sir Hugh's marshal in the same way and when she had accompanied her mistress on a visit to the Duke's palace she seemed uninhibited by the ties of matrimony. My mother said no more but Doctor Giovanni described to me, with some relish, how he had come upon her sitting demurely in the undergrowth with Thomas Chope. I was glad Alys had returned to Danson by the time I arrived home and confess I thought Master Gregory would be well justified in taking a strap to her if her knew of her behaviour.

A year later our studies at the university were complete and Arthur was to go to Calais to join his father, who was undertaking business for the King there, accompanied by the Duchess and a sizeable retinue. I was to return to Greenwich by easy stages, for I suffered from the saddle-soreness of a novice, and I was delighted when a messenger intercepted me with a request to spend the night at an inn in the City of London, before completing my journey, in order to sup with Doctor Swanwych who was staying there. He and I spent a joyful time, into the early hours, while I poured out much that I had learned at Oxford and he questioned me on my own views on many matters. He told me of a newcomer to the palace, another Italian, Tito Livio of Friuli, who was writing a life of the late King, Duke Humphrey's brother, and as the night wore on he shared with me some erotic verse which Antonio di Beccaria had written. Such a conversation between us was unprecedented and, as we talked and drank, I realised my old shyness was less pronounced, while the doctor treated me more as an aspiring equal than the youthful assistant I had been. It was very gratifying and I chuckled at the bawdy poem quite openly.

Next morning I awoke later than intended and the doctor had already left for the meeting he was to attend. My head was not as clear as I would wish for negotiating my way across London Bridge and through the unruly streets of Southwark, south of the river, so I took my time in setting out from the inn and it was mid-afternoon before the wall of Duke Humphrey's park came into view. As soon as the watchmen caught sight of me, the gate was flung open but, when the chamberlain himself approached, I knew something was wrong and dismounted.

'Harry, I thank the blessed saints you are come. Doctor Swanwych sent word you were to be expected. I wish I had a better greeting for you. Sit down on the bench, lad, for I have sorry news.'

I shook the weariness from my head. 'My mother?'

'She is frantic with grief and you must go to her.'

I saw him bite his lip and a wave of terror passed through me. 'What has happened?'

'My daughter, the Lady Blanche de Grey, came here two days ago, with her husband and little Hugh, her son. Duchess Eleanor said they might stay a week or two while she and the Duke are across the Narrow Sea.' He hesitated but I knew now where his ponderous words were taking me.

'My sister?'

'Mistress Alys accompanied her ladyship. Her husband remained at Danson with some commission from Sir Hugh.' Again he paused.

'What has happened?' I repeated.

He drew his gown across his chest and pulled himself upright as he took a deep breath. 'Mistress Alys was missing from the palace during last night and this morning a search was mounted throughout the park and outhouses. At length she was found, that is her body was found, in the wooded area upon the ridge. A foul deed has been done, Harry. Your sister has been barbarously murdered.'

Chapter 3

'The villain has been apprehended.'

I was so stricken by the news of my sister's death that it took me a moment to comprehend what the chamberlain had said. He saw my confusion and spoke more gently. 'Some fellow engaged on the building work in the park. There is irrefutable evidence. He will assuredly hang.' As I rose he patted my arm. 'You will go to your mother?'

'Soon. Where is my sister?'

'She is laid in the chapel now, in the chaplain's charge.'

'I should like to see her.' I think I said this to buy time before I had to face my distraught mother but I also knew I owed Alys personal tribute for the happiness she gave me in childhood. Perhaps I already felt a twinge of that guilt, mixed with anger towards her, which oppressed me in the next few days – guilt for the ease with which I had shrugged off concern for my wilful sister. The chamberlain clearly approved my choice and summoned a groom to lead away my horse while I crossed the courtyard to the chapel.

There were two men beside the bier which stood in front of a side altar and they looked round quickly as I stepped across the threshold onto the tiled floor. The tapers on the gilded candelabrum fluttered in the draught, flecking the painted screen with light. The chaplain raised his hand in blessing but Doctor Giovanni dei Signorelli hurried forward, flinging wide his arms, and clasped me to his chest. 'Mio povero amico,' he said. 'I am so sorry.' He seemed much distressed.

I knelt with them in prayer below the chancel steps before turning back to the open coffin. A heavy sheet had been laid over my sister and only her face was visible but the sight of her battered features was shocking and I gasped. 'He is monster,' the Italian said. 'Savage beast.'

I struggled to stay calm. 'She was raped?'

26

'Brutally,' the chaplain answered. 'May God have mercy on her soul. She died unshriven.' He moved away from the bier, wagging his head, and fell to his knees.

I ignored the note of rebuke in his voice and took hold of the covering which shrouded her body. 'It is ugly, Harry.' Giovanni sought to restrain me but I shook my head and lifted the cloth.

I swallowed the bile in my mouth and tried to control the trembling in my legs but I could not stop my tears. Her ripped and bloodied dress I had expected but not the nature of the way she died. 'She was stabbed,' I said foolishly. 'I thought her strangled.'

'Seven times he plunged the knife into her body and used it to mutilate her private parts.' The doctor's voice was steady and his English impeccable as the chaplain crossed himself. 'There was much hate in him.'

'Who found her in the wood?'

'Every man here joined the search and it was a forester who found her, lying in beech mast beneath the old trees on the hill. I was not far away, scouring through bracken and brambles, when he called.' He glanced for a moment at his scratched hands before thrusting them into his gown. 'It was most horrible to see.'

I was grateful Giovanni had been quickly on the scene to treat Alys with delicacy and respect because I knew that for many of the men on the demesne her fate would be the subject of ribald jests. I could not bring myself to kiss her ruined face but I raised her right hand and brought it to my lips in farewell. Her fingertips were muddy and I imagined them groping helplessly on the earth while her attacker abused her. I detached a cluster of darkened threads from beneath her nails and, when I replaced the covering and lifted my head, the Italian was looking at me intently.

'You are holding a remnant of the proof,' he said. 'When we found her she was gripping a piece of woollen cloth. It matched a tear in the scoundrel's jerkin. The sheriff has taken it, with our statements.'

'The sheriff was called? To the Duke's palace?'

The chaplain had re-joined us. 'The Duke will undoubtedly wish to pronounce judgement as the atrocity occurred on his land but the sheriff was known to be nearby, in Deptford, so he could gather evidence without delaying matters. Your sister can be laid to rest without waiting for the Duke's return. If you will excuse me, I will set in hand the necessary arrangements.' Once more he raised his hand in blessing.

'The women will come to prepare her,' Giovanni said, after the priest had gone, and then he paused, twisting the ties of his gown. 'I wondered if you would permit me... That is, I could make her more seemly before they see her. Down below, you understand.'

I am ashamed to say that my first thought was that he would gain some lewd satisfaction from handling her privates and he read my thoughts. 'I am physician, Harry. As you will be. My trade is with the living but the dead should have their dignity.'

At his gentle words my fragile self-control gave way and I sobbed. He put his arm round my shoulders and took a phial from inside his robe. 'You will be going to your mother now? Give her a few drops of the potion. It will help her sleep. Perhaps you should take some too.' He held me at arms' length and a puzzled expression came into his eyes. 'You know who the villain is, Harry?'

I shrugged. 'Some workman, they said. She was known to be over-familiar with many.'

'It is Thomas Chope they have arrested. Maybe that does not surprise you. But do not judge Mistress Alys too harshly. I do not think she was as some make out and she brought merriment wherever she went. Come, I will take you to your mother. She needs your comfort.'

I let myself be led away, my head spinning from all I had heard, too numb to know whether I was surprised or not.

*****

My mother was sitting on a stool in the ante-room to the Duchess's chamber, surrounded by her fellow servants. The cellarer's wife, whom she had known from girlhood, knelt by her feet, clasping her hands, and round them twittered a bevy of weeping maids. I saw at once that my mother's cheeks were dry and her face blank of expression, as if what she contemplated with her inner eye was too grotesque to acknowledge. When I entered the room a susurration of grief rose from the attendants but they fell back from my path and I was grateful that my mother's old friend clapped her hands to dismiss them. 'She will say nothing, Harry,' the goodwife said. 'It is as if she has turned to stone.'

I pressed her hand as she turned to leave, then I knelt beside my mother. 'They were troubling you with their wailing, I expect. Would you like me just to sit quietly at your side?'

There was no response but after a few minutes of silence I reached up to touch her face and felt the tremor that passed through her body. Her mouth trembled and she focused her eyes on me. 'Harry? You have come?'

'Of course, mother. You still have your son.'

She reached out to grasp my arm. 'And I am so proud of him. So proud. But pride is sinful and perhaps it is because of this that such terrible shame is come upon me.'

I stroked her brow, brushing back a few hairs that had escaped from her coif. 'The shame is not yours,' I said.

'She was my daughter. The shame is mine. You know what she was?'

29

'I know what some have said of her but I don't know the truth. If she was done to death so cruelly it is more likely she was defending her virtue than making free with her favours.' My words surprised me even as I spoke them, trying to offer my poor mother some comfort, for there was a logic to what I said that had not occurred to me previously.

My mother clutched me in her arms. 'Is it possible? They say it was Thomas Chope and I think he had been after her since before she moved from Greenwich. She was always too free and easy, even when she came here as a married woman. Could she have teased him once too often? Did he force her when she refused? Oh, tell me that is possible, Harry!'

I did not entirely follow my mother's reasoning but it seemed to revive her spirit. 'It may be so,' I said. 'We are unlikely ever to know the truth but that could explain what happened.'

'She had a fondness for him, I'm sure of that. She hinted it to me once but there were so many stories of her flirtatious ways, I did not want to hear. Then Sir Hugh's marshal asked for her and I thought that the end of the matter. I was wrong. She was much at fault if she encouraged Thomas Chope after she married but if she died resisting him, I am a little consoled.' I watched in wonder as, with this solace, my mother's tears began to flow.

I stayed with her while she wept and until she had calmed herself. Then I gave her a beaker of small ale and added three drops of Giovanni's medicine. I asked the cellarer's wife to get her to bed, with my promise to return in the morning, and I left the Duchess's apartments wrung out with weariness and ready to seek my own pallet.

*****

It was to be some time before I could rest for when I descended to the courtyard I found two pages waiting with

30

messages for me. One came from the Duke's chief warder conveying the news that the prisoner had asked if I would visit him, for he wished most earnestly to speak to me, and indicating that the chamberlain had granted permission for the visit if I was willing to make it. I was disgusted by Thomas's Chope's effrontery and dismissed his request brusquely. The other message I did not relish either but there was no question of disobeying that command and so I presented myself immediately at the chamberlain's lodgings.

A small maid-servant, no more than twelve or thirteen years old, was waiting to escort me and she showed me into a comfortably furnished room with drapes on the walls, a turkey carpet covering the heavy table and two carved chairs, one each side of the hearth. In one chair sat Dame Margery, upright and thin-lipped, while in the other was a beautiful young woman who seemed greatly distressed, dabbing frequently at her eyes with a sodden kerchief. Although I scarcely recognised her I knew this must be Lady Blanche de Grey and I was touched that she should so mourn the death of her attendant. The little maid presented me and moved back to stand in the shadows beside the door.

'We are sorry at your loss, Master Somers. You may take that stool.' I bowed and thanked the chamberlain's wife but I was bewildered by being so addressed, registering in surprise how differently my position in the household was now viewed following my sojourn at Oxford.

'Mistress Alys was dear to me, Master Somers, and I am much disturbed by her loss.' Lady Blanche's voice quavered and I saw her grip the arms of her chair to steady herself.

'I am grateful, my lady. She was fortunate to serve you.'

'Sir Hugh has ridden to Danson to inform your good-brother of the tragedy. They are detained overnight by some business but will be here at first light.'

It took me a moment to realise she was speaking of her husband's marshal, for I had never thought of him as my good-brother. 'I am very grateful to Sir Hugh.'

'Oh, he is dreadfully concerned, knowing how much I valued Alys, and the marshal has served his family since his father's day.' Her fingers scrabbled at the beads around her neck. 'That such a bitter misfortune should afflict us all!'

'It is well that you are here, Master Somers, to bring your mother consolation at such a time.'

Dame Margery's astringent tones contrasted with her daughter's passion and it was Lady Blanche who brought these pleasantries to an end, rising from her chair so unexpectedly that I kicked the stool in my haste to stand as she did. 'Foul things are being said of Alys and I am wrenched apart by the humiliation of it.'

I misunderstood her words. 'My lady, no one could attribute blame to you for your servant's waywardness.'

'No, no, the humiliation is for her and she did not deserve it. I wished to tell you she was a loyal and diligent maid, whose service I treasured. She was merry and open, perhaps too open, but I know she meant no harm. Whatever you may hear, do not credit the calumny. I wished to tell you this. There is much that could be said but it cannot be.' She had started to rip the lace on her kerchief and I was disconcerted by her vehemence but it occurred to me that she might be with child again, and therefore inclined to be irrational in her feelings; I was pleased with my medical insight.

As if reading my mind, Dame Margery rose. 'Master Somers, we are obliged to you for waiting on us. As you can see my daughter is greatly upset by what has happened. You will excuse her as she shares your pain.'

Lady Blanche rushed forward at her mother's words and fixed me with her cornflower-blue eyes. 'Nothing can justify this barbarity. The rogue who did this... it cannot be allowed... if I were to...'

32

Her words had become incoherent and as Dame Margery signalled to the maid-servant by the door she commanded her daughter to be silent. 'Master Somers,' she added, causing me to turn on the threshold, 'the villain must be hanged without delay. I pray you see to it.'

I bowed. 'I will make it my duty to see that justice is done, madam,' I said – and to this day I do not know what put those words into my mouth.

The little girl followed me from the room, closing the door behind us, and then she leaned against the lintel and grinned up at me most inappropriately.

*****

I was troubled by this strange encounter with Dame Margery and her daughter and annoyed by the pertness of the ill-bred maid. More unforgivably I was irritated with Alys for bringing so much hurt to those who cared for her. Comments about her behaviour were inconsistent but it seemed clear she had teased and dissembled, charming many but provoking at least one to uncontrollable lust. I was inexperienced in such matters but I pondered whether there was a point at which winsome insouciance became incitement and, although I did not want to think badly of my sister, I could not hold her to be blameless. My ignorant exasperation reminded me of Thomas Chope, who would justly hang for what he had done, and it came to me that it was my Christian duty to visit him as he requested, however unpleasant it might prove.

His cell was at the base of the warden's tower in a room used for storage when there was no miscreant awaiting justice from the Duke. A faint smell of flour drifted from the floor as the door was unlocked and a high window-slit cast a beam of light on empty sacks piled by the wall. I held my taper in front of me as my eyes adjusted to the gloom. Thomas was sitting in a corner with one ankle manacled to a heavy ring fixed on the wall. He had clearly been manhandled by his captors for his face was bruised, with a trickle of blood visible on his temple; he was without a tunic and his shirt was ripped. He looked up at once as the door hinges creaked and he struggled to his feet.

'I didn't think you'd come, Harry. I'm grateful.' As he spoke I noted that one of his teeth was broken and his lip torn.

'Why do you want to see me?' I was already regretting my decision.

'I want to make my confession to you.'

'What nonsense! I'm not a priest. You can make your confession to the chaplain – and the sheriff too.' I turned back to the door, ready to rattle the handle for it to be unlocked.

'Not for the murder. Not for what happened to Alys. For what I did to you.'

'What on earth are you talking about?' But I knew. Even as I heard his words, I knew and I stood still.

'When you fell, all those years ago. It was my doing. I cut half through the ropes at the top of the scaffold before we climbed. I didn't care if you were killed. I thought of you then as the devil's spawn. When I was a boy I hated you for what you looked like.'

'So has something changed your mind? I channelled my anger into sarcasm.

'Alys changed my mind. She was proud of you. She loved you.'

'So you murdered her because she loved the devil's spawn. Is that what you're saying?'

'No! Listen to me. I was sorry for what I did to you but I'd never have been brave enough to tell you – until this happened. Now you're the only chance I've got.'

'I'm not staying to listen to this rubbish.' I moved back to the door.

With a clatter of the chain he fell to his knees and I saw the grimace of pain on his face as he came down awkwardly, twisting his shackled foot. 'You've always been honourable. I've known that since you refused to snitch on me to the Duke when I pushed you in the mud. Now you're educated too. You're the only one could help me. That's why I needed to tell you how it was my fault you fell and smashed your leg. I can't hide anything from you if I'm to beg for your help.'

'What the hell are you talking about?'

'Please, Harry, please. Find the man that did this to Alys. For her sake, not just mine.'

I rattled the door furiously. 'I will not listen to this.'

As the warder slid back the bolts, Thomas made a final desperate appeal, grovelling at my feet. 'I loved her and would never have harmed her, believe me. By the blood of our saviour Christ and his blessed mother, I swear I did not kill your sister.'

I thrust myself through the door, shouldering aside the attendant, and put my hands to my ears to drown out the shouts which echoed along the passage behind me.

Chapter 4

The little sleep I had that night was fitful and disturbed. The horror of Alys's murder was reason enough to keep me from rest but it was aggravated by the outpourings I had heard from others. My mother's agony was inevitable but the extremity of Lady Blanche's grief, even if she were with child, puzzled me and Thomas Chope's absurd protestation was bewildering. Did he think me such a dolt that I would bring ridicule on myself by trying to show his innocence? Was that his intention? Would it give him satisfaction, as he faced the gallows, to know I was once more the subject of mockery? I tossed about on my pallet and was glad Doctor Swanwych had not yet returned to Greenwich so I was alone in his chambers to struggle with these unanswerable questions.

While I lay awake in the early hours a wave of panic came over me and I remembered a story from one of the ancient works the doctor had read in the Duke's library: of a young man pursued by furies because of a murder he had committed. Was that to be my fate – hounded by demons that would never let me escape? Thwarted in pursuing the dignified profession I had chosen by my sister's legacy? Then my befuddled mind told me it was Thomas not me who merited that doom and I dragged myself out of bed to walk up and down the room, attempting to calm the hammering of my heart. I poured a goblet of ale, slopping it over my fingers, and opened my purse to find Giovanni's potion which might bring me respite. Nestling in a corner, caught on the rough lining of the pouch, was the knot of dirty threads I had taken from my sister's hand. I took it out and gazed at it stupidly.

I thought I was deluded at first as I looked at the tangled wool in my wet palm but then I rubbed at it, splashing more ale over my fingers, until finally I plunged it into the goblet and scrubbed at it with my nails. The mud which coated the threads drifted into the liquid and the ale was too weak to replace it with a new dye. Excitedly I dried the strands on my sheet and smoothed them out on my bolster, feeling their texture with care. This was not coarse wool from a workman's buff-coloured tunic: it came from some finer material and its hue was richer, almost golden. Did Thomas Chope possess such a garment? Of course he might, I told myself, for he could well have acquired the cast-off of some superior servant, but it would be easy to confirm what sort of torn jerkin had been taken from him and handed to the sheriff. I separated the threads and replaced two or three in my purse but the others I rolled into a ball and secreted behind some dusty bottles in the doctor's cupboard. Instinct was telling me to be cautious.

*****

I made an early call on my mother in the morning and was relieved to find her already at her needlework which she said was soothing to her spirit. She asked me to see that Alys was laid to rest as soon as possible and I promised to see that it was done that day, provided the widower, Gregory, agreed. Sir Hugh and his marshal were expected within the hour and, with some misgivings, I went to greet them at the gatehouse.

Sir Hugh rode ahead of his officer, all panache and self-importance I thought: a stocky, good-looking young man, handsomely dressed in blue velvet. He leapt with agility from his horse and offered me courteous condolences without staring at my disfigurement, which gave me a favourable opinion of him. My good-brother was at least two decades older than his master and of contrasting appearance: tall, although meagre in build, gaunt of face and wearing a black robe. When the groom helped him dismount the furrows beside his mouth pulled down its corners so strongly that I doubted if he had ever learned to smile. His

37

sour expression did not change at the sight of me but I was not convinced this reflected bad manners rather than indifference.

'Master Gregory, we share grief at the circumstances of our meeting.' He grunted. 'Would you wish to see your wife? She is laid in the chapel.'

'Her corpse you mean. I hear it is badly mauled. I do not wish to remember her in her state of shame. I shall not view her remains.'

I bridled at this description of Alys but was not surprised that such an austere man would judge his murdered wife with severity. A woman raped on a hillside by night, when she should have been with her mistress inside the palace, was bound to be held guilty and her husband may well have heard gossip about her errant ways.

'I can be ill spared from Sir Hugh's house at Danson,' Gregory said. 'I have ceremonies to arrange for a visit by the Lord Archbishop next week. I should like the obsequies to be conducted so I can return there before dark.'

'There is no impediment,' I replied, matching his pomposity. 'The chamberlain hopes you will dine with him at twelve and the burial can take place soon after.'

'Why don't we go to see where the deed took place?'

Sir Hugh's enthusiasm seemed misplaced but it was more straightforward to handle than his marshal's self-containment and I too was anxious to see the scene of my sister's death. 'If you would care to take a cup of wine, I will arrange an escort and have the forester who found Alys summoned to attend us. Would you wish to ride up the hill?'

'Capital,' the young knight said. 'We'll walk. I've a fancy to stretch my legs. That is if you can manage it, Master Somers.'

When we set out Sir Hugh marched ahead, chattering with the chamberlain who insisted on accompanying us, while I hobbled at my fastest rate to keep pace with Gregory's long stride. I was grateful that he did not choose to converse. Although I did not like him I felt sorry that a man of his rigid outlook and unimpeachable honour should be put in this appalling position, for he had no reserves of compassion on which to draw. The forester joined us at the edge of the wood and led us, ankle deep in mouldering leaves, to a little clearing beneath tall beeches. We stood, peering down at what might have been a slight hollow in the ground-cover, a shape in which a person – two people – might have lain. Imagination was not needed to spot the faint darkness along one side of the depression and I remembered there had been no rain for the last forty-eight hours which could have washed away that tell-tale sign.

I swallowed hard as I pointed to the stain. 'That is my sister's blood.'

Gregory drew his gown closer round him and the slight colour which had come into his cheeks on the ascent vanished. 'This is horrible. I wish to see no more.'

Sir Hugh had stepped aside and I saw him clutch his stomach as if a spasm was curdling his guts but he straightened quickly and kicked the leaves nonchalantly. 'Hullo, what's this?' he said and bent down to burrow his fingers into the decaying vegetation. 'It's a ring.'

Gregory had turned to leave the wood but at these words he span round angrily. 'My wife's ring?'

'I shouldn't think so. It's no more than a twist of wire, a cast-out fragment from the forge perhaps.' Sir Hugh held it out to show me and I noted that it looked sticky on the inside.

'My wife's wedding band was of pure gold from the goldsmiths of Cheapside in the City.'

'And it was still on my sister's marriage finger when I kissed her rigid hand in the chapel yesterday.' I was glad to give the marshal that comfort for I suspected that underneath his impassive exterior he was torn apart by emotion.

'I thank God,' he said.

39

'The trinket is nothing to do with her then. I fancy this has been a trysting point for others from the palace, nicely concealed as it is. I doubt many will come here from now on.' Sir Hugh raised his hand and the base metal caught the sunlight briefly before he hurled the ring down towards the roots of the largest tree.

Gregory walked rapidly by his master's side as we descended the hill and I followed with the chamberlain who had stayed silent throughout the visit. When the pair in front of us moved out of earshot I took the opportunity to draw him into conversation.

'My good-brother is deeply upset', I said.

'A sorry business for everyone.'

'Seeing that blood-stain on the ground, I was wondering, sir, if the accused's jerkin was also covered in gore.'

He snorted. 'It was so filthy and discoloured I did not notice. Doubtless the sheriff will have had it examined.'

'It was Thomas's working tunic, I suppose?' I tried to sound as casual as I could.

'I'd be surprised if he had another. It was an old woollen thing, tattered and scruffy, such as workmen customarily wear.'

I did not dare enquire further, for fear my interest should seem unusual, but I was uneasy at what I had heard.

*****

The chaplain said Mass for Alys's troubled soul and we laid her to rest in the graveyard outside the palace walls. Immediately afterwards Gregory rode off to return to Danson. He had not spoken to my mother on his brief visit, which I thought lacking in courtesy, but she was probably relieved to be spared the encounter. Sir Hugh and his father-in-law accompanied me back through the palace gates but the younger man excused himself, to re-join Lady Blanche, and I was anxious to renew my conversation with the chamberlain.

'You gave me permission to call on the prisoner, sir, when he requested it yesterday. Would you object if I were to do so again?'

His thick eyebrows beetled towards each other as he frowned. 'Why should you wish to see him, after what he has done? '

'It's true I left him angrily when I saw him,' I said. 'But now I've reflected over my sister's grave and heard the blessed words the chaplain repeated, I feel it is my duty to hear him out. Before he faces the judgement of his peers and of God.'

I thought I must sound horribly sanctimonious but the chamberlain was persuaded by my humility. He patted my arm. 'You're a good fellow, Harry. Few in your situation would show such loving kindness. If you wish it, you may certainly see him but don't let him distress you. I'll send word to the warder to admit you whenever you choose to go.'

I bowed my head in gratitude but was glad that he excused himself to go to his study where, he explained, numerous documents awaited his attention. I needed time to think before I was ready to visit Thomas Chope and I wished Doctor Swanwych had returned to Greenwich, so I could share with him the doubts growing in my mind. Unfortunately for me my master had sent a message saying he had been summoned to Oxford by Gilbert Kymer, the Duke's principal physician, and would be away several days; he bade me be at home in his chambers and have free use of his books and apparatus. Alas, I thought, it was his wisdom I needed not these secondary aides. I considered confiding in Giovanni dei Signorelli but did not feel I knew him well enough to place such trust in him. Besides, I remembered how he had ogled my sister and I decided I could not count on him giving dispassionate advice. I decided that the only suitable person to consult about my misgivings would be the chaplain so I turned into the chapel and knelt in front of the rood screen until he appeared. He greeted me in a kindly manner.

'You are right to pray for your wretched sister, Harry, for she succumbed to the sin of Eve, as frail women are prone to do. Her fate in purgatory is likely to be dire and only our prayers can lessen the torments she will face there.'

I contained the fury that his derogatory words about Alys aroused, so great was my need for the priest's guidance, and I said 'Amen' after he prayed in patronising terms for her soul. Then I moved with him to the stone bench built out from the wall, for the infirm to sit on during services, and when we were seated I told him of my wish for his counsel. I explained my puzzlement concerning the prisoner's jerkin which had been taken as evidence but appeared not to match the threads in Alys's hand.

He put the tips of his fingers together and pressed his mouth against them, pursing his lips. 'I think you could be mistaken, Harry,' he said, looking up after a pause. 'A grimy workman's garment might have all kinds of dyes spilt on it. The painters may have splashed it; oil used to treat the woodwork that Chope shaped may have soaked into it. Only a small piece of the material may have been stained the colour you describe and it is fortuitous that your sister grasped it.'

'A coincidence then?' I attempted to keep the disappointment from my voice.

'Just that, my lad. You are being sorely tested by the circumstances of Alys's death but I advise you not to rake over the evidence in your head. It will be examined in full by the sheriff and put in front of the Duke and twelve jurymen. They are the proper ones to give judgement and you may have faith in the process of the law. Have faith in God to direct them so that they discern the truth.'

I shut my eyes forcing back the response I wished I could make. 'Pray with me, Father, that I may be strengthened to do as you recommend for I am less clear-headed than I would wish at this time.' Once more I thought my pious sentiments must sound insincere but the chaplain fell to his knees at my side and thanked the Blessed Virgin for leading me towards holy obedience.

Again I murmured 'Amen' but I remained utterly unconvinced by his explanation for the discrepancy, plausible though it might be, and I found it troubling that he seemed unwilling to contemplate any other possibility. At least, I thought, consoling myself, if Thomas's trial was to await the Duke's return, there was no urgency and I could delay any action until I had availed myself of Doctor Swanwych's reliable counsel. I returned to his chamber and buried my head in a tome of medical knowledge, translated into Latin from the Arabic, concentrating fiercely to put all other concerns out of my head, until I fell forward over the table in welcome sleep.

*****

Next morning, after checking that my mother remained in reasonable spirits, I made my way down the spiral stairs from the servants' quarters in order to re-cross the courtyard. Just above the ground floor I needed to compress myself into a niche to permit the passage of a maid ascending the flight with a large pile of bed-linen in her arms. Her burden obscured her face and hid me from her and it was only as she squeezed past that we saw each other and she stopped. It was Dame Margery's little attendant, whose familiarity had made me uncomfortable when I encountered her previously, and I was disconcerted by the look she gave. Instead of proceeding up the turnpike she flattened herself against the wall beside me.

'Does it hurt? Your face?' she asked in matter-of-fact tone.

'Not at all. I forget it unless someone draws attention to it.'

She ignored my rebuff and, moving the weight of the linen onto her right arm, she extracted her left hand and held it out to me. It was badly misshapen and lacked the smallest finger. 'People get used to it,' she said, 'but newcomers stare.'

I felt myself flush. 'You were born like that?'

She nodded. 'Some say my mother slept with the devil, like yours.'

'They are ignorant. Is that why you smiled at me the other day, because we'd something in common?'

'That and the fact I were sorry for you, for what happened and the way they was trying to pull the wool over your eyes.'

I shivered. 'What do you mean?'

'Thomas Chope weren't the only one your sister went with, not by a long chalk, but you won't thank me for telling you.'

'I'd thank you very much if you're telling the truth. I want to know what really happened. Who else did my sister go with?

'Why, any number of the workmen, I'd say. She were seen with half a dozen. Specially that big mason with the bald head, Randolf, I think he's called. She went up the hill with him more'n once. And then there were...' She paused and shifted her bundle onto her other arm.

'Go on.'

'No, you won't want to know.'

I gripped her shoulder. 'Please, I want to know everything.'

'Well then, it were the doctor.'

'Doctor Giovanni?' The lascivious Italian wretch, I thought.

'No, not him. Your master, what's his name?'

I nearly slipped from the narrow step. 'Doctor Swanwych?' I caught my breath pronouncing it.

'Yes, him. I saw her go to his room a week back, late in the evening, stayed there quite a while. I watched to see when she'd come out. And she'd got her skirt tucked up a bit at the back. She pulled it down as she crossed the yard. I weren't spying exactly but...'

'That's all right. I'm glad you've told me. What's your name?'

'Grizel.' She smiled at me and this time it seemed entirely proper. It was a very pretty smile.

'Thank you, Grizel. There's no need to tell anyone else about this, not at the moment. But if you learn anything further that I might be glad to know, please find me. Do you understand?'

She winked. 'I weren't born yesterday, Master Harry.'

She said my name with a curious intonation, half-mocking, half-respectful, and went on her way up the stairs, leaving me shattered by the news she had given me. Doctor Swanwych had not been at Greenwich on the night of Alys's death but he could no longer be regarded as an impartial witness able, without any self-interest, to advise me what course of action to take. I had no doubt Alys had offered herself to him and he had taken her, like any of the other ruffians who had abused her generosity. He was a noted scholar and physician but he must also be a base and lewd philanderer. I found there were tears on my cheeks and knew I was alone in facing the conundrum of my sister's murder. At any rate there was now no reason to wait or resist what instinct told me to do. I set my footsteps towards the tower where Thomas was imprisoned.

Chapter 5

The foul smell hit me as the door to the cell was opened and I signalled to the warder to remove the odorous bucket of waste. Thomas was lying, crouched in the dirty straw on the floor, and it was only when the man approached him and lifted the pail that he rolled over and realised I was there. His right eye was shut beneath dark bruising and his bottom lip was swollen. As I exclaimed and the door clanged shut behind me, he struggled to his feet. 'I never thought you'd come back. My thanks for making him take the shit away.'

'Did that man do this to you?'

'No, one of the sheriff's bully boys, sent specially to extract a confession. If it wasn't for you I think he'd have put a hot poker up my arse so I could be found dead and no questions asked. That would've happened on his next visit, I expect, if the food they give me hadn't curdled my guts completely by then.' He gripped his stomach.

'What do you mean: if it wasn't for me?'

'They know you came to see me before and you might have been suspicious if I died too suddenly. They didn't think you'd come again, no more did I.'

I brushed rank straw aside and sat on the gravelly earth. 'You made me a solemn vow. Can I believe it?'

'I face the gallows, Harry, for something I didn't do but my soul is in peril for all the sins I have committed. I beg you to believe that I wouldn't add to them by swearing a false oath to deceive you.'

'It isn't just what you said that's brought me here. There are questions I can't answer without your help. But I need to be sure I can trust what you say.

'I can only repeat my vow.'

'I need to know everything that happened between you and Alys.'

'Everything?' One battered eyebrow was raised and the old mischief came into his voice.

'I don't mean the detail of your coupling.' Embarrassment swept over me.

Thomas gave a weak chuckle but a bead of blood appeared in the corner of his mouth as he smiled. 'Alys said you were a prissy lad.'

It sounded so like my sister that tears came into my eyes. 'How long were you lovers?'

He sank down on his knees. 'We used to flirt a bit before she went to Danson. You know what she was like, teasing all the boys and letting them put their hands up her skirt. But no more. I think there was only one she went further with.'

'Who was it?'

'That lout, Randolf, the mason. She was his doxy. Us younger lads all knew about it and called her names but we were jealous too, at least I was. I thought they might get wed but then she upped and went to Danson with Lady Blanche. Randolf was soon shagging the fuller's daughter and didn't seem bothered when Alys came back to say she was marrying Master Gregory but I was a bit older by then and I knew I wanted her.'

'Did you lie with her then – when she was already hand-fasted to Master Gregory?'

'No, she wouldn't have me. She was full of her good fortune, marrying Sir Hugh's marshal. She was going up in the world and she wasn't going to risk that. She still flirted, mind you, and went in the bushes with me. She let me suck her nipples and I was frantic to bed her. But I didn't. I never forced her.'

I let out a feeble groan at my sister's wickedness and Thomas gave a thin, careful grin. 'Prissy,' he repeated. 'Never been with a girl, have you?' I shook my head and he went on with his story. 'Sir Hugh and Lady Blanche came here for the New Year festivities, seven months back, invited by Duke Humphrey, and Alys came with them, without Master Gregory. She'd lost enthusiasm for her marriage by

47

then and was ready for any randy bugger who would take her. She went after Randolf first. He'd moved on from the fuller's daughter and the chandler's wife and I don't doubt he was only too willing to tup her but I went after her too and she found me to her liking. Randolf and me came to blows but she decided it for us and I thanked heaven for her choice. I was mad with frustration when she went back to Danson and she was desperate for me but we had to wait until she came here again.'

'Danson's not many miles away. Didn't you manage to meet?'

'Not so easy when she was under Master Gregory's eye. I fancy he knew the way she was inclined and kept a close watch on her.'

'Did he beat her?'

'I don't think so. She never spoke of it. But he locked her in their room if he had to be away from Danson and he was forever forcing his attentions on her, trying to get her with child. By the time she came here three weeks ago she couldn't stand the sight of him, still less his prick.'

'So you took up with her again three weeks ago?'

'It's not difficult to find an empty outhouse here or to wander up into the woods. We had pleasure of each other half a dozen times and never tired of it. We talked of running off together, heading west to Bristol where there'd be work for a carpenter and we'd not be traced. That last evening we began to make plans and she seemed so eager, though nervous too.'

'You were with her that evening – in the wood?'

'We lay together for an hour or more as darkness fell and she was as passionate as I'd ever known her. My God, Harry, I hope that when you are ready for a woman she'll come for you as sweetly as Alys did for me.'

I shifted uncomfortably. 'When did you leave her?'

'We walked back to the edge of the wood at sundown. She was to go straight back to her mistress and I was to walk along the ridge and return by a different path. We'd done it before. Someone must have lain in wait for her and dragged her back to the dell.'

'Someone who knew what you did? Someone who'd seen you? Who do you think it was? Randolf?'

'I don't know. I've no proof and there were others with lust in their eyes when she smiled at them. But Randolf hates me for worsting him with my fists and for taking Alys.'

'Does he have a buff-coloured jerkin?'

'Mother of God, of course he does. It'll be covered in dust and probably torn like everyone else's. But the sheriff was satisfied it was my jerkin that Alys seized.'

'And so she did, I suppose – in her passion.'

Even though it was painful for him, Thomas chortled. 'The way you said that! "Passion." As if it was the pestilence. The devil of it is that she didn't clutch my jerkin that evening because I took it off.'

'There was a piece of material in Alys's hand and the sheriff thinks it comes from your jerkin. I took some threads from under her nails.'

'Whatever threads she held were from her attacker's tunic, not mine.'

'But your jerkin was torn?'

'In several places: under the arms where I ripped a seam and more than one tear where I've caught it on a nail or sharp corner. I remember now I jabbed a hole in it with my chisel the other day when I was working on a ceiling boss in the new tower in the park. That might have been where a strip came off.

'Would there be dye on your jerkin from anywhere?'

'I don't think so. What is this, Harry?' He sounded suddenly truculent and struggled to his feet. 'Has the sheriff sent you to trick me into incriminating myself? Are you deceiving me with this show of sympathy? Go and report back that I'm not playing this game. I'll answer no more questions.'

I stood to face him. 'I promise you I'm here only on my own account – and Alys's – and to see justice is done. I don't believe those threads I've seen came from your jerkin but I wanted to be sure. If you're telling the truth and you're innocent, I want to help but I need all the information you can give.'

He stared at me and pulled at the quiff of hair which had drooped over his forehead. 'You can tell me one thing I'd like to know. When they found her, was Alys still wearing my ring?'

It was my turn to stare. 'Your ring? She wore her husband's on her wedding finger, no other.'

'Mine wasn't a proper ring, just a twist of wire, but we made believe it was a golden band and she put it on her hand when we lay together. She was wearing it when I left her.

'But she would have taken it off when she returned to her mistress?' He nodded and I said no more, judging it unwise to mention that his ring had been found – at least until I had examined it more closely. More than anything else he had said this persuaded me he was speaking the truth but a sense of foreboding had come over me and I needed to see if it had any basis. 'Have you told me all you know now?'

He slumped on the floor, clutching his stomach again. 'I swear it and I pray God you're being straight with me.' He began to retch and I banged on the door.

'Bring back the prisoner's bucket,' I shouted and when the warder appeared I spoke to him as authoritatively as I could. 'I am a doctor and will send balm for his injuries and a potion to calm his guts. I shall return to see him tomorrow and if he has not been treated with my remedies, it will be the worst for you. I have the ear of the chamberlain.'

The man inclined his head with a show of deference and Thomas lifted his hand as I left the cell. 'I thank you

Doctor Somers,' he said and I knew it was not wholly ironical.

*****

As fast as my inadequate leg would carry me I hastened into the park and up the hill. I did not make directly for the wood but turned right towards the tower still under construction, on the crest of the ridge to the west, and I slowed my pace as I approached it. I noted with pleasure that the workmen were sitting outside munching their midday meal and I hailed them as I drew near. 'May I look inside?'

The mason who said I was welcome to do so was a burly, bald-headed man and I guessed he was Randolf but I did not seek to speak to him at that point because I wanted the opportunity to go into the tower alone. The building was well advanced and, although the upper storeys awaited completion, on the ground floor the walls were panelled and there were painted bosses on the ceiling. I walked to and fro but I was studying the ground, not the artistic work above me. There was a good deal of debris on the beaten earth and I began to doubt whether my search would reveal anything but on my second perambulation I saw what I might be looking for and dropped to my knees. Carefully I disentangled the fragment of woollen material from the curls of shaved wood on which it was caught and I smoothed it on my palm. It was grubby and tattered but there was no doubt that it came from a workman's buff-coloured jerkin and its presence in that spot bore out what Thomas had told me. Directly above my head was a finely carved wooden boss displaying the Duke's favourite armorial crest, the swan.

The workmen were returning to the tower as I left it and I lingered a moment to thank the bald mason as he shook crumbs from his napkin. To my delight he chose to respond by initiating conversation. 'You're Harry Somers,

51

aren't you? I'm right sorry about your sister. That bloody swine should have his balls cut off before he's hung.'

'It's a terrible time, especially for my mother. I'm wandering about trying to think of other things. That why I came here to look at the tower. You knew Alys?'

He made a sucking noise with his mouth as he considered my question. 'Yes,' he said at length, 'she was always friendly when she lived here and I liked to see her when she came back with Lady Blanche.'

'And you worked with Thomas Chope?' I tried to sound casual.

'If I'd known what he'd do, I'd have cut his fucking throat. He was always making up to her, even years ago, but she had more sense than to go with him. God rest her soul and send that bastard to hell.' He drew himself up to his full, impressive height and strode into the building. I recognised I would get nothing more helpful from him as things stood and I resumed my walk along the ridge.

Once in the wood I found the dell without difficulty and identified the roots of the great beech where Sir High had hurled what I now knew to be my sister's love token. It took a few minutes to grope through the deep leaves, which tumbled back as soon as I lifted them, until I set about my task more systematically, sifting them heap by heap and removing them from the pit I created. At last my diligence was rewarded when I glimpsed the dull glint of metal in a fork of the roots and I carefully extracted the coil of wire. The leaf mould had kept it moist but on the inside of the ring there was still some stickiness. I wondered what that fragment of base metal would be able to reveal, if it had comprehension like a living creature, and I swallowed hard as I slipped it into my pouch to join the scrap of woollen material I had found in the tower.

In order to conceal where I had come from, in case curious onlookers observed my return to the palace, I chose not to descend the hill by the most direct route. Instead I traversed the wood and followed the wall of the park down the slope at the extremity of the Duke's estate. This took me along a rough track, through scrubland, until I was near the side gate into the grounds, where the earth was churned by the wheels of wagons bringing stone from the quarry for the building works. I needed to traverse the ruts with care, given my unequal stride, and kept my eyes fixed on the treacherous terrain. The breeze was rustling the undergrowth and I was concentrating so hard on my steps that I heard nothing until the swish of the bludgeon through the air accompanied its contact with my head and I fell senseless onto the hard-baked mud.

The sun was lowering towards the west when I became conscious again and, with my head throbbing, crawled onto my knees. At my waist the belt hung limply and the straps which had attached my pouch to it were cut. My purse and its precious contents were gone.

Chapter 6

I dragged myself downhill, scarcely aware how I did so, hoping not to encounter anyone before I had brushed my muddy clothes and washed my face. My cap had fallen off as I got up and when I replaced it I could feel the dampness of blood in my hair; fortunately my body seemed otherwise undamaged except for minor bruising on my face. My mind, on the other hand, was frantic with worry. I went straight to the well in the corner of the courtyard and, in the shadows, did not at first see the small figure bending over the parapet to haul up a pail of water.

Inevitably Grizel exclaimed when she saw me. 'Lord love us, what's happened to you, Master Harry.'

'I fell over on the rough ground. I must look a sorry sight.'

She tilted her head to the side. 'Bumped your head back and front, did you?

'I fell awkwardly.' I cursed her acuteness.

She accepted my feeble explanation but I never thought her persuaded by it. 'Let's give you a swab down then. Take off your cap. That's a nasty cut you've got there.'

I flinched as the cold water entered the wound but she took hold of my chin and dabbed at it again with her apron before starting to clean my face. 'That's better,' she said, standing back to appraise her handiwork and I began to mutter thanks. 'Dear heaven, you've lost your purse! And don't try telling me it broke from your belt when you slipped over. Them straps have been cut. You been jumped, ain't you? Someone bashed you and stole it.'

It was no use pretending and I raised my hands in surrender. 'There were very few coins in it.'

'Anything else?'

She was infuriatingly persistent. 'A keepsake I'm sad to lose. Of no value but precious to me'

54

'Your sister's?' I nodded for that was literally true. 'Well, it won't be no good to a thief, will it? He might have slung it down near where he sloshed you. You'd better go and look in the morning.'

I wasn't quick enough to agree with her suggestion and she let out a squeal as she read my expression. 'Wait a minute! You think it weren't no ordinary cut-purse, don't you? Were it evidence, this keepsake?'

'I don't know. It might have been but I can't be sure. It's a bit far-fetched to think some rogue set on me because he knew what I'd got. I hadn't long had it. I'm trying not to let wild ideas run away with me. I can't think very clearly as it is.' I leaned back against the parapet and closed my eyes.

'Here, you're proper under the weather. Let's help you back home.' She took my elbow and propelled me across the courtyard to the door of the doctor's rooms but as I took hold of the handle, she stretched up to whisper in my ear. 'I reckon you don't think Thomas Chope is the villain and you may be right. But be careful what you're tangling with. If someone's trying to fit him up with what he never done, they won't take kindly to you sticking your oar in.'

'I've thought the same myself.' I gave her a weak grin.

'I'll keep me ears open in case I hear anything that'll help. Mind you, it don't have to be anyone who's at the palace now.'

'What does that mean?' I couldn't cope with puzzles.

'Why someone could have had poor Alys done in without doing it himself. That Doctor Swanwych, for instance. He could have set it all up, paid some ruffian to do it and then made sure he was well away from Greenwich when it happened. Clever!'

'That's nonsense.' I was cross with her for imagining such a thing.

'Have it your own way. I won't barge in if I'm not wanted.'

I pulled her back as she turned to go. 'I didn't mean that. I'm grateful for your help. I'll think about what you said. But I'm very tired now.'

She gave me one of her delightful smiles. 'Water off a duck's back, to me, it is.'

Then I lifted the little maid's withered hand to kiss it and she gave me a deep curtsy in return.

*****

I fell on my bed in exhaustion and slept without stirring until the sun was high in the sky next morning. Although the back of my head was still sore when I woke, I felt refreshed and, to my relief, my mind seemed to be working properly. I was in no hurry to seek company and did not stir from my room even though, through the window, I saw the usual procession of serving men carrying the midday meal on platters from the kitchen to the hall. I could not smell the roasted capons, geese and pork and I tried not to imagine the savoury sauces and spiced accompaniments, settling instead to eat pieces of stale bread and hard cheese which I had left from my journey four days earlier. At least Doctor Swanwych's flagon of ale was in good condition.

I decided I must review all that I had learned to see if I could draw any conclusions. It seemed unlikely I could achieve any sort of certainty but I needed to clarify for myself where the contradictions lay, so I started by running over in my mind what Thomas Chope had told me and the circumstances leading to his arrest. I had to admit it was entirely possible that he had killed Alys and was seeking skilfully to deceive me, as he had in the past. What he told me of his last meeting with my sister could be a pack of lies for, rather than planning to run off with him, she might have decided to have no more to do with him and provoked his murderous fury. The strange matter of the material in her hand, which did not match his jerkin, was the only slight evidence countering that conclusion and it seemed he had torn his coat in the tower where he was working. Certainly her public dalliance with Thomas might have roused the jealousy of other workmen with whom she had flirted – or done worse – and Randolf was foremost among these potential suspects. Again I had no proof that the anomalous threads had come from his clothing, nor any other explanation for them. The chaplain's idea that dye had been spilt on a labourer's old tunic was not borne out by the fineness of the wool.

Then there was the curious business of the wire ring and here I had my own observation to help, even though the object was no longer in my possession. I was convinced that the stickiness I had felt inside the twisted metal was congealed blood and that suggested that Alys was wearing the ring when she was attacked and it was then wrenched from her finger as she lay dying. Thomas might have reacted in this vicious way but, if she intended to leave him, would she have worn the token of his devotion at their final meeting? If Randolf or another had attacked her, after seeing Thomas depart, would he had known the significance of the worthless hoop and been so enraged by it that he tore it from her stiffening hand? Her husband's gold band remained untouched on her wedding finger. Without doubt her murderer was frenzied when he stabbed her but who, other than Thomas, might have been driven to that barbarous extremity? Grizel had suggested that Alys could have been the victim of a hired assassin, working for someone like Doctor Swanwych – although I could not entertain such a base suspicion of my master – but surely no paid cut-throat would indulge in superfluous violence?

All these considerations were bewildering enough but now I had the added puzzle of the attack I had suffered and the theft of my purse. Was it fortuitous that I was robbed for money at that time and in that place? Who might have surmised that the other contents of my pouch would be of greater value to them than a few coins? Who, except the murderer, could possibly want to remove a coil of wire and a tangle of woollen strands? But if someone did, he could not be Thomas Chope and the poor relics of my sister must have more significance than I had discovered. At least I still had the remaining threads which I had secreted in Doctor Swanwych's cupboard but they were of uncertain importance in pursuing my thankless quest for the truth.

My analysis took me little further in deciding what to do but some irrational instinct told me that, even though I lacked any vital clues, there were mysteries still to be unravelled. I remained at a loss how to pursue them and concluded I was unlikely to make progress unless I discovered some new evidence. I had reached this unsatisfactory conclusion when a banging at the door required my attention and I was glad to be diverted from my fruitless mental exercise. I was surprised to find a servant from the chamberlain's household who told me Sir Hugh de Grey was about to leave Greenwich to return to his estate and wished to bid me farewell. Furthermore, I was informed, Lady Blanche was to remain with her parents for a few more days, accompanied by a handful of attendants from Danson, and she requested my attendance in her chamber at my earliest convenience as she had need of my assistance. Hurriedly I splashed water on my bruised face, brushed myself down, put on a cap over my head wound and made my way to the stables where I found Sir Hugh already mounted.

'Master Somers. Capital, I hoped to see you. Just wanted to give you best wishes. Dreadful business. Gregory's taken it very hard and I don't like to see him so distracted. We're relying on you to see justice is done – and speedily. That scoundrel should swing for it without delay. Make sure they get on with it. Don't let them create a field-day for the lawyers. Sure you feel the same. Anything you need us for, Danson's not far away.'

He slapped my shoulder and wheeled his horse towards the gatehouse without waiting for a response. I called goodbye and set off for the chamberlain's lodgings.

This time Lady Blanche received me, without Dame Margery, in the bedroom she had shared with her husband, and she was attended by one of her own ladies. There was no sign of Grizel. Her ladyship seemed as agitated as at our previous encounter and moved about the room restlessly while she spoke, fingering table-tops and drapes as she passed.

'Master Somers, I am grateful you have come and I was sorry to hear of your accident.' I regretted that Grizel must have reported the incident but was re-assured to hear it described in those terms. 'I am still distressed by your sister's death. I can hardly banish the awful deed from my mind. She was dear to me and did not deserve such a horrible fate. Oh, it's monstrous that I intrude upon your grief at such a time by making so frivolous an enquiry – but I am bound to ask you. It is a trivial thing but I wish so much to find it. Forgive me for my inconsiderate claim on your assistance but I beg you to help me.'

I must have looked completely bemused and, once she realised I had no idea what she was asking, she fluttered her hands apologetically. 'I fear I am not coherent. I will speak more plainly. I have lost a tiny pomander, Master Somers, an exquisite thing in filigree silver which I wore hanging from the belt of my richest gowns. Sir Hugh gave me it and he does not know it is missing. I must find it before I return home.'

She paused and I muttered regrets, hesitating to ask what in the world I could do about it, and then she continued. 'All I can think, Master Somers, is that it must have slipped from my belt and fallen into the bundle we made of poor Alys's effects. I beg you to look for me or bring back the bundle so my woman can search it. I am so sorry to trouble you.'

I caught my breath. 'My pardon, Lady Blanche, I did not know there was such a bundle.'

'It would have been delivered to your mother when Master Gregory said he could not bear to have it.' She seemed to suppress some further comment and made a tiny squeak as she thrust her fist to her mouth. 'Please will you help me?'

'Of course, madam. I will go at once to speak to my mother and look for your pomander. I hope very much I can find it for you.'

'Oh, thank you, thank you,' and as I bowed and turned to the door she subsided onto her bed with her face in her hands. I did not envy Sir Hugh his excitable wife.

*****

I found my mother, as expected, busy at her needlework in the Duchess's rooms and, after I had explained my mission, she confirmed that a pack of Alys's things had been delivered to her. 'I simply put the bundle in my box, Harry. I couldn't bear to look at it. There's very little. Just a gown and a kirtle with bits and pieces rolled up inside – a comb, I suppose, and maybe stockings.'

'Could a small pomander have fallen inside?'

'I'm sure it could if Lady Blanche was bending over the bundle. Fancy her taking such trouble with a servant's belongings. She thought so well of poor Alys, bless her. She must be fair worried to have lost something her husband gave her. Come with me now and I'll show you my box. You can take the bundle back to your room to look at. I don't want to watch. I'm not ready to set my tears off again.'

She took me up to the servants' garret at the top of the west wing, above the floor where three old retainers remained in lodgings, excused from the journey to Calais with the Duke and Duchess. My mother slept at the far end of the long room under the rafters and kept her possessions in the ancient painted box I remembered from childhood. She handed me the bundle, averting her face from it, and to distract her from miserable thoughts I remarked on a great mound of damp bed linen beside her pallet.

'That's to keep me busy when I've no fancy stitching to do for ladies' gowns or men's tunics. The laundresses bring them here for me to fashion into new sheets. I cut out the holes, turn them end-to-middle and re-hem them to serve us for another dozen years. The silly girls don't always check they're dry when they deliver them so I have to spread them out or they'd go mouldy.'

I made a quip about the Duchess's frugality in purchasing household goods compared with the Duke's extravagance in buying books and my mother laughed. 'It's more Dame Margery's influence than Duchess Eleanor's,' she whispered, as if sharing a solemn secret. Then she giggled like a girl and added, 'I'm speaking out of turn – mind you don't tell a soul.' So I was able to leave her in a good humour which pleased me.

Ten minutes later I had my sister's few effects spread before me on the floor of Doctor Swanwych's study and I had soon satisfied myself that Lady Blanche's pomander was not among them. I understood why my mother had shunned the task of examining the bundle, for the sight of the little comb, with some of Alys's dark hairs still clinging to it, made tears spring to my eyes and the discovery of a tattered rag doll, which I remembered from my childhood, caused them to course down my cheeks. I prepared to roll everything up again when my hand detected something knobbly sewn into the neckband of a shift. It wasn't big enough to be the missing pomander but it was hard and round and it intrigued me, so with my knife I carefully snipped a stitch and made a small opening in the cloth. I eased the object

61

towards the hole, squeezed it out – and into my hand fell a beautiful, valuable pearl.

I gazed at the jewel in amazement and growing concern for I could not understand how it came to be there. It was worth far more than Alys could have afforded and, whatever her faults, I was sure she was no thief. She must have been given it and I had no doubt what services she had rendered to be rewarded by such a gift. Only a man of some means could have paid her so generously and, with a heavy heart, I realised that man was likely to be Doctor Swanwych, whose family was well-to-do and who was seen to entertain her in his chamber. I had not wanted to admit that my master could be as lecherous as any common workman but the evidence was in front of me. Alys must have hidden the pearl to keep it safe until she wished to sell it and the thought came to me that, if she was truly planning to run off with Thomas Chope, it would furnish funds to see them on their way.

This possibility fitted well with Thomas's story but it gave me no pleasure, so disillusioned was I by my master's behaviour, and I decided I must seek some diversion to distract me from absorption in my sister's murder. Only one person in the vicinity might offer amusement sufficient to do this and I hurried to the neighbouring chambers to beg that Doctor Giovanni dei Signorelli join me in a jar of ale. I had not seen the Italian since the funeral and I feared he might be absent from the palace so it was with great relief that I greeted him as he flung open his door.

'Mio amico! I was coming to see you. I have message for you from John Swanwych. He has written from Oxford. He received letter from Duke Humphrey, while he was in London, asking that he take a consignment of books to the library the Duke has founded in the university. These books the Duke had sent from Calais. Most of them are by my countrymen, notable scholars, full of wisdom.

'What does the doctor's message say?' My mouth was dry as I referred to the man I wasn't allowed to forget.

'Only that he will return before the week is out and you are to be free to work in his rooms. He also asks that you supply me with some particular ingredients that I need to make up the potions which he usually prepares for Dame Margery.' I knew about the medicine my master provided to ease the aches in the old lady's joints and I nodded. Giovanni lowered his voice as he went on. 'Other things as well – I will show you the list – for the chamberlain's daughter.'

'Lady Blanche?' This surprised me.

'To help her...' Giovanni faltered as if something else had occurred to him. 'To help her conceive again, you understand. She is most anxious to bear another child to Sir Hugh.'

'And Doctor Swanwych knows the means to do this?' It was an aspect of alchemy of which I knew little and I found the idea distasteful.

'Harry, when you are fully-fledged as a physician, you will welcome payment for attempts to cure – many different conditions. Sometimes to humour our patients is as beneficial as to purge them and who knows but our efforts may successful.' He laughed as he poured me a goblet of wine, rather than the ale I had in mind, and he made me sit on his one upright chair while he sank down on a stool. 'This topic it reminds me – I have wondered whether to say it but I think you have right to know, especially as I hear you ask questions about poor Alys. It is, you understand, confidential matter. As doctor I am bound to keep it – but she is dead and...'

'If it concerns Alys I should like to know.' But I dreaded what he might say.

'You gave me permission to tidy her private parts before the women made her ready for burial.' He took a hefty swig of his wine. 'She was most badly torn. I had to venture very intimately. No one, I think, would know but your sister was with child.'

Chapter 7

I suppose it should not have been a surprise but I was not prepared for this news and my hand shook as I lifted the goblet to my lips. My voice sounded strained. 'How long? Could you tell?'

'Not yet three months, perhaps ten or eleven weeks. Almost certainly she would have been aware of her condition.'

A ridiculous shiver of relief passed through me. 'So it was not at Greenwich that she conceived.' But my relief was short-lived as I realised the implication and remembered her coldly withdrawn husband who so longed for an heir. 'I wonder if Master Gregory knew. What a terrible loss for him to bear.'

Giovanni raised a fluttering eyebrow. 'Unless some other man at Danson had enjoyed her favours.'

'Thomas told me Alys was closely constrained by her husband.'

'Ah! So she came to Greenwich for some diversion, so lively a lady.' He registered my disapproving expression. 'Oh, I am sorry, Harry. I make improper joke. Forgive me. I meant no harm. She was so popular here, you understand. I hear so much of her charms. Myself, alas, I did not experience them.'

I bit back the sour reply that he might have been unique among the men at the palace if he had not lain with her. Instead I begged him to change the subject and tell me of his recent studies into constriction of the bowels and he regaled me for some time with the success he had achieved by trying different combinations of rhubarb, senna leaves and cloves. Before long he launched onto the most fitting mixtures to be prescribed according to the proportions of the four elements within a man's make-up, of earth, air, fire and water, and whether his disposition was, in consequence, sanguine, choleric, phlegmatic or melancholic. I listened enthusiastically to this outpouring of knowledge and practical experience, asking questions, and seeking details of where he had found it best to make incisions for blood-letting, depending on the movement of the celestial spheres. Even as the wine made me light-headed I recognised that some of Giovanni's proven treatments varied from the theoretical learning I had absorbed from academic treatises. I leaned back in my chair, happily engrossed, only dimly conscious that the sunlight was beginning to fade while we still talked.

The tap at the door and the shrill peremptory voice made us both jump. 'Master Harry, you in there?'

'It's the little maid, Grizel,' I said, trying to blink away my stupor. 'She serves Dame Margery.'

'I think I know the one, a cheeky minx.'

She must have heard his words as Giovanni opened the door but she ignored them, erupting into the room dragging a scruffy, snot-bespattered urchin behind her. She was waving a sodden article in her hand, the occasional muddy drip falling from it to splatter the immaculate rushes on the floor. It took me a moment to realise it was my pouch that she was thrusting into my hand.

'See, I were right. The bugger what took it threw it away. There ain't no coins in it, I looked, just some tatty rubbish. Rendell here found it.' She pushed the boy forward and added proudly, 'he's my brother.'

I managed to stammer my thanks while opening the purse and seeing, to my delight, a coil of wire, slightly tarnished, and a damp knot of threads. 'Where was it, Rendell?'

The boy, who I judged to be about eight years old, compressed his mouth and held out his hand. Although Grizel cuffed him he maintained his attitude until I had slipped a groat into his palm. He showed no gratitude but did then open his mouth. 'I were fishing where the creek joins the river. Walked out on the mudflat when the tide were out. This were caught in the reeds. Reckon it were slung from a boat. Griz had said a purse were missing so I guessed what it were. Weren't there yesterday.'

'See! Now you say I were right, Master Harry. Shame you were conked on the head for the sake of a bit of small change but the cut-purse'd be worse narked, I'd say, if he was hoping for more.'

'Certainly, I'm most grateful.' I couldn't tell them how much, for they must not know how greatly I valued the contents which had been returned to me, nor the relief I felt at knowing the thief had been interested only in money. Rendell's hand had advanced once more and I accepted that my benefactor shared that monetary interest. I found a few smaller coins and gave some to Rendell who promptly bit them to reassure himself of their quality but Grizel stepped back in annoyance as I offered the others to her.

'I don't want paying. I ain't helped you to get some reward. I reckoned I were your friend, Master Harry.'

'And so you are, Grizel, indeed you are,' and I seized her distorted hand and once more kissed it.

Giovanni was watching with interest but it was not my gallantry which caught his attention. 'Your hand, little mistress, may I see it?'

'No, you can't,' Grizel said, snatching her fingers from mine. 'You bloody doctors are all the same, like that other one always wanting to look at my hand to see if it could be straightened somehow. Fat chance of him growing me my missing finger!'

I suppressed a smile, understanding why Grizel disliked my master, but Giovanni was bowing low before her, full of apologies. 'It was most remiss of me. I had no right to ask. I beg forgiveness, Madonna. Scusi, scusi.'

Grizel tilted her head, looking at him coyly, and I felt a rush of irritation that such a young girl might be beguiled by the effusive courtesy of the Italian. Giovanni had not finished making amends for his indiscretion. 'You have most fine names, you and your brother, very high-sounding. I admire them.'

Grizel gurgled with pleasure. 'Taken a lot of stick for them, we have, I can tell you. Proper fancy, aren't they! Me mother were a pie-woman outside St Paul's in the City but she had la-di-da ideas and picked up our names from some of the gentry she served. Do you like them, sir?'

She rolled her eyes at Giovanni in an infuriating way but he never answered her question for at that moment Rendell, who had drifted over to the window, gave a shout. 'Fire! There's a fire! Look at all that smoke.'

It was quite difficult to see, for there were no flames visible, but against the leaden sky there were dark plumes of smoke curling out from the uppermost storey of the west wing of the palace. 'It's the servants' quarters,' I shouted, jostling my way into the courtyard. 'My mother's there.'

Quickly Giovanni was at my side and we were running, followed by the children, towards the building from which people were emerging, some coughing and spluttering, while other brave souls were hurrying in the other direction with buckets of water and ladders from the masons' compound. As we reached the entrance to the block a bevy of women were ushered across the threshold by a soot-covered workman and among them was my mother who staggered into my arms.

'Thank the Blessed Virgin,' she gasped, 'we were not yet in our beds and the old ladies who sleep on the floor below are with Dame Margery. We had just lighted our tapers to go up from the hall when we smelled the foul smoke.' She clutched my arm. 'But Mary's up there, one of the brew-women. She felt unwell and left us to lie down. Pray God they find her safe.

'Amen,' I said and kissed her as she moved off with her companions. Then I hurried as best I could to follow Giovanni and a crowd of other men up the spiral stairs.

The smoke billowed more thickly as we climbed and we were soon gasping for breath but a sensible fellow had held back one bucket in which to dunk rags, before handing them out to clamp over mouths and wipe eyes. Even so, as we reached the second landing, I thought it unlikely we could get much higher and attendants, who had been ahead of us in trying to douse the fire, turned to push their way down, croaking that they could do no more. Some carried garments and boxes which they had rescued and the bulkiness of their burdens, when they squeezed past us on the narrow stair, risked trapping everyone in imminent danger of suffocation. I recognised Randolf's grimy face above an armful of objects but gave him no greeting as he trod on my toe in passing. Somehow I struggled to the top of the staircase.

I felt the fumes choking my throat and was terrified that I would be asphyxiated when, all of a sudden, the crash of splintering timber was followed by a cool breeze which momentarily dispersed the wall of smoke in front of us. On the opposite side of the garret I glimpsed men outside the building, balanced on a high ladder, who wrenched off the shutter they had smashed and clambered across the window-sill. The draught thinned the smoke, blowing gusts about us, but it also enlivened the blaze and I saw flames leap up from the steaming pile of cloth, at the other end of the room, which was clearly the source of the fire. Filling my lungs with God's blessed air I struggled onwards and joined a chain of helpers, quickly established to pass buckets, hand to hand, to quench the conflagration. It was then that I made out the shape of a woman collapsed on top of the burning debris and knew that she was dead. The thought flitted through my mind that Mary, the brew-woman, had stumbled or fainted and her taper had ignited the linen which awaited my mother's attention.

There was little time for conversation while we were engaged in controlling the flames but, as we gained the upper hand and our eyes ceased smarting, several men expressed surprise that, given the volume and intensity of the smoke, the fire had not caused more damage. Of course everything was covered in soot, many pallets were shrivelled to ashes and the rafters were badly scorched but the destruction did not match the inferno we had expected to encounter. It was no great puzzle for me, for I knew that linen had been damp, but I had other questions in my head and, when we were stood down from our labours, I moved closer to where my mother's bed had been and where Mary's charred body lay, face-down across the smouldering heap of cinders. Giovanni emerged from the gloom and joined me.

The corpse was too hot to lift but we managed to turn it slightly, ready to look on the inevitable ruin of Mary's burned face, and I forced down the cry which rose in my throat at the sight I was not prepared for – the gaping hole in her ravaged chest where some sharp weapon had plunged into her heart. Giovanni's eyes held mine and in silence we laid her back where she had been and crossed ourselves. 'Would you fetch the chamberlain?' I asked. 'I'll stay with her. Tell the other men to leave.'

Giovanni drew himself up, draping his charred gown around him, and, with a physician's authority, he led the other men back to the stairs while I looked about me. My mother's sleeping place and its immediate surroundings had been destroyed but, strangely, her box with its faded pattern of painted flowers had survived and was standing some yards away, in the centre of the room, coated with smuts. It was overturned, its lid hanging broken from its hinges, and at first I thought it must have been kicked aside by the first fire-fighters to arrive, who might have stumbled against it as they rushed forward. Then it struck me that this was improbable, for the box's normal position would have put it close to the outbreak and the inferior wood of which it was made would have been rapidly consumed. It must have been moved before the fire broke out, which was odd but for which there might have been some fortuitous explanation – had not a murder been committed nearby. Closer inspection revealed that the contents of the box had not simply tumbled out where it fell but they were strewn about, as if they had been removed and examined one by one.

'That your mother's box?' Grizel's cheerful voice interrupted my reverie and I looked down on her filthy face. I nodded although I was annoyed she must have slipped past Giovanni to enter the garret. 'Looks as if it were rummaged. Always are rogues after loot when there's a calamity. Not that there's going to be much good stuff in a servants' attic. Here, you've singed the side of your face – not the marked side either – and your tunic's a bit scorched on the shoulder. You'd better come down to the well and I'll patch you up again. Becoming a habit, this is.'

'I need to wait here for the chamberlain. He will want to see for himself what damage has been done. Doctor Giovanni has gone to fetch him. If you'd like to go and wet some rags, I'll be down as soon as I can.'

To my surprise she made off obediently but she had probably heard the chamberlain's voice on the stairs for no sooner had she gone than he appeared in the doorway with Giovanni. My head was buzzing with anxiety. The canny little maid had recognised at once what I had deduced – that whatever had happened to my mother's box was not accidental. It was convenient to think of it as the action of a looter but he would have needed to be very quickly on the scene to move the box before it was burned. I could not make myself believe that explanation, not when I was certain that the fire had been started deliberately. There was an alternative and much more troubling reason for my mother's possessions to be searched – by someone looking for a particular thing he expected to find – for a valuable pearl which might offer incriminating evidence if its donor were to be identified. The wretched brew-woman had

71

chanced to return before the villain's work was done and paid the price for interrupting him.

I held back these thoughts while we showed what remained of Mary's body to the chamberlain. 'Thieves,' he said, 'caught in the act of rifling the servants' possessions. Poor woman!' He was an intelligent man and his knitted brows suggested to me that he was not persuaded by his own words. 'I have ordered the guards to watch all doorways to ensure there is no attempt to repeat this atrocity but I do not propose to announce to the household how the victim died. Not immediately, anyway. Are you physicians content with that? It will allow me to conduct enquiries without causing undue nervousness. Make her a decent as you can and I'll send some strong fellows to carry her down the stairs.'

We gave our agreement and the chamberlain left us to wrap the brew-woman in a shroud Giovanni had fetched from the chapel. I was glad news of the murder was to be suppressed for the time being, for I too had enquiries to pursue and misgivings to resolve, which I was not trustful enough to share with the Duke's representative. Perhaps I should have drawn his attention to my mother's box and its scattered contents but it made no sense to do that unless I was willing to tell him about Alys's pearl – and, at this stage, I was not.

I paused in my descent behind Giovanni, grasping the ledge cut into the wall for support as my speculation continued. Was there a connection between the fire and the cutting of my purse? Had the thief thought the pearl was in my keeping and, when he did not find it, stolen my money to disguise his real intent? Had he then decided to ransack my mother's things? He had not intended the fire to spread quickly but to create a fog of smoke in which to hide his actions and facilitate his escape. After he had murdered the hapless intruder and realised his quest had failed, he had simply joined the servants running from the building, unobserved in the hubbub. Only the man who gave it to my sister would know about the pearl other, possibly, than Thomas Chope who must be held blameless of this outrage. Yet, as Grizel had suggested, it need not be the villain himself who carried out these violent deeds. A wealthy man could be miles away while his paid minion executed his brutal orders.

A few hours previously, when I learned that Alys had been got with child at Danson and my purse was returned with its worthless contents untouched, I had thought I could dismiss my most horrible imaginings. Now they returned with renewed force to centre on my own respected master. Perhaps he had not contrived her murder and he could not have foreseen Mary's, but if he was ready to employ men of violence to recover his gift, in order to prevent his licentiousness being made public, he was in my eyes abominably culpable.

*****

I spent a restless night, tormented by demons in my dreams and worse terrors in my waking mind, obsessed with my broken trust in Doctor Swanwych. At least my mother should not be in further danger, for the serving women had been taken under Dame Margery's wing and the guard had been strengthened at all entrances. If the unknown attacker deduced that I had acquired the pearl after my purse was taken, I might be at risk but surely the doctor would not countenance an attack on his own chambers. Perhaps I would be safe until he returned to Greenwich. At all events, I concluded, I must use what time I had to obtain evidence which could be shared with the chamberlain and by the time I dragged myself from my bed I knew what I must do next.

It was not difficult to find the mason, Randolf, for he and his colleagues had already been set to work on the damaged building and I met him at the doorway to the stairs. 'You were quickly on the scene here yesterday,' I said, attempting to keep any hint of accusation from my voice, and I was relieved he was willing to reply.

'We'd just got back to the courtyard and saw the smoke. We'd stayed late up at the tower in the park, finishing the crenellations along the roof-walk. I went straight up the stairs while others fetched ladders. We didn't know if people were trapped inside but no one could last long in that fug so we grabbed what we could save and ran down again while we still had breath.'

'The chamberlain believes it was arson. Did you see anyone when you first got to the garret?'

Randolf whistled. 'Is that so? In that murk it was difficult to see anything but I reckon there were two men who pushed past us at the top of the stairs. I didn't recognise them but they could have been servants I didn't know. I never thought anything of it at the time.'

'Would you recognise them again?'

'Christ, no. They had their hoods pulled well forward – we all did, to protect us from the smoke.'

'Were they in livery?'

'Not the Duke's. It looked like they were in dark grey. That's why they didn't show up against the smoke.'

'Will you make a statement about this to the chamberlain? You said you had colleagues with you? Did they see the men?'

'Course they did. Swear on Saint Edward's relics at Westminster, they will.'

The irony in his voice undermined his encouraging words and I wondered if he was mocking me with lies. If what he said was true, it was useful information but I thought it just as likely that there were no mysterious men in grey hoods. I did not doubt that Randolf could secure the witness of his companions in whatever terms he required, by fair means or foul, and I could not dismiss the idea that he and his lackeys might well have been the arsonists.

His next comment strengthened my doubts. 'Have to be quick taking our statements though,' he said, stroking his stubbly chin. 'We've finished at the palace and all us masons are off to the Duke's house in the City when they've helped clear up the mess here. I'm going ahead right now to make sure our quarters are ready.' He moved to the side of the doorway and picked up a bulky bundle of goods bound together with a strip of leather. As he slung the strap over his shoulder the contents clinked and he chuckled. 'All me worldly goods in here: platter and chisel, mallet and drinking horn. Need to go now to catch the turn of the tide. I bid you farewell, Master Scab-face.'

*****

I made my third visit to Thomas's cell with a heavy heart, apologising silently to Alys for what I was about to say to him. It was a different warder who admitted me this time and I was pleased to see that the prisoner had acquired no more obvious injuries and looked less unkempt. His mood, however, was surly.

'I doubted you'd come today after all the excitement I've heard about. Do they think I set the servants' room ablaze by conversing with the devil and invoking the use of his fiery breath? Am I now deemed an evil wizard as well as a murderer?'

'No one has suggested anything so stupid.' He grunted and turned his head away, as if to discourage dialogue, but I could not indulge his churlish mood. 'Thomas, I have discovered a number of things which may be to your benefit but I need your help if I am to pursue them effectively.'

'Are you forsaking medicine and turning to the law? I am impressed by your countless talents.'

'Why are you cantankerous with me today?'

'I suppose you expected thanks for the improvement in my treatment? I have a warder who is civil, clean water to drink, your salve to treat my bruises and food that teases my taste-buds. I am profoundly, obsequiously grateful, kind Master Doctor.'

His sarcasm was more hurtful than Randolf's blatant rudeness but I contained my annoyance. 'I'm not looking for thanks but I would have thought these improvements would be welcome.'

'You know nothing. I am the cockerel fatted and sleeked, ready for the pot. Will you feel better to see my well-nourished carcase swinging on the gibbet?'

'If you have told me the truth, I want to save you from the gibbet.'

He glared at me but sat down on the floor. You're a strange one, Harry Somers. I've told you all I can.'

'There's one more question I need to ask. You told me that you and Alys spoke of running off together. Did you have money to pay for your flight?'

He dropped his voice to a growl. 'Damn you, it was Alys had the means. She'd managed to get hold of something valuable. She said she'd been given it. I didn't ask for details.'

'What was it?'

'I've no idea. I didn't expect it to be much.'

'She never showed you a fine large pearl then?'

He looked genuinely surprised and his mouth trembled. 'A pearl?'

'I recovered it from her things. I believe someone is looking for it. Who do you suppose gave it to her?'

'I've told you I know nothing about it.'

'I imagine it was someone she gave her favours to. You knew she was a whore.'

He shot to his feet, clanking the chain which restricted his movement, and he lunged towards me although I kept out of reach. 'Christ damn you! She never sold herself to any man. You pompous, prim cripple! Her own brother to call her harlot! May you roast in hell for eternity, you pompous scum.'

I stood stock still. 'Thank you, Thomas. You have told me what I wanted to know. May God forgive me for maligning Alys and for testing you but I couldn't think of another way to be sure.'

'Of what?'

'Of the circumstances in which Alys acquired the pearl I don't doubt it was a free gift, not payment, and that she took it because it offered you a future together.' I paused as a stray idea came to me 'When did she tell you she had secured something of value?'

'Not straight away after she came back to Greenwich. I told you we'd just began to talk of going off and thought of Bristol. It was only that last night we lay together when she said she could pay for us to get horses. Hours later she was dead.'

I heard myself exhale and closed my eyes. 'I must leave you. I have much to attend to but I give you my word that I am now convinced you did not murder Alys and I will do all in my power to prove who did.'

While he was still swearing at me and shouting questions, I was hobbling fast along the passage from his cell, attempting to steady myself for what lay ahead – for what I saw as my ultimate disillusionment and sorrow.

Chapter 8

I joined the rest of the household for our midday meal in the hall but I was not good company, sitting silent at the end of a bench while thoughts churned in my mind, and the little I took from the serving bowl lay unregarded on my platter. I was very young and had limited experience of men's foibles but I had become obsessed with the fear that Doctor Swanwych had arranged my sister's murder to conceal his shame at sleeping with her. If this was true it followed that he would wish to recover the costly token he had given her, in order that it could not be traced back to him, and so the ruffians he had hired to do his bidding had assaulted me and then set a torch to the servants' garret. It would have been comforting to believe my master had no part in Alys's death and merely wished to cover his tracks after the event but the timing of his departure from London made that improbable. He could only have set in hand those attempts to recover the pearl if he already knew she was dead and it beggared belief to think he could have heard so quickly when he was far distant on the road to Oxford. My misery at learning that a man I respected was capable of such infamy was overpowering but I told myself honesty required me to confront sordid reality and ensure that the villain was brought to justice.

Of course I had no hard evidence of the doctor's guilt and there was one remaining possibility which needed to be discounted before I considered how to denounce him. As the dishes were cleared from the table I rose to speak to the chamberlain but a workman, entering from behind the screens at the end of the hall, reached him first with a message that caused him to bang upon the board for silence. He turned towards the trestle where his wife and her women were sitting and announced that the second floor of the fire-damaged wing had been cleaned sufficiently for the elderly retainers who slept there to return. The servants' garret which required structural repair and much more thorough scrubbing would remain out of use for some days. Three withered crones pulled themselves to their feet and were escorted to the door, the tallest, a lean upright woman, giving her arm to a bent-backed companion.

'Difficult to credit that bag of bones once shared a royal bed, ain't it?' I looked down at Grizel's wicked grin and she winked. 'Fifty years ago old Joan Coverdale was a sprightly strumpet, they say, and served our Duke's grandfather, John of Lancaster, between the sheets. Course you know what was said about him, don't you?' I shook my head, confessing the inadequacy of my education on this subject. She hooted with laughter. 'Why his genitals putrefied on account of his frequenting so many women. A great fornicator, he were.'

I knew I was blushing and excused myself in order to speak to the chamberlain but I heard her final, giggling sally. 'Mind you he lived nigh sixty years and Joan Coverdale has lasted as long since she first entertained his mouldy cock.' I was appalled to hear such bawdy jests on the lips of the little maid and I drew my gown close around me as if to keep myself from contact with all that was ribald and obscene. I scuttled awkwardly towards the high table.

I explained my wish to ride to Danson, in order to return to my good-brother something of Alys's that he might like to keep, and the chamberlain made no objection. 'My daughter, Lady Blanche, is to return home in the morning,' he said. 'She is still fragile and Sir Hugh is resolved to come in person to escort her, despite the attendants he left to accompany her. They are to be hosts to the Lord Archbishop himself in two days' time. A great honour! His Grace is a relative of Sir Hugh's mother. Such a distinguished family.' His eyes focussed on me as if he had only just noticed I was still there. 'Yes, go this afternoon, Harry, so your sad business can be concluded quickly. They will all have their minds on the archiepiscopal visitation thereafter.'

Grizel was waiting below the dais and she fluttered her eyelashes at me. 'Fragile,' she said delicately, 'fragile. I'd say Lady Blanche were more than fragile. Skimble-skamble, more like. Nearly off her head, she is. Nothing better to do than fret herself silly.'

I had no wish to be delayed by the girl's chatter and was glad that she was summoned to attend Dame Margery just as I set off for the stables. When my horse was saddled I trotted into the courtyard and crossed to leave by the gatehouse but at the sound of the woman's scream I pulled on the reins and turned to see what had happened. The ancient attendant I now knew to be Joan Coverdale had emerged from the west wing waving her arms and keening loudly. At the same moment the chamberlain came out from the hall and hurried towards her while I rode back to see if I could help.

'Whatever is it, mistress?' the chamberlain asked, looking round in the hope that Dame Margery or one of the other women might appear.

'Robbery! Theft! My cincture! My precious girdle! Gone! Stolen.'

'Quietly, now, mistress. Are you saying something has been taken from among your possessions?'

The furrowed chin quivered but Joan Coverdale collected herself. 'My chain, set with fine stones. The late Lord of Lancaster gave it to me. It was in my chest. It is not there.'

The chamberlain sighed. 'My daughter thought she had lost a pomander the other day and caused much to-do before it was found in a shoe. Many articles will have been misplaced during the fire. Perhaps your belt is with your companions' things.' I noted his comment about the pomander with interest.

'We have looked. It was deep in my chest and nothing else has been removed. Someone knew it was there!'

'Well, I dare say we all knew that, mistress, you have told us of it many times and worn it on feast days for us to admire.'

'There are thieves in the palace. They must be caught. I demand my girdle be returned. There were looters and vagabonds hidden by the smoke, making off with our valuables.' She swivelled and pointed at me. 'Why is that evil-faced man mounted? He was one of them at the fire. Search him! He may have my chain in his saddle.'

Wearily I slipped to the ground and allowed my person and my horse's accoutrements to be patted and squeezed until the old woman was satisfied I had concealed nothing of interest to her. Fortunately she did not trouble to examine my crumpled purse as it was too small to contain the fine belt she was seeking, so Alys's pearl was not revealed – otherwise she might have accused me of extracting it from her girdle. I was allowed to proceed on my way while the chamberlain directed that a search be conducted throughout the palace. It was only as I crested the ridge beyond the park and glanced towards the distant tower, where I had first encountered Randolf, that I remembered how his bundle had clinked when he was leaving the palace. I could prove nothing of course and I had no intention of further delaying my journey in order to advise the chamberlain how the mason might have taken Joan's treasured gift; I had matters of more immediate and personal concern to pursue.

As I rode across the wide heathland beyond the park I noticed a group of urchins skimming stones across the surface of a pond and at the sound of my horse's hooves one of them turned and placed his fingers between his teeth to give piercing whistle. Then he executed an elaborate and, I thought, mocking bow. I ignored any intended impudence and gave young Rendell a cheery wave.

*****

81

Years earlier I had accompanied Doctor Swanwych on the short journey to Eltham Palace when he had been requested to examine one of the senior servants stricken by a seizure. Sir Hugh's manor lay a few miles beyond the curtilage of the royal residence, across ground I did not know, but I had been advised to keep to the circuitous track which avoided the wooded hill, where bandits were said to lurk, and the swampy land at its foot. The manor house was set among orchards, where the ripening fruit was beginning to dip the branches of the trees, and I could see its uneven rooftop from a distance. The demesne had been in the ownership of the de Greys for generations and their home had been added to over the years so that the old stone keep had long since disappeared within a shell of brick and timber, tiles and plaster. The exterior of the building had little regard for artistry but the bustling dovecote and a string of well-tended fish ponds gave Danson an appearance of prosperity and confidence.

I was greeted courteously at the lodge by a retainer wearing crisp fawn livery with the crest of an eagle picked out in silver thread on his chest. I was not disappointed to learn from him that Sir Hugh was absent from the manor hawking and would not return until nightfall. It spared me the need to give him an explanation of my visit and listen to his expressions of robust bonhomie. The gatekeeper had me shown to the marshal's small office behind the newly built great hall, where Master Gregory rose to his feet as soon as I entered, shuffling a number of rolls into a tidy line on his table. The side of his mouth twitched but he gave no other sign of surprise to see me.

'I am sorry to disturb you, good-brother,' I said, intent on conveying the utmost sincerity. 'I know you are occupied with important business. My visit need only be short. I have found something of my sister's which you must have given her and I wanted to return it without delay.'

Gregory held my gaze but his expression did not change so I continued without hesitation. 'She had sewed it into one of her gowns to keep it safe and it did not come to light at first. Alys must have valued it greatly.'

I drew the pearl from my purse and held it out in my palm, its milky surface catching the sunlight. The marshal did not reach out at once to take it but nor did he repudiate knowledge of it. 'It is indeed of much worth,' he said after a pause. 'You are a man of honour and honesty to bring me it, Master Harry.'

I drew breath while he stared silently at the jewel, for I had expected him to deny it had been his gift, and I admired his self-control at what must have been a painful moment. Then, with faintest of sighs, he took it in his thin, tapering fingers and held it to the light. 'Perfect, as my wife's beauty was perfect.'

I concentrated on disguising my surprise. 'You were most generous to her, Master Gregory. Her wedding ring was of the finest gold from Cheapside, I remember.'

He ignored my pleasantry. 'Thank you for this, good-brother, in very truth.' His voice sounded hoarse but he slipped the pearl inside his gown and moved to a side table, set below a sloping beam, where there was a flagon of ale and some goblets. At once his tone became matter-of-fact. 'You will take some refreshment? You must be thirsty from your ride?'

'I should be glad of a drink before my return. I'd like to be back at Greenwich before nightfall.'

He nodded and poured me a generous draught but I sensed he was not anxious for me to linger. I wondered if he would permit himself a tremor of sadness when I had gone, the slightest moistening of that sharp eye, the least crack in his impassive façade. I could not warm to him and found something unpalatable about his icy calm but I was sorry for the dreadful circumstances of his loss and sensed he might be capable of emotion in private. On my own account I was gradually coming to terms with immeasurable relief that it was not my master who had given Alys the pearl, purchasing her services like any drab. While I drank the strong ale with decent speed I asked Gregory about the arrangements for the Archbishop's forthcoming visit and he seemed thankful to speak of the administrative details he had in hand, relaxing to describe ceremonies he planned with an ease he found impossible when discussing personal matters. As I rose to leave I had a foolish impulse to give him some morsel of comfort to hold on to, while he reflected tenderly alone, and it may have been the effect of my hasty quaffing that I did not recognise the double-edged nature of my information.

'My sister's body was made seemly for burial by my colleague, Doctor Giovanni dei Signorelli,' I said. 'He told me something you should know. Alys was with child, perhaps ten weeks in term.'

I saw his hand tremble before he clenched his fist to quieten it and a strange gurgle came from his throat which he converted into a cough. 'Of course,' he said, 'of course. She would have borne me a child, the child I have longed for.' His voice had become quite different from that of the impersonal man of business and I suffered a qualm of fear that I had made a serious misjudgement in mentioning his wife's pregnancy, expecting him not to know of it already. As quickly as before his self-discipline was re-asserted and he smiled thinly, grasping my shoulder. 'I am most grateful to you for your visit. God go with you, Harry Somers.'

*****

My head was spinning when I turned away from the hamlet of Danson and without conscious choice I turned north, rather than retracing my route to Eltham, until I found myself at the foot of the track which led uphill, straight back to the great heath. It was the most direct way to Greenwich but, like all prudent travellers, I had avoided the steep wooded slopes on my outward journey, for fear of encountering the bands of thieving outlaws who frequented the area. Now I was too obsessed by confused thoughts, and perhaps a degree of inebriated foolhardiness, to pay much attention to prudence as I turned my horse's head towards the rough climb. In the distance across the flatter land which stretched towards the river I glimpsed a group of horsemen moving in the opposite direction and, noting their light coloured livery, I guessed they were Sir Hugh de Grey's hawking party returning home. I was pleased to miss them.

A breeze had developed which whipped fronds of hair escaping from my cap against my forehead and I stopped for a minute to tuck back the irritating strands. I had gone to Danson expecting to confirm that Alys must have received the pearl from a lover (in my mind Doctor Swanwych). I had even readied myself to denounce the villain on my return. For, if Thomas Chope was innocent, this generous lover was the obvious suspect who had instigated further murderous violence in an attempt to recover his incriminating gift. My theory had been rubbished by Master Gregory's tacit acceptance that he was the donor but, the more I thought about it, his excessive self-restraint seemed unconvincing and something about his manner did not ring true. Yet why should he imply that he gave his wife a costly present if he did not? I couldn't believe he was greedy to acquire the pearl for himself. Was he trying to protect Alys's reputation by disguising the fact that she had played the whore? Was he unable to face the truth of her behaviour and denied it even to himself? Or was it possible that he was intent on protecting another?

I started to walk my horse slowly up the narrow track, the reins loose in my hands, while my head cleared and I reasoned through the alternatives. I was concentrating so hard on an alarming possibility which had just occurred to me that I was oblivious to my surroundings and did not see the cord thrown to entangle leisurely lifting hooves. I was jolted forward in the saddle with such force that I banged my nose on the pommel and in the same moment I was dragged sideways from behind and a sack thrown over my head. I caught sight only of mud-coloured hose and a scuffed boot. My left foot caught in the stirrup as I was hauled down, causing an agonising bolt of pain to shoot through my lame leg, but my cry of distress was swiftly muffled by a gag tied over the blindfold, wrenching my mouth open and compelling me to breathe through my nose. The hessian was so close to my nostrils that I was terrified I would suffocate and I struggled desperately to pull it aside but my arms were pulled back and my wrists bound fast. My throbbing ankle was then strapped to its partner and I was flung across another rider's horse. When I wriggled and tried to raise my head he fetched me a stinging blow with his whip across my shrouded face before wheeling his mount and spurring it into a gallop. Further resistance was useless and I drooped, half-conscious, my neck under intolerable strain as my head dangled, consigned to miserable captivity.

*****

We had not travelled far when we stopped and I was dragged from the horse up a step into what seemed to be a small building, where the men's voices sounded confined and did not echo. Before the door was closed I fancied I could hear water lapping in the distance and, from the forward jolting I had received on the journey, it made sense that we had descended the hill towards the river. I thought hard to remember any structures I had seen near the bank but was certain there was nothing notable and concluded I had been taken to some brigands' hideout or fishermen's hut. I supposed I would be held there while a ransom was sought from the Duke's chamberlain, assuming I had been identified as a member of his household, and I wondered gloomily how long the transaction would take. On the other hand I had little of value in my purse and it might not be deemed worthwhile to enquire as to my credentials. A useless prisoner could easily be disposed of with a knife to the throat and his carcase hurled into the ebbing tide. I must ensure they knew I had patrons who would, I trusted, purchase my freedom but there was small chance of making myself understood while the gag throttled speech.

I felt movement at my feet and realised a chain was being fixed to the rope which bound them together and fastened to something firm, presumably on the wall. There was grim irony in being shackled like Thomas Chope, the man whose liberty I was seeking to secure. The release of my wrists was unexpected but, before I could attempt to tear the cloth from my mouth, my arms were seized and held by a man on each side while I was kicked sharply in the groin to teach me compliance. My captors' next actions were startling as I felt my points undone and my clothes taken from me, robe, jerkin, shirt, drawers and hose, until I stood naked except for the sack over my head, trembling and fearful of some horrible assault. I thought there were three or four men but they said little between themselves and I could not be sure. I gathered from the rustling of the material that they were examining my gown and other faint sounds suggested that all my garments were receiving attention, so I imagined them sharing out my things as pathetic booty. Then fingers groped my privates and I tensed in terror but my reaction was met with a guffaw.

'Christ, he thinks I fancy him! No such luck, changeling. We'd not soil ourselves fucking the devil's spawn.'

Another voice spoke sharply, the voice of one in more authority I thought 'He's nothing hidden on him. Pull on his shirt and hose and bind him tightly. I'll send a message to see what should be done with him.'

With frantic groans and snorts I tried to persuade them to unmuzzle me but they ignored my efforts and trussed my limbs so that I could not move. One bade me a mocking 'God speed,' as they slammed the door and rode away, leaving me full of dread that some robber-lord would decide my fate without troubling to interview me. Just when I had gained some insight into the mystery of my sister's death, I was faced with the prospect of my own demise, pronounced unserviceable as booty to my abductors and rendered useless in my quest for the truth. Inside the coarse sacking I began to weep and begged the Blessed Virgin to help me, not for my own pitiful sake but in order that the evil-doers might be brought to justice.

Chapter 9

I had no inkling how long I would have to wait and feared my limbs would become numb, as I was scarcely able even to wiggle my fingers, so I was both surprised and apprehensive when I heard shouts not long after I had been abandoned. Distant cries sounded peremptory and the tone was vaguely familiar but if this was the principal who had ordered my capture, his anger did not bode well. I heard the growl of aggrieved underlings, protesting at their master's strictures, but could make no sense of what was happening outside, except that there was a good deal of chinking of bridles as horsemen drew near. Then the door crashed back against the wall and the command was given. 'Untie him at once and take off that blindfold!'

I could not credit my ears until the sack was removed from my head and my eyes confirmed that Sir Hugh de Grey stood before me, in the guise of rescuer, it seemed, not captor. He had with him a number of personal attendants who had taken hold of four disgruntled looking colleagues, all wearing his livery, among whom I noted the wearer of a scuffed boot which I recognised from the ambush. My astonishment that it was men from Danson who had taken me prisoner in the wood was momentarily overridden by another shock of recognition, when I observed that the fawn jackets of Sir Hugh's recalcitrant followers were begrimed by dust and looked grey – just as they would if they were dirtied by smoke. I struggled to gather my wits as the young knight pointed at the weal across my face and rounded on his prisoners.

'Whoever did that to Master Somers will be flogged. Page, fetch him a flask so he may drink and bring those stools here so we can sit. Sergeant falconer, take these four men in charge and convey them under escort to the cell at Danson. The rest of you, wait outside and see to the horses.'

He moved to his chief henchman and spoke more quietly into his ear so that I could not hear his final orders.

I sat down gingerly, stretching my cramped legs in front of me, while Sir Hugh remained standing. 'It is fortunate my hawking party caught sight of these miscreants as they left the hut where they had no business to be. You have been shamefully mistreated and I fear will hardly wish to have a conversation with me'.

I felt life returning to my limbs and was pleased that I could summon an ironic smile. 'On the contrary, Sir Hugh, you are the one man in all the world I wish to speak with.'

He raised an eyebrow uncertainly. 'I can understand your indignation if you recognised the de Grey colours when you were taken. My men have been misdirected and disgraced their livery. I apologise.'

'I didn't know who assaulted me. I assume there was some misunderstanding. But I should tell you I had already resolved to seek you out, for there are questions only you can answer.'

He sighed and sank onto the stool facing me and I knew that his immediate comprehension of my meaning was significant. 'I owe you the courtesy of a hearing. I do not promise to answer your questions.'

I ignored his qualification and drew on my resources of courage, reminding myself that in the past I had needed to criticise and upbraid a Duke's son and so should not be daunted by confronting a mere knight. 'It concerns my sister.' A vein on his temple throbbed but he did not speak. 'I wish to ask you whether you ever gave her a gift.'

'My wife rewarded her women on her own account. She was quite free to do so.'

'I understand, but the gift I have in mind seems unlikely to have come from Lady Blanche. I am speaking of a pearl, of some value.'

Sir Hugh stood impatiently. 'Why should I give your sister such a gift?' I caught his eye and he had the decency to flush.

'I don't think I need to explain, sir. I pass no judgement. I know of my sister's generosity with her favours.'

He frowned. 'She was not a wanton, Master Somers, whatever you may have heard, but she was wasted on my desiccated marshal. She did not throw herself at me. Indeed, she resisted my overtures at first, for the sake of her mistress, but I took her unawares one night and we found pleasure in each other. After that we met by arrangement on other occasions. Such things are not unusual, as you must know. Many lords make free with the womenfolk in their service.' His voice rose with truculent bravado and I thought how youthful he sounded, despite being my senior by half a dozen years.

'Did Master Gregory know of this arrangement?'

'Christ's bones, of course not! One doesn't trumpet such things. Alys waited on Lady Blanche in the evening until my wife retired, so she was usually late returning to her husband's bed. In the meantime she often graced mine. Are you so ignorant of such affairs?'

I was irritated by his veneer of sophistication and the cavalier acceptance of his right to tup any servant he lusted for but I knew I must not lose my temper. I was on the verge of crucial discoveries. 'Did Lady Blanche know?'

'You impertinent pup! How dare you? That is no business of yours.' His chin was quivering with assumed indignation.

'My sister was murdered, Sir Hugh, and Lady Blanche's father has authorised me to make enquiries. I am aware that the circumstances are more complicated than was at first thought.'

'The murderer is locked in a cell, is he not? Why are you delving into matters that are irrelevant?'

'There is good reason to believe Master Chope is innocent and there are others who may have wished her dead.' I dragged myself upright and took a step towards him. 'Did you you kill my sister, Sir Hugh?'

His eyes were bulging at my unexpected effrontery and I noticed him grasp one trembling hand with the other but he had the grace to reply. 'No, I did not.'

'Did you give her the pearl?'

'Yes.'

'Did Lady Blanche know of your congress with Alys?'

He stared at me as the implication dawned on him. 'That is outrageous,' he said but his protest lacked vigour and he did not look me in the eye.

'Whose were the men that captured me on the hill?'

'Mine.'

'And did they come from Danson – or from Greenwich? Were they the attendants you left with your wife? Were they her orders they were obeying, not yours?'

'You have no proof.'

'Did she know about you and Alys?'

He made a desperate attempt to regain the bluster he had shown earlier. 'A gentleman does not need to explain his bed-mates. A wife's duty is to accept his nature.'

'Did Lady Blanche know?'

'Christ damn you! Yes, of course she knew. Why should I trouble to disguise it?' He strode backwards and forwards in the narrow space while I stayed motionless, my heart pounding. 'I refuse to believe my wife had her slaughtered.'

'Lady Blanche has been very nervous lately. I could see that she was distraught when she spoke to me.'

'I know that! She has been terrified that I killed your sister or, at any rate, that if my gift was found in Alys's possession, I would be suspected of murder. That's why the good woman has been a bundle of nerves. Not because she instigated the deed.'

This made sense and I acknowledged it. I understood now that Lady Blanche had been responsible for the attacks on my person and for the fire, although her followers may have used more violence than she would have countenanced, but I too found it difficult to see her as her maid's executioner. I could not believe that her sorrow at my sister's death was feigned and it was credible she feared for her husband's safety and honour. Besides, Alys's murder was undoubtedly a crime of passion, not cold-hearted assassination.

Sir Hugh was crouched on the stool, his head in his hands, and I went to him, brusquely shaking his shoulder. 'The men you left at Greenwich have been guilty of several crimes, at your wife's behest. If accusations are laid against them it will be impossible to keep her name out of the matter. Your honour and hers will be destroyed. But I do not think those men murdered Alys and I need to prove who did. That is more important to me than anything else. Do you understand what I am saying? I need to know that you have told me the truth in all respects.'

His truculence returned at my threat and he rose. 'Of course I did. You can prove nothing. What have you done with the pearl? That would be what my wife was seeking. She thought it would incriminate me.'

I smiled as he framed the question but there was no amusement in my heart. 'I have given it to the person who I assumed had presented it to Alys. I have just returned from Danson, where I went to see my good-brother. He acknowledged it as his gift.'

We held each other's eyes as we both considered possible reasons for the contradictions in what the marshal had told me and I think we reached the same conclusion simultaneously. 'Merciful Heaven,' I said under my breath. 'Is Master Gregory capable of such barbarity? Could he have come gone to Greenwich that night without being missed at Danson?'

'Very easily. He has been a doughty soldier in his day. I had left him at the manor in charge of the arrangements for the Archbishop's visit, with only a small staff to assist him. No one would have queried his comings and goings and several of my men went back and forth between Danson and Greenwich while I was there.'

'He may not have known of your dalliance with his wife, Sir Hugh, but I imagine he heard tales from your messengers of her misconduct with Thomas Chope. It was common currency at Greenwich. Perhaps he knew of earlier gossip too. I fancy he is a proud and jealous man.'

'Which is why I sought to spare him from knowing I had boarded his wife. I respect him as a competent marshal. Now he is under no illusions. He will have recognised the pearl.'

'And he is capable of frenzied violence when roused. You may be in danger.'

He gave me a supercilious look. 'I think not. Loyalty to his lord is an article of faith with such a man. He would sooner die than betray his guiding principle. But he must be taken in charge. Will you accompany me to Danson to see justice done?'

We moved to the door and Sir Hugh snapped instructions to his escort that a horse be provided for my use but, before we had mounted, we heard shouts across the marsh and identified a large posse of retainers in the Duke of Gloucester's colours who were approaching. They were led by the chamberlain in person and by his side an attendant rode, conveying in front of him on his saddle, a grimy and dishevelled urchin who let out a yell of triumph when he saw me.

'It's 'im! He's safe. Glory be!'

There was no point in hiding my bewilderment. 'Rendell, how did you know?'

'Your horse, Master Somers. It came back across the heath without you – from over the hill where there's said to be bandits. I jumped up on the saddle and rode him down to the palace. I telled them what I'd seen. So we came to rescue you. I done well, ain't I?'

'Very well. I'm profoundly grateful, Rendell, and will see you're rewarded.' I turned towards the Duke's senior representative. 'And my thanks to you, Chamberlain. As you can see Sir Hugh found me first but if he had not, I would have been in dire need of your services.'

'Chamberlain,' Sir Hugh said, addressing his father-in-law with formality, 'we need to go at once to Danson and see a great wrong righted. I should be pleased if you would come with us and advise me. I will explain as we ride.'

The chamberlain gave his agreement and beckoned his men to follow, spurring ahead of them beside his daughter's husband. I took Rendell onto my horse, ruffling his filthy hair, and dropped behind the leaders. I did not wish to eavesdrop on what Sir Hugh was saying and nursed my anxiety about what we would find at his manor for I knew, as he did not, what information I had given Master Gregory, in addition to the pearl. Nonetheless I was not allowed to dwell on my sombre thoughts for Rendell was full of news he had learned at the palace, squeaking at me eagerly as he persuaded his tongue to repeat some fine-sounding phrases before lapsing into his more usual figures of speech.

'That mason, Randolf they call him. He's pronounced thief and vagabond. The chamberlain made enquiries, then sent to apprehend him at the Duke's house in the City but he never showed up there. He's run off and Joan Coverdale's girdle's run with him, they says. What a caper, eh! Cor, I wish we had excitement like this every day.'

*****

Sir Hugh deployed his men at the entrance to his demesne and around the house, with orders to apprehend the marshal if he attempted to flee. I did not think this likely and was unsurprised that, when we burst into the hall, the only occupiers were maids strewing fragrant herbs among the rushes on the floor. All was peaceable and Master Gregory was nowhere to be seen. I steadied myself and suggested quietly that the young knight and the chamberlain should accompany me to the small office behind the service passage but I opened the door with foreboding for I sensed what we would find there.

Gregory's body hung from the sloping beam I had noticed on my previous visit and it had clearly been there for some time. His scraggy neck was twisted in the coil of thick material which held it and his eyes bulged from their sockets, fixed with a look of stark horror. Beneath him on the floor lay a document which seemed likely to have fallen from his fingers as they contorted and, while my companions exclaimed with shock at the scene, I bent to pick it up and read its message aloud.

I and no other effected rightful punishment on my unfaithful wife. I have no remorse for her death but, may God forgive me, I did not mean to kill my child, my only child.

He had signed it with his full name.

Sir Hugh turned aside to lean over his marshal's desk, choking back the bile in his mouth, and I saw him reach out to take a small packet resting on the neatly stacked rolls of parchment. He grasped it in his fist while asking the chamberlain to fetch men to cut down the sad carcase but as soon as the older man had left us he uncurled his palm and held it out to me. 'This has my name on it. Open it, Harry.'

He nodded as I took a hesitant step forward and I did as he asked. There was no message, simply a twist of cloth and inside it, a single luminous pearl. Sir Hugh gulped and collected himself. 'He was true to his master, you see, as I knew he would be: a loyal servant to the end.' He lifted his head and held my gaze. 'If Alys was pregnant, I think it probable the child was not his.' Then, he took the pearl from my hand. 'Will you find it necessary to refer to this wretched token?'

'I don't think so,' I said as I considered hastily what might be involved in keeping silent 'But Lady Blanche knew of it and the men she set to look for it...'

'My wife will hold her peace on the matter, you may be sure. Our honour is at stake. As for the men who took you captive and carried out atrocities beyond their remit, they have already reaped their reward.'

I did not immediately understand and began to ask how he could be sure they would not name Lady Blanche as the instigator of their crimes but, as we heard footsteps approaching, he held up his hand. 'I was their lord and had every right to execute judgement upon them. My officer carried out my decree as soon as they were brought to Danson. They will say no more. As for you, Harry, I trust I may make the claim of friendship in return for what we have done for each other.'

The chamberlain bustled back into the room, with his troop of followers, and he grasped my hand as if I were of equal status with himself and his son-in-law. His cordiality led me to suspect that he knew more of the situation, from his daughter no doubt, than he would ever admit. 'Well done, Harry, well done,' he said. 'You have achieved all you set out to do. You have unmasked this most unlikely murderer and exonerated the lad who was wrongly accused. I have sent word to the sheriff and dispatched a message to Greenwich for the release of Thomas Chope. He should be your acolyte for the rest of his life. His debt to you is very great.'

'We are all in your debt, Harry,' Sir Hugh added, making the understanding between us needlessly explicit. 'You know how much we owe you and we shall strive to repay you as you deserve.'

Thus it was that I became the hero of the hour, but a hero who knew himself compromised by keeping silent about the whole truth, shielding my betters from their wrong-doing. Nevertheless I welcomed the plaudits and the relief which I felt. The tragic episode of my sister's death was over and I had no way of foreseeing that, in time, it would have significant consequences for me.

Part II – 1439-41

Chapter 10

As we moved along the corridor towards the door of the Duke's chamber, retainers wearing his badge of the swan on their livery flattened themselves against the wall and men at arms stood to attention with their halberds upright at their sides. It was right and proper they should show the utmost courtesy to the chamberlain and Doctor Swanwych but these gentlemen were my escort, conducting me to audience with Humphrey of Gloucester in his private study which I had never dreamed I would enter. I was clad in a fine black robe, like a fully-fledged physician, and crowning my neatly cropped hair was a silk cap of superior design. The feeble November sunlight flecked my gown with patches of pale grey as we passed the high windows and I appreciated its warmth in the chill air. The fullness of the material concealed my uneven gait to some extent but, more importantly at that moment, it hid the trembling in my legs; no one need know of the churning in my stomach.

'Courage, Harry,' my mentor said and he squeezed my elbow to give me reassurance but, as the door was flung open before us, the chamberlain glared quickly to indicate that we must remain motionless until the Duke beckoned us forward. I took a deep breath and lowered my eyes, awaiting the prolonged silence which I had been advised to expect, but almost at once his Grace rose and stood beside his desk while we advanced, in halting step with each other. In unison we bowed. It was only then I noticed that the Duchess was also present, seated in the shadowed recess beside the fireplace, and I quickly repeated my obeisance to her. It was three days since they had returned to Greenwich, bringing with them a large company of new attendants to augment the splendour of the ducal household.

'Master Somers, is it not? You are welcome.' The voice was melodious and his hand gesture elegant as he acknowledged my companions. They fell back a pace and allowed me to proceed alone. I dared not keep my gaze directly on Duke Humphrey, closer to him than I had been since boyhood, but I noted the pointed chin, broad forehead and penetrating eyes, beneath hooded lids. Then he laughed. 'Why, of course, I should have remembered. You are the mudlark who shielded your tormenters long ago. You had a sense of what was just and honourable even then.'

'I did not think you would recall such childish pranks, my lord Duke.' I prayed he would not recall who my chief tormenter had been.

'You are much like your father. He would have been proud of you. I was pleased with the reports I received when you accompanied my son to the university but, now I have been informed of all that happened during my absence from Greenwich, I am grateful for what you have done to see an evil-doer identified and an innocent man freed.' His hand moved to the medallion round his neck. 'I am sorry, of course, for the loss of your sister.'

I bowed awkwardly. 'You are gracious, my lord.'

A rustle of silk brocade from beside the hearth caused the Duke to turn as his wife came to his side. I had never seen Duchess Eleanor at such close quarters and I was overwhelmed, as much by the brilliance of her smile as by her beauty. 'Master Somers, it is the more commendable that you could keep a cool head and dispassionate judgement at a time of such distress. Despite your youth, you are to be admitted to the guild of physicians before long, I hear.'

'By special dispensation, my lady.' I could not banish the pride from my voice.

The Duke nodded. 'We have made representations. From now on we purpose to reside more regularly at our Palace of Pleasance here at Greenwich. I shall be less encumbered by affairs of state and will indulge my love of learning and debate in the company of scholars from far and wide. I should be happy if you would make one of our number for our disputations and listen to the wisdom of the ancients from the Italians who have renewed acquaintance with their works.'

'I am honoured, your Grace.' I could scarcely speak for excitement at the prospect of sitting alongside Doctor Swanwych and Giovanni dei Signorelli when some of the world's most learned men shared their knowledge with the Duke and his chosen followers.

Humphrey of Gloucester relieved me of the need to say more. 'We are making new dispositions in our household. Doctor Swanwych will be more often absent from Greenwich, fulfilling commissions concerning the books I am giving to the University of Oxford – as he did so successfully recently. You will wish to work with another physician while he is away and this can be arranged.' I nodded, expecting him to refer to Giovanni, but he took his wife's arm and drew her in front of him. 'A worthy man who is both priest and physician will be attending us from time to time – Doctor Southwell – he is knowledgeable and you should learn much from him. Duchess Eleanor also has a new clerk, Roger Bolingbroke, who is conversant with the mysteries of the heavens and how they govern our humours and whose loyalty to us is unsurpassed. I propose therefore, Master Somers, that you be attached to her household while you continue your studies and widen your experience.'

He paused as if seeking my agreement and I stammered thanks, bowing to his wife, but she moved forward and extended her hand for me to take and kiss. Her fingers were slender and tapering and their gentle touch filled me with a surge of unfamiliar excitement. 'My lady, I am privileged to offer you my service.' She rewarded me with an enigmatic smile and fixed her eyes on my blemished face.

*****

The Duchess's personal attendants were housed across the courtyard from John Swanwych's rooms and it was arranged that I would lodge where Doctor Southwell was to be accommodated. This gentleman was a physician of renown and held a number of clerical positions, including as Canon of St. Stephen's Chapel in the Palace of Westminster and rector of St. Stephen's, Walbrook, in the City of London. He was likely to be an irregular resident at Greenwich, I thought. It took me only two journeys to carry my few possessions to their new home and on my second traverse I was hailed by a raucous shout as Grizel ran to my side. I had encountered her several times in the months which had passed since our adventures in the summer but she had been more reserved in her approaches and I imagined this reflected her growing maturity.

'Gone up in the world, eh? Joining the Duchess's household. Suppose I'm too lowly to be in your presence, sir. Excuse my base company.' She curtsied.

'Don't tease, Grizel. I've been greatly honoured but I'm just the same as I was and I'm still your friend.'

'Maybe for now but you'll change, mark my words. Hobnobbing with them scholars and all, you'll not be the same six months hence.' I shook my head but she went on with her lecture. 'Don't know nothing about this Doctor Southwell but you'd do well to steer clear of that new clerk, Roger Bolingbroke. Dame Margery says he's trouble – come across him before when she were younger, I imagine.'

'What kind of trouble?'

'Dunno. I couldn't overhear no more. She weren't talking to me.'

'No, of course. Still, thanks for the warning.'

'You're laughing at me. See, you're already getting too grand for me.'

She flounced away but I was reluctant to let her go in a bad mood. 'How's Rendell?' I called.

She turned her head with abroad grin. 'Thank'ee kindly, sir, for asking. Rendell's gone into the kitchens, old enough to be a scullion now, he is, and well thought of for the help he gave you.'

'Quite right too. I owe him a great debt.'

Her smile was almost coquettish and I did not care for it. 'Maybe he'll take you up on that one day – or I'll do it on his behalf. Remember what I've told you. Us lower orders have our uses.'

*****

The Duke had commissioned Doctor Swanwych to travel to Italy to confront Pier Candido Decembrio, who had agreed to translate Plato's work, *Republic*, into Latin but appeared to be making slow progress. Before he departed from Greenwich John, as I was now invited to call him, suggested we spend the evening at the tavern in the City where we had parted on the night preceding my fateful return to Greenwich in the summer. I remained wary of my former master in view of his apparent relationship with my sister (although he had never admitted it to me) but it seemed churlish to refuse his invitation so we took the boat upstream and occupied ourselves with light-hearted conversation over the ale-jug.

After a while silence fell between us and I dare say my eyes were as bleary as John's but he rallied himself first and pushed his goblet aside. 'Harry,' he said and his speech was only slightly slurred. 'There is something I should have told you. Maybe it will distress you but I cannot feel wholly at ease, keeping it from you.'

I stiffened. 'There's no need. I have no claim to know who lay with my sister.'

His voice dropped to a whisper. 'You believe I did?'

'Please, John,' I protested, trying to stand but finding some difficulty.

''I was never Alys's lover. I swear it.'

'She was seen to visit you.' My truculence overcame the difficulty of speaking clearly.

'She did and that is what I need to tell you.'

'You spurned her! You thought her unworthy of your bed!'

'Stop it, Harry. You are on quite the wrong tack. I am a physician, am I not? Some physicians dabble in matters they should leave alone – or consign them to old women who do the devil's work with their potions. Alys came to beg my help in such a matter but I have never countenanced those vile practices and could not help her. Do you understand what I am saying?'

I sat very still in my drunken blur. 'I know she was with child. Giovanni told me after he made her wounds decent for burial.'

'I should have guessed.' John sighed and his voice thickened. 'The child was not her husband's – she did not tell me whose – and she did not wish to deceive him by foisting a bastard on him as his own. I respected her for that. She asked me for some mixture that would procure a miscarriage. When I refused, she wept and begged me most poignantly. She offered me her body in an attempt to persuade me and I confess I was tempted to take her, although I would never have abetted her in defying God's law. It eases my mind to have made my confession to you.'

I had the advantage of John in knowing who had fathered my sister's baby but I would never disclose it. 'I am no priest,' I said lamely.

'It is long since I made full confession to a priest.'

I stared at the man I had admired for so many years and I do not know whether, in my befuddled state, I was more appalled by this new tale of my sister's waywardness or John's last admission. I bowed my head and he, seeing my confusion, said no more, letting me slip into temporary oblivion. When I awoke he had left the inn and taken a boat to Deptford for his journey across the Narrow Sea.

*****

Immediately after his release from imprisonment Thomas Chope had been sent away from Greenwich, not as punishment, for he had been exonerated, but to mitigate the embarrassment the chamberlain felt at his mistreatment. He was despatched so speedily to join the household at the Duke's residence in the City that I had not seen him before his departure and I regretted this. Accordingly, after spending the night for the second time at the inn John Swanwych favoured, I determined to pay a visit to the magnificent house by the riverside, just west of Paul's Wharf, known as Duke's Wardrobe at Baynard's Castle.

Above the entrance, as at the Palace of Pleasance, the Duke's heraldic device, of England and France quartered, were impaled with the Cobham arms, to honour his wife. On the right side the shield was supported by a leashed greyhound and, on the left, by a chained antelope bearing a ducal coronet. I had little time to admire the workmanship of the carving as the gatekeeper demanded my business and, on hearing my name, admitted me at once. My reputation had spread beyond Greenwich, it seemed.

I was shown into an anteroom and offered refreshment while Thomas was sent for but I had hardly set the Venetian goblet to my lips when he bounded in, sawdust still clinging to his shabby tunic, and flung himself at my feet. 'For goodness sake, get up,' I said, deeply embarrassed. 'How are you?'

'How am I? Free! Free and alive and pursuing my trade, thanks to you who owed me nothing but disdain. They hustled me from Greenwich with such speed I had no chance to give you thanks. I left a message but it was a poor response to your efforts to save me.' He pulled himself onto his knees. 'I never thought to see you here. What is it you want of me? I am your man for life, Harry Somers, and will do whatever you ask.'

I was amazed by his display of emotion. 'I don't want anything, Thomas. I was in the City and thought to come here. I also regretted that you had already been taken away by the time I returned from Danson. But you don't owe me anything. I wanted to make sure justice was done – and ultimately it was.'

'You may not see it that way, Harry Somers, but I know my obligation. I deserved your enmity and you gave me my life. I mean it in all solemnity: you have every right to call on my services whenever I can help you. I shall gladly obey – in token of what you did for me and for Alys.'

The seriousness in his voice and the loving way he spoke my sister's name convinced me that I must reply in similar terms. 'I cannot think I shall need to call on your assistance but I'm grateful for your offer and I accept it.' Then I abandoned the note of formality and slapped him on the back with familiarity I never thought to show towards Thomas Chope but which was worthy of the brother-in-law he should have been. 'I hope we can be firm friends in future. Tell me of life in the City.'

We talked for half an hour and I gleaned a good deal of information from him, not least about my new master, Doctor Southwell, who was well esteemed by the citizens he served both as pastor and physician. 'A mild-tempered man, eager to please and devoted to God's service, so I've heard,' Thomas said, but when I mentioned Roger Bolingbroke he pulled a face. 'He's attended the Duchess on visits here once or twice. He's not well thought of and there are stories about him tangling with things best left alone. Still, it's not for me to believe all the bad-mouthing I hear, not after what happened to me.'

I left Thomas cheered that previous difficulties between us had been swept aside and untroubled by his pledge of support which I did not take seriously. I promised to call on him again when I was in the City and he vowed to introduce me to taverns with a livelier reputation than the one frequented by John Swanwych. All in all I was surprised how easy it was to revise my previous opinion of him – perhaps we had both learned the virtues of tolerance.

*****

I was disconcerted to hear at the gatehouse that my new master had arrived at Greenwich during my absence in the City and I hurried to his rooms, preparing my excuses for not being there to greet him. I expected he might be engaged in supervising the arrangement of his possessions and when I opened the door, somewhat timidly, a bird-like little man darted towards me, retort and beaker in hand. He waved aside my stammered apologies and began to address a series of rapid questions towards me while pouring liquid from the larger vessel into the cup.

'What humour do you associate with autumn? Which blessed apostle governs it? Would you expect one born under the sign of the crab to be of melancholic disposition? With what season is yellow bile linked? Can you answer, lad? Are you tongue-tied?'

I gathered my thoughts quickly to respond to this elementary catechism, based on the teachings of the ancients I had long ago absorbed. 'Black bile; the Apostle John; no, one born under the crab is likely to be of choleric disposition; and yellow bile is linked to summer which is hot and dry in nature.'

'Hee, hee!' Doctor Southwell slopped the last of the liquid into the beaker while emitting a high-pitched giggle. 'All correct, nothing omitted and extra information I did not ask for. Welcome, Harry Somers. Here sniff this and tell me what you think.'

He thrust the cup into my hand and I had no doubt what it contained. 'The urine is discoloured and diseased. The patient probably has some pain while passing water.'

'Well done. I am prescribing an infusion to counteract the gross imbalance in his humours. Do you know that fellow in the stables with the face of a lion? You have seen a lion? Do his features denote a leonine temperament? I should dearly like to examine his cranium, a most interesting shape.'

I judged there was no need to reply to all these questions, especially as I had never seen a lion, albeit there were drawings of this animal in some of the manuscripts I had studied. 'I know the man you mean. He seems of a placid disposition. He'd be flattered if an eminent doctor asked to feel over his head. I'll speak to him if you wish.'

'Practical as well as erudite! We shall do well together, Harry Somers. Come, let me show you where everything is kept. These jars, for instance. Why are they this shape do you think?'

'They are waisted to make it easy to take them from the shelf. Doctor Giovanni dei Signorelli says they are called albarelli.'

'Hee, hee! I'd forgotten Giovanni was lodged here. I met him years ago in Padua. Now kneel with me and we will ask God's blessing on our endeavours for I am grateful He has sent you to me and you, I hope, will benefit from our efforts to serve the Duke and his household. Let us praise His blessed name.'

I knelt beside him, remembering that he was a cleric as well as a physician and marvelling at his liveliness of mind and body. I knew I should miss the calm sagacity of my former master but I fancied I would enjoy completing my studies in the practice of medicine in the company of this idiosyncratic tutor. At any event I was unlikely to have leisure to be bored.

*****

A year had passed since my sister's death and I was admitted to the guild of physicians. I was filled with pride and a solemn intention to fulfil every obligation implicit in my oath to uphold the highest standards of medical practice. For weeks at a time Doctor Southwell left me alone to look after the health of the Duchess's household and I was generally content, knowing myself favoured to have such responsibilities when still so young. Only two circumstances troubled me. I told myself that Grizel's increasing reserve was quite fitting as she blossomed visibly into young womanhood but it annoyed me to see her dallying more than once with a tall, well-built guardsman who was often posted at the entrance to the Duke's apartments. When I saw him reach out his hand to stroke her cheek I felt a ridiculous surge of anger, all the more so because she offered no objection. Yet I knew I had no business to concern myself on her account.

The other cause of discomfort was more personal and difficult to handle. Among my professional charges were the Duchess's ladies, a dozen well-born females of varying ages some of whom, especially the younger and more comely, were inclined to tease me in a way I thought unbecoming. It was obvious they found it amusing to have so youthful and inexperienced a doctor to consult on their minor ailments. Chief among my tormentors was Lady Maud Warrenne, a girl near my own age and, I understood, betrothed to a nobleman away on an embassy to the French court; when he returned they would marry. In the meantime she showed none of the decorous modesty one would have expected in behaviour towards her physician. It seemed to me she invented maladies in order to call upon my services and, although she was of course always chaperoned when she summoned me, she thrust out her bosom as she described her symptoms and made darting movements with her tongue, between sharp little teeth, which diverted my mind considerably from my medical diagnosis. I had been slow to mature with masculine desires and was still unpractised in satisfying them but the longing I felt for Lady Maud became almost overpowering.

One night I trudged up the stairs to Doctor Southwell's rooms after a bibulous carousal in the hall, carrying a taper to light the uneven steps, when a sudden movement extinguished its light. A finger of moonlight remained from a window slit on the landing above and I saw the slender arm which reached for my shoulder as sweet-scented lips found mine. I was hard with lust for her but forced myself to push her away.

'Lady, I beg you. This is wrong.'

'My friends said you would be stuffy,' she giggled, taking my hand and putting it on her breast where I could feel the pounding of her heart. 'You have never had a woman, have you? I will show you how.'

'You are my patient, lady. It is not proper.'

She wasted no time in argument but slid her fingers between my thighs and I convulsed. 'See, you are ready, Master Harry. You are alone in your chamber tonight, are you not? They will not miss me for half an hour. Let us make merry. She grasped my privates and I could resist no longer. I swept her into my arms and carried her to my pallet where, under her instruction, we pleasured each other richly.

Next morning I felt deep remorse that I had undermined my integrity so soon after swearing my physician's oath. I berated myself for moral frailty and fell on my knees to implore God's help in resisting such temptation in future. Yet even as I prayed my manhood rose and I ached to bed Lady Maud again, my mind obsessed with the fascination of her body in a way that was far from professional. Only when I ventured across the courtyard and encountered a bevy of her younger colleagues did I appreciate that my chagrin was not to be suffered in private, for they tittered and covered their mouths with their hands while a bolder maiden made crude thrusting movements with her pelvis. My mortification was complete.

Much worse was to come. During the last few months the Duchess's clerk, Roger Bolingbroke, had been a lugubrious presence at Greenwich but he had not intruded on my peace of mind. He scorned to acknowledge me when we encountered each other and I was content that he should deem me beneath contempt, for stories of his unpleasantness abounded among even the highest grade of attendant at the Pleasance. Two days after my shameful encounter with Lady Maud my complacency was shattered.

I met him coming from the Duchess's private rooms after I had been counselling an elderly serving woman on the proper proportions of the ingredients for an ointment to treat piles. I bowed as usual but this time he did not ignore me, coming close to speak in a low voice, his meaty breath filling my nostrils.

'Master Somers, you have been most unwise. You lay yourself open to all sorts of mischief.' I stared at him, unwilling to believe the sense of what he said and irked by his use of my old title. He flicked the lapel of my gown. 'The Lady Maud is an engaging little whore but one you have been ill advised to tup. If the Duchess were to learn of your misdemeanour I fancy you would not long remain at Greenwich.'

I gulped at his obvious menace but said nothing. He sneered at my silence. 'You will do well to accept counsel on avoiding such a woeful outcome. Come to my chambers after we have dined this afternoon. We will find an accommodation, I doubt not. Do not attempt to evade me, boy.'

He strode away leaving the insulting attribution to ring in my ears but, more alarmingly, his threat hung over me. Stupidly, for a few moments of ecstatic delight, I had put myself in the power of a man notorious for dubious pursuits and malignant influence – but I had no idea where my foolishness would lead.

Chapter 11

Roger Bolingbroke received me in an antechamber, divided from his study by a curtain which was drawn back, giving a glimpse of apparatus in the larger room. I registered that in addition to the expected raised desk with rolls of paper and writing implements, there were flasks, pestles and elaborate charts of the heavens and the celestial bodies. I had no chance to study these for my host directed me away from the arched doorway and pulled the curtain across it. 'Sit,' he said, indicating a stool carved with the heads of strange beasts at its corners, and he gave me a chalice of what proved to be very indifferent small beer.

'Canon Southwell will be mightily disappointed to hear of your escapade, Master Somers. Weakness of the flesh is not something that worthy man comprehends.'

'I can but hope he will not judge me too harshly. I will make full admission of my fault to him.'

Roger Bolingbroke gave a wolfish grin. 'That would be most ill-advised. Why proclaim a youthful indiscretion when it could be kept close and your esteemed master left unperturbed by the errors of his pupil?'

It was not the moment to protest that Doctor Southwell was no longer my master but what the Duchess's clerk had said made no sense and I wondered if he was testing me. 'It is scarcely a secret when Lady Maud has shared news of our liaison with her companions. They twitter and point at my groin with vulgar amusement.'

'That you have deserved, foolish boy, but they are unimportant. Southwell will pay no attention to their chirping, even if he hears it; they are full of wishful imagination. As for Lady Maud, I can ensure she boasts of her conquest no further.'

'You sir?' I sounded naïve, even to myself.

Roger Bolingbroke crossed his legs and let his robe fall away from one shapely calf. 'I have some credit with the lady and she will not wish her fiancé to know of her lewd behaviour. Do you understand what I am saying?'

'What is it you want from me in return for your good offices?'

'Excellent! You are quicker in comprehension than I feared. I want your services, Harry Somers, in whatever I require from you.'

'What do you mean?'

'Simply what I say. If I have need of your services I will let you know and you will comply with my wishes.'

'I will do nothing dishonourable or unlawful,'

'You are in no position to set limits to your indebtedness. May I remind you that you, as a physician, have already indulged in dishonourable and illicit concupiscence? However, I am unlikely to require you to commit murder or lay in wait for an innocent wayfarer. I have minions better fitted for such activities than you. Your value may lie in other directions and you may see and hear matters which could interest me.'

'You are asking me to spy on Doctor Southwell.'

'Not at the moment. I will let you know when you can be of use to me.'

I rose and slammed down my chalice, slopping ale on the turkey carpet which covered the table. 'I will not do it. I am not your chattel.'

He came to my side and bent his head close to mine. 'Oh, but you are, Harry. You are my chattel, body and soul. Do you wish to be cast out from the profession you have so lately joined?' I shrugged but my distress would have been evident. 'Do you want your dear mother dismissed from Greenwich with no provision for her old age and only your disgrace to comfort her?' My horror must have been visible. 'I have the power to arrange this, boy, do not doubt it. Now give me your word you will do my will.'

'I wonder at your willingness to accept my word when I have already broken a more sacred oath.'

114

'Bravo! I like spirit in a man, even when he is utterly defeated. For your mother's sake, you will comply. Now give me your word.' He took my wrist and twisted it slightly, sadistic enjoyment gleaming in his eyes. 'I have a follower who would gladly rape Widow Somers despite her being past her prime.'

I tried to dislodge his grip but he was surprisingly strong and forced me to my knees by kicking my weak leg. 'Swear.'

'I swear,' I echoed, hating myself as I did so.

'Good, Harry. I know you will not forget. You will not come near Lady Maud again. That is understood. She will leave Greenwich for a period. In recompense I can procure a clean girl from the village to service your needs. As Doctor Southwell has not yet returned, I will send her to you tonight.'

'No! I have no need of your trollop. I won't admit her.'

When he smirked the corners of his mouth turned down to disappear into his heavy jowls. 'Still so prim, crooked physician? Your maidenhead has gone, remember. It cannot be recovered. Do not forget to whom you are beholden for silence on its grievous loss.'

He was still chuckling as I staggered from the room, blinded by fear and hate.

*****

My misery was intense for the next few days and when Doctor Southwell returned to Greenwich he had cause to complain of my inattentiveness, while he fired off his usual catalogue of questions as to the medicinal properties of comfrey and what ailments might be denoted by subtle changes in a man's complexion. Hourly, I feared receiving Roger Bolingbroke's summons and an order to perform some unpalatable task on his behalf. On the other hand,

115

when I was called to appear in Duchess Eleanor's private chambers I trembled from head to foot, believing that her clerk had deceived me and, after all, denounced me to her Grace. I gave an audible sigh of relief on discovering it was the oldest and most senior of her ladies who wished to consult me on a dizziness she had experienced.

I listened carefully to the matron, prescribed a suitable potion and advised some relaxation in her busy round of duties for a few days; then I made my way across the outer waiting-room, through the cluster of chattering serving women. Lady Maud detached herself from the group and glided past me at an arm's length. She was flushed and I saw how her bosom heaved. 'I'm sorry,' she murmured hurriedly. 'He is a demon. I am leaving the palace tomorrow.'

I pondered her words as I descended the stairs for it was obvious she knew what had happened. Did she blame herself for gossiping about our encounter? She was evidently unsurprised that Bolingbroke had sought to make use of this information but she seemed genuinely upset and I found that comforting.

Only one diversion absorbed me sufficiently to make me forget my anxiety – and that pleasure was double-edged, for I dreaded losing the privilege of sharing in the conversation of learned men. The Duke had collected about him such a miscellany of scholars and writers, each supremely confident of his own opinion, that disagreements flourished and were enlivened by erudite wit and scathing sarcasm. Tito Livio, a naturalised Englishman by letters patent, read from his *Vita Henrici Quinto,* commissioned by Gloucester, and then engaged in fierce dispute with John Capgrave, who had dedicated his *Commentary on Genesis* to the Duke. Thomas de Norton, only a few years older than I was and recently appointed chaplain and chancellor of the ducal household, discussed religious topics with the Abbot of St. Albans and alchemy with Gilbert Kymer, whom I revered as Chancellor of Oxford University and an eminent physician. It was a remarkable honour to listen and I was avid for knowledge. I found myself exchanging grins of delight with another observer, John Home, who came to Greenwich frequently, serving as chaplain and secretary to both the Duchess and her husband, despite his occasional commitments as Canon of Hereford Cathedral.

Home seemed to share my enjoyment of conflicting views and skilful repartee, while modestly saying little, and we quickly became friends. He was in his thirties and had risen from humble beginnings, which I thought at first might account for his timidity in the presence of distinguished men, but then I realised he was quite capable of expressing a divergent opinion on occasion. It occurred to me that such occasions coincided with the absence of Roger Bolingbroke from the assembly and I wondered if Home had also put himself, albeit inadvertently, in Bolingbroke's power. I told myself not to exaggerate Bolingbroke's malignant influence but, once conceived, the thought would not leave me and I had fellow feeling for John Home. Bolingbroke, when in attendance at the debates, seldom spoke, but sat regarding all the participants from beneath his thick eyebrows, with what I took to be a predatory leer. I imagined him identifying his next victim and plotting how to trick the man into unwise behaviour.

As the weeks went by without Bolingbroke imposing any requirement on me or, indeed, showing the slightest sign of recognition, I began to relax. Perhaps the man was merely a perverted prankster who took delight in taunting his inferiors and boosting his own esteem – circumstances known to derive from a disturbance in the balance of humours in the mind. I tried to adopt a physician's impersonal detachment and to regard him as suffering from a puzzling and distasteful medical condition but I did not wholly convince myself. My burden was lessened by the fact that I now had a small circle of friends with whom to share lighter moments: Giovanni dei Signorelli, who remained a jovial companion, John Home and Geoffrey du Bois, the newly arrived apothecary who nurtured the herbs and mixed the remedies we physicians prescribed. We four regularly drank together, both in the palace and, perhaps in a more uninhibited fashion, at the tavern in the village beyond its walls. Our discourse was sometimes unflattering towards senior members of the Duke's household but none of us mentioned Roger Bolingbroke and I lacked courage to be the first to do so.

One evening when a heat mist rose from the waters of the Thames and sweat collected on brows and under arms, John Home had excused himself from coming to the inn while Giovanni soon disappeared into the back room of the establishment with a trollop who had entertained him on several occasions recently. Geoffrey and I declined the services of two of her companions, although I was tempted by a dark haired minx who sat herself on my lap and licked her lips as she felt my manhood rise. If my apothecary friend had not been there I might have succumbed but I was still nervous of the carnal act, following the escapade with Lady Maud and its consequences, so I decided to walk back with him to the palace.

He took my arm as we walked along the quayside and pointed to a barge making towards the bank where we stood. 'Look at that! The Beaufort arms and the Cardinal's own insignia. What message can he be sending to the Duke? You know they have always been bitter enemies?'

I expressed surprise. 'I thought that was long ago. The Duke has withdrawn himself from affairs of state this last year.'

'He had but I heard something has sparked the old animosity. The Cardinal is strong for making peace with France but the Duke is still set for war. He can't abide the idea of yielding what his brother won at Agincourt and surrendering his royal nephew's claim to the French throne.

He's roused himself from his studies to go to court in recent weeks and speak against Beaufort's plans.'

We watched the barge moor at the landing stage and an official in clerical robes stepped ashore to make his way daintily towards the palace. My apothecary friend snorted.

'Sending that rogue as emissary smacks of insolence. He was deeply involved on Beaufort's behalf fifteen years back when the Duke accused the Cardinal of defrauding the King.' Geoffrey winked at me. 'Our Humphrey revived that accusation last week. He reminded the Council of his claim that Beaufort had purloined some royal jewels, taken in pawn in return for a loan to the King's depleted coffers, but used to his own advantage and not returned.'

That story was not new but I was intrigued by Geoffrey's knowledge of state affairs and one particular thing he had said. 'You spoke as if you recognised the cleric who just landed.'

'Oh yes, I do. You may not realise, Harry, that when I was a lad I lived in the Beaufort household. My father was cook there and my mother a laundress. I was an inquisitive boy and learned things I did not like. To do him justice, the Bishop, as he was then, enabled me to pursue my studies but I did not return to his service. The sight of the Beaufort arms still causes uneasiness in my belly and makes me want to spew.'

I nodded, thinking that Roger Bolingbroke had a similar effect on me. We had entered through the gatehouse and were headed towards our quarters when we stood back to allow Dame Margery and two of her attendants to cross in front of us. The chamberlain's wife looked distressed and did not acknowledge us; she held a kerchief to her face and one of her maids was weeping openly. Geoffrey raised an enquiring eyebrow but I had no more idea than he had of why the lady allowed herself to appear tearful in public, in such an uncharacteristic a manner.

We did not have to wait long for an explanation for Grizel came hurrying behind her mistress, clutching an over-mantle which Dame Margery had probably discarded in the warmth of the evening. 'Why, Doctor Somers! Haven't seen much of you in a while. Have you come to offer your condolences and join in the mourning?'

'What do you mean, Grizel?' I asked, ignoring her first comment.

'Dame Margery's son-in-law is dead and her poor daughter become a widow.'

I rocked back on my heels. 'Sir Hugh de Grey is dead?'

'Nah! Not him. Lady Anne's husband. He were a knight with land somewhere north of the river. He were miles older than her.' Then I recalled that Lady Blanche's elder sister had left Greenwich years ago but I had heard little of her since. Grizel noted my surprised expression. 'Don't think Lady Anne has ever seen her mother from that day to this. Word is they didn't get on and Dame Margery were that relieved to be rid of her. Now she's to come back here – at least until she gets a new husband – and the Duchess has offered to take her as one of her ladies. Dunno how it'll work out. They say Lady Anne's a bit of a bitch. Any rate, that's what her mother's blubbing about.'

I smiled at Grizel's familiar irreverence in referring to her superiors but I noticed that Geoffrey looked uncomfortable and I started to move away from her. I need not have bothered for at that moment two soldiers, just relieved from their guard duties, emerged from the entrance to the Duke's apartments and the girl ran to greet the younger fellow. He grasped her under the armpits and swung her round, so that Dame Margery's mantle flew out behind them like a ceremonial train. The sight annoyed me unreasonably.

'A disrespectful little minx,' Geoffrey said.

'She has proved a staunch friend to me,' I replied stiffly, 'but I fear she is changing as she nears womanhood.'

'Not jealous of the guardsman, surely?'

'Of course not.' My annoyance grew.

I returned to my room, nursing my irritation, without a second thought for Lady Anne's bereavement and her impending return to Greenwich. I never suspected this event would have significance for me and for my already fragile peace of mind.

Chapter 12

The arrow flew straight to the mark, slicing between two others skewered closest to the wooden Frenchman's heart. Fragments of feather fluttered down from their shafts. 'Bravissimo! Giovanni shouted, waving his fist in the air. 'Is good, that soldier, yes? I think he win. I give you wager, Harry.'

I shook my head. 'I'm not betting against a certainty.'

I must have sounded curt and John Home looked up with surprise but Geoffrey du Bois diverted our Italian friend's attention to one of the buxom serving maids carrying flasks of ale towards us. The afternoon was hot and we had stood for some time watching the competition at the butts so we were all thirsty but Geoffrey held me back as our companions moved away. 'That's Grizel's admirer, who's carrying all before him, isn't it?'

'His name's Dickon but Grizel's too young to have an admirer.'

Geoffrey gave an awkward laugh. 'Where are your eyes, Harry? She's as marriageable a girl of fourteen as any lusty guardsman might tumble in the long grass.'

I bit back my irritation and began to move towards Giovanni but the apothecary held my arm. 'I think this Dickon is fond of her and she is certainly sweet for him. I know how she helped you last year, after your sister's death, but you cannot stop her from becoming a woman and acting as women do.'

'Meaning?' I snapped and strode off without waiting for an answer. I could not bear to think of Grizel ruining herself – as Alys had.

Only a few days later it was announced that at Michaelmas great festivities would be held at Greenwich to mark the marriage of the Duke's natural daughter, Antigone, to Lord Tankerville. Antigone was full sister to my old charge, Arthur: both children, it was rumoured, of a noble

Frenchwoman whom Humphrey had taken as his mistress before he met Duchess Eleanor. Antigone was a regular visitor to Greenwich, treated with honour by her father and step-mother and I knew of her brother's devotion to her. We welcomed the news of her nuptials and the opportunity for merrymaking but I did not envy the chamberlain the workload this entailed in organising pageantry, masques and feasting.

In the meantime the widowed Lady Anne arrived at the palace and took her place among the Duchess's attendants. I saw her from a distance, and thought her sour expression denoted ill humour as much as grief at her bereavement, while I pitied a slender serving maid with long black hair coiled below her coif, who attended this vinegary mistress. A few days later I was surprised to hear that Lady Blanche de Grey had come to Greenwich to visit her sister, for neither she nor her husband had ventured to the palace since the events of the preceding year. I understood, as others would not, that there was good reason for their tact. Besides, Lady Blanche had been brought to bed of a second healthy son since then and had been unwell for some weeks thereafter. Now, it seemed, she was recovered enough to bring commiserations in person for Lady Anne's loss. In view of the secret knowledge she knew I possessed I did not imagine she would wish to encounter me so I was startled by the message, brought by a page, to attend the ladies in the chamberlain's apartments; but the meeting was to be brief.

Dame Margery was not present with her daughters but each of them was attended by a servant standing in the shadows to the side of the high windows. Lady Blanche was thinner than I remembered but still beautiful and she greeted me cordially, presenting me to her less well-favoured sibling in gracious terms. 'Doctor Somers is a respected physician in the household and he did us great service last year following the sad demise of his sister, who

123

served me.' She gave me a conspiratorial smile as she spoke and I knew she was confident of my discretion.

'I have heard the story,' Lady Anne said dismissively. 'If I have need of medicinal services which my woman cannot supply, I shall remember your good offices, Doctor Somers. We need not detain you now.'

Lady Blanche shook her head apologetically but I signalled my sympathy to her and bowed low before leaving the room. The serving woman I had seen before with Lady Anne held open the door but, as she saw my face in full sunlight, she gasped and to cover her confusion she followed me into the antechamber coughing loudly. Her eyes were dark pools of terror but she had the fairest face I had ever seen.

'My pardon,' I said. 'I am apt to forget how horrifying I appear on first acquaintance. The alarm passes with familiarity.'

'It is I should ask your pardon. I was unmannerly.' She raised her hand towards my disfigured cheek. 'Is the condition painful?'

'Not at all. It is merely a crusty cover, like a shell, for a small part of my exterior.'

'Like a tortoise has?' She smiled and I caught my breath at the radiance in her face. Then she blushed. 'I must return to Lady Anne, Doctor Somers.'

'You have the advantage of me, mistress. What is your name?'

She looked down bashfully and for a moment I thought she would not reply. 'Bess Barber, sir.'

'Bess, attend us this instant.' Echoing her name, Lady Anne's angry cry shattered the magical interlude. Without a word the girl gave me a bob and hurried back into the inner room.

*****

Lady Anne kept strictly to the Duchess's chambers, as befitted her status and, although I looked constantly to encounter Bess again, I did not succeed. On one occasion I was summoned to attend the elderly lady I had advised previously and I entered the ladies' quarters in a state of excitement but there was no sign of the maid I longed to see. In the grounds of the palace the hurly-burly in preparation for the wedding was enough to deter any modest woman from venturing out among the workmen erecting stands, from which jousting would be viewed, while musicians tested their instruments in the open air, less than tunefully. I despaired of meeting Bess again until the day of the nuptials but I prayed solemnly to Our Lady that she might be permitted to join the revels then and that I might have courage to approach her. Even timid John Home recognised that I was preoccupied in some way but he was too courteous to question me.

I had ceased to concern myself with Grizel's welfare and was taken aback when, as I crossed from the apothecary's chamber towards my own, she erupted into the courtyard and ran towards me, shrieking with delight. 'Master Harry! You're to be the first, d'you hear? First to wish me well!'

'Why so I do, Grizel, always. But what especially requires my..?'

'Cor, you're so slow! I'm to follow where Lady Antigone leads. What d'you think of that?' I stared at her stupidly. 'I'm to wed, you dunderhead. Next year. Dickon's asked and Dame Margery has said I may go with him to the church door in a twelvemonth. He's been made one of the Duke's personal bodyguard and is free to take a wife. What d'you think of that?'

Her repeated query annoyed me and I answered brusquely. 'Are you sure this is wise? You're still very young.'

'Young! Girls of my age have borne their husbands heirs by now. Dickon don't think I'm too young for what we do.'

'Stop this! You're a fool if you're letting Dickon bed you. Think of my poor sister.'

She touched the side of her nose. 'Reckon me and Dickon are a bit more canny than Alys ever were, God rest her.' She rolled her eyes at me. 'Ways and means, there are, Doctor Somers, ways and means.'

I strode way in anger, furious at Grizel's loss of innocence and perhaps jealous of the ease with which she had lost it. Of course I wished her well, even though I had said nothing to this effect, but I regretted the circumstances that required me to do so.

*****

There were three days of continuous festivities. Choirs sang – some from the chapel most melodiously and others from the village with raucous enthusiasm. Processions of colourful characters wound their way through the passages before presenting their diversions in the hall: dragons, green men, devils, angels, mermaids purporting to come from the deep with seaweed in their hair, holy damsels and pious matrons – both these last showing their heavy boots beneath womanly garbs. In the grounds knights rode in the lists, artisans took part in wrestling matches and soldiers competed at the butts in a competition which would reach its finale on the last day of the celebrations. I did not venture near that display. The thought of it only added to my loneliness.

On the third day the activities spread out into the park, where villagers and anonymous wayfarers swelled the crowds, and they became more unbridled in their nature as the nobles kept within the palace and left the menials to their own pursuits. The archery competition had ended with

126

the inevitable shouts of 'Dickon', acclaiming the winner, and shortly afterwards I saw him, clasping Grizel's hand, capering up hill to the woods and heathland, where Alys had been done to death by her husband. I felt a horrible sense of premonition, ridiculous though it was, and turned back to the palace disconsolately.

As I approached the postern gate it opened slowly and a figure stood in its portal looking up towards the rumbustious merriment on the hill. I held my breath, not daring to go forward, but as Bess Barber moved to retire and close the gate I stumbled forward as fast as I could. 'Mistress Barber, please do not withdraw. There is much to watch and enjoy. Let me escort you. You will be quite safe in the company of her Grace's physician.'

Bess's lips began to form the words of refusal but I think she took confidence from the solemn expression on my face. 'I have been granted half an hour by Lady Anne,' she said. 'It would be kind of you to accompany me. I had not expected such a throng. I shouldn't care to venture to the ridge alone.'

'Nor should you,' and I gave her my arm, hoping she would not feel it trembling as she laid her hand very gently on my sleeve.

We walked in silence, both no doubt nervous of our proximity, and we climbed to where people from the village were dancing to an accompaniment of viols and flutes. We stood to watch and I noticed Bess's foot tapping. 'I am no practised dancer, Mistress Barber,' I said, 'but this is not a setting where skill is required. Would you allow me to lead you into the round?'

She was near my height and smiled into my face with such open pleasure I could scarcely stop my knees from knocking together. I took her hand and we joined the nearest column of couples setting and whirling, parting and regrouping, her feet as light and skilful as mine were heavy and ungainly – but I saw from the enjoyment gleaming in her eyes that my clumsiness did not matter.

All too soon she insisted she must return to her mistress and I escorted her back to the postern. She did not wish me to go with her beyond the gate and I understood her reluctance but for that moment I was content. Surely this brief episode would permit us to encounter each other again and the thought gave me great comfort, so I wandered aimlessly back up the hill, breathing deeply and wondering at the marvel which had come about, the coming of an emotion I had never experienced before.

As I climbed I became dimly aware of people nearby, young lads and maidens running about, chasing each other and screaming with laughter as they caught their quarry. I was oblivious of who they were but I fancied I saw Grizel scurrying through the multitude and guessed Dickon would be close behind her. I sat down with my back to a tree, letting the world of lovers twirl around me, and I did not begrudge them their joyfulness.

I had no idea how long I sat in my happy stupor before I heard the shout from higher up the hill. 'Doctor Somers! Doctor Somers! Please come. Someone is hurt.'

Reluctantly I returned my thoughts to the reality around me and pulled myself upright. A red faced blacksmith pounded down the slope to join me. 'Summat's happened, sir,' he said. 'Maybe dead, he is.'

At once I was scrambling up the incline as the fellow led me onto the stretch of heathland beyond where Alys died. A cluster of villagers and attendants from the palace stood round the figure on the ground and I could see at once that he was past my help. His head was hidden by the lower branches of a gorse bush but the dagger protruded from the centre of his chest in a pool of congealing gore. He wore a soldier's livery and I realised with a sudden qualm that under that scarlet stain was the Duke's personal emblem of the swan: this was a member of the ducal bodyguard. When

I knelt beside him and eased his head from the prickly canopy concealing his features, my misgivings were confirmed and my stomach lurched. Grizel's betrothed, Dickon, the man I had unjustly resented and knew not at all, would trouble me no more but bring her devastation. Without any doubt, the handsome guardsman, jocund lover and most talented archer at the palace had been murdered.

Chapter 13

I stayed with the body until a young priest and the chamberlain had come to perform their respective offices – obsequies for Dickon's soul and sharp enquires as to the circumstances of his death. Then I accompanied the cortege back to the palace, all of us stunned by the sudden violence shattering the merriment of the day, and I heard Grizel's desperate screams as we entered the courtyard to approach the chapel. Her companions could not hold her; indeed it would have been unkind to restrain her from expressing the enormity of her grief. She ran forward, halting the litter-bearers conveying the corpse, and flung herself on her lover's mutilated chest. She had already torn her hair loose from its coif and she rocked back and forth as she held Dickon, shrieking denial of what she saw, sobbing wildly and uttering blasphemous imprecations. Quite unreasonably I resented her behaviour but I tried not to show my embarrassment at such excessive passion. John Home had joined us and, although his brow was furrowed at hearing her profanities, he prevented the other priest from chastising her. Only when she began to tear her face with her nails, incising deep scratches beside her nose, did I deem it prudent to intervene.

She fought me at first when I tried to lift her from the body and quieten her ranting but I did not release her. 'He would not wish you lose your reason, Grizel. He would want his murderer brought to justice and you, above anyone, can help with that. You had been with Dickon on the hill I think.' I hoped these practicalities would bring her to her senses.

She scowled at me but stopped wailing and brushed her sleeve across her tear-stained face. 'Course I had. We'd been cuddling each other as umpteen other couples were. Then I teased him and said he must count to twenty before coming to find me. We both knew I meant to go to the outhouse beyond the potter's kiln, where it'd be quiet and we'd often done it together.' Grizel's tone was defiant and John put a cautionary hand on the young priest's arm, for this was no time to castigate fornication.

The chamberlain also wisely ignored any moral transgressions by the betrothed pair and bent down beside Grizel. 'Did you see anyone nearby as you left Dickon?'

She shook her head but turned to look him in the eye. 'I've said there were others around, haven't I? Besides there's bushes all over, up on the ridge. Half a dozen could have been hiding there. But it weren't half a dozen, was it? Only needed one or two buggers to jump him from behind and take him unawares.'

'Have you any idea who could have done this?'

She snorted. 'Course I have! Them bastards as he beat in the archery. Same ones he'd thrashed at the butts the other week. They had it in for him on account of him being made one of the Duke's bodyguards. Told him to watch his back, they did. He thought it were just a lark.'

The chamberlain noted two names and Dame Margery joined us to take her maid into the palace but as she rose Grizel gave another squeal. 'Where's his purse? It were hanging from his belt. Had his prize money in it. Them fuckers must have taken it, God damn them.'

The chamberlain's wife was stony faced as she led Grizel away but she did not utter a word of rebuke. Her husband immediately instituted further enquiries and took statements from those present at the merry-making, as to the whereabouts of the two men named, but it soon emerged that there were numerous witnesses to attest that they had participated in the dancing throughout the afternoon and there was no evidence whatever to incriminate them. When the Duke, sitting in judgement as lord of his domain, considered the case and interrogated the men in person, he declared them innocent and concluded that some ne'er-do-wells had joined the festivities, seen Dickon pocket his prize money and followed him up the hill intent on theft and, if necessary, murder. This seemed entirely probable but there was little hope of identifying the villains, given the number of strangers in the crowd, and it was to be expected that they soon disappeared from the vicinity.

Poor Grizel refused to be comforted in her distress and after a week I heard that Dame Margery had sent her to serve Lady Blanche at Danson, away from the scene of her shattered dreams. I thought this mightily generous of the old lady towards a humble serving girl but I missed encountering my outspoken and lively young friend while I went about my business. It troubled me greatly to think of Grizel as the young woman she had become, blithely experienced in carnal matters, but I remembered with affection the inquisitive, bright child she had been a twelvemonth since.

*****

My interest in Bess Barber had in no degree waned and I looked for her wherever I was in the palace but it was clear that Lady Anne was a demanding mistress who decreed that the seclusion appropriate to her widowed state must apply also to her serving woman. Nevertheless, after our dinner in the hall one afternoon, I managed to speak to Bess when she was sent back to recover a wrap Lady Anne had left behind. I was sorry to see how startled she was at the sound of my voice over her shoulder, expressing the hope she was in good heart, but the smile she gave as she realised who was addressing her was rich compensation.

'Doctor Somers! Please forgive my alarm. I hadn't realised you were there.'

"You are of nervous disposition, Mistress Barber? I shall need to prescribe an infusion to calm the spirit and soothe the digestion.'

She blushed and the heightened colour in her cheeks was most becoming. 'I do not think I need call on your professional services, master physician.'

I was tempted to bandy words with her and enquire if my personal services might be more to her liking but instinct told me she would take such a jest amiss. 'I have hoped to see you,' I said instead, cursing the lameness of my words. 'I should be honoured if you would walk with me in the garden one day, before the air grows chill – if you can be spared from your duties.'

'I have little opportunity and my mistress would not approve. Excuse me, sir.' Then as she stepped to the side and my heart plummeted into my boots, she half-turned and undid the hurt she had caused me. 'I am uncivil, Doctor Somers, forgive me. I cannot come but I beg you to believe, this is not of my choosing.' I stared after her as she scurried away and I felt the acceleration in my pulse.

*****

I soon discovered it was not only Bess who seemed strangely on edge in my company: but she was still largely unknown to me, whereas my mother's preoccupations were normally crystalline to her son. I visited mother in the servants' quarters every week and I tried to persuade her that she had no need to stay there for, now I held a respected position, I could provide for her. She declined my offer, saying it was not fitting I should be encumbered with an ageing and unworthy parent – which pained me – but adding that she found pleasure in the company of her colleagues, some of whom she had worked with since girlhood – and this I understood. So I simply continued to pay my regular visits and we were both content with our arrangement.

On this occasion I could tell at once that something was wrong and, as I embraced her, I asked if she was well.

133

'Perfectly, perfectly.' She paused as if realising this lacked conviction. 'Just a small headache,' she added quickly. 'Nothing to need your ministrations, Harry. Tell me what you have been doing. Have they caught that poor soldier's murderers yet?'

'No, nor are they likely to. There seems little doubt they were intruders to the park who made their escape rapidly. No names have been put to them and there's small chance more will be discovered.'

I was surprised to see her shudder. 'Such villainy – and on the Duke's own estate! What are we coming to when honest folk cannot be safe on their lord's domain?'

'There's no cause for anyone here to be concerned for their safety,' I said in an effort to reassure her. 'No one's going to break into the palace and terrorise the serving wenches.'

She shuddered again and I realised that my attempt to laugh off her improbable fear was misdirected. She clasped my arm and squeezed it. 'You're not in trouble, Harry? You've not offended any of the powerful men?'

'Of course not! Whatever are you talking about?' I began to worry that her wits were become prematurely confused and she would end like the old biddy who customarily sat by the hearth in the chamberlain's lodging, muttering to herself and forgetful of her own name.

Mother rubbed her fingers back and forth across her knees until with an obvious effort she stilled them in her lap. 'I hear things, Harry,' she said. 'That the Duke is out of favour with the King, that his old quarrel with the Cardinal is revived, that all is not as it should be between him and the Duchess... Her voice faded.

'None of this has anything to do with me, mother.' Then curiosity got the better of me. 'I've heard nothing of any breach between the Duke and the Duchess.'

'They say he has a sprightly new mistress in the City. He is often at his house there.'

'Duke Humphrey has always been free with his affections but it has never caused any serious difficulty in his marriage, to my knowledge. He is devoted to his wife.'

'She is no longer as young as she was.'

It was unlike my mother to trouble herself about such matters and I had the impression she was trying to deflect our conversation from other topics. 'Is there real concern among the serving women about their safety?'

'Not... not generally.' She rose. 'You'd best be getting back to your duties. I will be calmer when you come again.'

'I shall not leave you until you tell me why you are far from calm now. What is it?'

She sighed and subsided onto her seat, straightening her skirt. 'It's nothing. Just an old woman's imagining.'

'You are neither old nor given to fancies. Tell me.'

She breathed deeply before answering. 'It is mere foolishness, no doubt. A man came yesterday. He asked for me by name and I was summoned to the antechamber in the Duchess's quarters. I'd never seen him before.' She paused and I did not hurry her, for I was bemused by her story and where it might lead. 'He made enquiry of my health and mentioned you, Harry. He said I was to tell you of his visit. I did not understand why he could not tell you himself but he brushed aside my question. He said you would understand.' She choked slightly before continuing and I put my arm round her in horrified comprehension. 'He said that your welfare and mine would depend on your actions. Oh, Harry, what does it mean?'

I ignored her enquiry. 'What was this man like?'

'Not a gentleman or an educated man but not a ruffian either. Perhaps a tradesman or a man at arms. Tall and well built.'

Not Roger Bolingbroke himself, I thought, but undoubtedly his minion, intent on reminding me what I had promised, even though nothing had been demanded of me – yet. I shivered. 'The man is some joker,' I said, improvising

135

quickly. 'I think I can identify his master. He should not have visited and frightened you. I will register my protest. Don't worry, mother, it is a trivial business – related to an ill-advised wager. Put it out of your mind.'

She looked at me uncertainly but she wanted to be comforted so she held me close and kissed me, before sending me on my way with a feeble injunction against the evils of making wagers. I wished I merited her advice, deeply concerned by the incident she described but reluctant to beard Roger Bolingbroke about it, lest it provoke him to some further mischief. I had managed to persuade myself that he was simply a malicious jester who amused himself by taunting lesser men over whom he had secured some hold, but there had been no sign previously that he would carry out his menaces. I had concluded he gained pleasure from the fear he engendered in his victims but now I was outraged that he should extend his malevolent influence to my mother. What if this was only the beginning? As I walked back to my rooms, my stomach heaved when I glanced towards the entrance to the Duchess's chambers, where Lady Anne and her winsome attendant were lodged. Heaven forbid Bolingbroke should discover my feelings for Bess Barber! If he was as perverse as I suspected, relishing the distress of his victims, he must never know that she would offer fresh opportunity to secure me under his control.

*****

It seemed there might be some truth in the rumours my mother had heard about disharmony between the Duke and his wife for, as Yuletide approached, Humphrey of Gloucester was absent from Greenwich for much of the time and Duchess Eleanor was reported to be considerably agitated. I mentioned these circumstances to John Home who, as her chaplain and secretary, might be expected to know where the truth lay.

136

He laughed nervously at my enquiry. 'Are you asking me to break the sanctity of a confessor's silence?'

No, of course not. But you may have information from other sources which you can disclose.'

He gave a weak smile. 'Well, that's so, Harry. I can say nothing of matters between husband and wife but you may be reassured that there is good reason for the Duke's attendance at court. Old antagonisms have revived.'

'With Cardinal Beaufort? I'd heard the Duke tried to move against him earlier this year.'

'It is more intense now and affairs of state are at the heart of it. The Cardinal wants to secure lasting peace with France, not just a continued truce. The Duke is virulently opposed to this.'

'Surely there's nothing new in this?'

'Do you know of the King's prisoner, the Duke of Orleans?'

I stared at John for Charles d'Orleans, kin to the French King, had been in honourable captivity at the Tower since before I was born. 'I'd forgotten his existence.'

The Cardinal is resolved to set him free and return him to France as proof of England's commitment to a treaty. King Henry seems likely to agree, for he is a peaceable, mild man who favours the end of all discord. Duke Humphrey is adamantly opposed.'

'So he is away from Greenwich in order to argue his case with his royal nephew.'

'He has followed the court on its journeys from Westminster to Windsor to Leicester. He is discontented with the reception he has received and has complained that old slights to Duchess Eleanor have been revived – not just by Beaufort but by the King himself.'

'Surely at last New Year the King gave the Duchess a lavish gift – a garter of gold and pearls, with a flower made of diamonds and a ruby on the pendant. She exhibited it to the household when she wore it on Easter Day, lifting her skirts to show the jewels gracing her leg. That generosity does not suggest the King considers her an unworthy consort for his uncle or their marriage irregular.'

John Home took my arm. 'Personal kindness does not preclude bowing to the dictates of prudent policy. The King is an unworldly man, more fitted for the cloister than the court. He leans much on his chief advisers and great men cannot be governed by their personal inclinations if affairs of state require otherwise.' He looked me straight in the face and his eyes were momentarily troubled. 'Nor indeed can lesser men if fate decrees they shape their destinies to the dictates of the more powerful.' Then he slapped me on the back and hurried towards the chapel. I was struck by the breadth of his knowledge but feared there was a warning in his final words.

Next day welcome news was brought to the palace that John Swanwych was on the last leg of his homeward journey, bearing the first five books of Plato's *Republic*, which the Duke was so anxious to receive. I looked forward to listening to the translation of this ancient work but even more to the prospect of seeing my former master once more. My rancour towards him for his role in Alys's wretched history had cooled and felt I would be able to confide in him as in no other man, if the necessity arose.

In an unexpected gesture of generosity, one day after we had dined in the hall, the chamberlain invited me to take wine with him and a small party of other guests in his chambers. I quickly brushed crumbs from my gown and smoothed my hair below my cap as I crossed the courtyard, for if the ladies of the family were present their attendants were likely to be there also. Sadly, however, only Dame Margery was in attendance but she greeted me kindly and after more general talk with some of the Duke's retainers I re-joined her on the fringe of the assembly.

'I trust your daughter is in good health, Dame Margery.'

'It is kind of you to ask, Doctor Somers. Lady Blanche is with child again and does very well.' She spoke smoothly, fixing me with her basilisk eye and I had the impression she could read my true intent. 'She is most fortunate to have a husband as attentive as Hugh de Grey and to live in matrimonial harmony.'

I could not completely suppress my smile and she glared at me. 'And Lady Anne?' I asked quickly. 'She is not often seen about the palace.' The assumed innocence of my question seemed artificial, even as I spoke.

'My eldest daughter observes the proprieties as a widow. But by summer she will be a wife again and gone from here. My husband is in discussion with a prospective suitor – a younger man than the late Sir Bertram, a knight with land in Hertfordshire.'

'She must be hopeful of bearing children,' I said while my heart pounded.

'What woman is not?' Dame Margery replied caustically and moved to join the elderly keeper of the Duke's seals.

I was disheartened by what she had said for it set a term to my opportunities for courting Bess Barber. I was in no doubt this was what I wanted to do but the constraints on her freedom and my own timidity were huge barriers against my success. I was pondering my unhappy position when, as if it were a harbinger of improved fortune to come, Dame Margery's page rushed into the room followed by Bess herself. A quick glance drove away my momentary cheerfulness. She was ashen faced and her dress was splashed with mud but, while the boy spoke to his mistress, Bess ran to my side with a look of relief. 'Thank heaven you are here, Doctor Somers. Please come. Lady Anne is desperately ill.'

I followed her at once, taking the direct route across the sodden courtyard, squelching through the mire left after heavy rain, and asked the nature of the lady's illness. 'She is most violently sick,' Bess said. 'For half an hour or more. I've never seen such revolting matter as she has brought up. Not just what she has eaten but foul smelling dark liquid.'

'Black bile. What of the other ladies?'

'No one else is ill and we all ate together at dinner.'

We had reached the entrance to Lady Anne's chamber. 'What was the meal?'

'She took mainly shellfish.'

I had treated many cases of overburdened stomachs turned by a surfeit of ale or food no longer fresh, but I was startled by the sight of Lady Anne's drawn and pallid features, still more by the noxious material she had spewed into the pail beside her bed. She seemed only half-conscious but her body continued in spasm as she retched uselessly, unable to bring up more of the fetid bile. 'She became ill soon after the meal?' I asked Bess.

'She suffered awful cramps in her inside and writhed about in agony. At first she tried to stop herself from being sick but I put a feather into her throat – I thought it best.' Bess looked at me nervously as if I might criticise her action.

'You did right. You may well have saved your mistress's life.' I scribbled on a scrap of paper I always keep about my person for such eventualities. 'Send a page to fetch these items from Master du Bois. Mix them with a little honey and give it to her at once. If her stomach rejects the first dose, wait a little then try again.' When the lad had departed I spoke again in a low voice, so the other ladies who had collected at the entrance to the room should not hear. 'It is not uncommon for shellfish to bring about severe sickness but it is strange no one else suffered. It may be wise to take especial care of what she eats in future.'

I had not dared to voice my fear more explicitly, but Bess understood at once. 'You think she has been poisoned?'

'I cannot be certain. I shall take a little of the substance she has voided to see if I can tell more. It is a precaution merely.' Bess was looking at me with huge frightened eyes but there was intelligence behind her alarm. 'Does she have enemies at the palace?'

Bess lowered her eyes and folded her hands together. 'I did not think anyone would seek to kill her but she is not popular. She is a pious lady and does not approve of frivolity. Some of her companions have earned the rough edge of her tongue. They say she pokes her nose into matters which do not concern her and then criticises what she does not like.' Bess blushed. 'I should not speak of her in this way.'

'To her physician, you should. It is helpful to me. She is most fortunate to have you at her side.'

'She has always been kind to me. She took me into her service when my father was killed.'

I hoped Bess would share more details of her background but Dame Margery had entered the room and I was immediately occupied in describing Lady Anne's condition and the treatment I prescribed. In my summary I attributed the malady to toxic shellfish and this was not queried. I stayed at the patient's bedside until the page had brought the medicine and the first dose had been administered; then I left her in the charge of her mother and Bess came with me to the door where the gawping ladies were clustered. 'Thank you, Doctor Somers,' she said with formality. 'We are most grateful. I shall remember all you advised.' Without adding anything, she smiled with that dazzling curve of her lips and twinkle in her eyes which enraptured me and sent me joyfully on my way.

Before returning to my room I called on Geoffrey at the pharmacy and discussed Lady Anne's case with him. Together we studied the sample of her bile and, while we could not confirm the cause of her malady, we shared our suspicions. Geoffrey raised his eyebrows. 'Why on earth should anyone want to poison Lady Anne?'

'Her maid says she is not liked.' It sounded tame.

'Must be more to it than that. I know women are catty bitches but this smacks of something more serious. I'd like to know more.'

I shifted in my seat. 'You won't start asking questions though, will you? If there is someone with evil intentions, we don't want to alert him or her to our concerns.'

He laughed. 'I'd forgotten you are expert in such enquiries. I've heard about your exploits in determining guilt and ferreting out felons. I'll leave it to you, Harry, but I'd be interested to be kept in touch with your progress. Here have some more wine.'

We changed the subject and drank another goblet of Gascon nectar before I left him. I called on Dame Margery to enquire as to Lady Anne's progress and was pleased to hear she was now sleeping peacefully. Then, with my mind in a whirl of conflicting thoughts, somewhat heightened by the wine, I returned to my room.

As I opened the door I sensed a slight movement by the window and stood still, peering into the gloom beyond the range of my taper. A figure moved forward, with no attempt to conceal its presence. It was enveloped in a mantle falling to the ground, its head covered by a hood. My hand slipped inside my robe to the small dagger I carried in my belt.

There came a trill of merriment from my uninvited visitor. 'You will not need a weapon, Harry,' she said. 'Only one instrument of yours will suffice for our business.'

Chapter 14

I rocked back on my heels. 'Lady Maud!'

'I am returned, as you see, and fervent for your embrace.' She took a step towards me, letting her mantle fall slightly open to reveal her swell of her bosom.

I flung open the door. 'Go! You should not be here.'

She came to my side and placed her hand on mine as it grasped the handle. 'You pay me no courtesy, Doctor Somers, to dismiss my advances. Would you really send me from your chamber to traverse the courtyard like this?'

Her free hand tugged at the girdle encircling her waist and the sides of the garment parted. While I stood shaking she shrugged it from her shoulders and, naked, stepped free to press her body against me. 'I think you will not be so discourteous.' She put her hand to my privates.

I forced her back but the door had closed behind us and every sinew in my body was quivering. 'I owe no courtesy to a woman who has trumpeted her conquest throughout the palace.'

She pouted and touched my cheek with her fingertips. 'It was not of my choosing, Harry. Believe me.'

'Whose, if not yours?' My fury was befuddled by wine and lust.

Her golden hair had cascaded over her shoulders when she threw back the hood and now she lifted it to fall behind her, stretching her arm and bringing her firm nipple into view. 'Do you still not understand, physician? This is an affliction you cannot cure. We are both his creatures and must comply with his will if those we hold dear are not to suffer.'

'You?' As understanding dawned I tried to draw back but the wall was behind me.

'Roger Bolingbroke commands all I do, as he will control you when he decides it is time. He bade me seduce you in the first place but I assure you the performance was

143

more pleasurable than a mere duty. Now I have been compelled to visit you tonight and I am to stay with you until dawn breaks. It will be enough for his purposes that my presence utterly compromises you but I suggest we use the time to satisfy the desire that threatens to consume us both.' She giggled and pointed to my swollen crotch.

She had moved across the small room to sit on my pallet and with her last words she spread wide her legs and beckoned. As if in a trance I came to her side. She reached to unclasp my belt and loosen my points but I clutched her wrists. 'How can you be Bolingbroke's chattel?'

'He rescued me when a child from my guardian who abused me, so I have cause to be grateful. But then I was foolish and put myself in his power.'

I was already on my knees and nuzzling her breasts. 'Did he take you by force?'

She giggled a second time and placed my hand between her thighs. 'I have not lain with Roger Bolingbroke. He would never put himself at hazard by incontinence. There were others who flattered me and sought my favours. I was very young and my nature is to be generous. But then I bore a child.'

I paused in my fumbling as I registered her words but she drew me up onto the mattress and in a few moments I was lost in the oblivion of my pounding blood. After we had spent our passion a wave of revulsion and shame passed over me but she began again to caress me and I was too weak-willed to resist. 'Your child?' I murmured, stroking her luxuriant hair.

'She is the hold he has over me. He provides for her but if I do not carry out his wishes he will do her harm.'

'That's monstrous.'

'He is a monster. He has entrammelled many in his web and they do his bidding. As you will, Harry.'

'Perhaps I will not. Perhaps I will defy him!'

'And see you mother ravished and pretty Bess Barber serve the turn of some common cut-throat?'

I wrestled myself free from her embrace, staring in horror. Again she giggled. 'You thought no one would notice? She may not realise the strength of your affections but others have eyes and yours have betrayed you, Harry. You will do as Roger bids you, master physician. You have no choice.'

I would not have believed myself capable of violence towards a woman but I took Maud then with as much force as I could muster. I did not care whether her cries were of pain or delight but when I had finished trickles of blood ran from her throat into the recess above her collarbone and her body was discoloured with bruises. My fragile hopes of a happy future had been shattered and I wanted only to cause suffering to equal mine. 'Perhaps you will bear another child,' I spat at her. 'A misshapen, devil-scarred brat with my dishonourable features.'

She drew her disordered tresses back as she crouched beside me. 'I shall bear no more children. I am barren now. My second infant died in my womb.' She paused and dabbed a trace of blood from her neck. 'Roger had Doctor Southwell get it from me with a speculum.'

She pronounced the name of the physician's instrument with sarcastic precision but it was not that which riveted my attention. 'Doctor Southwell is one of Roger Bolingbroke's minions?'

She lifted her mantle from the floor. 'I should not have told you that but I can trust you not to repeat it. I've no idea what hold Roger has over him.' She glanced up. 'It is still dark outside your window and I am bound to stay here until dawn. Since my body encourages you to such viciousness, I shall roll myself in my gown and lie on the floor. I have done what I was enjoined to do.'

Overcome with remorse and anger I slipped onto the rug beside her. 'I don't know how much you are to be pitied

145

or blamed but you have shattered my dreams. My hatred and my desire for you have become one.' The sob in my voice disgusted me.

She did not reply but drew the mantle round us both and there we slept an hour or two, intertwined, until the first gleam of light showed in the sky. Before she left we made love once more and our love-making then was gentle and kindly.

*****

I thrust my head into the bowl of water from the well and wished it was deep enough to drown me. I was consumed with disgust for my actions and horror at my predicament. I must go about my business, seeking to cure others of their ailments, advising, giving reassurance, while knowing I was the basest profligate and libertine. I had betrayed the first stirrings of what I knew to be true love and, carelessly, exposed Bess to grave danger. I had put myself thoroughly into the power of a villain: I was weak, faithless, worthless. There was no value in my continued existence. I could only do more harm to those I loved. I shook the water from my hair and for a moment pondered the church's ordinance against self-destruction. I understood the wickedness of seeking to extinguish what God had created, and that continuing to live with the knowledge of my sin was a fitting prelude to the agonies of Hell, but surely that should be balanced against the benefit my early death would bring to those I had imperilled. My mother and Bess would be released from the menaces they did not know existed.

I rubbed my face dry and knelt to pray, as was my custom, to repeat the words of contrition and entreat blessings and forgiveness, but the words would not form in my mind. I had used them in the past with reference to insignificant offences; now I had desperate need of Heaven's

146

mercy I dared not make that trite petition. Instead, on my knees, I wept.

My misery was interrupted by hammering on the door and, although I thought of ignoring it, my physician's duty asserted itself and, towel in hand, I undid the latch. A page in the Duke's personal livery stood there. 'Doctor Somers,' he said, bowing, 'I am commanded to bid you attend his Grace at noon when he will ceremonially receive the works of the great sage, Plato.'

The boy was word-perfect in his message and its implications jolted me back into the wider world. 'John Swanwych has arrived with the translation?'

'He landed in Deptford at dawn and has ridden here with the great work. The Duke is entertaining him at this moment.' The page bowed again. 'Excuse me, sir. I must call on several other gentlemen to bid them attend at noon.'

I waved him on his way and flung on my jerkin and gown to cover my nether garments. Despite my despondent musings I was anxious to see John Swanwych again, to hear about his travels, to become acquainted with the translation he had brought from Italy, and somehow this revived interest in life fired me with courage. I owed it to myself not to accept my fate with supine resignation. Degraded and damned I might be but I would not submit mildly to the consequences. I would not wait to be manipulated. I would demand to see Roger Bolingbroke and be told what he expected of me. Death by my own hand might still seem the appropriate response but my decision would not be reached in ignorance – moreover, my hope would be to contrive his downfall to accompany mine.

Heartened by these intentions I went at once to Bolingbroke's chamber but was informed that he was closeted with the Duchess and would remain there, dealing with her correspondence, until the ceremony at noon. Swallowing my impatience, I left a message and made my way reluctantly to the corridor where Lady Anne was lodged.

I dreaded to encounter Bess and hailed a servant carrying a pile of soiled linen to enquire for news of the invalid.

'She's taken a little food, sir, and is sitting propped on pillows now.'

'That's good news,' I said, with a sigh of relief that I could justifiably make my escape without visiting her.

'Mistress Bess has been sent to find you,' the girl continued. 'Lady Anne's that keen to reward you for your services.'

Silently I groaned but I hoped I might see the lady briefly and be gone before Bess returned, so I was ushered into the room where my physician's pride was boosted by the hint of colour in my patient's cheeks. She extended her hand graciously.

'Doctor Somers, I am in your debt. I have a purse here for your pains.'

'There is no need, Lady Anne. Your recovery is sufficient recompense.'

'No need for courtesies, physician. I know how much I owe you. It was no ordinary malady I suffered.'

'You owe much to Mistress Barber. She acted promptly to bring about your sickness. Unpleasant though it was, her remedy was timely.'

Lady Anne nodded. 'She is a loyal and intelligent attendant. I am fortunate. Have you established that I was intentionally poisoned?'

Her forthright enquiry took me by surprise but I answered honestly. 'There is no way to be certain but it is possible.'

'As I suspected. Doctor Somers, I know there are those at the palace who would welcome my demise. I will not stand idly by when I observe those who plot villainy and treason.'

'Treason?'

'Hush!' She silenced my startled cry as the door-handle rattled and, to my distress, Bess entered.

Her expression was troubled but at the sight of me Bess gave a radiant smile. 'I failed in my search, madam,' she said, 'but my quarry has made his own way to your bedside.'

I froze the joy in my heart and acknowledged Mistress Barber stiffly. To my relief Lady Anne allowed me to depart. 'I must not intrude on your time, Doctor Somers. Others need your ministrations, no doubt. But I pray you will come again when you have leisure. There are matters I would like to share with you. I remember my sister's recommendation of your services.'

I bowed and retreated, biting my lip and deliberately scowling at Bess when she held open the door. I do not know how I bore the pain to see her blush of embarrassment as she lowered her eyes at my rebuff.

*****

The gathering at noon in the Duke's private apartments was impressive. All the luminaries of his personal court were present, some summoned at short notice from the City and Westminster. Gloucester sat in his cushioned chair with John Swanwych at his side and in front of them, set out on a bench, lay five volumes of Plato's *Republic*, only a little travel-worn. A clerk read extracts from the translation, so we could admire the wisdom of the writer and the fluency of Pier Candido Decembrio in rendering it easily accessible to us in Latin, but now was not the occasion for detailed dissection of the treatise. Candido had dedicated the books to the Duke and sent with them a letter of effusive praise for his love of learning and a recommendation for the purchase of one hundred other works, indispensable to a complete collection.

Duke Humphrey laughed when John Swanwych read out this part of the missive. 'And who does he propose to undertake this lucrative commission? Himself perhaps?'

149

John confirmed this had been mentioned. 'Candido is also pressing for the payment he claims in due to him for the work he has completed but the agreement was for payment when the contract has been fulfilled. One volume is yet outstanding, your Grace.'

'A plague on these grasping Italians!' Despite his words the Duke sounded jovial and he waved his hand towards the group of men around me. 'Giovanni come here and tell me how to outmatch this rogue in bargaining. Are you not glad I arranged your naturalisation as a civilised Englishman?'

Giovanni bowed with an extravagant flourish. 'I am forever grateful, my lord. But I modestly suggest that you are wise to employ Italian scholars to bring the fruits of their learning to your Palace Pleasance. They interpret the writings of the ancients in order that they may illuminate the glories of your court.'

The Duke chuckled loudly. 'No one can match an Italian in smooth flattery,' he said.

'It sounds even better in my language,' Giovanni whispered as the Duke turned away to converse with John Home. 'Harry, my friend, you look solemn. You should learn the beauties of my tongue. One day I pray you visit Italy. Why not I teach you?'

Abstracted, I said I should like to try but I was conscious of other eyes fixed on me and, as I spoke, Roger Bolingbroke advanced. 'You wish to see me privately, Master Somers? Follow me to my rooms when we are dismissed.'

*****

The curtain covered the entrance to the inner room and the antechamber was gloomy in the December afternoon but Roger Bolingbroke did not light a taper. Although he pointed me to the strangely carved stool I had used before, I remained standing, facing him across his encumbered desk. 'Well, boy, what do you want?'

I bridled at his patronising rudeness but checked myself. 'You know why I am here.'

'I know you spent the night in bawdy copulation with Lady Maud Warrenne and that you have turned the little fool's head with your ardour. Fortunately I do not need to engage her services on your behalf again. She has done all that was needed. In fact the vessel that brought your old master, Swanwych, to Deptford also conveyed her betrothed husband who has been absent in France. They are to wed before Candlemas and he will carry her to his fastness in the wilds of Norfolk where she will doubtless take a greasy rustic to her bed for want of better entertainment. She does not know this but her future lord has no interest in womankind and keeps a stable of lads to gratify his appetites. Are you not sorry for your lusty paramour?'

I tried hard to show no emotion. 'She is your victim. As am I; and I wish to know what you want of me that justifies your gross manoeuvring and vile threats.'

'Well spoken, master physician. Your spirit substantiates my wisdom in selecting you for my enterprise.'

'What enterprise?'

'That is not for you to know. You will do what I bid you, as I told you before. You are wasting my time.'

I stood my ground. 'You have not yet asked me to do anything.'

He came close to me so I could smell the rankness of his breath and knew his guts must trouble him. 'I do not ask, boy; I direct. But you are asking for a commission? That is novel. I am not yet ready for the exploit in which you will play an invaluable part.' He paused and I said nothing, refusing to give him the satisfaction of a useless protest. 'But perhaps, Master Somers, there is one small service you could perform to make you feel part of the endeavour. You have cause to go to the City from time to time, I believe.' I did not reply and he continued. 'I require a message to be delivered, verbally and not by a liveried messenger. You will do this, will you not?'

'What is the message?'

'Oh, it is simple and nothing sinful. You are to say 'Roger is ready for Mistress Jourdemayne to come.' You can commit this to memory?'

'To whom is this message to be given?'

'Why, to the woman's husband: a former cowherd now working as ostler at the Joyous Regard on Cheapside. A charming name for an inn, do you not think?'

'If this message is innocent why does it need to be delivered so secretly?'

'There you exceed your licence. You have asked for a role, Harry Somers, to test me and for me to test you. Deliver this message and we shall see how next to proceed.'

I did not answer at once. The commission was ludicrous, maybe deliberately insulting, but without doubt there was more to it than appeared from Bolingbroke's description. What I wanted more than anything was to bring this scheming wretch to some form of retribution but to do that I needed to know more of what he intended. I held his gaze. 'I am content to carry your message.'

He smiled thinly. 'Well done, Harry. You show good sense. Who knows where your compliance will lead you?'

Who indeed? I thought then and I think still.

Chapter 15

The ostler, Jourdemayne, was a surly fellow, a poor recommendation for the hostelry which employed him, and indeed the Joyous Regard had been optimistically named, perhaps many years previously before it had weathered. The man forked a truss of hay into a feeding trough and did not look at me when he confirmed his name, nor when I delivered my message.

'Do you understand?'

He looked at me over his shoulder. 'Oh, aye. I was expecting to hear. She'll come.' Then he continued filling the manger and began to whistle.

I waited a few moments, while he continued to ignore me, before withdrawing from the yard. I stepped carefully to avoid soiling my gown or, still worse, slipping over. I felt stupid and wondered angrily if Bolingbroke had devised this pointless exercise simply to demean me. To cheer myself I stumped towards the river and the Duke's mansion, called the Wardrobe at Baynard's Castle, where Thomas Chope needed no second bidding to join me in a jug of ale at a more salubrious establishment than the inn where Master Jourdemayne earned his pittance. I told Thomas I had needed to conduct a little business in the City but did not explain further and, instead, enquired whether the Duke had been a frequent visitor at the Wardrobe in recent weeks.

Thomas looked solemn. 'He's had good need to. Cardinal Beaufort has unsheathed his talons and is after Humphrey's blood in their dispute over the French prisoner. Charles of Orleans has been packed off to France at last, despite Gloucester's protests, and our noble lord needs to be constantly in attendance at the court to keep a step ahead of the holy man's tricks. I've heard it hinted that the Beauforts may even have an informer within the Duke's household.'

I poured us more ale, trying not to be resentful of Thomas's superior intelligence on affairs of state. 'You're well informed. The Duke's not delayed in the City by a new light o' love then?'

'Is that the Greenwich gossip? Rustic imaginings! In the City we hear what's nearer the truth and we're more sophisticated in our knowledge of the world.'

I gave him a light-hearted cuff. 'The Duke sleeps chastely alone, you're saying?'

'Of course not, dolt. There's three or four he beds when he's inclined but none of them mean a thing. They say he writes every day to Duchess Eleanor and he's never content until he's heard from her on the next tide.'

'Someone's spreading rumours at Greenwich – even though the Duchess must know the truth of it. Would that be the work of a Beaufort spy?'

Thomas crossed one leg across the other thigh and I envied him the elegance of his limbs. 'Unlikely. When you came here before you mentioned a fellow I'd heard ill of – Bolingbroke. I've learned a bit more about him.' I was at ease with Thomas now and I did not disguise my interest, leaning across the table to catch every word when he spoke softly. 'He's a very learned man.'

'Well, that's no secret!'

Thomas held up his hand to calm me. 'He's thought to speak with the dead and they help him foretell the future.'

'Necromancy!'

'Yes, that's the word. Mind you, there may be nothing in it. He's not popular.'

'The church will not approve if it's true!' I gripped my companion's arm. 'Bolingbroke has made himself my enemy, Thomas. I should welcome being privy to evidence that would disgrace him but I dare not risk acting on mistaken information. Could you find out more without drawing attention to yourself or me?'

He gave a guffaw. 'You're dark horse, Harry Somers. Tangling with great men now, are you? It might be a dangerous pastime but, by the look of you, you know that.

I'll make enquiries. Don't worry, I'll be tact itself. I have contacts who'll keep mum and never ask whose interests I'm following. I'd be glad to do something to help you.' He reached for the jug and winked. 'Have you lost your maidenhood yet?'

I spluttered a mouthful of wine and he slapped the table with enthusiasm. 'You have, by God! Merciful heaven be praised! Is she a bawd or are you enamoured and like to be married within the year?'

I burbled helplessly, unable to give a straight answer to his question, except in one respect. 'No prospect of marrying,' I said finally.

'I hope you're wrong there,' he said, 'but I can see it's not plain-sailing so I'll not press it.' He drained the jug into my cup and shortly afterwards I left him to return downriver.

*****

Over the Feast of the Nativity the weather turned bitter cold and two days before the festivities of Twelfth Night it was reported that the ponds on the heath were frozen solid enough for a bullock-cart to cross. 'In consequence,' the chamberlain announced, 'his Grace, the Duke, has been pleased to agree that revels be held in the forenoon, upon the hill, where there will be sliding on the ice, roasting of oxen, numerous games and contests, and, beyond the ponds, butts will be set up for the young men of the household to show their skill with the bow.' He paused as he made his announcement on the steps of the hall. 'His Grace and Duchess Eleanor will be pleased to attend the proceedings and all the household are at liberty to do so, subject only to the permission of their immediate superiors.'

I had no pleasure in these pursuits and dreaded tumbling over on the slippery ground but I was anxious not to attract Bolingbroke's attention by my absence. He, I was sure, would be in close attendance on the Duchess and her husband, observing everything. Besides, Doctor Southwell was unexpectedly eager to venture up to the ridge in my company.

'I have a care of souls out at Ruislip in Middlesex,' he said. 'A rector serves there on my behalf but I go to see how he fares from time to time and a few years back we had much amusement during my winter visit when the villagers disported themselves on the frozen stream. Lads were skimming stones along the solid water and some were most agile in their movements. I tried my hand at the game and also fishing through a hole in the ice. Who do you think span his stone so skilfully it travelled furthest, eh? And who do you think caught most tiddlers with his line? Eh? Eh?'

I was obviously expected to show amazement when he declared he had been the winner of both competitions and certainly such prowess seemed out of character. I entertained the base suspicion that the astute villagers had somehow contrived to ensure their eminent vicar secured the victory but, at any event, he was anxious to try his hand and foot on the ice once more and I was bound to accompany him.

Needless to say he scurried on ahead of me while I trudged carefully, grasping a switch of ash to steady my steps, but I nearly dropped my staff when I was greeted from behind with a harrumph by way of greeting. 'Doctor Somers! I ain't seen you for weeks. You don't look too happy on the frosty ground. Wait till you get to the sheet ice. Then you can slide free. I'll give you a push to set you going.'

I gritted my teeth for conversation while attempting to climb the treacherous slope. 'Rendell! How are you? You've grown taller.'

'Should hope I had. Got muscles coming too. See!'

I took a hasty glance towards his arm, flexed like a wrestler's, and immediately regretted it as I felt my boot slip backwards. He hooted with good-natured laughter. 'Here take hold of my shoulder to lean on, you poor cripple. Them muscles come from me turning the spit. Trusted to do that now, I am, turning great carcases above the fire. Warm work, it is.'

I made an effort at humour. 'Unlike our present activity.' With my stick on one side and Rendell's stout person on the other, I felt more secure.

'All one to me, it is.' He lurched a little to the side and chuckled when I clutched his shoulder more tightly. 'God's bones, you're a scaredy one.' He bent towards me to pat my arm reassuringly. It was humiliating to be so dependent on a boy not yet nearly a man. 'Grizel's coming back.'

I dared not lose the rhythm I had newly acquired. 'To Greenwich? Is that wise?'

'She's bored at Danson. Went to see her, I did. Got a lift with a carter. She's more cheerful now. She's not one to pine for long. Quite a young woman now, more's the pity. Got a touch of the airs and graces.'

'I wouldn't like Grizel to lose all her spirit.'

'Nah! She won't do that. She's set on revenge. Reckons she's learned summat what'll help catch Dickon's killers. She'll be after you to help follow it up, mark my words.'

I shuddered at the thought of taking on such a vain task and incurring Grizel's frustration when it led nowhere.

'She's all right, I reckon,' Rendell said cheerfully. We had come to a stretch of frozen mud and he leapt ahead to haul me up the glissade. 'Here, it's flatter now. You'll manage with your stick. I need to get to the fire they've lighted by the side of the pond. There's a spit for me to turn! No rest for wicked, ain't that right?'

I was sorry to lose his help but the path was easier and within a few paces I reached the outer ranks of the onlookers from the palace. I knew I must continue further, so that I could claim to see Doctor Southwell at his unlikely exploits on the ice, but first I had to pass through a group of excited ladies in their furs who had been conveyed up the hill by some intrepid horsemen and their sure-footed mounts. I exchanged pleasantries with several of the Duchess's attendants, noting there seemed no sign of Lady Anne, which did not surprise me, but then I recognised a voice behind me that I had hoped never to hear again.

'Doctor Somers, how brave you are to venture up the hill in such conditions. May I present you to my future husband?' Lady Maud was glowing beneath her sable hood and she sat gracefully, to the side, with her arm around an elegant rider swathed in rich silks. 'Sweet lord, this is the physician I told you of, Doctor Harry Somers, who is highly esteemed in the household. The Lord Walter Fitzvaughan.'

I bowed as best I could, terrified by her words, wondering what on earth she could have told him of me, but he seemed unconcerned. 'Doctor Somers. The ladies make a pet of you, I think. I trust we shall become better acquainted before the Lady Maud and I enjoy our nuptials. Pray call upon me while we remain at the palace.'

I bowed again as they rode off, leaving me pondering whether her fate would be as dire as Bolingbroke had foretold. Lord Walter appeared a cultivated man whatever his propensities. If he treated his wife with respect, she might fare no worse than a host of other noble ladies married to lords whose interests lay elsewhere, whether with mistresses or bawds or boys. It was a harsh conclusion but I had lost some of my sentimentality. I moved on towards the pond.

An awning had been erected over an open-sided stand, near the edge of the frozen water, so that the Duke and Duchess, with their closest attendants, could view the diversions on the ice in comfort. I made my obeisance as I drew beside them and they graciously acknowledged me but as I lifted my eyes I realised that on Duchess Eleanor's other side sat the widowed Lady Anne herself. This was a high honour for the chamberlain's daughter. She raised her hand to me and simultaneously beckoned a page to her side. I moved a few steps to the right and began to make sense of the varied activities in front of me. There was much rough-and-tumble merriment among those lacking the gift of balance, or whose skill was impeded by the quantity of ale they had imbibed, but there was also grace and a degree of competence at which I could only marvel. Most impressively, in the centre of the pond, Doctor Southwell pirouetted, leaning from side to side as necessary, twisting his feet at just the correct angle to cut shapes upon the ice with the bones strapped beneath his boots.

I watched my colleague in fascination but also became aware of the archery in progress on the far side of the pond and thought again of the wretched Dickon who had excelled at the sport. Just then a piping voice below my shoulder made me look down. 'The Lady Anne Wenham bids me speak to you.' The page indicated that we should move away from the crowd on the bank and I followed him dutifully. When he was satisfied that he had observed his mistress's instructions, he stopped. 'Lady Anne reminds you that she bade you call upon her and you have not done so.'

I shuffled, quite unable to dispute what this miniature assessor declared. I knew well enough why I had chosen to ignore a gracious but casual invitation, as I deemed it, for I could not bear to risk encountering Bess face to face and needing to scorn her publicly. 'I am at fault,' I muttered.

'Lady Anne requires that you remain here and I will lead her to you in a short time when she is released from attendance on her Grace. You will comply?'

I assured the solemn boy I would comply and watched with amusement as he returned, towards the ducal stand, full of pert importance and decorum. I turned back to the revels on the ice but I could not concentrate on them, so fearful was I that Bess would accompany Lady Anne. I had not seen her on the heath but she would doubtless be waiting in attendance somewhere for her mistress to summon her. I found I had begun to loosen slivers of bark from my staff in my nervousness and, as the period of waiting became prolonged, I was tempted to desert my post. While I still dithered I heard those piping tones again and looked round to see the page leading Lady Anne, alone and otherwise unattended, to my side. In great relief I bowed.

'Wait here,' the lady instructed the boy and indicated that we should walk on a few paces out of his earshot. 'My complaint has been delivered, I think?'

'Indeed yes, my lady, and I am contrite.'

She looked at me sternly and lowered her voice. 'You will not have realised the importance of my request. There are things I wish to tell you. Oh, damnation! How has he contrived to come here? Quickly: stretch out your arm as if you were indicating something to me.'

I did as she asked, pointing to Doctor Southwell and speaking his name, in time for Roger Bolingbroke to hear as he approached from behind the nearest knot of onlookers. 'Your servant, Lady Anne,' he said as he bowed. 'Is it not remarkable that a medical man should possess such unexpected talents on the ice? I would beg a moment of your time, my lady.'

She could do no other than accede to his request and I could do no other than ignore his snide remark and withdraw, to allow my superiors to converse. I bowed and moved away towards her small attendant, still waiting where she had left him.

Just as I reached the boy he screamed and his cry seemed to echo round me. In the same instant he flung himself forward, spinning me round to face the ill-assorted pair I had left and, as I did so, I saw the full horror of what had occurred. Roger Bolingbroke was still standing, pasty-faced and shaking, his hand covering his mouth, but Lady Anne lay crumpled on the frozen ground and from her

160

throat protruded a barbed arrow. I hurtled to her side as Bolingbroke collapsed into the arms of others who rushed to help.

The second cry I heard had come from the lips of the dying woman but a flicker of life remained and she fumbled for my hand. Blood bubbled from her mouth as she struggled to make herself understood and I put my ear to her mouth. 'Tell,' she hissed. The next word sounded like 'treachery' but I could not be sure. I soothed her brow but knew she wished me to receive her message. With a great effort, through a jet of crimson liquid, she gasped, 'woe is come... which will do it.' Then her whole body convulsed and when Doctor Southwell pushed to my side it was too late for him to give her the final rites, only to join me in praying for her soul.

Chapter 16

The pallor of the Duke's cheeks was heightened by the black velvet of his pourpoint and it rivalled the whiteness of the ermine around the neck of his gown. He had assembled all the senior men of the household in the hall, within an hour of Lady Anne's death, and he paced to and fro upon the dais before speaking, awaiting a signal from the chamberlain that everyone was present.

'Only Roger Bolingbroke is absent, your Grace. He was carried from the heath in a state of shock and put to bed. Doctor Swanwych has given him a sleeping draught.'

The Duke nodded. 'What are the results of your immediate enquiries?'

'The marshal at arms is here and will vouch that no participant in the archery, beyond the frozen pond, was responsible for a stray arrow.'

The burly official stepped forward. 'Indeed, your Grace, I'd stake my word that this was no stray arrow but one most carefully directed.'

'From what position?'

'The eastern end of the pond, where the bushes are thickest, about a furlong away from the victim. A good bowman would have a sure aim over the distance.'

The Duke held up his hand. 'Do the medical men confirm that the injury is consistent with an arrow from that direction?' John Swanwych and I bowed and gave our confirmation. Thank you. Pray continue, master marshal.'

'Your Grace, the soldiers engaged in the archery and we who were officiating were absorbed in the competition. We did not know anything was amiss until we heard the shouting from across the ice. It took several minutes before we understood a murderer was to be sought from near the butts. I ordered a search to be made but nothing definitive could be found. There were signs that horsemen had ridden from the scene in various directions but the frost on the

162

ground was churned and there was no clear evidence as to where the villain might have fled.'

'You assume he escaped on horseback?'

'It might be expected – for speed – but in that case he would have been handicapped by his bow. There were dozens of bystanders on foot but my men fanned out to bring them in for examination and none was carrying a longbow.'

'Could the bow have been concealed in the bushes?'

'I ordered a thorough search, your Grace, and my men beat through the undergrowth with their swords. I despatched riders to follow the hoof marks which radiated from the site and some have not yet returned but I cannot hold out a promise of success.'

'Thank you, marshal, you have done well.' The Duke turned back to the group of men standing with the chamberlain, which included John Swanwych and me. 'Insofar as you saw what happened, gentlemen, is it your opinion that the arrow was aimed at the Lady Anne?'

'No one can be certain,' the chamberlain replied. 'Hardly anyone observed the moment of impact. Perhaps only the lady's page here.' He drew the lad forward and put a kindly hand on his shoulder. 'Courage, my boy. Tell his Grace what you saw.'

The page's first attempt to speak came as a squeak but, after he had swallowed and coughed, he mastered his voice. 'I was watching my lady,' he said, 'as she turned towards Master Bolingbroke when he came to join her. Doctor Somers was walking towards me and screened my view for a moment but I heard the swish and I think I screamed. I rushed forward to clutch hold of the doctor.'

'This accords with your testimony, Doctor Somers?'

'Absolutely, your Grace. It was the lad's cry which caused me to turn.'

'Roger Bolingbroke was standing close to Lady Anne?'

'No more than a yard from her side. He had asked to speak to her and I had just left them so they might do so in private.'

'Is it possible the arrow was intended for Master Bolingbroke?'

I had been pondering the same possibility and cleared my throat. 'No one could be sure, your Grace, but he was half turned away from its flight, whereas it struck Lady Anne squarely in the centre of her neck. If the bowman was expert, as the marshal suggests, his aim is likely to have been true. He loosed only one shaft.'

'Yet Roger Bolingbroke fainted?' I wondered if I imagined a hint of disdain in the Duke's words.

John Swanwych took a step forward. 'The feathers passed close enough to graze his cheek and he was spattered with the lady's blood. I do not find his collapse surprising.'

The Duke inclined his head. 'I meant no criticism. Eleanor's clerk is no warrior after all. Chamberlain, marshal, you will both continue your enquiries and no one will leave the palace overnight except under your instruction. We reconvene here at nine in the morning. In the meantime let continuous Masses be said for the lady's soul.' He signalled that we were dismissed and we filed silently from his presence.

*****

I walked across the courtyard with John Swanwych and Geoffrey du Bois and at first we were silent, lost in our own thoughts, but before we reached the opposite range of buildings my apothecary friend could contain his suspicions no longer. 'Is it possible that Roger Bolingbroke lured Lady Anne to stand where she did – where he had arranged a bowman would target her?'

John gave a gasp of disbelief but I answered quickly. 'Lady Anne had come to the spot of her own volition.'

164

'That does not mean the bowman was not watching her every move and awaiting a signal from Bolingbroke.'

'In theory I would be very ready to believe that but the evidence of my eyes disputes it. I saw Bolingbroke's look of horror as Lady Anne was struck. Whether it was simply his alarm at the sudden violence or personal fear that the arrow had been meant for him, I cannot tell, but I do not believe he mimicked terror or surprise.'

John Swanwych looked from me to Geoffrey and pursed his lips. 'You obviously have reason to doubt Bolingbroke's integrity. I know little of him but since my return to Greenwich I have become aware how greatly the Duke and Duchess lean on his advice. You'd best be careful of throwing accusations in that direction.'

Geoffrey raised his hands in a gesture of surrender and I repeated that I saw no grounds for implicating Bolingbroke in the atrocity. John's reaction was a timely reminder of the clerk's privileged position and I was glad I had no role in trying to untangle the mystery of Lady Anne's death. Nor, for her sake, must I show any interest in Bess Barber's future, now her mistress was dead, although it was that which tugged at my heartstrings.

*****

Next morning we reassembled in the presence of the Duke. The chamberlain was not standing at his side on this occasion but Roger Bolingbroke, looking solemn but healthy, took this place. Two new pieces of information were reported. First to be hauled forward was a sharp-eyed scullion, who had been turning the spit beside the pond where its bank curved towards the butts, and who was quite unintimidated by appearing before his royal-born liege. Rendell winked at me as he passed and he gave his testimony with aplomb.

165

'I'd been watching some carts, yer Grace, across the ice. At the far end of the pond, opposite where the lady were. There'd been a bit of a kerfuffle when they turned them round. It looked like a horse slipped or a cart got caught. T'any rate next thing I knew, after the lady screamed, them carts took off at a fine old caper.'

'Which direction did they take?'

'Down the hill. Towards the City perhaps.'

'Well done, boy.' The Duke signalled for him to be rewarded and Rendell's eyes grew round at the sight of the silver coin put into his hand. The lad bowed deeply and I felt proud of him, as if I had some proprietary interest in his behaviour, but I needed to pay attention to another witness presented by the marshal at arms. This was one of the soldiers sent to search further afield and his witness supported what Rendell had seen.

'Your Grace, I followed the tracks towards Deptford and lower down the hill, where the frost had melted, it became clearer that two or three carts had travelled that way in a hurry. Nearer the river it was difficult to follow them with certainty, because there was a jumble of ruts, but on a jetty, where the barges pull in, I found this.' He flourished a leather wristlet, such as is worn by an archer to protect his left wrist from chafing by the bowstring. There was an audible intake of breath around the hall.

'So the bowman hid in a cart and then took to the water to complete his escape. I fancy we shall have difficulty tracing him further.' The Duke paused as the chamberlain entered from the back of the dais and bent to whisper in his master's ear. I noticed Bolingbroke lean towards them but Gloucester stood up abruptly. 'Gentlemen,' he said, 'I will adjourn these proceedings once again in order that the Duchess may pursue some matters she has in hand. We must not forget that the sad victim was one of my wife's principal ladies and she is right to take her own initiative.'

We all bowed and began to file towards the external door but the Duke halted our progress. 'Doctor Somers,' he said in a loud voice, causing many eyes to turn to me, 'Duchess Eleanor particularly requests your presence in her chambers. The chamberlain will accompany you.'

I felt Bolingbroke's gimlet stare fixed on me but I did not look towards him. I concentrated on presenting a calm demeanour to the company – after all it was entirely proper for the Duchess to send for her ladies' physician at such a time – but my heart was thudding and my throat was dry.

*****

The chamberlain hustled me across the courtyard but gave no indication of any particular service to be required of me. All he said was, 'my daughter, Lady Blanche, has come,' and I remember thinking, in my innocence, that it was kind of her to offer support to her parents at such a time. When we entered her chamber I was surprised to see the bevy of women attending the Duchess, but even more so to realise that Sir Hugh de Grey had accompanied his wife on the journey from Danson. He stood with Lady Blanche and Dame Margery at the foot of the platform on which the Duchess's chair was placed and he greeted me courteously. I noted he had broadened and put on weight since our last encounter. Just behind his wife and her mother was another face I knew well but Grizel was thinner than she had been in the summer and she stared ahead with unfocussed eyes. Two dozen other women, of varying status, were clustered round their mistress and most did not disguise their curiosity as they peered at me. Only Lady Maud Warrenne openly smirked as I approached and bowed. A plainly dressed older woman, whom I did not recognise, muttered something in her ear and, as Maud suppressed a giggle, I fought down my unease.

The Duchess wasted no time on formalities. 'Doctor Somers, it is not your physician's wisdom which we seek at this moment. Strong commendations of your ability to pursue justice and discern the truth have been made to me by Sir Hugh and his lady, who are known to you. They have urged me to place the investigations which must follow this heinous murder in your hands, with orders to all members of the household to assist you as necessary.'

I struggled not to panic at the thought of what would be involved. 'Your Grace, the little experience I gained, after my sister's death, was in very different circumstances.'

'Lady Blanche said you would be modest but she is confident in your skill. Sadly, it is her sister who has been so cruelly done to death on this occasion.'

The lady of Danson extended her hand towards me. 'I ask for no more than you did for Alys. Your honesty and integrity are the only guarantee I seek.'

I noticed Sir Hugh's leg twitch as he shifted position and dared not catch his eye, for he knew my honesty had not been absolute when I suppressed information about his own part in events eighteen months previously, but his wife took a step forward and clasped her hands to her chest. 'Doctor Somers, I implore you to help us. My sister was a woman of rigid rectitude. I am distraught at her fate and my poor mother is bereft, as yours was when Alys died.'

There was no escape, no possibility of spurning this eloquent, clever plea but I sighed. 'My lady, I am your servant. I will do what I can but I beg you not to overestimate my talents.'

The Duchess rose with a satisfied smile. 'Thank you, Doctor Somers. All my ladies and their attendants are ready to answer your questions. The Duke will endorse these arrangements and confirm your authority within the rest of the household. You will no doubt wish to begin at once and you can do no better than start with Lady Anne's personal maid-servant. The ante-chamber is at your disposal. You will have met Bess Barber, I think.'

My stomach somersaulted as Bess emerged from behind the group of ladies and I saw the crimson blush sweep across her pale features. 'Dame Margery,' I said hurriedly, 'would you be willing to be present while I interview the female witnesses? It will not be too painful for you?'

The chamberlain's wife drew herself up and I knew I had judged her resilience correctly. 'That will be entirely proper, if her Grace is content'.

We moved to the ante-chamber and Dame Margery summoned a flask of small beer to sustain us. She positioned a stool for Bess and took her own place on the window seat nearby. I too accepted a stool in order not to loom over the two women. I declined a goblet for myself but pressed one into Bess's hand.

'If this is too difficult for you, Mistress Barber, we can defer our talk until later.' I thought I sounded cold and pompous but my hand was shaking as I gave her the drink.

Bess shook her head. 'Duchess Eleanor said I must be the first to be seen and I owe that duty to Lady Anne.'

'What would help me most,' I said as impersonally as I could, 'would be for you to tell me what you know of Lady Anne's relationships, here at Greenwich and elsewhere, her friendships and, if she had any, her enemies.'

Bess took a sip of ale, then set down the goblet and folded her hands in her lap. 'Lady Anne was not comfortable at the palace. She never confided her feelings to me but I knew she was forced to mix with ladies she did not respect and saw things of which she disapproved. She said to me once that she hoped we might leave here in the summer.'

'She came to Greenwich after her widowhood. It was necessary for her to leave her husband's estate I suppose?'

Bess's huge dark eyes opened wide and for a moment held mine. 'It was not necessary in the sense you mean,

169

Doctor Somers. Young Sir Bertram, her step-son, and his wife were fond of her as she was of them. They are much of her age and became close friends while her husband was alive. They would never have compelled her to leave Dunmow. She believed it was her duty to accept Duchess Eleanor's invitation to become one of her attendants and she understood her father would wish to arrange her re-marriage in due course.'

This was not what I had expected to hear and I found it puzzling. 'She came here simply from a sense of duty?' I echoed.

'I believe so. She remained in contact with young Sir Bertram and Lady Mary. They often sent messages to each other.' Bess blushed and looked down as if afraid she had said more than she should. Lady Margery had shifted position on her seat.

Deeply embarrassed, I made myself pursue the point. 'To your knowledge, Mistress Barber, was there anything improper in this relationship?'

Bess shook her head and screwed the cord at her waist into a ball. 'Absolutely not,' she said softly, 'but she may have feared there would have been malicious gossip if she had stayed at Dunmow.'

I thought it best to change the subject. 'You had been her attendant for some time, I believe?'

'Since soon after her marriage to Sir Bertram. My father was chief forester on his lands but he was killed by rogues who raided the land to take deer. I was left without a protector and Lady Anne took me into her service at once. I owed her gratitude but it was no hardship to give her my loyalty.'

I heard Dame Margery give an approving murmur and wondered if she would offer Bess a place in her own household. I hoped she would. 'What will you do now?' I asked, stepping beyond the strict confines of my inquisitorial role.

Bess looked me in the face again and she was completely composed. 'The Lady Maud Warrenne has asked me to become her maid-servant and when she marries in two weeks' time I shall accompany her to Norfolk.'

My stomach heaved and I tasted bile. I dreaded what Bess might already know about Lady Maud and dared not ask her if her choice was wise. 'What was Lady Anne's opinion of Duchess Eleanor?' The abruptness of my question, covering my confusion, startled us all and Dame Margery gave a gasp of protest.

Bess pressed her lips together before replying. 'Lady Anne never spoke of this,' she said, 'but I believe she served the Duchess from obligation, not affection.'

'You have described Lady Anne's discomfort at the palace. Do you think it possible she had made enemies who might seek her death?'

Bess drew herself up straight on her stool. 'I think the idea is ridiculous. There are always jealousies and rivalries between attendants but they do not lead to murder. I find it difficult to credit the arrow was meant for my mistress.'

'You did not witness the attack?'

'No. Lady Anne had given me leave to remain at the palace. I have suffered with the rheum and did not welcome an afternoon in the icy air. But I have heard descriptions of her death.'

'You believe the arrow was meant for Master Bolingbroke?'

She looked at me sharply. 'Lady Anne's page told me the Duchess's clerk had only just joined her. A moment before that you had been at her side.' Her voice cracked and she put her hand to her mouth as if to stifle unseemly emotion. 'Isn't it possible that when the bowman loosed his arrow, you had been his target?'

I was devastated, seeing how it upset her to think I had been in danger, and it was all I could do to resist the instinct to take her in my arms. I thanked heaven for my foresight in asking Dame Margery to be present for I must preserve the illusion of my coldness towards Bess. I had no idea where Roger Bolingbroke's malevolent scheming fitted into the strange picture which was emerging but I felt certain he would make use of anything he saw as offering him advantage.

'I think I had moved away before the bolt was loosed,' I said and rose. 'Mistress Barber, I am grateful for your help. I do not wish to distress you further but it is possible I will have more questions to put to you.'

She nodded as she stood and Dame Margery advanced to put her arm round Bess's quivering shoulders. When I opened the door for them to leave, a page in Gloucester's livery was waiting outside and he delivered his master's command to attend without delay in the Duke's study. I could not disobey and, although my head was in tumult after the painful interview I had just conducted, I followed the boy dutifully down the stairs and across the courtyard.

*****

I was admitted at once and was surprised to find Duke Humphrey alone, pacing backwards and forwards in the small room. He made no attempt to summon other attendance but continued his uneasy progress while I stood in awkward silence until he thumped his fist on his desk and turned to confront me. 'Doctor Somers, the Duchess has told me you have been charged to conduct enquiries into the unfortunate lady's death.'

'If it please your Grace,' I stammered, trying to stop my knees from knocking together.

He gave a brief laugh and flung himself into his chair. 'I am not displeased. Not with you, Harry. If anyone can untangle this horrible business it will be you. But there are all manner of inconveniences likely to be involved and I have anxieties. I have no knowledge whatsoever of what lies behind this fiendish deed and I assure you I stand for justice and the rule of law in all things. You must have a free hand to pursue the truth but I have an uncomfortable feeling that you may uncover malfeasance within my household and that concerns me. I have asked to see you, Harry, to ask for your discretion. I cannot be more specific because I do not know what you will find and I place no qualifications upon your task, but I do seek your discretion.'

I was bemused how to reply and extremely nervous that I had ventured into territory beyond my comprehension. 'Your Grace, if you wish me to withdraw from the enquiry...'

'No, no. I have confidence in you, master physician. But if you find that wickedness has been committed on my account, as I fear may be the case, I ask that you consult me before bringing the miscreant to justice.'

'My lord Duke, you are the overlord of your household and any misdeeds would be brought before you as a matter of course.'

'Certainly. I am content to rest on your judgement and this is merely hypothetical but, should it prove to be relevant, I ask for discretion. I can do no more.'

'I am your Grace's humble servant.' I was at a loss what else to say but as I bowed he moved forward to grip my shoulder. 'God go with you, Harry Somers,' he said. 'I am content.'

He rang a handbell and I was shown from the room in a state of great perplexity. If Duke Humphrey was content, I was not. I could make no sense of his words or what lay behind them. Only one interpretation seemed possible and that was so improbable that I could not credit it – and yet it fitted with some things Bess had said. Was it possible Lady Anne had been the Duke's mistress? Was that why she disliked Duchess Eleanor and why she was unpopular among her companions? Nothing I knew of Lady Anne suggested she was unchaste but would any noble woman resist Gloucester's overtures – he was notorious for his amours? She had been no beauty but her virtue might have seemed a challenge to be overcome, which a determined rake might relish. Was the Duke fearful that she had been killed because of their liaison? If that was so, where might the guilt lie? The implications were too appalling to contemplate.

Chapter 17

When I left the Duke I turned towards the apothecary's chamber. As soon as it could be arranged I needed to interview Roger Bolingbroke, the closest witness to Lady Anne's death. This was a prospect which filed me with alarm and I was determined not to see him alone but it was no role for Dame Margery, so I had been pondering who should best accompany me. In many ways John Home would have been my preference, for I judged his quiet intelligence would be calming in a sensitive situation, but I could not disregard the possibility that Bolingbroke had some hold over him and, even if this was imaginary, I must not take the risk. I had therefore determined Geoffrey du Bois would be a safer choice, as I had never found cause to doubt his independence, and I went at once to seek his agreement. I found him weighing small heaps of what looked like coloured sand, his usual soft bonnet askew on his head, and he hailed me cheerfully.

'Are you come to question me about the gruesome deed, Harry? I can add very little to what you already know. I was at the other end of the frozen pond from Lady Anne, with a group of astonished bystanders admiring Doctor Southwell's skill on the ice.'

'No, I don't need to speak to everyone who was on the heath. I'd be occupied for weeks if I were to attempt that. But I need a companion to come with me to see Roger Bolingbroke and hear his testimony. Would you do that, Geoffrey, perhaps this afternoon?'

He set down his scales abruptly, spilling some of the powder and dropping one of the weights. He bent to retrieve the fallen disc and, to my surprise, I could see his hand was shaking as he rummaged on the floor. When he straightened his face was ashen. 'I'm sorry,' he said, 'I am about to take the wherry to the City. I have to deliver these minerals to a

175

colleague near the Tower. His need for them is most urgent. I beg you will excuse me.'

He poured what remained in the scales into a twist of cloth, seemingly unconcerned that the quantity was diminished from what he had measured, and his movements were agitated. I did not believe his explanation for one moment but my undertaking required a willing participant so I merely nodded. 'Think nothing of it,' I said. 'I'll not delay you,' and I moved back into the courtyard.

I was rattled by this unexpected rebuff but knew I must concentrate on the task in hand so I turned towards John Swanwych's rooms and there I received a genial and accommodating response. I knew I would be less at ease in the company of my former master, than with one of my closer friends, but I had renewed my trust in his integrity, so I was content to pen a note to Roger Bolingbroke asking that he receive us after we had dined that afternoon. I started to walk back to my own chamber when the sound of scurrying feet caused me to turn and Grizel hurtled to my side, panting.

'Thank the Lord. I thought you'd vanished from the palace. You're to come at once, to the chamberlain and Dame Margery. Here, let me get me breath a bit.'

'It's all right, Grizel. Of course I'll come. You've not returned to Danson then, with Lady Blanche?'

She gulped air and winked at me. 'Nah. I'm back with Dame Margery. It were good to be away for a while after I lost Dickon but Danson's too quiet for my liking – except when it's too lively.'

I raised an eyebrow. 'I'm not sure I follow you.'

She tucked a strand of hair behind her ear. 'That Sir Hugh: he's as randy as a stag at rut. Three times I've had to make a run for it when he'd got his hand up my skirt and his tongue down my throat. Reckon Alys must have known a thing or two about that.'

I ignored her too perceptive comment but, as we approached the chamberlain's quarters, she gripped my sleeve to check our progress. 'I'm glad you're charged to enquire into Lady Anne's death. But I want you to take Dickon's murder on board too.' I began to demur but she persisted. 'There's more to it than we thought. A pedlar came to Danson who'd been in the park on the day Dickon were attacked. He heard men talking in a waterfront inn at Deptford later that night who said the archer were killed because he knew too much. So did Lady Anne know too much, I reckon. There could be a link.'

To my relief the door was flung open before we knocked and Grizel was sent away while I was shown into the chamberlain's study. Dame Margery was seated beside her husband, as expected, but a third person was also present and I swallowed hard to stay composed when I saw Bess Barber's white face. The older woman seized the initiative and with no preliminaries pushed Bess forward. 'Repeat to Doctor Somers what you have told us.'

Tears overflowed from her eyes, rolling down her cheeks, and I longed to comfort her. 'When I returned to my room after you had questioned me, sir,' she said in a low voice,' I found that Lady Anne's things had been disturbed. She had a box with a few keepsakes, nothing really valuable, and I took charge of it when she was killed. It was never locked. There was nothing secret in it. But it had been opened in my absence. I could tell. Everything had been put back but it was not as it had been.'

'What was missing, Mistress?'

'Nothing, nothing at all.'

'You're sure? Were there no jewels?'

'There are some simple chains and necklets, pretty but not costly. They are still there. So are two letters from her late husband which she treasured. I am certain nothing has been taken.' She paused as if she was gathering her strength to say more. 'It may be that thieves were looking for something they expected to be there but it was not.'

'And you can guess what it might be?'

'I don't know but there was one thing which she gave me on the morning of the day she died. I delivered it to the chamberlain as she asked.'

The old man took a packet from his desk. 'Lady Anne corresponded with her step-son regularly. A messenger came from Dunmow most weeks, bringing her letters from young Sir Bertram Wenham and taking her replies. I dealt with the fellow on her behalf. As she said, Mistress Barber handed me a sealed communication to go with the next delivery. It has not left the palace yet and so I have enclosed it with my notification to Sir Bertram of his step-mother's death. The messenger will probably call here tomorrow.'

I turned back to Bess who was wiping her eyes with Dame Margery's kerchief. 'Where are Sir Bertram's letters to Lady Anne?'

'She destroyed every one of them, as soon as she had read them. She held them to a taper until they fell in ashes.'

'Do you know what they said?'

'No, sir. I can only read a little but Lady Anne never let me see them.'

'Why did you not tell me of these letters earlier?' I did not intend to sound harsh but her lips quivered and, with distress, I realised I had frightened her.

'I did not think they signified. They were family matters and I am sure they were harmless. But when you questioned me you suggested there might have been impropriety and I was upset to hear my mistress's reputation defamed so vilely.' Fresh tears flowed in the grooves beside Bess's reddened nose. 'I'm sorry, sir. I am sorry.'

I wanted to tell her she must not call me 'sir' and I held her in no way blameworthy but I had my hateful part to play. 'I understand you meant to protect your mistress.' I turned to the chamberlain and held out my hand. 'If you will permit it, I should like to extract Lady Anne's letter from your packet and read its contents.'

Duke Humphrey's official looked affronted and he drew his gown around him with a haughty gesture but Dame Margery rose and stood at his side. 'Our daughter has been murdered,' she said quietly, laying her hand on his wrist. Her husband passed the papers from hand to hand while he considered his duty until, at length, he broke his own seal and removed the enclosure from his letter. He held out the small folded document and I took it. I snapped open Lady Anne's seal and smoothed the creases in the communication while I stared at the brief message it contained. Then I passed it back to the chamberlain so he and Dame Margery could see it.

'*WOE is come to Greenwich*,' the old man read aloud.

Bess gave a gulp of pain and sank to her knees. 'Poor mistress, poor mistress,' she sobbed. 'She was so unhappy here. I told you so. She had no one else to tell of her misery but her friends at Dunmow.'

Dame Margery helped Bess to her feet and consoled her while the chamberlain offered the paper back to me. 'I take it we do not need to forward this sad missive in the circumstances.'

'I suggest you send your letter to Dunmow as soon as possible, without the insertion, but I believe Sir Bertram is entitled to know of his step-mother's last message and, once I have completed my initial enquiries here, I will take it to him and explain why it has been opened. There are questions I should like to put to him.' I spoke softly but was conscious that the women could probably hear so I raised my voice for my final words. 'I wish no one outside this room to know of my intentions or the contents of this letter, is that clear?'

All three gave their promise and I left them, carrying with me the memory of the distraught and resentful look Bess gave me as I passed her. I was sure that, if she had ever felt any fondness for me, my assumed coldness must have destroyed it utterly.

*****

Roger Bolingbroke had consented to receive me, as I requested, but he looked narrowly at Doctor Swanwych when I presented him as my companion. Since John's return to Greenwich there had been little opportunity for them to make each other's acquaintance but the Duchess's clerk would have known how highly the Duke valued the services of my former master. Although it had not been my first plan, I thought John's presence a shrewd move but I had no time for self-congratulation as Bolingbroke was not prepared to give me the advantage of speaking first.

'I understand you are charged with investigating the atrocity of Lady Anne Wenham's death. I have grave reservations that your appointment is appropriate and I hereby reserve my right to refuse to answer your questions.' He remained standing and offered us no seats.

'If we are to note your reservations, we need to understand the reasons.' I spoke mildly but, I hoped, with firmness.

'You had been at the lady's side moments before I joined her. If you propose to suggest that I had some part in her murder, the same accusation could be made of you.'

'I had no intention of being so provocative. I am well aware that Lady Anne selected the place where she asked to speak to me, the place where you joined us and she was killed. Neither you nor I could be held responsible for where she chose to stand.'

'So you say.'

I was conscious of John's impatience with Bolingbroke's hostility but I did not wish him to intervene. 'I have no theories of motive or guilt. I wish to interview you as the closest witness to her death. Nothing more.'

'So you can taunt me for the feebleness of my response? It must please you greatly to know I fainted like any green girl at the sight of a speck of blood.'

'You do us both an injustice. Doctor Swanwych attended you at the time and found it entirely natural that the shock caused you to collapse. In fact I want to ask you whether you believe the arrow reached its intended target – or whether it was meant for you?'

I was gratified to see the tic which distorted his mouth briefly as he swivelled away from us and strode across the room but when he turned back he had mastered his expression and his voice. 'I am no expert on the skill of archery. No doubt, if it were known where the bowman stood, it could be ascertained how quickly he must have loosed his dart before it reached its fatal mark. You or I or Lady Anne might have been the intended victim.'

'And can you offer any suggestion why you or I or Lady Anne might have been targeted?'

'That is the evidence you need to collect, my boy. My speculations on the matter are of no consequence for they would be uninformed – except by prejudice, as I conceive yours would be also.'

I bit my lip to stop me rising to his sarcasm. 'I am prepared to listen to anyone's speculations at this stage. I retain the discretion to come to my own conclusion but must consider the full range of possibilities.'

Bolingbroke rolled his eyes. 'You cut a heroic figure, Harry Somers. I admire your aspirations.' He planted himself, feet apart, in front of the window so the winter sun glowed behind his head and made it difficult for us to look at him directly. 'But I am not prepared to indulge in childish guessing games. By all means listen to the spiteful imaginings of others and take your pick from their malicious fancies. I have no more to say.'

'But I have one more question. You may say it is irrelevant but I should be glad to know what it was you had wished to say to Lady Anne after I left you.'

He smirked and I had the sudden impression that this was a reply he had rehearsed. 'It is irrelevant and impertinent but I am content to share my message with you. Sadly, it was never delivered to the dear lady it concerned. I was aware that her father, the chamberlain, was considering marrying her to a young fellow in Hertfordshire. It happens that this knight is known to me and he had charged me to convey to her his dutiful service and hopes that their contract would be soon concluded. Does that satisfy your prurient curiosity?'

'I am obliged for your frankness,' I began but he flung open the door.

'I shall be obliged if you will now leave me. Good-day to you, Doctor Swanwych: I am sorry you have wasted your valuable time. I suggest you advise this foolish boy to resign the ambitious commission he has been given before he fails in it ignominiously.'

As soon as we were across the courtyard and out of earshot, John gripped my shoulder. 'For heaven's sake, Harry, whatever lies between you and that snake? He is a dangerous enemy to have made.'

'I know it, believe me. But I'm not displeased with our visit. I have seen Roger Bolingbroke flustered and dissembling. That's interesting. I owe you a flagon of wine for your company.'

'I'll hold you to that but you'd best get back to the horde of nubile beauties awaiting your attention. I've heard you are popular with the Duchess's ladies and they have been drawing lots to determine the order in which they present their evidence to you. Some may wish to present more than evidence, eh?'

182

I laughed off John's jest but when I resumed my interviews with the young women I kept Dame Margery closely at my side in case there was any truth in his innuendo. For the most part what they had to say was repetitious and unenlightening until, inevitably, the final attendant to be seen glided into the antechamber amid a tumble of exquisite jewels and a miasma of alluring perfume. 'My name is Maud Warrenne,' she simpered.

'Thank you, my lady.' I was content to take part in her charade but resolved to keep the initiative. 'Did you witness the tragic event yourself?'

'No. I was in the stand with her Grace. I saw nothing.'

'How well did you know Lady Anne Wenham?'

She gurgled with girlish insouciance. 'None of us knew her well, Doctor Somers. She did not choose to seek our company. We were too frivolous for such a stern, unbending lady. We could not meet her high standards, alas. We have known temptations of which she had no concept.' She lowered her head and fluttered her eyelashes. 'Young women are troubled by temptations of the flesh, Doctor Somers, such as should not be mentioned politely but, between ourselves, we sometimes whispered of carnal matters. Lady Anne was appalled.'

Dame Margery coughed loudly and Maud put her hand to her mouth in a parody of coy embarrassment. 'Forgive me. I am trying to be truthful.'

I wriggled awkwardly as my manhood became hard and I longed to send her away but I needed to go through my usual recital of questions. 'Can you think of any reason why Lady Anne should have an enemy who would seek to kill her?'

'Oh dear!' She mimicked distress. 'It is a horrible thought but if she had upbraided a young person for the loss of her maidenhood, or for his forceful ravishment of a

183

serving maid, her manner could be so severe, it might have impelled a villain to wickedness.'

'You know of nothing more specific?'

The expression in her beautiful eyes became serious. 'Personally I doubt that the arrow was meant for Lady Anne.' She paused but I did not prompt her. No other attendant had made such a suggestion. 'Do you not think Roger Bolingbroke a much more likely target?'

This was dangerous ground to explore in front of Dame Margery, as Maud well knew, but I could not tell if she was still simply teasing me. 'Is that pure conjecture on your part?'

'Conjecture, yes,' she purred, 'but perhaps not pure.' She folded her hands demurely in her lap.

I could tolerate this no longer and, pulling my gown loosely in front of me, I rose. 'If you have reason to make any precise accusations, I encourage you to do so, but otherwise I need not detain you, Lady Maud.'

As she stood she bunched together the front of her skirt at her waist, pulling down her bodice to show the swell of her breasts, and she sidled towards me. 'I have offered a position to Lady Anne's pretty attendant, Mistress Barber. I hope you consider that appropriate. When I am in my new Norfolk home, far from the fascinations of Greenwich, I shall welcome a charming companion with whom to share memories of our earlier life. I am sure you will figure in our reminiscences, Doctor Somers.'

I knew I had turned crimson and as Maud sashayed from the room I gathered my papers quickly. Dame Margery made no comment but she regarded me with tight-lipped indignation and it was clear she had understood perfectly what lay behind the mortifying badinage she had heard.

Chapter 18

I was pleased to be alone in Doctor Southwell's quarters that evening for my misery at losing any chance to court Bess was profound. The only way I could divert my thoughts from this wretchedness was to concentrate on reviewing what I had learned from my enquiries and to seek clues which might help explain a multitude of inconsistencies. I had discovered little enough to help me but I suspected there could be layer upon layer of mystery to be solved. I could not even be certain of the intended victim but the coincidence of the possible attempt to poison Lady Anne a few weeks earlier strengthened the likelihood that the arrow had found its mark.

Duke Humphrey himself had asked for discretion, as if he or the Duchess might be touched personally by my findings, but I still found it difficult to accept the only plausible explanation for his concern. On the other hand I found it all too easy to believe Roger Bolingbroke had some malign role in Lady Anne's death and I was convinced he had lied to me but I had no justification for my belief, other than prejudice against a man I loathed. Without better proof, I must not discount the chance that the arrow was intended for him. I felt a nagging disappointment that Geoffrey had been unwilling to help me and might have cause to fear Bolingbroke but I tried not to let myself be distracted from dispassionate assessment of the facts. Facts? There were few enough of those.

The victim's last brief letter to her step-son suggested the weight of her sadness, using the same word 'woe' which she had whispered to me as she lay dying; but it seemed incomplete. I could only presume it referred back to the subject of previous correspondence and Sir Bertram, as her confidant, would understand what she meant. There were also the lady's other words, spoken to me and known to no one else. They too were puzzling. She had wished me to give someone a message, and it now seemed probable that the recipient was intended to be Sir Bertram, but the rambling words of her death throes made no sense. Had she really said 'treachery' or did I imagine it? Could her anxiety have been about 'lechery' and those guilty of it? How could any of this be connected to her murder?

I slept only in snatches but I rose early and, with a small bundle of possessions, made my way to the jetty in time for the first boat, on the turn of the tide, to the City. This customarily carried the Duke's correspondence from the previous evening and there were rarely any passengers other than his herald, so I was surprised to see a pair of men-at-arms further along the quay and two hooded women waiting by the steps – even more so when I made out the women's identity.

'Don't be alarmed, Harry,' Dame Margery said softly as she advanced towards me. 'We are not travelling with you. I merely wished to be certain of catching you. I was sure you would set off for Dunmow today.'

Clearly she had not construed my injunction to keep my proposed visit secret as applying to her maid-servant and Grizel grinned at me mischievously. 'I wished to leave unobserved,' I said glancing towards the soldiers.

'They know nothing of your plans, I assure you, but they are at your disposal. You should be accompanied on your expedition. There may be danger – on the road or at your destination.'

I smiled, touched by her concern. 'You are thoughtful. I promise you I will not travel alone but I don't want military men at my side.'

Dame Margery narrowed her eyes. 'I understand; but who will go with you?'

I spoke in a whisper. 'I thought of asking Thomas Chope.'

The chamberlain's wife inclined her head. 'That is sensible,' she said, while Grizel gave a squeal of excitement.

'A master-stroke! He'd do anything for you,' the girl giggled.

I jumped down into the boat. 'Thank you for your kindness but send those men back to their duties.' When we cast off I was relieved to see the women move away to speak to the soldiers and soon there was clear water between us as the rowers pulled on the oars to take us upstream.

*****

Thomas was eager to join me and I used my position as the Duke's representative to secure him leave of absence from his work at Baynard's Castle. He hired us horses and helped me check our route to avoid the more notorious Essex forests which were known to harbour bandits. Later, as we rode north-east from the City, I outlined to him the task I had been given, even speaking of Roger Bolingbroke's baleful influence at Greenwich, and I suggested, as neither of us was an accomplished horseman, that we divide the distance over two days. We made reasonable progress on the first day, where the track was fairly well maintained, and we spent the night at a commendably clean inn at Ongar. This, I hoped, would enable us to arrive in Dunmow next day while there was still daylight but I had not allowed for the worsening conditions underfoot. We encountered no brigands but the frozen ground of the previous week had thawed into a quagmire and the heavy going made us much slower than I planned. The short-lived winter sun was already sinking when we entered the Wenham demesne and halted in a stand of trees with a distant view of the manor-house.

Thomas urged that I delay my visit until the following morning but we had laid our plans and I was impatient with the delay we had already suffered. 'No, I'm not wasting more time. You go into the village and find us beds at the inn, then come back to this spot and wait for me here. If the church bell rings for Vespers before I return, call at the house with a message for me, just as we agreed.' I sensed he was not happy with the plan but he accepted it.

I was admitted to Sir Bertram's home without difficulty and received by him and Lady Mary in their principal chamber. This was a well-appointed room with a fire burning in the hearth beneath an impressive overmantel carved with a row of coats of arms. I was surprised to glimpse what looked like the lions of England quartered on several of them but they were crossed by a bar which probably denoted a bastard line. I was no expert in such matters and I could not look more closely because Sir Bertram showed me to a cushioned seat at an angle to the fireplace, so that I could face my hosts. He was a bluff and courteous young man, who immediately offered me refreshment, but his wife seemed nervous. I noted that she was with child.

'The Duke's chamberlain informed me of my step-mother's death and named you as the official charged to investigate the circumstances. I did not expect a personal visit and I am obliged to you for coming. Are you able to give us more details?'

'I have established very little as yet. I've found no reason why anyone should seek to kill Lady Anne and it is possible the arrow was meant for another who stood nearby.' Sir Bertram tilted his head as if about to speak but I decided to forestall him. 'The Duchess's clerk, one Roger Bolingbroke, had just asked to speak to her.'

I heard Lady Mary's intake of breath but her husband did not react to my statement. 'You wish to ask me questions?'

'It might help me to understand more about Lady Anne. I believe she was happy at Dunmow.'

'She brought great joy to my father's latter years and I shall always be grateful to her for that. She was like a sister

188

to my wife and me. We were sorry she felt bound to accept the Duchess of Gloucester's invitation to serve her.'

This accorded completely with what Bess had told me and I proceeded to explain about Lady Anne's last message to her stepson and how I had intercepted it. I held out the missive to Sir Bertram and he read it out loud: '*WOE is come to Greenwich.*'

Lady Mary fluttered her hands. 'Woe? Oh, I see. Poor Anne.' I fancied her husband caught her eye and she twisted the signet ring on her right hand as she composed herself. 'I wish she could have stayed with us. Our way of life was to her liking.'

'Indeed,' Sir Bertram said, 'she was comfortable with my father's simple loyalty to the King. But of course her own father, the Duke's chamberlain, had always served Gloucester.'

'Surely that was no problem to your father? He was content to take her in marriage?'

'He had known the chamberlain for many years and he had no personal quarrel with the Duke, although he disapproved of what he heard concerning Gloucester's lechery.' I noted Sir Bertram's use of that word and nearly lost the import of what he said next. 'My father never recognised Eleanor Cobham as Duke Humphrey's lawful wife. He had met her in his youth and believed her unworthy of a ducal bed.'

'Yet Lady Anne went to serve the Duchess after her widowhood?'

Sir Bertram shrugged. 'Her father is the chamberlain and she had a most honourable sense of duty.'

This seemed strange but I sensed he would say no more on the subject. 'Lady Anne corresponded with you regularly after she went to Greenwich?'

'I believe she welcomed contact with her former life, especially as my wife and I await the birth of our first child. She would have stood sponsor to the infant.'

'Were her letters always as sorrowful as this last one?'

He drummed his fingers on the arm of his chair as if he disliked my impertinence but he answered my question calmly. 'She was free to share her discomfort with us.'

'Did you give her advice in your replies?'

He crossed his legs. 'You have not seen them?'

'Her maid told me she always destroyed them.'

'It was what we agreed. In seeking to entertain her and lift her spirits, I was sometimes incautious in what I wrote – making fun of distinguished men and woman, you understand.'

The idea of Sir Bertram writing light-hearted slanders to amuse his solemn step-mother did not ring true but I did not query it. He was firmly in control of his narrative and I knew nothing with which to disturb his confidence. I therefore drew our conversation to an end and thanked him for his help. I promised to let him know my conclusions as soon as possible and he responded with equal blandness. He showed me to the door and pointed me my way towards the village, warning me of treacherous, uneven ground to be crossed at the edge of the wood, particularly as there was no moon.

*****

I quickly realised that Thomas was not waiting where I had left him but I had not been long at the manor-house and I imagined him quenching his thirst at the hostelry before re-joining me. At first I could make out hoof-prints going in the right direction but on the rough ground Sir Bertram had mentioned the mud was churned and tracks led off along several paths. This was not a difficulty, however, for by now I could glimpse the lights of the village and I urged my tired nag towards our resting place. The inn commanded a central position in the high street and its entrance led to a large courtyard, from which a number of staircases climbed up to sleeping accommodation. An ostler came at once to take my horse and called the landlord who confirmed that Thomas had taken the inn's best room for us. He showed me to steps in the corner of the yard where, despite the chill air, an unsavoury looking fellow lounged by the doorway. I took him to be a local simpleton who peered at me as we went inside but he did not impede our access and the landlord ignored him.

The room was unoccupied although Thomas had left his bundle of belongings on the bed and I laughed. 'I suppose he's drinking downstairs. I'd best go to join him.'

'No, your man went out, half an hour ago or more. He never stayed here above a few minutes when he took the room. He said he'd to meet you.'

'We must have missed each other,' I said with more confidence than I felt. 'He'll soon discover the mistake so I'll wait here. If you've got some cheese and bread and a flagon of ale they'd be welcome.'

The man nodded cordially and left the room by an inner door, through which shortly afterwards a boy brought meat and drink. I settled on the window seat and took a hunk of bread to assuage my hunger while looking down into the yard, hoping to see Thomas arrive. The scruffy ruffian still stood sentry by the outside staircase.

As time went on I became worried that Thomas had suffered some mishap but I was wary of leaving the inn to look for him in the dark and I was uncomfortable with the way the wretch downstairs often cast up his eyes as if to check I had not moved. I was relieved when at last there came a faint scratching on the inner door and watched expectantly as it opened.

'Don't stand up, Doctor Somers, and don't give any sign you're not alone. You're being watched and he's not to know I'm here.'

I stared at the newcomer as he lifted his cape to show the crest on his jerkin and I recognised Gloucester's swan. I turned my head away from the window. 'You're from Greenwich? You were with Dame Margery at the jetty yesterday.'

'She insisted we follow you and your friend from the City. Just as well we did too.'

'Where is Thomas?'

'He's along at the mill on the edge of the village. He's had a nasty blow on the head but he'll do. My mate is with him. We managed to drive away his attackers before they finished him off. Reckon they'd have been waiting for you under the trees if we hadn't.'

All at once I remembered how Bess's father had been killed in those woods by poachers after the Wenham deer and I was annoyed with myself for forgetting this hazard. Then I realised it was not an adequate explanation of what the soldier had said. 'The man in the yard is up to no good?'

'My guess is that after you've put out the candle and turned in for the night he'll be up those stairs with his dagger poised to slice your gizzard. If you get my meaning.'

'Most graphically. What do you suggest I do?'

'Stay where you are while I wait on the back stairs leading down to the kitchen. Then make it look as if you're going to your bed. Pull the bolster down to look as if you're in it and blow out the light, then bunk through this door to join me. That rogue'll wait a bit to make sure you're asleep and by then we'll be on the road back to London.'

'With Thomas?'

'Yes. My mate'll take him on his horse, seeing he's not fit to ride alone. You'll need to leave your horses here.'

'Why don't you just deal with the vagabond downstairs before he comes after me?'

The soldier drew back his lips in a ferocious grin. 'Because there's a dozen of his cronies at the entrance who'll back him up – just in case you're not quite asleep or turn out handier with a knife than might be expected. In battle, master physician, retreat is sometimes the wisest course of action. Do what I tell you and we'll be away from Dunmow before they have a clue you've gone and you might offer up a little prayer to thank the Lord for Dame Margery's forethought.'

'Amen,' I said to that with great sincerity.

Chapter 19

At Dame Margery's instruction, conveyed to us when we reached the Duke's house in the City, I brought Thomas Chope back to Greenwich to complete his recovery, pleased to have him at hand because of my confidence in his disinterested loyalty. I found the palace in a ferment of excitement for the wedding of Lady Maud Warrenne and Lord Walter Fitzvaughan, which was to be celebrated next day in some style. My preoccupations had caused me to forget it entirely, and I was not disposed to join in the robust jollity which accompanied such occasions, but I received a personal message from his lordship reminding me that he had invited me to call on him and I felt bound to comply.

He received me in his chamber in company with a handsome tousle-haired young man of about my age, whom he introduced as Gaston de la Tour from Rouen, and he settled me on a chair by a reading-stand on which he set a large manuscript. 'This is what I wished to show you. I've already displayed it to your fellow physicians while you were away from the palace. Is it not fine?'

I turned the pages with care, scarcely daring to touch the exquisite vellum, lost in admiration of the beautiful illustrations. I read the inscription at the beginning of the Latin text and exclaimed aloud with surprise. 'It is translated from the Greek!'

'Yes, as you know, the language has been learned afresh in Italy in recent years. This is a tome of ancient medical lore and astronomical charts. I thought it would interest you. I propose to give it to the Duke when I leave Greenwich after tomorrow's ceremonies. I think he will approve it.'

'He treasures such works and will be delighted. It is a generous gift.'

'I have stolen a march on Gilbert Kymer in obtaining it for I know he covets having it for the University at Oxford.'

'The Duke will doubtless donate it to his library there.'

Lord Fitzvaughan gave me time to study the manuscript before pouring wine and inviting me to drink a toast to his marriage. 'It is the King's command, you understand,' he said, shrugging his shoulders. 'I have passed my thirtieth year and have no taste for matrimony, having all the companionship I want, but if I am to continue to have a role at court, serving King Henry, he requires me to have a well-born wife.' Gaston opened his mouth and was about to speak but his lordship held up his hand to silence him. 'I value the position I have won and believe there is great need for one to hold the neutral ground between our worthy Duke of Gloucester and the magnificent Cardinal Beaufort: which I have shown I can do. Their quarrels are likely to intensify over the proposed settlement with France, with the Cardinal pressing the King to make a French marriage and ratify a peace treaty. It would be natural for the Duke to resist that idea. He will be in no hurry to see a royal child while he remains his nephew's heir. I wonder how many of Humphrey's followers consider the implications of that relationship. Some do, you may be sure.'

I was uncomfortable to hear such delicate matters talked of casually and I tried to deflect the conversation into safer channels. 'Do you intend to remain at court then? I had understood you would be going to your lands in Norfolk.'

He guffawed. 'Lady Maud told you that, no doubt. It was what she believed until I told her otherwise. Now she delights in thoughts of a place at court, although I fear she will be disappointed when she sees the pious solemnity of King Henry's daily life. It will not offer the sensual entertainments she would like but it will doubtless please her better than rural solitude. You must visit us at Westminster. She thinks highly of your talents.'

I did not know how to interpret his cryptic words. Was it common courtesy or a jest or was he offering me the services of a wife he did not want? Behind my confusion and alarm lay the insistent throb of useless hope, for Bess would also be at Westminster, where I would be free to visit, not a hundred miles away and forever inaccessible. It was as well that I could not allow myself to daydream for Lord Fitzvaughan's next words required all my attention.

'Did you find what you were looking for at Dunmow?'

'I did not have any particular expectations. It was a visit I was bound to make.'

'In my opinion Lady Anne Wenham was not the intended victim, poor woman. Would you not think that rat, Bolingbroke, a more probable target?'

'I keep an open mind,' I said, 'until I find compelling evidence.'

'Very diplomatic, Doctor Somers. You are deserving of a place on some future embassy to France. In the meantime may I give you some advice? I think you have learned to be wary of the Duchess's clerk. Make sure that you correctly identify those who have cast in their lot with him and treat them with equal circumspection.'

'Are you willing to be more specific, my lord?'

He swilled his wine in his goblet before swallowing a large draught. 'Not with certainty and I am not sure we are well enough acquainted for me to abandon my professional caution by indulging in idle conjecture.' He smiled and set down his glass, beckoning Gaston to his side. Our interview was at an end.

I gave a weak smile as I rose and excused myself. I was grateful for the sight of his wonderful manuscript but I did not enjoy a conversation which might be either harmless banter or loaded innuendo. I was further discomforted as I walked back along the corridor outside their chamber to hear Lord Fitzvaughan and Gaston de la Tour laughing heartily.

*****

196

The marriage was solemnised, the newly-weds bedded (to what effect one could only speculate), the splendid gift was bestowed on the Duke and next morning the Fitzvaughan entourage left Greenwich. I had no chance to speak to Bess before their departure, and tried to persuade myself this was just as well, but I did feel a lightening of the atmosphere knowing that Lady Maud was no longer at hand to torment me, so I was happy to join my friends in a convivial celebration that evening.

John Swanwych was to set off on his travels again, on the Duke's behalf, as soon as the weather was settled fair. He would carry with him further orders for translations from several academic worthies and part-payment to encourage the recalcitrant Pier Candido Decembrio to complete his work on Plato's *Republic*. It was therefore appropriate for Giovanni dei Signorelli, Geoffrey du Bois, John Home and I to drink his health and send him on his way with good wishes for a safe but stimulating journey. To my relief Doctor Southwell was missing from this group of my associates but he was seldom at Greenwich at that time. Giovanni was in characteristically ebullient mood, speaking soulfully of the delights Doctor Swanwych would encounter in Italy, without ever showing the slightest inclination to return there himself. Despite his contentment with exile, he had long ago whetted my appetite for his native land, which I was most unlikely ever to see, but when he turned his inebriated attention to me it was to introduce a different and unwelcome subject.

'Are you not pining, mio amico, for the loss of the lovely Lady Maud from our midst? I heard many gossips about her liking for her physician with the devil's mark.'

John Swanwych looked at me sharply and I felt myself flush. 'The Duchess's ladies have been known to tease me,' I said lamely.

'I have wondered if the teasing blossomed into action.' Giovanni made crude movements with his groin. 'She is generous with her favours, I believe.'

'I trust that is a joke, albeit in the poorest taste,' John Swanwych said. 'It would be gross impropriety if their physician lay with one of the Duchess's ladies.'

My stomach heaved but Giovanni was quick to make amends for his indiscretion, in his inimitable and ambiguous way. 'Of course: a joke. I meant no harm. Harry knows I am always merry. How should I be aware with what men the ladies fornicate – or even whether Doctor Somers has yet tupped a ewe?'

Doctor Swanwych looked annoyed and John Home intervened to change the subject. 'I hear the King has declined the Cardinal's recommendation for an immediate treaty with France. The Duke's resistance to Beaufort's pressure has carried the day, for the moment any way.'

'Humphrey wrong-footed his old rival despite the rumours of a Beaufort spy here in the palace.' Giovanni was always surprisingly well informed and he raised an eyebrow towards Geoffrey du Bois.

It was the apothecary's turn to look uncomfortable and I realised Giovanni must know of his old allegiance to the Beauforts. I concluded that the Italian in his cups was determined to embarrass his companions for his own amusement and I felt sympathy for Geoffrey but I too had drunk well and was prepared to be incautious. 'Why don't you turn your biting wit on Roger Bolingbroke, Giovanni?' I asked. 'We could all relish the jest then.'

To my surprise it was Geoffrey who responded to my challenge. 'I could tell you a strange thing about her Grace's clerk. He's been making some unusual purchases lately. More the sort of ingredients you physicians ask me to mix as potions for your patients.'

The memory came to me of Thomas Chope saying that Bolingbroke was reputed to be a necromancer who

198

spoke to the dead. 'He's said to practice the dark arts and he certainly studies the mysteries of astrology. He has amazing charts of the heavens in his sanctum.'

'You've been in there?' John Home had become agitated at my words, renewing my suspicion that Bolingbroke had some power over him.

'No, only glimpsed beyond the curtain – when I went to his outer room to interview him.' I remembered in time to give a plausible reason for being in the clerk's chamber, while hoping that John Swanwych had also seen beyond the drape.

The doctor said nothing but shortly afterwards he brought our conviviality to an end by leaving for his bed. Giovanni now began to recount tediously bawdy stories, some of which might have been true, and when John Home rose shakily to say he also needed to retire I offered to escort him across the courtyard. Giovanni seemed unabashed by his disappearing audience and Geoffrey was content to sink his head upon his chest and let the torrent of words flow over him.

*****

Next morning my head was heavy and I struggled to concentrate on my enquiries but the prospect was depressing as I had made so little headway. I prescribed some invigorating fresh air for my condition and persuaded Thomas Chope to join me for a walk by the riverside. Although his pate was still bandaged, he seemed in good spirits. 'Dame Margery says I can stay at Greenwich if I wish. She's spoken to the chamberlain and he's happy – there's plenty of work for another carpenter here and no one's bothered now about what happened two years ago.'

I started to say how pleased I was when Grizel came bounding along the path from the servants' quarters. 'The Duchess's page is looking for you, Master Harry, or Doctor

199

Somers, I suppose I should say.' She paused, looking up at Thomas. 'Ee! Well I never! I heard you were back but you've changed, Thomas Chope, grown quite solemn, I'd say.'

'Older and wiser. But if you are who I think, you've changed a great deal more. I remember a cheeky little lass, now I see a passable young wench.'

'Passable! You insolent bastard!' They were laughing at each other and I joined in but Grizel pointed me up the slope, to where the Duchess's page had just rounded the corner, so I left them to their repartee and, in a state of considerable apprehension, followed the lad to his mistress's chambers.

Duchess Eleanor was attended only by the plainly dressed older woman, whom I remembered vaguely from the previous occasion when I had been summoned to see her. She looked troubled, with dark shadows beneath her eyes suggesting lack of sleep, and her hands moved restlessly on the arms of her chair as she bade me take a stool. 'Have you come to any conclusions, Doctor Somers?' she asked as soon as I was seated.

'Not yet, your Grace.'

'I'm relieved to hear it for I feared you might have been led astray by gossip which has been brought to my ears. Some malicious slanderers are suggesting that the arrow was not intended for Lady Anne but for Master Bolingbroke, my trusty clerk. That may be wishful thinking on the part of malcontents he has had occasion to rebuke but it is nonsense. I hope you will dismiss such calumny and not let it deter you from your objective.'

'Your Grace, I am bound to consider any evidence put before me.'

'And is there evidence to suggest Roger Bolingbroke was the target?' Her voice was shrill.

'There is little evidence one way or the other but I believe the archer was a skilled marksman and so on balance

I surmise Lady Anne was his intended victim – until it can be proved otherwise.'

The Duchess sank back onto the cushions on her chair and beckoned her attendant. 'Mistress Jourdemayne assures me your surmise is correct.'

A tremor passed through me as I realised this was the woman Bolingbroke had sent me to summon from the City. Ludicrously, I felt responsible for her presence and at the same time afraid of her. 'You have information, which could help me, Mistress?'

She took her place beside the Duchess, tossing her neatly coifed head. 'I have consulted the stars, physician, and they tell me there was no evil practised against Master Bolingbroke.' Her tone was dismissive, almost pitying, and her hooded eyes bored into mine in a most disconcerting way.

'I am obliged to you, Mistress. Have you consulted the stars about Lady Anne?'

'I do not have exact information as to the time and place of her birth.' Her thin mouth stretched into an unpleasant smile. 'But the lady was deeply unpopular.'

I bit back the obvious riposte that Bolingbroke must have many enemies, because I was unnerved by the familiarity between the Duchess and this alarming practitioner of secret arts. Mistress Jourdemayne's knowledge of these mysteries would account for her link with the clerk but I was puzzled by the hold they both seemed to have over Duchess Eleanor. 'I shall note your words well,' I said. 'Have you advice as to where I should look for the murderer?'

That disturbing smile played on her lips once more. 'Perhaps Lady Anne had disappointed those close to her.'

I tried not to show surprise. 'Would you explain?'

'You have been to Dunmow. Do you not think it probable that Lady Anne Wenham and her lusty stepson have made sport together? Her importunity may have become an embarrassment to him, or his sweet lady wife may have decided to remove a rival. We may conclude that one or the other decided to dispose of Lady Anne.'

I knew I needed to be very careful, even though her suggestion did not match my own conclusions about relationships in the Wenham family. For, if I was wrong, it might explain the attack on Thomas and the plan to kill me, which I had been reluctant to attribute to Sir Bertram or his wife. 'It is possible,' I said. 'There are many matters I need to investigate more fully.'

'Do that, physician, and bring them speedily to justice.'

The Duchess grasped her attendant's hand. 'Mistress Jourdemayne is a wise counsellor. Do as she advises.'

'I have no proof as yet, your Grace.'

'You will obtain it, Doctor Somers, I have no doubt.' Her certainty brooked no denial.

*****

During the next night, while I slept soundly, a paper was slipped under the door of my chamber and I picked it up while still drowsy, staring with horror at the careful script as I read and re-read the vile words. It was addressed to the Lady Anne Wenham.

Your lewd entreaties must cease. We can have no more to do with each other. Mary knows you have sucked my cock and guesses my seed swells in your belly as well as hers. I have begged her forgiveness and there is no division between us. If you persist in pestering me, you must reap the consequences.'

At the end of the missive was the letter '*B*'.

I staggered to sit on my pallet, thrusting the hateful letter aside. I knew it was a forgery but didn't doubt it matched Sir Bertram's writing well enough. I did not believe for a moment Lady Anne had been pregnant; so long had elapsed since she left Dunmow that she could not have concealed a swollen belly by the time of her death. But I knew none of that would matter in the face of this overtly incriminating admission. The Wenhams were scapegoats and I was enmeshed in a plot to destroy them. Mistress Jourdemayne and Bolingbroke, with at least the Duchess's tacit blessing, had determined what my findings should be and, if I defied them by trying to expose the fraud, without question I would be derided, threatened, and probably eliminated.

When my mother appeared at my door, not half an hour later, white-faced with terror after a man had seized her by the throat as she came down the stairs from the servants' quarters, I understood how completely I was trapped.

Chapter 20

My mother was a woman of great simplicity but she was nobody's fool and she was staunch in defending what she believed was right. After she had nestled in my arms and cried for a few moments she wiped her eyes and held me at arms' length. 'Are you in trouble, Harry?' she asked with that shrewdness I recognised from boyhood.

I knew I must be as honest as I could with her and I nodded. 'Influential men are trying to make me say what I am certain is wrong. They hope I will give way to their threats.'

'Against me?' Again I nodded. 'Then you must resist them. You must do what is proper and let them do their worst.' She stood back from me, her frail body upright and defiant. 'I am an old woman and of no account.'

'You are of every account to me and I will do nothing until I have made sure you are safe but I need you to help me.'

She looked at me doubtfully. 'What can I do?'

The words tumbled out as the thoughts formed in my mind. 'I need you to leave Greenwich for a while. I'd like you to go to Danson. Sir Hugh de Grey will ensure you are safe and I will be free to do what's right, as you'd wish me to. I'll arrange everything with the chamberlain and Dame Margery. Thomas Chope will take you secretly. Will you do this?'

I knew the prospect of leaving the household at Greenwich would alarm her but she showed no fear. 'I'll do whatever helps you. But you will be in danger, won't you?'

'Perhaps, but I promise to be careful.'

She gave me a hug and then blessed me, which made our parting seem ominous with hidden meaning. She asked for further instructions and when I watched her return across the courtyard with downcast eyes, visibly trembling, as I had suggested, for the benefit of those who would be watching, I needed to wipe a tear from my cheek.

I guessed my movements would be scrutinised but it would be judged entirely normal for me to visit the chamberlain's quarters where I was accustomed to attend members of his staff. I was fortunate that both he and Dame Margery were at hand so, without going into details, I was able to outline what I wished to arrange and he penned a letter to his son-in-law at Danson. Shortly afterwards Thomas Chope, who had been summoned to the servants' entrance of the tower, was admitted by the back stairs to join us. I explained his mission and he accepted it enthusiastically, furious that my mother's well-being was threatened.

'When you return from Danson,' I added, 'I'd be glad if you'd pay a visit to the City. I have small hope that we can find any trace of the bowman but it's probable he landed there and someone might remember something useful.'

Thomas slapped his thigh. 'If there's anything to be discovered, I'll find it. While I was at Baynard's Castle I met a number of the watermen, drinking at the inns they frequent. I'll use my contacts. Give me a couple of days.'

The chamberlain issued instructions for a covered cart to be placed at Thomas's disposal and they both went about their business, leaving me with Dame Margery as she gathered together cushions to make my mother's journey more comfortable. 'What will you do next, Harry?' she asked.

I paused, uncertain of my answer, watching her stiff fingers grappling with tassels and loose threads which caught on her rings. She set down the cushions and turned the rings, so that their prominent stones were facing inwards, before tucking the bundle under her arm. As she did so a recollection came to me of other hands twisting a different ring in the same way. I had thought nothing of it at the time but perhaps there had been a reason for that gesture, when Sir Bertram caught his wife's eye: a reason for Lady Mary to hide the crest on her signet. I remembered the carved shields above the fireplace, with their indications of royal blood somewhere in the Wenham family, and the way my chair had been positioned so I that I could not examine them closely. An astonishing idea came into my mind.

'I am going to Westminster,' I said.

*****

Never before, since I left it as a child, had I sought admittance to the Palace of Westminster but I was prepared for long delays as I was passed from official to official, anteroom to anteroom. Fortunately my credentials as a physician from Duke Humphrey's household were sufficiently respectable and the name of Lord Walter Fitzvaughan so distinguished that, although my request to see him was met with scepticism, it was not dismissed out of hand. Attendants came and went, assuring me that my message had been conveyed to him, and eventually I was told he would see me after he had attended Vespers with the King. I was made to stand in an alcove along the corridor to wait for his emergence from the chapel, and I watched in some puzzlement as servants hurried about carrying chests of tableware, wall-drapes and rolled turkey carpets. These minions made themselves scarce when the door to the chantry was opened and I saw my sovereign lord for the first time, as King Henry led his courtiers from their prayers with a cloud of incense wafting around them. I was struck by the young monarch's humble demeanour and pious expression and I bowed as low and as gracefully as my disability allowed. To my relief he paid no attention to me.

The King swept past and turned to the right, where the corridor divided, leaving all but his personal attendants to disperse and go about their own affairs. After he had exchanged a few words with his colleagues Lord Walter broke free and crossed towards me. 'Are you come so soon to entreat me to let you see my wife?'

I spluttered some sort of denial and he roared with laughter. 'Come, you shall see her all the same but I suspect you have some other motive for your expedition to Westminster. We will go to our chambers. The place is in some turmoil as the court moves tomorrow to Windsor.'

On the threshold of the Fitzvaughan rooms we met Gaston de la Tour, swathed in a loose gown and glistening with sweat after a bout at wrestling. He looked askance at me but Lord Walter steered him through the door with a hand on his shoulder, promising to join him after he had bathed and my business had been completed. Then the baron sent an attendant to invite Lady Maud to grace us with her presence and, while we awaited her, I explained the purpose of my visit and admired the remarkable set of tapestries covering every wall.

'They tell the story of the great King Alexander. I ordered the weavers to copy the illuminations in the wonderful history, *Le Roman d'Alexandre*. I can assure you King Henry has nothing so fine to decorate his own apartments.' He held out an exquisite goblet of Venetian glass filled with deep ruby wine.

Before I could reply Lady Maud entered the room alone. She was as opulently dressed as the figures in the tapestries, with threads of gold shining through the transparent fabric of her overskirt, and a huge pearl hanging from her headdress in the centre of her forehead. She was pale but her eyes were gleaming. 'Doctor Somers,' she purred. 'This is an unexpected pleasure. Is Greenwich already so dull a place without me?'

'Incomparably dull,' I said, schooling myself to play this mannered game, 'but I confess a serious aspect of my investigation also requires me to put further questions to you and your attendant, Mistress Barber.'

Maud pouted prettily and rang a handbell. 'But I hope you will then stay and entertain us with the latest gossip from the Palace of Pleasance. You must excuse our disarray. Even these draperies you were admiring must be removed for transport to Windsor.'

'I am grateful and honoured to be received at such a time.' I went on quickly with my business. 'My lady, I should like to ask you what you know of Mistress Jourdemayne.'

It was disconcerting to hear Lord Walter's chortle while Maud pursed her lips. 'She is reputed a wise woman, whose aid her Grace has invoked. Roger Bolingbroke had her brought to Greenwich. I had little to do with her but found her ingratiating. I suspected her affability concealed a wish to pry into matters which did not concern her.'

Lord Fitzvaughan was still chuckling as handed his wife a goblet of wine. 'Mistress Jourdemayne is an evil, malicious termagant. She dabbles in the work of the devil and preys on the innocent trust of simple folk who believe she can perform magic cures for the sick and curse their enemies to perdition.'

'Walter! How do you know this? You never warned me while we were at Greenwich.'

'I had every faith in your ability to identify an unctuous harridan, sweet wife, as you clearly did, being neither simple nor perhaps entirely innocent.' He raised his goblet to honour Maud and gave an enigmatic smile. 'Mistress Jourdemayne began her fiendish practices in her native village, in the north of Suffolk, not twenty miles from my lands. I heard much of her mischief while I was a lad. "The Witch of Eye" they called her.'

I was aware that Bess had entered the room and felt distress when she flinched on seeing me but for the moment I ignored her. 'Lady Maud, do you know why Duchess Eleanor has sought her services?'

Lady Fitzvaughan sipped her wine before answering, her composure unruffled. 'Yes, poor woman, I know what troubles her peace of mind night and day. She will clutch at any possibility that may give her a child. The Duke has no lawful heir and when she sees his grown bastards, healthy and robust, envy and grief churn inside her. Mistress Jourdemayne is said to weave spells and devise potions that can quicken a barren womb. That is why Roger Bolingbroke sent for her – to give her Grace some solace and entrench his own position.'

'She is versatile, this witch,' Lord Walter murmured. 'Her reputation has more often been secured by bringing about the termination of unwanted pregnancies.'

I saw Maud's hand tremble as she set down her goblet and I wondered if her husband knew of her history and the children she had borne, one of whom still lived. I shook my head to drive away the troubling thought and bowed. 'My lady, I am grateful for your frankness. I understand the Duchess's predicament.' I half-turned towards Bess who was standing with downcast eyes by the door. 'Mistress Barber, there is a question you may be able to help me with as well.'

Bess gave a small bob and for the first time looked me fully in the face. In front of the Fitzvaughans, I felt no need to put on a pretence of hostility towards her and as our eyes held for a moment the terror in hers faded. 'Mistress Barber, can you tell me what Lady Mary Wenham's name was before her marriage? What family she comes from?'

Bess looked surprised but not anxious 'Her name was Neville, sir. She came from the same family as young Sir Bertram's mother, Lady Joanne.'

Lord Walter moved to my side and I heard his intake of breath. 'The Nevilles are acolytes and relatives of the Beauforts,' he said.

'The mother of the late Sir Bertram's first wife was a Beaufort, my lord,' Bess continued. 'When I was little Lady Joanne would tell us children on the estate stories of how she and her son carried royal blood in their veins. She was proud to claim the great Duke John of Lancaster as her grandfather.'

'Albeit the offspring of John of Gaunt's third marriage were barred from the royal succession,' Lord Walter added. 'From this derives the grudges fostered by Cardinal Beaufort and his brother, Edmund of Somerset.'

'Duke Humphrey's mortal foes.'

Lord Walter endorsed my comment and I went on with my conjecture. 'So is it possible the good Lady Anne came as a viper into Gloucester's nest: an informer, feeding information to Dunmow for transmission to the Beauforts? When I called there I was told how readily she had embraced the interests of her husband's family.' This seemed to be far more credible than the concocted story of lechery with her stepson.

'If this is so, who would have found advantage in the lady's death?'

Lord Walter's question required no reply for it was obvious to everyone and, remembering the Duke's appeal for me to exercise discretion in my investigation, I felt acutely uncomfortable.

*****

When I left the Fitzvaughans' chambers I was delighted that Bess showed me along the corridor, to point out the easiest way of departing from the rambling palace, and I grasped the opportunity to speak to her alone.

'Mistress Barber, there is something I should like to explain. I must have seemed unpleasant to you in your last weeks at Greenwich and I am very sorry for it. Circumstances forced me to appear unkind to you. Threats had been made by an influential man against anyone whom I esteemed and I dreaded embroiling you in this wickedness. You are safe here at Westminster and I am deeply relieved. Please try to forgive me for any hurt I caused you.'

Bess stared at me in uncertainty until her lips tilted into a glorious smile. 'Doctor Somers, are you saying you esteemed me?' Even while she spoke she was gripped by embarrassment and lowered her eyes as if she feared a reprimand for frivolity. 'Oh, that sounded presumptuous.'

'I esteem you always and forever and would have told you so weeks ago.' I took her hand and bent over it, brushing my lips against her fingers. 'But I must still dissemble until I have rid myself of the threatened perils. Can you believe this?'

'I have longed to hear you speak such words.' She was blushing and withdrew her hand from mine. 'You see what a forward hussy I am! It must be Lady Maud's influence. She is a very different mistress from poor Lady Anne.'

Her comment filled me with confusion for I could not tell if she spoke from maidenly innocence or complete knowledge of my liaison with Lady Maud. Could she be chiding or teasing me? I didn't know. 'If my feelings really give you joy, I must ask for your patience until I can speak freely, without putting you at risk. May I hope that you will grant me a little time and that I may then ask you to join the dance again, as I did after the wedding of the Lady Antigone?'

She reached her hand to touch the deformity on my face and again she smiled. 'Yes,' she said, 'but I beg you not to put yourself at hazard to save me from some malicious threat. Do not underestimate my strength, master physician. Nor my wish to join the dance once more.' She laughed and her eyes sparkled in the sunlight pouring through the window high above us.

There were royal guards approaching so I did not dare to do more than kiss her hand again but the radiance of her face as we parted gave me the resolution to face whatever challenges might lie ahead.

*****

While I sat in the boat sweeping forward on the flowing tide towards Greenwich my mind veered between joy and anguish. My delight at Bess's response, my feeling that we had achieved some delicate understanding, was counterbalanced by my alarm at the need to confront the Duke and perhaps be instructed to compromise the integrity of my investigation. I wished I could postpone the inevitable interview and decided that it would be justifiable to await Thomas Chope's return and see if he had been able to discover anything of relevance about Lady Anne's killer. Nevertheless I disembarked with a heavy heart which only lightened when I learned that Duke Humphrey had left his palace that morning to join the court at Windsor and was not expected to return until after the celebrations for Easter. At least as gratifying was the news that Roger Bolingbroke was attending to business of his own in the City and would be away for several days.

Doctor Southwell, by contrast, had arrived at Greenwich and, after catechising me about the patients I had treated during his absence and the treatments I prescribed, he declared he would visit them all to satisfy himself I had acted appropriately. He knew of my commission to probe the circumstances of the murder and assured me I must commit whatever time was required to my enquiries. He seemed in jovial mood but I was disconcerted when he referred excitedly to Roger Bolingbroke's 'enterprise'.

'You may not know of it yet, Harry, but time will tell, time will tell. I have only a hint of what is intended but, mark my words, it is a worthy enterprise. Master Bolingbroke has intimated you will have a part in it, as will I, and believe me we are both privileged to serve in so auspicious an endeavour. We will speak again when we are free to do so.'

I pressed him to explain what he was talking about but, with much tapping of his nose and unsuccessful attempts to wink, he declined. 'Until the propitious moment, Harry,' he said, 'until the propitious moment.'

I had no wish to endure more of this bothersome innuendo so, with Doctor Southwell's enthusiastic agreement, I took the opportunity to visit Danson and reassure myself as to my mother's welfare. I found her content and made welcome by Lady Blanche, who valued her skill with the needle in fashioning garments for the growing brood of small de Greys. Sir Hugh and his wife insisted that I stay two nights at their manor and the relaxation was helpful, clarifying my mind and stiffening my resolve do what I knew to be right. If I am truthful some of the restful hours were also filled with daydreams of a happy future with Bess at my side but I tried not to hope too greatly, for fear of dreadful disappointment. My leisure came to an abrupt conclusion early on the day I had planned to be my last at Danson, when I was summoned to the hall to receive a visitor who had ridden from Greenwich to see me.

Thomas Chope was grimy from his travels but beaming broadly and, despite the interruption to my respite, I was glad to see him. 'You need not have come out here specially,' I said.

'Wait till you hear my news; then tell me so.' He flopped onto a wooden settle and stretched his legs in front of him. 'I've drunk in every waterside tavern from the Temple steps to St. Katherine's Church. Soused in the line of duty, you might say.'

'A hard imposition.' I grinned. 'Do you mean to say you've discovered something?'

'Oh, yes. It took a dozen or more encounters but I finally found a man who knew of the bowman who landed in the City on the night of Lady Anne's death. Knew where he went and what happened to him.'

I waited while Thomas savoured the moment of suspense. 'Guess where he landed?'

My stomach somersaulted as I shook my head. I was certain of the answer.

'The jetty at Baynard's Castle. What d'you think of that?'

'You say you know what happened to him?'

'A strange coincidence, you might think. He was knifed in a brawl outside an inn two days later, died in the gutter, not a stone's throw from the Duke's house.'

I put my head in my hands but quickly rallied myself. 'You've done well, Thomas. I'm grateful, but this is ominous news. It confirms all my suspicions. Can the fellow who told you be trusted to keep his mouth shut?'

'He's just put to sea for the Low Countries. He'll be out of the way for a bit.'

'But a good many more know you were making enquiries. You'd better watch your back. Perhaps you should stay at Danson until I see which way the wind blows when I speak to the Duke.'

Thomas stood and punched my shoulder. 'My job is to watch your back, Doctor Somers. I'm returning to Greenwich with you.'

I did not argue with his rash decision.

*****

Roger Bolingbroke returned to Greenwich well before Gloucester and I appreciated that a confrontation with him was bound to take place before I could see Duke Humphrey. Sure enough I was soon summoned to attend him and reluctantly acquiesced but I was surprised to meet Geoffrey du Bois descending the stairs from his chambers. The apothecary was pale and he stared as if he did not recognise me before scuttling past without an acknowledgement. It was dispiriting to think that he had

214

somehow placed himself in Bolingbroke's power for I had looked on him as an upright man whose honesty could be relied on unreservedly.

'Doctor Somers, come in.'

I noted at once the use of my proper title and wondered what store of irony it concealed. 'You wish to see me, Master Bolingbroke?'

'Of course. To congratulate you.'

I was wary of this unexpected cordiality. 'I'm not aware that I've done anything worthy of congratulations.'

'Ah, but I'm confident you have. I have been following your progress with admiration.' He waved me to a seat. 'I underestimated you, Harry. I readily admit it. When I first came here my attention was drawn to you as a lad of intelligence whose ability had solved a sad little conundrum two years back. That's why I paid some heed to you; but I was not impressed by what I saw and, when I set a simple trap, you abandoned all your scruples to enjoy the carnal delights of Maud Warrenne's much-visited flesh. That confirmed my belief that you were a foolish boy who put bodily satisfaction before ambition of the mind.'

'Do you imply you've changed your views?'

'Your new-found boldness complements your unexpected skill. You have chosen your supporters well. The ruffian Chope, whom you saved from the gallows, was an obvious choice but he's proved adroit in the rougher aspects of your enquiries. I had not appreciated what staunch allies you had in Sir Hugh de Grey and his lady and that was my error; they have given your dear mother secure sanctuary. More surprising to me is the way you seem to have won the trust of the austere Lord Fitzvaughan – as well as his harlot bride. I gather you have been admitted to their private quarters at the court and, as you were not ejected forcibly therefrom, I surmise that you neither assaulted the bountiful Maud nor suffered the attentions of his lordship or the ingratiating Gaston.'

215

As he drew breath I interrupted. 'I am impressed by the information you have assembled but I'd like to know the purpose of your recital.'

'Ah, the impatience of youth! Very well Doctor Somers, I shall come to the point. I have recognised my mistake in underestimating your capacities. Now I wish to make a new start in my dealings with you by offering you a full part in a most auspicious enterprise, not as a mere dogsbody but a principal player.' With a considerable effort to suppress my curiosity I did not respond and after a long pause he continued. 'I assure you from the beginning that it will redound to the advantage of Duke Humphrey and Duchess Eleanor. You need have no qualms on that account.'

'Then the instinctive qualms I feel must be on my own account.'

His lip curled derisively. 'Over-caution, I promise. I do not expect a reply immediately. I understand you will wish to consider if you are bold enough to step into the arena with combatants of the highest standing.'

'I am no sort of combatant. I am entirely peaceable.'

'But you bandy words aggressively. Enough of this! Go, Doctor Somers, and ruminate on what I offer. I will remove any anxiety you feel for your mother's sake and you will reap a rich reward.'

'Don't you think I might make known your offer, as you call it, to others?'

'What could you make known? You have no idea to what I refer and if you were foolish enough to mention our discussion, I have a fine tale ready to show how you rejected the chance to serve the Duke's interests. You can be certain your position at Greenwich would be at an end.'

'You sound more convincing when you threaten, Master Bolingbroke.' I rose and stood as straight as my crooked leg allowed.

'You may think so but my offer is genuine. Think about it. And if you are a prayerful man, physician, remember the Duchess in your orisons.'

I was shocked by the implications of his words. 'Is she ill?'

He smirked at me in his former, patronising manner. 'It is early days but there is hope she is to bear a child. Ponder that too, my boy.'

Chapter 21

I had given Bolingbroke no answer when the Duke returned to Greenwich at the end of April and I made my inevitable request to see him privately. I had hoped that the volume of business awaiting his attention at the palace might defer our meeting for several days but he summoned me immediately to his study. I thought he looked older, certainly tired, and I wondered how difficult a time he had experienced at court, parrying Cardinal Beaufort's attempts to persuade the king towards peace with France and a royal marriage. He waved aside my formal words pledging service to his Grace and came at once to the point of our conversation. 'I hear you have made progress in your enquiries Doctor Somers.'

'I have formed some tentative conclusions, my lord Duke, but fear it may not prove possible to reach certainty.' He nodded for me to continue. 'I have concluded that the murderer intended to kill Lady Anne and no one else and that he had been employed to do this by someone who had your interests at heart and believed his victim was guilty of working against you.'

'You doubt that she was?'

'It is possible but as yet I have found no proof. Her late husband's family bear allegiance to the Beauforts, being related by marriage to them, and Lady Anne corresponded regularly with her stepson after coming to Greenwich. That might be thought to offer grounds for suspicion but the correspondence seems to have been destroyed, except for one brief and apparently innocent communication: so there is no evidence of malevolence on her part. On the other hand when I visited Dunmow there was a concerted attempt to curtail my pursuit of the truth.'

'I am glad you escaped that plot but I am confident someone at the Pleasance has been spying on my plans and activities. Before the Feast of the Nativity the Cardinal displayed detailed knowledge of my intentions which went beyond the bounds of reason for him to have divined without secret information.' The Duke did not disguise his irritation.

'May I ask if this has occurred again since then, your Grace?'

'As you would say, master investigator, I have no evidence but I believe the informer has been silenced. If that is so, the episode is at an end.'

'Would you not wish the principal in the lady's assassination brought to justice?'

'You implied that could not be done.'

'Not without further enquiries – but there is an opening for me to pursue the matter, if you agree.'

Duke Humphrey rose from his chair and walked to the window. For several moments he stared across the courtyard while clasping his hands behind his back. I heard him sigh before he turned and faced me. 'You'd better tell me what you mean although I have no stomach to hear it.'

'My lord, it has been possible to trace the route taken by the bowman in his flight. It leads to your palace of the Wardrobe at Baynard's Castle in the City.'

'You have apprehended the man?'

'No. He was killed in a brawl soon after Lady Anne's death.'

The Duke let out his breath slowly and a faint smile played around his lips. 'So you do not know who commissioned him?'

'No, your Grace.'

Gloucester returned to his chair and fingered a stylus on his desk. 'Do you remember what I said to you, Master Somers, when you were first commissioned to look into the occurrence? When I asked for your discretion?'

'Yes, my lord Duke. That is why I am consulting you now.'

He tossed the pen from one hand to the other. 'Good, Harry, good. Who else knows where your enquiries have led?'

'No one else knows the full position although those who have assisted me are aware of some part of it. If I am to proceed I shall need to put questions to members of your household in the City.' I paused before adding, 'and here at Greenwich.'

'I see that and I also see I could be mightily discomforted by the answers to some of those questions. You were right to come to me at this juncture. Will you obey my decision?'

I drew breath but I was prepared for this demand. 'My lord, you are the seat of justice for your domain. You have the power to determine the fate of your servants.'

The Duke grimaced. 'You do not give me a straight answer, physician, but I deduce you have concluded resistance to my will would be useless.' I bowed my head and he continued. 'Then I hereby revoke your commission at this point, with gratitude and commendations for what you have ascertained and the risks you have run. I shall acquaint the Duchess with the outcome and explain my conclusion. You need trouble yourself no longer with this wretched affair but return to your medical practice and concern yourself with the health of the living, not the circumstances of a single grievous death. Do I make myself clear, Doctor Somers?'

'Absolutely, my lord Duke.' Despite the throbbing in my temple, there was clearly no more to say.

*****

Thomas Chope was outraged when I told him of the Duke's directive and he tried to persuade me to disregard it. We had walked by the riverside away from the palace and he tore a cluster of twigs from a willow which overhung the water, ripping off the new grown leaves in his annoyance.

220

'The King's uncle should be the first to uphold the law and ensure malefactors are brought to justice. Is he protecting that reptile, Bolingbroke?' He spat on the grass and ground his foot onto the sputum.

'I fancy his main purpose is to prevent accusations being made against the Duchess. Of course I suspect Bolingbroke of arranging Lady Anne's murder – although not perhaps the precise circumstances, an arrow's length from his chest – but if that was shown to be true, her Grace could well be thought guilty by association, or even design.'

'Is she capable of executing one of her own ladies?'

'I scarcely know her but, if it favoured the Duke's interests, I imagine she is.'

'Christ! I don't envy you mingling with the nobility, Harry. They're dangerous beasts. But I understand why you must obey Gloucester. If you're to keep your position, you have no choice.' He jumped down the bank onto the shingle beneath the trailing branches and picked up a stone which he skimmed across the water, just as I'd seen him do when we were lads. Then he looked up at me with an unexpectedly fierce expression. 'You'll not prevent me pursuing enquiries into another violent death though.'

With one hand on the trunk of the tree I let myself down gently to stand beside him at the river's edge. 'What do you mean?'

'Grizel's betrothed wasn't murdered resisting robbery. She's no doubt of it and she's told me what she heard from the pedlar at Danson. I'd like to see whether I can find out anything more. I'd start with the inn at Deptford, where the pedlar overheard the admission, but I wouldn't be surprised if there's a link to someone in the City – you know where. Grizel reckons Dickon knew more than was good for him. It's mighty like Lady Anne, if you ask me.'

'I didn't know Grizel had been trying to claim you as her knight errant.' The idea amused me. 'I don't believe there's any basis for her theory. Dickon was killed for his prize money.'

'Maybe, but I'd like to follow it up. She'd be happier to know someone had.'

'I can't stop you but I think you'll be wasting your time. Just promise me that if you do find some link with people at the Pleasance or the Duke's house in the City, you won't take any action without letting me know.'

'I've no problem with that. Thanks, Harry. She'll be pleased.'

Something in his voice caught my attention and I realised his face was crimson. 'By the saints, Thomas, are you getting sweet on her?'

He kicked loose earth from the bank. 'Don't read too much into it but we've both lost someone dear to us. She deserves support. We'll be going together to the May Day festivities in the park. Will you come too?'

I laughed and held his arm to scramble back up the bank. 'Three's an awkward number for such an outing. I'm glad for you both.'

Thomas hauled himself up beside me. 'You don't mind? I mean Alys was your sister and...'

'It's nearly two years since Alys died. Watch out for young Rendell though. He may think it's too soon for Grizel to be tripping about with another rogue.'

'Rogue! If you weren't such a distorted runt, I'd thump you!'

Hooting with laughter, he seized me round the waist but I succeeded in tangling my foot round his ankle so that we fell into the grass, mock-wrestling, rolling over and over until we broke apart to draw breath. It was a long time since I had indulged in such boyish pursuits and it did me good, lightening my too heavy spirits and reinforcing my pleasure at having at least one true friend.

*****

Over the following days I concentrated on my duties as a physician and tried to push aside the anger which the Duke's attitude had provoked but which I had hidden from Thomas. I did not venture out to join the merriment of May Day and kept to my quarters when I did not need to visit patients. On two evenings I drank with Geoffrey and John Home but neither was good company, each seemingly obsessed with his own thoughts, and I was no better. I regretted that Giovanni was absent from Greenwich at the time, sent to Oxford on some errand for the Duke, for his ebullience could disperse the dullest of moods. Despite my efforts my mind dwelt on the information I had gleaned and the gaps which prevented me coming to a final conclusion and I chafed at my inability to conclude my task.

When a message was brought that Dame Margery wished to see me I assumed she was unwell and set off for the chamberlain's chambers with my bag of ointments and potions. I was always glad to meet the intelligent old lady and hoped I would not find her badly ill so I was reassured to see her rosy cheeks and clear eyes as she greeted me. I was surprised she was not attended but she knew me well and I feared she might have some delicate internal problem to discuss. I looked at her solemnly.

'You need not peer at me as if I were at imminent danger of expiring. It is not your physician's expertise I wish to consult, Harry. Sit down and take some wine. I've not seen you for a while but I deduce you are somewhat aggrieved.'

'You know the Duke has curtailed my investigation?'

'I surmised it and can guess why. I should not dare to intrude into what is Gloucester's business but there is another concern I want to put to you. I think you have made the acquaintance of Mistress Jourdemayne?' I nodded and she continued. 'I spent an hour yesterday with old Joan Coverdale. You remember her? She is not always in her right

223

mind these days but I was fortunate to see her when she was clear in her memory of things in the past – less so about recent happenings. I chanced to mention Mistress Jourdemayne as one whose company seemed most unsuitable for Duchess Eleanor and Joan immediately began to recount a history about which I knew nothing. It concerned that sinister woman.'

'Is Joan Coverdale's recollection to be trusted?'

'On this, I think so, and it would not be difficult to find others to confirm the facts. She told me that some years ago Mistress Jourdemayne was held in the Fleet prison on charges of witchcraft and then moved to the castle at Windsor where Joan was living. Others had been arrested on grounds of sorcery at the same time and met their doom at the stake but after a period of incarceration Mistress Jourdemayne was released, without penalty, on condition that she refrain from witchcraft in the future. Is that not strange?'

'Unusual, certainly. Proven witchcraft attracts the harshest sentences.'

'She was arrested in company with a friar, John Ashwell. The pair of them had forecast that the sun would be obscured on a certain day, plunging the earth into untimely darkness. It came about as they foretold.'

'Such things do occur and astronomers can calculate when they are due. It may smack of witchcraft to the ignorant but it can be explained.'

'I don't doubt that but it seems to have been the accuracy of this forecast which secured Mistress Jourdemayne's freedom. Fortuitous, perhaps. Joan thought the woman's original offence had been malicious in intent.'

'This is not the first time I've heard her described as a witch,' I said, remembering how Lord Fitzvaughan named her "the witch of Eye". 'Has there been any suggestion she is engaging in such evil practices now?'

224

'I confess I've heard none but I do not understand why the Duchess keeps her by her side.'

'I understand she is skilled in helping wives to conceive and the Duchess no doubt credits her with assisting her pregnancy.'

'Her what?' Dame Margery leaned forward in her chair, gripping its arms. 'Where did you hear that nonsense, Harry? The Duchess is not with child and never has been. She continues sylph-like and barren, more's the pity for her and the Duke. Who is spreading such a vile rumour?'

'Roger Bolingbroke told me, some weeks ago.'

'Bolingbroke! False hope or wishful thinking, I suppose. The man's ambition is boundless.'

I decided to risk a direct question, even though it might rebound on her maid-servant. 'Grizel told me once you referred to him as "trouble". Do you know something of his past?'

Dame Margery's eyebrows shot up and she grunted before answering. 'That girl needs to learn prudence in what she overhears and then repeats. I may well have said something of the sort but it did not refer to Bolingbroke's past – I know nothing of that – but to events immediately after his arrival here. One of his first acts at Greenwich was to try to suborn my husband. Bolingbroke offered to make it worth his while if he consented to report on matters privy between Duke and chamberlain.'

'To inform on the Duke! Whatever for?'

'You may well ask. Bolingbroke received a downright refusal of course and he had no way of forcing my husband to do his will. In the case of some weaker members of the household, I suspect he has gleaned embarrassing information to hold over them and coerce them to do his bidding.'

I prayed silently that I would not blush and reveal my guilt. 'You could be right. I know people in awe of him.'

'He is the spider drawing those who might be useful to him into his web, putting them under his control. That gratifying sense of power may be all he seeks or he may have some more malignant intention. Mistress Jourdemayne is another minion, no doubt, but she is surely here for a purpose and I do not like to think of her dabbling in the black arts at the palace.'

'If she restricts herself to improving Duchess Eleanor's fertility, she will do no harm. Have you told others of your concerns?'

'Only my husband. My reason for speaking to you, Harry, was to bid you take care and to bear in mind what I have said as you continue your searches.' My mouth opened of its own accord, such was my surprise. 'Oh, I know you will not give up, however discreetly you proceed. I am sorry I cannot give you more specific assistance but I am sure there is something unsavoury afoot and you must discover what it is. God go with you, physician.'

*****

I left Dame Margery in a state of confusion, tempted to look further into the mysteries which puzzled us both but nervous of disobeying the Duke's command. In any case it was unrealistic to think of prying into Bolingbroke's activities when he exerted such influence within the household and, together with Mistress Jourdemayne, enjoyed the Duchess's protection. I pondered the old lady's motive in sharing her anxieties with me and, when I tried to reconstruct our conversation in my head, I realised it was highly likely that her husband knew exactly what she intended. The chamberlain could not go against Gloucester's decree but if his wife had his tacit blessing to invoke my services, it put a different, and serious, complexion on the matter. I knew then that I would succumb to the challenge she had set but decided I needed some diversion before I

226

committed myself to such a rash undertaking. I decided that when evening came I would seek out John Home and Geoffrey du Bois and offer them refreshment at the village tavern.

In the event it was John who sought me out, as twilight was falling, and I was startled to see how worried he looked as he pulled me out into the courtyard. I guessed he had glimpsed Doctor Southwell working at his experiments in the inner chamber and wanted to speak to me privately. 'I was about to call on you,' I said. 'Is something wrong?'

'I'm afraid it might be.' His fingers were scrabbling along the folds of his cape as if he lacked the ability to still them. 'It's Geoffrey. I saw him this morning and he invited me to take wine with him after Vespers. We intended to send a page to see if you were free to join us. But he's gone.' He clamped his mouth shut and appeared to swallow several times.

'Gone? What do you mean? Perhaps he's been called away from his rooms.'

John lips twitched as he made the effort to speak and his voice was hoarse. 'Come and see.'

He led me to the apothecary's rooms where the outer door into Geoffrey's dispensary stood slightly open and he gestured to me to enter. In view of John's strange behaviour I did so with some caution but I quickly gasped in horror at the scene that confronted us. In one corner broken retorts and phials were strewn on the floor, lying in pools of the liquid they had contained, creating weird swirling patterns of orange, green and brown, with mounds of disintegrating powder and globules of mercury adding bulk to the fluid mixture. Across the room precious books were scattered and sodden, and the delicate scales on which Geoffrey weighed his ingredients had been trampled on the damp tiles. The table on which the apothecary worked had been upturned and his chair, flung against toppled shelving, was smashed into pieces. The door in the far wall, leading to his private chamber, was closed.

'Have you been in there?' I asked.

'I didn't dare,' John said, making the sign of the cross.

I picked my way through the debris and turned the handle to reveal a sight every bit as alarming. Papers had been tossed about, the bed linen appeared to have been slashed and some of Geoffrey's clothes were hanging out of his chest in a crumpled heap. Of their owner there was no trace but as I tiptoed across to his desk I stopped with my knees trembling and pointed. John came hesitantly to my side. 'What is it?'

'Spots of blood. There on the torn manuscript. Go and fetch the chamberlain. You can run faster than me.' John nodded and gathered up his cassock to take to his heels.

When he had gone I turned back to Geoffrey's desk in order to examine a paper I had noticed, screwed up and thrust into the ink horn as if to obscure its contents. I straightened it and found only the top half was legible but it did not appear to be suspicious. In a clerkly hand it recorded the first words of a prayer:

Lord Jesus, think on me
By Care and Woe oppressed.

I was about to put it down as wholly innocuous when some trick of my mind made me stare at it more closely. Could it conceivably be more than a coincidence? Lady Anne had whispered that word, given some emphasis, and her last message to her stepson had said 'WOE is come to Greenwich'. Now it appeared Geoffrey was in trouble and sought consolation, using the same word. Or had he written it to pass to someone else or received it from another? Could it contain a message? Could it even be a cipher? I gulped and stared again, remembering how Lord Fitzvaughan had described Mistress Jourdemayne and, at that moment, I remembered Lady Anne's other words. I had heard them as 'which will do it'; now I suspected I had misunderstood. The word could have been "witch" and WOE stood for "Witch of Eye". A dreadful possibility occurred to me and I stuffed the paper into my gown as John Home and a number of attendants entered the dispensary.

When he had examined the rooms the chamberlain ordered that they be barred on the outside, a search made throughout the palace and checks undertaken at the jetty and the gatehouse to ascertain those entering and leaving the Pleasance during the day. Then he led me away to his study to speak in private. 'This is a nasty business,' he said, shaking his head. 'I fear for the apothecary's safety.'

'So do I – Geoffrey is my friend. Yet there is something strange about it. It seems clear a struggle took place in his rooms with the furniture knocked over and all those bottles smashed but I'm surprised no one nearby reported hearing unusual noises. The dispensary is normally a very peaceful place. Perhaps your enquiries will find someone too frightened to come forward earlier but it's odd a tussle like that could happen in broad daylight without being noticed. What puzzles me even more is how the intruders managed to get Geoffrey out of his chambers without anyone observing it.'

The chamberlain patted my arm. 'I fear it was Geoffrey's body they were moving. In a sack over a man's shoulder it would not draw much attention. There are workmen with sacks wandering through passages every day.'

I nodded. 'We'll have to ask questions widely to eliminate as many as possible. But Geoffrey is a tall man. It wouldn't be easy for one fellow to carry him.'

'So we may be looking for two men or one very hefty lad.'

'And Geoffrey must have been taken somewhere, in the palace or the park or away by boat or across a horse.'

'We'll find out which, Harry, I'm confident.'

At that point we were interrupted by banging on the door and, to my surprise, a servant asking to speak to me. On behalf of Doctor Southwell he requested my attendance in the soldiers' quarters where my colleague needed assistance in treating an injury.

'There's too much larking about with weapons among the guards,' the chamberlain said. 'I've had cause to complain to their officer about louts wielding lances and swords in the corridors. They're always scratching each other. Off you go, Doctor Somers, do your duty. I'll let you know as soon as we hear something definite from the search.'

*****

I was not taken to the main area where the soldiers were lodged but to a vaulted storeroom at the base of their tower and I found Doctor Southwell preparing to stitch a jagged gash in a man's left arm. The man lay not on a pallet but a pile of grubby sacks. 'I need you to hold him down while I do what is necessary,' Southwell said. 'It'll be painful and I don't want him wriggling.'

There was nothing unusual in the procedure, although the surgeon-barbers objected to physicians undertaking such operations, straightforward though they were. What was peculiar was Southwell's request for me to assist him when any sensible attendant could perform the function equally well. This was not the moment to seek an explanation and I did as I was bidden but I peered carefully at the man's injury.

'Caught by a dagger accidently,' Southwell said as he observed my curiosity. 'Nasty slash. He's lucky it didn't go deeper. Hold still now.' The man groaned as the needle pierced his flesh and Southwell thrust a rag into his mouth. 'Bite on that. Try not to call out.'

I was baffled by the need for silence but the task was soon completed and Southwell strapped the man's arm across his chest. 'You know where you're to go,' he said as he did so. 'Your officer's been told you're on an errand for Master Bolingbroke. In a day or two you'll be taken to Baynard's Castle while you recover. I'll come to see you before you go. You understand?' I had never heard him speak so succinctly and with such authority.

The man grunted and staggered to the door where the attendant who fetched me was waiting to fling a capacious cloak over him and help him up the stairs. As they disappeared Doctor Southwell collected his things and thanked me for my help but I was not prepared to let the occasion pass without comment.

'Why did you need me? And why attend to him here, in a storeroom?'

'You're to forget everything you've seen, d'you understand, Harry Somers? If you know what's good for you and yours, you'll say nothing. We're here at Bolingbroke's special request. Just a favour to him, you see. The soldier's given him service in the past but it's a matter where tact is needed. Don't worry, we've done nothing wrong. We're bound to assist the afflicted, are we not?'

I knew it was injudicious to persist but could not prevent myself. 'I find it all very strange.'

'Then I advise you to stop doing so. I understand Bolingbroke has invited your participation in matters of great significance but he still has a hold over you, does he not? He mentioned that he has a letter ready penned to John Swanwych outlining some of your indiscretions. He intends to send it to your esteemed friend if you are difficult. But you won't be, will you, Harry?'

'He has a hold over you too?'

'That's none of your business. You should be clear that it is not just your carnal incontinence he would reveal if you are troublesome. He has written a second letter, to be sent to the Duke, stating that you have been negligent in your enquiries, refusing to expose the Lady Anne's incestuous relations with her stepson.'

'That was a false allegation, based on a forgery. Bolingbroke knows that!'

'Unwise, my boy, unwise! We are in no position to challenge one in so powerful a position. Much better to ally ourselves to his interests and make them our own. I can assure you, there will be abundant benefits to come, if you join me in this enterprise.' He hustled me through the door. 'Meanwhile, Doctor Somers, keep your mouth shut about what does not concern you.'

Chapter 22

The events of the previous few days had disturbed me deeply but the revelation that Doctor Southwell was now prepared to be open about his commitment to Roger Bolingbroke was unsettling because it was so unexpected. I worked alongside him, shared his accommodation and believed I knew his character: I had thought him amiable, learned and bumbling. Yet, in the space of a few minutes, I had seen him capable of overbearing authority and intransigence. He seemed to be enmeshed in Bolingbroke's affairs by his own choice, anxious to see them come to fruition, whatever that might involve, and he expected me to obey his directions. I felt bewildered on my own account as well as extremely worried about Geoffrey du Bois and I dreaded having to converse with Southwell again when he returned to our rooms.

I went directly from the wounded soldier to see the chamberlain and learned that there had been no sightings that day of anyone conveying a burden, which might contain a body, leaving the palace on foot or horseback, or by boat. Only one unusual departure had been noted, in the late afternoon, when an unidentifiable man, with his hood pulled down to hide his face, took a horse from the stables and rode from the palace at speed. A lad who helped the groom was the only witness and he claimed the man sent him on a wild goose chase to fetch a different saddle but when he returned the impatient rider had gone. There could be a dozen explanations for such an episode but the chamberlain and I agreed that it might have been a murderer escaping after secreting his victim somewhere at the palace. A search of the entire building had begun but would take several hours and gaining access to the private areas used by the Duke and Duchess – and their closest advisers – might not be straightforward. There would certainly be opportunity for a shrouded corpse to be shifted between hiding places without detection.

I could not share my misgivings about Southwell with the chamberlain but he recognised how troubled I was and suddenly asked if I needed respite away from Greenwich, to review all that had happened. I must have sounded feeble when I replied.

'I can't leave the palace, now my enquiries have been aborted, without giving a reason.'

'Then perhaps I should give you an impeccable one. You are always welcome at Danson and I will let it be known that Lady Blanche and Sir Hugh are concerned to receive a second opinion about the health of one of their infants, so I have asked you to oblige. You can stay a few days if you wish – while the child recovers of course. Messages pass to and fro between Dame Margery and our daughter frequently so I can send you any information we glean here in the meantime without arousing any suspicion. Would this be helpful?'

'It would be invaluable!'

'Good. Be on your way as soon as you're ready. I'm sure the de Grey child is feverish and needs your urgent ministrations.' He dipped his head and, with his expression as imperturbable and incorruptible as ever, the worthy old gentleman turned back to the rolls of paper on his table.

*****

Everyone at Danson made me welcome and no one required my professional attention. My mother was delighted to see me so soon after my last visit and asked no difficult questions about my purpose in coming, while my hosts waited tactfully for me to tell them as much or as little as I wished. Next morning Sir Hugh insisted that I accompany him to view the hawks in his mews where I listened patiently while he and the falconer described the skills of the various birds and flew them for me to appreciate their prowess. I made appropriate comments, although knowing nothing of the techniques I was meant to admire, and despite my ignorance I was impressed by the way the raptors swooped accurately on their prey. I wished I was capable of doing the same. I was less happy when they fitted me with a cumbersome gauntlet and made me hold a bunch of feathers with meat hidden within it, so that a small merlin would be encouraged to return and alight on my unsteady wrist. I found the experience frightening but, as the falconer slipped a hood over the bird and relieved me of its weight, I reflected that what I needed was a lure to trap Roger Bolingbroke.

Sir Hugh then took me to see his orchards, heavy with ripening fruit, and these I could review with more confidence, relaxing enough to tell him how the Duke had banned me from completing my investigation. 'It's infuriating,' I said, 'for I feel sure there is something profoundly wrong to be uncovered and I am on the brink of revealing it.'

'If your performance two years ago is anything to go by, you'd unravel it if anyone could.'

'It's very different from two years ago. Then I had to work my way through confusing clues and was often misled before I identified Alys's murderer. Now I'm convinced I know the villain but lack evidence, while he smirks at me and plots who knows what mischief.'

Sir Hugh swung himself up onto the bar of a gate. 'You could appeal to someone able to overrule the Duke's decree.' I felt my brow pucker as I stared. 'Do you know anyone who could present your case to the King?'

I shook my head and started to reject the impossible idea when I realised it was not impossible at all. 'There is one person who might help, I said. 'He has the King's favour and is at court. I believe him to be fair minded and not directly aligned with either Gloucester or the Cardinal.'

'Then he's your man. Go to him, Harry. The court has returned to Westminster so you could easily slip there while those at Greenwich believe you to be here. If the chamberlain sends messages I'll get a fast horseman to deliver them to you. In whose chambers will you be found?'

'Lord Walter Fitzvaughan's,' I said, dry-mouthed.

'Capital! You couldn't do better. He has a reputation for honesty unusual among the nobility. Come and dine with us and I'll have an escort ready to accompany you as soon as you've eaten. You'll want to avoid the vicinity of the Pleasance on your journey. No argument now. Take your case to the King. It's your only chance to trump his uncle.'

I knew he was right but the undertaking was more than rash; it was hazardous and foolhardy.

*****

It was evening by the time I presented myself at the Palace of Westminster but on this occasion there were no delays and I was taken directly to Lord Fitzvaughan, which was just as well because by the time I arrived, saddle-sore and weary, I was losing my nerve. It seemed outrageously presumptuous to seek the King's intervention, daring enough to bother one of his chief advisers with my request, and I knew I risked destroying all my credit with the Duke. The corridors seemed hushed compared with the bustle of my previous visit but Gaston de la Tour came to meet me and led me past all the intervening guard posts with an assertive wave of his hand. He poured me some ale and took a stool by his lordship's side as I was welcomed but, when I summarised my concerns to Lord Walter, I sounded apologetic and felt as I had when teased for my deformity in boyhood, longing to hide myself away and pretend nothing had happened.

I described the position frankly, only holding back the circumstances of Bolingbroke's hold over me, and Lord

Fitzvaughan sat silently after I had finished, with the knuckle of one finger pressed against his lip as if to assist consideration of my ridiculous appeal. 'If I may risk a pun,' he said at length, 'there is more to this than meets the Eye. Cardinal Beaufort is squawking of treachery to the King and, in view of what you say, it is plausible he's right, although how he has wind of it I cannot conjecture.'

'As she was dying Lady Anne said something that sounded like "treachery" but I couldn't be sure. She wanted me to tell someone but wasn't able to speak again.'

'We may surmise it was intended as a last message to Dunmow and thence to the Cardinal. She clearly knew of Mistress Jourdemayne and may have discovered a plot which is only now coming to light. Your arrival is timely, Harry. In the last day or so a highly dangerous prediction has been made known and, although attempts have been made to stop it spreading, the court is like a sieve. There is grave anxiety and the King is understandably distressed.' He paused and Gaston offered a goblet which he took but did not drink. 'The prediction foretells that King Henry will suffer a life-threatening illness in the next two months. It is not yet known who made this prophecy and reputable astrologers are being consulted to confirm or deny whether the stars truly hold this information. It is my belief the mischief came from Greenwich, uttered by the witch, Mistress Jourdemayne, and circulated unobtrusively by Roger Bolingbroke.'

Gaston stirred and shifted position. 'A man who stands to benefit if dear Duchess Eleanor were to become Queen and he remains her clerk. How charming. You've gone very white, Doctor Somers. Would you like more ale?'

I shook my head. 'Surely the King cannot be terrified into mortal illness?'

Lord Walter' elegant fingers caressed the stem of his goblet. 'Perhaps the plot leads into darker waters. We must take care. The Cardinal has wind of this but is known to be

Gloucester's enemy and the King will not lightly act against his uncle. Duke Humphrey is entitled to execute justice against offenders within his domain as he sees fit and I cannot suggest that Henry should overrule him.' I must have given a groan of disappointment for he held up his hand to silence me. 'Wait, Harry, I have not finished. What the King would do, I think, if sufficiently persuaded, would be to authorise enquiries to find the origin of this prediction and what it portends. I'd wager such enquiries would bring us close to the person who ordered Lady Anne' death and so would serve your turn as well. As they say, there's more than one way to skin a cat.' He rose and indicated to Gaston that he wished to put on his long surcoat. 'This is a delicate matter and I shall seek an ally in putting it to his Grace – not just the Cardinal because he will be seen as prejudiced. The King is showing favour to a cultured soldier returned from the wars in France, William de la Pole, Earl of Suffolk. He is an interesting fellow and I should be glad to know him better. Wait here while I pay a visit to his chambers. Gaston, come with me, I have a message for you to take. I'll send my dear wife to keep you company, Doctor Somers. I expect to be half an hour or so.'

I fancied he smirked as he spoke and he ignored my protest that it was unnecessary to trouble Lady Maud but my smile may have given the lie to my words, for I was joyful at the chance to see Bess again. I was disconcerted when Gaston winked at me as he held the door for his lord but, if it meant Mistress Barber had made no secret of her pleasure in my company, it was reward enough.

Before I had done more than sip my ale I heard the latch click and Maud entered the room. She was magnificently arrayed in a brocade court dress, with a capacious skirt and low-cut bodice, and on her head she wore a towering pyramid from which flowed diaphanous veils which rippled as she walked. She fastened the door behind her and glided towards me.

'My lady, you are unattended?' Panic overwhelmed my disappointment.

'I have sent sweet Bess to chapel to pray for us all, as I have been prevented from joining her by my lord's command that I attend you. I am sorry to thwart you, Harry, but I place my own desires before those of my maid.'

'Lord Fitzvaughan cannot have intended you should receive me alone. Excuse me, I will wait outside and you may join Bess in the chapel.'

She blocked my way as I moved towards the door. 'You misunderstand, Harry.' She reached across to the hourglass on her husband's desk and turned it. 'We shall have time enough, until half the sand has fallen through, for you to satisfy my desires – as you have so ably in the past. I'm sure you remember. You have never resisted me – despite your initial show of reluctance.'

I shuddered with disbelief and indecorous excitement, for what she said was true. 'This is madness, lady. The past is over. You are married to Lord Walter.'

'Who has no need of me. He is gracious and considerate but he does not come to my bed. I am as I always was and the sight of you causes my blood to race and my nipples to grow firm. Put your hand here and see that I am right.'

I stepped backwards but she pinned me against the desk and, instinctively, I put out my hands to grip her shoulders and push her away. I felt her body quiver at my touch and she seized my hands to slide them beneath the neckline of her gown, easing it from one shoulder and baring a breast. 'No, Maud, no!' but even as I protested my member was responding and she saw me jolt with its vigour.

'Foolish physician, have you not learned the impulses of our bodies?'

'Only too well but I must resist this depravity for both our sakes.'

239

She gave me stinging blow across my face. 'Do you call me depraved, you insolent deformity?'

My inward pain hurt more than the smarting of my cheek. 'You show your true colours, my lady. You taunt my blemish even when you seek to seduce me.'

'Your blemish, as you call it, excites me, Harry, more than any man's unscarred face. Your vivid stain makes me believe that when you master me the devil himself possesses my body and that is exhilarating.' She stroked the crusty skin on my cheek and nestled against my shoulder. 'My urge for you is unbearable. I insult you simply to rouse your passion. Don't pretend you do not share it.'

'For God's sake, Maud, stop. We should never have lain together but now you are married and...'

'And now you have the itch to tup my virtuous attendant. I promise I will help you to her if you serve me first. I do not indulge a common woman's jealousy. I will arrange for you to come to her by night and take your pleasure, even if she resists.'

'Never!' My exclamation was stifled as Maud fastened her mouth on mine but I forced her aside roughly and she gave a cry of anger.

'You dolt! If you refuse me, physician, I shall expose you as a rapist who forced me to your will while my husband was absent furthering your interests.'

'I don't think Lord Walter will believe you.'

'But Bess will, when I describe how you have been my paramour for many months – how you have come from smiling plaintively at her sweet face and thrust your prick inside me with all the violence you could muster. Do you recall the love-bites you left all over my naked body when you punished me for my effrontery in coming to your room? I shall explain each one of them to her.'

I broke free from her, horrified by her words but not knowing whether her angry threat should be treated seriously until she spat her next furious words. 'Roger

Bolingbroke has tutored me well. I mean what I am saying and will exact the uttermost retribution.' Then as I reached the door her voice changed. 'But come, I would not have you mount me under duress, dear heart. Let us be friends. For the sake of what has been, let us be reconciled.'

She stepped back and, stupidly, when she put out her hand as if to clasp mine in amity, I thought she was coming to her senses. I took a step towards her, eying her bare breast, as she smiled with beguiling charm, and I reached to touch her fingers and show our quarrel was concluded. Sinuously she stretched herself, leaning against the desk, and lifted her dress high to reveal her delectable pale thighs and the dark pelt above them. 'Come under the shelter of my skirt, physician, and let your mouth explore my secret lips,' she said. 'Bess will know nothing if you serve me well.'

She opened her legs and, as madness gripped me, I dropped to my knees in front of her. When she writhed in ecstasy at my caresses I pulled her to the ground and, while the sand trickled through the hourglass, our frantic coupling was accomplished.

We were standing apart when Bess tapped at the door but Maud was flushed and her headdress lay on the floor. Calmly she picked it up as her maid entered. 'The heel of these new shoes is unsteady,' she said. 'I have slipped over and bruised my leg.'

Bess did not look at me but she was pale as ivory. Without a word she fitted the pyramid on her mistress's head and smoothed its crumpled veils before withdrawing to a stool at the side of the fireplace, so that when, a few moments later, Lord Walter returned, he found a completely decorous scene. Only Gaston, entering behind him, showed from the malice in his expression that he might have divined what had taken place and, as Maud curtsied and left us, together with her maid, he sniffed the air and looked at me with venom.

241

'Doctor Somers,' Maud's husband said. 'You are to come with me. I shall present you to the King and then we are to converse with William, Earl of Suffolk.'

*****

I feared for my sanity as he hurried me along a network of corridors and I do not know how I survived the subsequent encounters without betraying my shame. If, at any time in my life, I had imagined I might be presented to King Henry I would have given thought to my appearance, replacing my shabby gown with the one I kept for ceremonies and setting my cap squarely on tidy hair. Instead I was grubby from my journey and befouled by fornication, weary in body and shattered in my spirit, struggling to compose myself and speak coherently.

When I raised my eyes from my low obeisance I noted how unwell the King looked. His face was grey and lined like an older man's and he held his hands rigidly clasped, perhaps for fear they would tremble if he released them. The large ruby at his throat and the varied gems on his fingers gleamed against his pasty flesh, taunting his weakness with their radiance, and a curl of hair over his ear looked damp with perspiration. Behind his gilded chair on one side stood the unmistakeable figure of Cardinal Beaufort, swathed in scarlet robes, peering down his hawk's nose as if I was some river flotsam washed up from Greenwich. On the other side the man in his forties had to be Suffolk, strongly built, a person of authority but with a surprisingly delicate mouth, hinting at some refinement. He regarded me with interest.

Lord Walter outlined what I had reported about both Mistress Jourdemayne and Lady Anne's only partially explained death. The Cardinal fixed gimlet eyes on me but did not acknowledge that any information on these subjects had already come his way. Suffolk, by contrast, pursed his lips and seemed to concentrate, before seeking the King's permission to question me. 'Doctor Somers,' he said, 'is it possible that the prediction about his Grace's health comes from the palace of Pleasance?'

'It is possible but I have no evidence, my lord Earl.' I had feared being tongue-tied and was relieved my voice obeyed me.

'If it were so, could it be that those at the Duke's palace might go beyond prophecy and seek to contrive what they predict?' The King shifted in his seat and Suffolk hastily spoke again. 'I do not for a moment cast aspersions on his Grace of Gloucester but a palace houses many followers, not all of whom may be as irreproachable in their loyalty as their principal.'

King Henry inclined his head. 'Our uncle of Gloucester is impeccable in his devotion to the crown.' I fancied he turned imperceptibly and addressed this comment to the cleric at his side. Then he indicated that I should speak.

'I know nothing of such things, your Grace.'

Suffolk was unperturbed by the interruption. 'Could you manage to find out, Doctor Somers? Is there any way you could infiltrate the inner sanctum of this fellow Bolingbroke's cronies?'

I must have rocked slightly on my uneven legs as I registered what was being asked of me. At the time when I felt most wretched and unworthy I was presented with the chance to serve my King, expose possible traitors, bring murderers to justice, seek revenge on the hated Bolingbroke and put myself in a position of the utmost peril. 'There is, my lord,' I said hesitantly. 'Roger Bolingbroke has attempted to draw me into his circle, on spurious grounds. I have rejected his suggestion but he has asked me to consider the matter further.'

The Earl smiled. 'You will now accept his offer?'

I was a lost soul and insanity loomed as I took a deep breath. 'I will, my lord'

The Cardinal folded his hands over his stomach and leaned towards King Henry. 'Your Grace, may I suggest, the physician submits his reports to me. I have well-tested routes for such messages to reach me.'

The slight figure rose from the throne. 'No, my good lord Cardinal, you are too well known for animosity towards our uncle. It will be safer to find another means of communication. Suffolk, we shall leave this in your hands.' The King came down the steps of the dais and we all bowed but he stopped and fixed me with a solemn, priestly glare. 'Serve us truly, Doctor Somers and you will find your reward.'

*****

It was late before the Earl had finished giving me instructions and I accepted the offer of a pallet for the night in his attendants' chamber. I intended to set out at first light to retrace my route to Danson and I sent a message to the stables to have my horse ready for an early departure. In my exhausted state I slept well but woke at dawn, full of guilt, and hurried to the quiet mews, where I was surprised to be hailed by a puffy-eyed groom who emerged from the tackle store and peered blearily at my black garb.

'Doctor Somers? There's a message. Your man'll be waiting for you at the Savoy Steps.

This was puzzling because, although Thomas Chope might have discovered where I was and described himself as my man, I did not understand why he would have chosen to meet me at the Savoy Steps. I knew of the renowned palace of the Savoy, which had been destroyed in Tyler's uprising some sixty years earlier, but since it was razed by the rebels its site had stood desolate and the steps down to the Thames were seldom used. The area had a reputation as a haunt of ne'er-do-wells and I was glad it was a clear day with no mist rolling in from the river. I recognised there could be some kind of trap but could not understand who had sufficient knowledge of my movements to contrive it. Intrigued, I trotted at a moderate pace until I needed to turn off the busy thoroughfare of the Strand to pick my way across ground thick with brambles and hidden pieces of masonry. Here and there hovels had been erected out of slats of wood and sacking and I did not like to think of the unfortunates who must live in such conditions. As I neared the bank of the Thames the undergrowth became so dense that I decided to dismount and lead my horse but I felt uncomfortable doing so it for I was then screened from view on the landward side. I was relieved to see a man crouching at the top of the steps but when I realised it was not Thomas I faltered until he called.

'Come over, Doctor Somers. I've something for you.'

Of the many incautious things I have done, heeding his words ranks high. When I approached he stood, revealing on his chest the blue and red of a crest I had seen recently, on the retainers of Cardinal Beaufort, and some time ago above the Wenham fireplace at Dunmow. At the time this seemed reassuring and I allowed him to lead me along the bank beyond the steps, as if to point out something to me across the river. Suddenly another ruffian sprang up from where he was concealed, under the overhang of the bank, seizing my feet and pulling me down, while, as I fell, the first man delivered a crushing blow to my belly and shackled my wrists behind me. My shout was cut off by the punch to my chin which had the desired effect of knocking me unconscious but the coldness of the water revived me as soon as I was flung into the river. This seemed no benefit at the time for I had never been a competent swimmer and with my hands tied at my back, flapping my feet wildly, I had no chance. I heard cries from the bank but as the tide swept me under for the second time I gave up hope, spinning helplessly downstream.

Chapter 23

When I came to myself I was being thumped on the back and as a spurt of murky water came from my mouth I heard cheers. I was sitting on a bed of shingle, held by a burly fellow I did not know, but the damp face that peered over my shoulder to ensure I was regaining my senses was that of Thomas Chope and, as soon as I had strength, I flung my arms round his sodden shoulders, spluttering thanks.

'I thought you'd ask why I took so long to get to you.' Thomas sounded husky.

'A life for a life,' I said. 'It's fair quittance.'

'No such luck. I'm bound to you until death. But you were daft to lay yourself open to attack in such a place.'

'How did you know? I don't understand.'

'When I came in search of you I was directed from Greenwich to Danson and I arrived there only a couple of hours after you'd left, so Sir Hugh sent me on to Westminster. They wouldn't let me past the outer ward at the palace but a groom told me you intended to set out at dawn so I asked him to let you know I'd be at the gate. He said you were much in demand because he had another message for you, which one of the Cardinal's attendants had left, and, being inquisitive, I asked what it was. When he told me you had a rendezvous at the Savoy Steps, I smelt trouble but wasn't sure what to do. I knew you'd want to find out what it was all about and, if I was seen to ride from Westminster alongside you, the meeting might have been aborted. I decided it would be best to get the Savoy and lie in wait, to see what happened and be ready to help if needed. I told the groom I'd meet you there anyway and not to bother giving you a second message.'

'That was cleverly contrived,' I said. Thomas's assistant wrapped some dry sacking round me and I thanked him as he helped me to my feet.

'Not clever enough.' Thomas kicked a stone in annoyance. 'Bernard here is a waterman and I got him to come with me. When we saw just one man waiting for you, we thought we could handle him with no problem, but we failed to notice the second lout below the bank. He must have crept along the edge of the water at low tide. The speed with which they bundled you into the river gave us no chance so I had to dive in after you.'

'What happened to the ruffians?'

'The one who dragged you down swam off quickly and got away. We've got the other though. Bernard's trussed him up nicely.'

I moved to the recumbent figure lying by a bush, with a gag in his mouth and feet and hands bound tight. His face was not familiar but something else drew my attention. In the fisticuffs which must have taken place, the man's jerkin had been torn and the Beaufort crest had come loose at one corner. I lifted it and pulled it free, staring at the different badge hidden beneath.

'We'll get him to the constable,' Bernard said.

Thomas understood the importance of what I had seen. 'Wait a minute, is he masquerading as a Beaufort servant? What's that crest?

'It's a tower,' I said reluctantly. 'I'd hazard a guess this wretch serves Gaston de la Tour.' My companions looked bemused. 'Give him a beating, Bernard, and then let him go. He can tell his master that his ruse failed but I have taken heed of his message.'

*****

We took refuge at an inn for an hour and Thomas acquired dry clothes for us both so we could complete our journey to Danson. On the way I gave him an abbreviated account of my activities at Westminster, although failing to satisfy him as to why Gaston de la Tour had sought to have me killed and why I had let the would-be assassin go free. I tried to divert him from that subject. 'You were looking for me, you said. Do you have news?'

He grinned sheepishly. 'Couldn't find out a thing about Dickon's murder. You were right there. The pedlar probably told Grizel a pack of lies. He's known to have a vivid imagination.'

'She'll be pleased you tried,' I said by way of consoling him.

He gave a half-smile and pulled on his reins. 'The main thing is, Sir Hugh asked me to tell you something. I'm sorry it's bad. They pulled a body out of the Thames down towards Gravesend. It was badly battered, with a broken neck, and had been in the water several days but it's almost certainly your apothecary friend.'

'Geoffrey. Sweet Mother of God,' I said and shivered despite the warmth of my dry jerkin, 'I nearly joined him in a watery tomb.' Then I fell silent for the rest of our ride.

*****

After spending one night at Danson I returned to Greenwich, with Thomas at my side, and I lost no time in sending a message to Roger Bolingbroke asking to see him. I could not conceal this request from Doctor Southwell, who dogged my steps, and he gave a small caper of delight. 'Have you come to your senses, Harry? I'd be so glad. There'll be rich pickings for us in the outcome.' I shook my head and said he must wait until I'd met Bolingbroke but he continued to make irritating, cryptic remarks until I was summoned, late in the evening when most folk were making for their beds.

For the first time I was shown into the clerk's inner chamber where a single candle on a high sconce threw flickering light onto the charts of the heavens, which covered the walls, and astronomical instruments glinted in the gloom. Bolingbroke's heavy-jowled face was in shadow but his voice was unmistakeably malicious.

'I think you would not have honoured me with a visit, on your own initiative, in order to reject my offer. Do I take it you have reflected and concluded you were hasty to deride my suggestion?'

'Perhaps. I may have been rash to judge so quickly.'

'Ah, there is rejoicing among the angels when a sinner repenteth.'

'I hardly think that quotation is appropriate.'

'You are not a sinner?'

I caught my breath, terrified that Bolingbroke was about to announce that he knew of my latest, unforgiveable transgression. The thought that Gaston de la Tour might be one of his informers turned my stomach. 'We are all sinners,' I said lamely.

'I do not choose to speak of sin. In a matter such as this we rise above the trivialities that common men define as reprehensible. You wish to join our enterprise?'

I risked taking the offensive. 'I would need to have confidence in my colleagues. You told me a lie when you said the Duchess was with child.'

'You put your finger unerringly on my blunder.' His tone succeeded in combining annoyance and sarcasm. 'Mistress Jourdemayne had assured me her potions were infallible. It proved not to be so. How did you come by such gossip?'

'The women of the palace are aware of such things.'

'The ineffable Dame Margery, no doubt. Well, I admit my error. I repeat my question.'

'I have more serious reasons to doubt your integrity. I believe you to have contrived the murder of Lady Anne Wenham.'

'That is the conclusion from your investigation?' His mouth curled into a confident smirk. 'I admit nothing and hazard the suggestion that you will never find proof of my culpability.'

'That I accept. Your hired assassin was conveniently done to death.'

'What a tenacious seeker after truth you are! The tiresome woman was an agent for the Beauforts. You should accept that her demise suited our Duke's interests.'

'Was that true of Geoffrey du Bois also?'

For the first time his composure was ruffled and he looked angry. 'I know nothing about the disappearance of that stubborn dolt of an apothecary. I had few dealings with him.'

'You mean you had no hold over him. I presume he declined your invitation to take part in your devious schemes.'

'That's as may be but he was of no significance. His family served the Beauforts.'

'But he had repudiated that service and was his own man.'

'Clearly his estimable independence incurred the wrath of someone else. I repeat I had nothing to do with his disappearance. I also repeat my question for the last time. Do you wish to join our enterprise?'

I was puzzled by Bolingbroke's denial of involvement in Geoffrey's abduction but recognised I could prevaricate no longer. 'I confess I am intrigued and attracted by a mystery.'

'This is not one for you to solve but to be part of. Our aims are ambitious. There is some danger.' He leaned forward and a gleam of light showed the perspiration on his brow.

'I have encountered danger more than once,' I said with perfect honesty.

'The penalty for failure in this case could be most severe.'

'My life has been in peril before.'

'You are quick to understand. You will join us?'

I stood and moved so that the fluttering beam of light fell on my discoloured cheek. 'They say I bear the devil's stain, so it may befit me to do the devil's work.'

He gave a contented sigh. 'How perceptive! But do not refer to our enterprise so dismissively. Victors create their own virtue and so shall we. We shall use our success wisely and that will justify our objective.'

'A convenient doctrine.'

'Stop bandying words, Doctor Somers, and give me a straight answer. Will you join us?'

'I will,' I said and I heard the long exhalation of his breath.

*****

'I want you away from Greenwich, Thomas,' I said. 'The chamberlain will arrange for you to go to Baynard's Castle until it's over. I may be able to send you a message when I find out exactly what's going on but it'll be better if you're seen to have nothing to do with it. I think it's some alchemy they plan to use. Bolingbroke dabbles in such pursuits and Doctor Southwell keeps burbling about rich pickings so I imagine they'll be trying to change base metal into gold.'

'But why do they want you involved and why warn you there's danger.'

'I suspect a plot to embroil me in their mischief – I don't trust Bolingbroke for a moment – but they may think there's some way I might help their devices. As for danger, there's always a risk when you invoke supernatural powers. I'm not comfortable about being involved with the dark arts but I gave my word to the King himself that I would find out what they were doing.'

We were walking by the riverside at the back of the palace and we paused as we saw two figures coming up the

252

steps from the vaulted storeroom beneath the kitchens. Thomas's face brightened at the sight of Grizel but the young person she held by the scruff of his neck looked anything but happy. Rendell had grown a good deal taller since I last saw him but he was snivelling and clutched one shoulder as if it pained him. We moved across to greet them.

'What's all this then?' I asked while Thomas drew Grizel away from her brother.

'Had a beating.' The lad sounded morose; as well he might, because I could now see blood seeping through the back of his shirt.

'Did you deserve it?'

'Don't think so. The under-cook's a bastard.'

Grizel turned towards us. 'Been thieving, he has. Took portions of bread and meat from the servants' table. Asking for a thrashing, that was.'

'Why did you do that, Rendell?'

He gave a rueful smile. 'Nobody ain't asked that before, Doctor Harry. It were for the beggars at the gate of the palace. Cook's ill so the under-cook's laying down the law and he's too mean to give the poor folk their usual rations. Only gave me dirty scraps to take them and I don't think that's right.'

'You sure that's why you took the food? Not because you were hungry?'

'Nah! I never ate a mouthful of it. I ain't a liar. Me back don't half hurt though.'

'Come with me, Rendell, and I'll put some balm on your cuts. Did the under-cook beat you himself?'

'Yeah. He's a cruel bugger. Get's pleasure from thumping us scullions but he ain't never done it so hard before. I've had enough of it here. I want to get away from Greenwich. I hate the kitchens.'

'Don't do anything foolish. If he's beaten you harder than he should have, I'll complain about it.'

'Nah, don't do that, doctor! Me life wouldn't be worth living if you did that.'

I nodded, remembering the torments of my own boyhood, largely at the hands of the lad who was now my friend and who, at that moment, was flirting outrageously with Rendell's sister. 'Be patient and I'll make enquiries about a different position for you.'

His eyes shone. 'Cor, would you really? I want to be a soldier but they won't take me yet.'

I led the aggrieved boy away, to treat his wounds, permitting Thomas to say his goodbyes to Grizel in private.

*****

Midsummer's day passed without any unusual events and I began to wonder whether Bolingbroke's plans had melted into thin air. Doctor Southwell was absent from Greenwich for days at a time, while the excitement he had shown about the secret enterprise had abated and he no longer plied me with questions. I was sufficiently lulled into complacency to wonder if it would be safe for my mother to return but I knew she had settled happily at Danson and might prefer to remain there.

I heard rumours from Westminster that the King had departed for Windsor in a panic about his health but it was normal for him to go to the country when the heat haze formed over the river, the smell of the palace middens became noxious and pestilence might infest the air. I found the Pleasance dull and lonely during those sweltering days. I missed Thomas and above all I missed and grieved for Geoffrey. John Home was agreeable company, from time to time, but he often seemed nervous and clenched his mouth shut if I mentioned Mistress Jourdemayne. Giovanni paid a fleeting visit to Greenwich before leaving again for Oxford and I spent one joyful evening in his company listening to his rapturous descriptions of the buildings, the culture and the intriguing women of Verona, Mantua and his own Ferrara. It was an attractive diversion from my preoccupations to imagine this Italian paradise which my friend conjured up delightfully from a safe distance.

So matters rested until the Duke left the palace to join the court and we were given to understand that he would travel on from Windsor to South Wales, where he had been made Chief Justice and was to hold assizes. I found his absence cheering for, if there was to be some attempt to invoke the black arts, I should not like to think of him being complicit with it. His interest in the astronomical tables was understandable but I hoped his intelligent curiosity about all kinds of learning would not lead him to pry unwisely into matters best left alone. Divination, to foretell the future, through horoscopes and astrology, was an absorbing science but the involvement of a woman said to be a witch hinted at the invocation of who knew what evil powers.

Three days after Gloucester's departure, I received the long-awaited summons to attend Bolingbroke's chambers at midnight and the hour specified was indication enough that this was to be the climax to the mystery. Doctor Southwell returned to the palace that afternoon and was immediately closeted with the clerk but, surprisingly, I met John Home hurrying to the jetty shortly after the message was brought to me. When I called out to him, anxious to know if he was to be present at the furtive ceremonies, he pushed past me rudely and never answered, instead leaping down into a boat and demanding that the ferryman cast off at once. I supposed he had some urgent errand to perform for Bolingbroke and would return before dark but I was shaken by the cold hostility in his face.

I was forbidden to speak to any other person about the forthcoming rendezvous but, after treating the boils on a page's buttocks, I could not settle to my studies and took myself to the chapel to pray silently that nothing vile was planned and that I might have the strength to confront what lay ahead. Only the knowledge that I had been commissioned by King Henry to find out what was afoot confirmed that it was legitimate for me ensnare myself with the clandestine and unpalatable but, if Bolingbroke discovered that I was pledged to report to the Earl of Suffolk, I gave little for my chances of survival. I had need of Heaven's grace to guide me.

*****

Only Bolingbroke and Doctor Southwell were present when I entered the clerk's quarters as the bell rang out at midnight. The inner chamber was better lit than it had been on my previous visit, with candles glowing from two double-branched candelabra set on the table as well as torches in the wall-sconces. The light illuminated a curtained gallery I had not noticed before, set high on the wall at the far end of the room, and it occurred to me that Mistress Jourdemayne might make a dramatic appearance from behind the drapes. Roger Bolingbroke gave me an ironic bow and my fellow physician twittered approvingly.

'You come well to time,' Southwell said. 'I'm glad you have not let us down, unlike another.'

Bolingbroke held up his hand to silence his companion. 'John Home has proved a feeble vessel. We should have been four to act as supporters to our esteemed enchantress but he has found some urgent business which keeps him from our observances. Never mind, he will count the cost.'

'You will make public the hold you have over him? You will proclaim him thief and scoundrel?' Southwell's eyes glittered with malevolence.

Bolingbroke glanced in my direction. 'The fool once pilfered from the poor-box when he was a deacon. He has been an obedient acolyte to me since that day – until now – but it seems he judges exposure to clerical justice less

256

daunting than participation in our merry japes. I am pleased you did not come to the same conclusion, Harry. Disclosure of your colourful exploits in the bedchamber would have been so very damaging to your unsullied reputation.'

My colleague ogled me with salacious interest but Bolingbroke rounded on him. 'You have no cause for prurience, Southwell, as you well know. Your wife and children preserve a decent anonymity, lodged close by your parish at St. Stephen's, Walbrook. It would ill become you to have their presence revealed.'

'Oh, Roger, I meant no harm, indeed I did not. Forgive me.' The silly, learned man flapped his arms uselessly while I tried not to gape at this revelation of his illicit family. Bolingbroke had made clear the scope of his authority over us both and neither Southwell nor I were in any doubt as to the message conveyed.

'We are quite clear, are we not?' Bolingbroke said in needless confirmation.

I noticed a slight movement of the curtain in the gallery and at once the Duchess's clerk clapped his hands. 'The hour has come,' he said. 'No more trifling. Prepare to welcome the wisest and most accomplished of women.'

I was still looking upward when the door from the antechamber opened and Mistress Jourdemayne glided silently into the room. She was dressed in a trailing, black gown, decorated with signs of the zodiac picked out in silver thread, and on her head she wore an ornate headdress of coiled brocade held by glistening crystal-headed pins. She looked from one to the other of us and scowled, setting down a bulky bag at her feet. 'Where is the fourth?'

When Bolingbroke explained John Home's absence she gathered up her skirt and turned to the door. 'I do not like it,' she said and pointed a long fingernail at me. 'I thought this one might shirk our rites, not Home. He left of his own free will, you say? He has not been abducted and put to the torture? Or has he proved false and betrayed us?'

'He fled in panic at what was required of him, nothing else.' Bolingbroke's voice was gentle, as I'd never heard it. 'I beg you to ignore his cowardice. He will pay the price. Dear mistress, all our design hangs on your willingness to continue. You alone can invoke the dark powers to achieve our purpose.'

For an instant his eyes flicked up to the gallery and, as I followed them, again the curtain twitched and, with foreboding, I understood. There would be a door at the back of the gallery and, at that level, it must lead directly into the Duchess's apartments. If someone was concealed there to overhear and join in the stealthy ritual, it could only be Eleanor of Gloucester herself. I turned back to watch Mistress Jourdemayne lift her bag and extract a number of articles, purring over them as if they were treasured heirlooms. Some I recognised as bones, probably from a chicken, and there were phials of soot and leaves of cinquefoil; others I preferred not to think about. She shredded various herbs which I suspected were those witches were said to use in order to procure visions – aconite, belladonna and water hemlock – and she sprinkled them over the other ingredients in a basin. I clutched my gown around me to prevent me shivering as she pounded them, while she muttered inaudible incantations and added liquid to the foul mixture. A pungent aroma filled the room and she gave a delighted chuckle. 'It goes well,' she said. 'Put your hands to the bowl and feel the vibrations of the blending. See how the bubbles rise.'

I had no choice but to join the others in placing my outstretched fingers over the seething ingredients while she continued chanting. Bolingbroke appeared entirely serene and unperturbed but Southwell's eagerness was so great that his hands dived towards the contents and the woman grabbed his wrists to restrain him. 'Not you,' she said. 'You are not marked by the devil to share his supper.'

258

Suddenly she swooped to seize my fingers and plunged them into the basin so they were coated with its contents. Despite my resistance, she exerted surprising strength, forcing my hands upwards to daub my birthmark with the glutinous, stinking substance and thrusting the oozing residue onto my clamped lips. 'You are chosen to bring success. We are favoured to have the devil's spawn with us,' she said. 'Drink in his excretions, physician. All will go well'.

I was sorely tempted to flee from the room in outrage and horror but some mad obstinacy, and my pledged duty to the King, compelled me to remain. To my relief the woman turned away from me and I was able to wipe my mouth on my sleeve, shuddering as I noted the discoloured stains on my gown where the mixture had dribbled down from my cheeks. Mistress Jourdemayne had returned to the table and she blew out the candles in the candelabra. At her signal Bolingbroke raised a long-handled snuffer to extinguish the torches, leaving a single taper to provide the only light for the rest of the ceremony. I had never given much credence to tales of witches communing with the devil but in the smoky, noxious atmosphere I was ready to credit this fearsome woman with unnatural skills. I shrank back into the shadows, scarcely daring to pray, even silently, for God's blessed forgiveness, because I feared her power to read my mind.

She delved into her bag and took out a small box which she stroked reverently before pouring some of her evil potion over it, rubbing the viscous concoction into the wood with circular movements. A new resinous fragrance wafted across the room and her murmuring grew louder until, with a shriek, she lifted the lid and removed a limp object which she set on Bolingbroke's reading stand. She began to gabble incomprehensible charms, her voice growing shrill, and she waved her arms wildly, dancing widdershins round her makeshift altar. By now I was convinced she was possessed by demons but worse was to come. When her fervour increased to fever-pitch, she ripped pins from her headdress, freeing her long grey hair to flop over her shoulders like slimy eels, and she snatched up the soft thing she had laid in front of her, prodding it with the pin-points, screeching with glee. Only then, cursing my slow comprehension, did I understand what her purpose was and I rushed forward to seize the anonymous doll from her hand. Studded with pins in heart and head and genitals, its body sagged and its pale woollen face stared up at me, its tiny tin crown drooping over its brow.

'He is doomed! He is doomed! Henry Plantagenet is smitten.' Mistress Jourdemayne screamed in triumph and sank on the ground as Bolingbroke strode forward with a shining face.

'Thus let him die,' he said in sepulchral tones, 'and we shall rejoice. Thus shall our glorious Gloucester mount the throne.'

Somewhere in the far corner of the room Doctor Southwell whispered 'Amen.'

'She has put a curse upon King Henry,' I gasped. 'We are complicit in treason...' but I never completed my sentence as the outer door flew back, thudding against the wall.

'You say truly, traitor!'

The sergeant at arms beckoned his men and a dozen soldiers, in Beaufort livery, ran into the room, brandishing drawn swords. He snatched the miserable manikin from my hand and landed a blow on my jaw, that span me hurtling against the wall. Traitorous conspirators deserved no mercy and we were fiercely beaten before they dragged us down the stairs. Stunned in mind and body, I was scarcely conscious as they flung me repeatedly against the newel while we descended but I heard the commotion at the outer door as someone tried to break free. I did not think at first that the yelp of terror could have come from Bolingbroke but, as my

260

captor pushed me into the courtyard, I saw the Duchess's clerk cringing beside a mounting block, clutching a bleeding arm and gibbering about his innocence. I registered with bleak relief that there was no sign of Eleanor of Gloucester.

The barges were waiting to take us to the Tower and it was evident the trap had been carefully sprung – though not through me. My remit had been to inform Suffolk if I found evidence of treachery at the Pleasance and I had made no report yet. It could only be that the Cardinal had settled on direct action to capture the plotters red-handed by infiltrating his own men into the palace. Although he had been witness to the royal assignment I was given, he might have concluded I would prove unreliable or perhaps he resented the royal favour shown to Suffolk. Some other agent must have supplied the information he needed to lay his plans and I thought regretfully of John Home, fleeing Greenwich in panic. Despite the fuzziness of my mind I realised that, in these circumstances, my own safety was not assured but I resolved to be passive and wait, until I was brought before men of authority, before explaining my presence and my role as King Henry's informer. I did not conceive what a thankless task that would prove to be.

Chapter 24

I was lodged at first in this dark cell with Doctor Southwell and I watched in frustration as he was taken away half a dozen times for questioning, while I was simply told my turn would come. I begged him to tell his interrogators that I wished to make a statement but I doubt that he did so, for he had become a crazed wreck and probably thought I intended to testify against him. We were denied visitors and I saw no one but our warders who laughed in my face when I asked to see the Constable of the Tower or his deputy. The only snippets of information they allowed us were calculated to add to our distress.

I gathered Duchess Eleanor had not been arrested when we were taken and I imagine there was no evidence she had been present in the gallery during the demonic rites. Wisely, she attempted to proceed with her normal activities, as if she was not affected by the turmoil in her household, and next evening she kept an engagement with City dignitaries, dining in high style at the King's Head in Cheapside. It was while she sat at table, I was told, that she received warning a warrant had been issued for her detention and she fled directly to sanctuary at Westminster. Our gaolers delighted in giving us a commentary on subsequent events.

'You're all done for now, mate,' the short, chatty man told us with relish. 'That Bolingbroke's been before the King's Council and confessed everything. On Sunday he's to be taken to St. Paul's Churchyard to make public repudiation of the Black Arts. All his magic instruments are to be smashed in front of him.'

'Will he be set free after that?' Southwell was quaking with renewed hope.

'Not bloody likely! He may think it'll do him good but we know better. He'll be strung up with the rest of you, don't worry.'

'Not a comrade I'd care to have.' The taller, lugubrious warder put his thumbs in his belt with a smug expression. 'He told the Council he'd been instructed by Eleanor Cobham to use his "powers of divination to discover what estate in life" she would achieve. Used those very words, he did. All done at the decree of the whore Duchess, he said. Seems she'd set her heart on wearing the crown and your little enterprise was to hasten her on her way by doing for King Henry, before he had a chance to wed and get an heir of his body.'

'Indeed, the Duchess of Gloucester is our mistress and we are bound to serve her. She is a formidable lady and commands our obedience. We are not free agents.' Southwell had quickly latched on to Bolingbroke's ungallant excuse and I despised their cowardice.

'Is she still in sanctuary?' I asked.

'Sanctuary's no protection for crimes of heresy and witchcraft, mate. She's cited to appear before the two Archbishops and the Cardinal, with soldiers sent to fetch her – by force if necessary.' The short man licked his lips. 'That's a mission I'd not mind. If she struggled it might be that her stomacher got torn apart and her comely breasts shown to all and sundry.'

'We've said enough.' His companion intervened and drew him to the door. 'Doctor Southwell, you're to appear before the Council in three days' time. Best prepare yourself, physician.'

Those three days were filled with my colleague's terrors, waking or sleeping, and by the time he was dragged from our cell he was so demented that I doubted he knew where or who he was. I had no potions to offer and could only speak mildly to calm him but it was useless. I prayed that he might not disgrace his honourable calling or lose his self-respect entirely and I thought his secret family, undoubtedly left in ignorance of his whereabouts and

263

condition. When he had not returned next day I asked the short gaoler what had happened to him.

'Had a seizure, they say. After his grilling by their lordships he foamed at the mouth and screamed for an hour. He's been put somewhere else. You've got this desirable accommodation all to yourself, mate.'

'Don't they want to see me yet?'

'Seems not. We've had no orders to take you for questioning. All we know about you is that no one's allowed to visit. Absolutely barred.'

I found that desolate prohibition strangely comforting because it had worried me that Thomas Chope had made no contact. Now I could imagine him fretting impotently at the gates of the Tower, trying to wheedle his way past the guards and cursing them roundly, and I felt sorry on his account that he could do nothing to help. I felt sorrier for myself as the prospects for my release were looking increasingly bleak. Surely Suffolk must know of my arrest and appreciate why I had been present in Bolingbroke's chamber? If he chose to disregard my plight it could only be because his interests were best served now by abandoning me. I had heard of nameless, forgotten prisoners languishing in the Tower until they died, if it suited the convenience of powerful men. I reflected that it was always dangerous to mix with matters of state for the honour of great nobles was different from that of humbler folk.

*****

With the blunt knife they gave me for my food, I scratched a faint record on the wall to show the passing of the days and I knew from this that nearly three months had passed since my incarceration. I could hear the autumnal winds howling round the Tower and occasionally I caught sight of a swirling leaf borne on an up-draught outside the high slit, through which a chill breeze found its way into my bones. Often the sky was dark, even at midday, while rain battered the stone lintel and seeped through the narrow opening. I begged to be given books and received a torn manuscript of devotions which I read and re-read, whenever there was sufficient light, until I knew every prayer by heart. At other times I recited to myself the uses of herbs, the humours of the body, the properties of the astronomical signs and as much of the ancient learning as I could call to mind. I was resolved to keep my physician's knowledge fresh, in case it could be put to use again, and above all to occupy my thoughts with constructive matters, lest they be possessed by despair and shredded into madness. I did not always succeed and then I sobbed at the futility of my wasted life. I wondered if Bess knew of my imprisonment and if she cared. I tried to persuade myself it was better she had already seen how gross a reprobate I was, so she would not grieve for me, but that idea was too painful to contemplate. I fretted for my poor mother and the humiliation she would feel if I was declared a traitor and I could not bear to think of her desolation.

One dark and depressing morning, not long after I had been given my meagre bowl of gruel, I heard again the clanking of the warder's keys as he approached the door of the cell. This was unusual for I was normally left undisturbed after I had broken my fast until the next meal was delivered and my slop bucket emptied. I did not dare to hope I was at last being summoned to appear before a tribunal but I raised my head as the bolt was drawn back and then I began to shake in speechless disbelief.

'Doctor Somers, this is abominable!'

'Good God, Harry, you're thin as a pike-staff.'

Sir Hugh de Grey and Thomas Chope were quickly at my side as I rose from my stool. 'I'm given enough to nourish life,' I said with absurd formality but, as Thomas flung his arms round me, I responded to the forgotten warmth of friendly contact. 'How did you get here? I was told no one could come to see me.'

'Too flipping right,' Thomas said. 'I tried for weeks to get in, offered all I'd got, but the guards refused. Seems you were worth more than I could pay. I should have gone to Danson earlier but I didn't think of it at first. Good job I did, though, because Sir Hugh was able to use influence. Even so we were kept waiting nearly a month before they'd take his money.'

'I wish I'd known the condition you were in,' the knight said. 'I don't understand what's going on. They won't tell us anything about your conviction.'

'I've not been convicted, I replied. 'I've not been taken before judges, or made my defence or allowed an opportunity to contact anyone.'

'That's unlawful!'

'I don't understand. The others have been brought to trial.'

They spoke simultaneously but I responded to what Sir Hugh had said. 'I've heard nothing. Tell me what has happened. Has anyone been sentenced?'

Thomas levered me gently onto the stool and knelt beside me. 'Bolingbroke is found the principal instigator of treason and heresy and is to be hung and gutted as a warning to others. The witch is to be burned. Doctor Southwell was to have been executed, as accessory, but we've heard from the gaoler that he suffered a seizure on hearing his doom and died in his prison cell. John Home is...'

'John Home! He wasn't present.'

'He was held culpable for knowledge of the plot and keeping it close until the last minute.' Sir Hugh had extracted a flask from inside his tunic and he held it out to me so I drank gratefully the finest wine I had ever tasted while he continued his explanation. 'Nonetheless he is pardoned and sent to Hereford, required to perform his duties as Canon more assiduously than he has done previously.'

As the wine warmed my belly my wits grew sharper. 'Home! As I thought. It was Home betrayed them! That's why he was rushing from the palace that day. He was another in Beaufort's service. The scheming wretch! He duped Bolingbroke into thinking he was his minion but all the time he must have been feeding information to the Cardinal. That's why he's been pardoned. I thought it had been Geoffrey who was Beaufort's spy. Poor Geoffrey! I decided he must have lied to me when he said he had rejected the Cardinal's service. Perhaps he found out what Home was doing and that's why he was killed – by Beaufort's ruffians, not Bolingbroke's.' I took another sip from the flask while Thomas unrolled a pack of bread and meat. 'I heard the Duchess was in sanctuary,' I said before biting into what I saw as delectable food.

'They took her from the abbey by force and arraigned her before the judges.' Sir Hugh spoke quietly and with maturity. 'She tried to escape downriver but was thwarted. Then they kept her confined until she appeared once more before the Archbishops. She denied all the charges put to her, except having recourse to the Black Arts, but she claimed she used the witch merely to procure potions to retain Gloucester's affections and help her conceive his child. She denied absolutely that she had treasonably encompassed the death of King Henry. Nevertheless the verdict of "guilty" was returned.'

'Dear God!' The savoury salt beef tasted sour in my mouth. 'Could the Duke do nothing to save her?'

'The Cardinal's position is unassailable. He secured an edict from the King forbidding interference in the proceedings against the Duchess. That was clearly aimed at Gloucester and the Duke's own position is gravely weakened by the accusations against his wife. She is not yet sentenced but she has submitted herself to the correction of the bishops and abjured her heresies and witchcraft. She is to appear next week to learn her fate.'

'Will they dare to execute her?'

'There are few precedents for arraigning a Duchess on such charges but Queen Joan, the widow of King Henry's grandfather, was kept close confined for the rest of her life after she dabbled in unlawful pursuits.'

'I don't understand why you are here at all.' Thomas's anger flared. 'You were only in Bolingbroke's room to find out what the others were doing. You told me the King sanctioned your involvement.'

'So he did, in front of the Cardinal and the Earl of Suffolk. But when I was taken prisoner I was holding his figure in my hand, a crowned doll studded with sorcerer's pins to bring about his death. King Henry may not even know I was arrested and I fancy the Cardinal has his own objectives to pursue.'

'It's not only that,' Sir Hugh said. 'You are also charged with bringing Mistress Jourdemayne to Greenwich so she could practice her pernicious evil.'

I remembered the innocuous message I had carried to the ostler at the Joyous Regard on Cheapside and understood how cleverly Bolingbroke had trapped me. 'I had hoped Suffolk would intervene, still more that Lord Fitzvaughan would help.' My voice cracked as I mentioned Lady Maud's husband for, in my solitary musings, I had concluded that he had abandoned me for dishonouring his marriage bed.

'Lord Fitzvaughan is in France,' Sir Hugh said, 'with his wife and his followers. The King dispatched him on another mission to the French court about the time of your arrest. I have sent a messenger to inform him of your plight but I've heard nothing in reply. It may be difficult for him to interrupt his embassy but I had hoped he would send word to vouch for you. I will write again. I have tried to gain the

Earl of Suffolk's ear but my rank is not exalted enough for him to heed me.'

'Christ, these bloody nobles are cautious about soiling their hands when they might lose out by it!' Thomas stamped across the cell. 'I won't give up, Harry. You stood by me when I faced an unjust penalty. You find out who your friends are when that happens. The chamberlain and Dame Margery are staunch on your behalf and Doctor Giovanni sends his regards. He bids you fill your mind with dreams of Italy – I imagine that's some private jest.'

Despite all I had heard, I smiled and nodded. 'One I understand well. I'm afraid I've been caught in a web of intrigue beyond my imagining. I was naïve.' I could hear footsteps outside the door and grabbed Thomas's arm. 'Is my mother distraught?'

Sir Hugh answered quickly. 'She knows nothing except that you are sent away on some mission. She thinks it a matter for pride. Lady Blanche will ensure she remains of that mind.'

I gave heartfelt thanks but the warders were at the door and I knew my visitors were about to be hustled out of the cell. 'Give my regards to all my friends and pay my affectionate respects to Grizel.'

'Respects, yes; affection, no,' Thomas said with a wink. 'She's pleased to accept my affection, no one else's. But I might make an exception, given your predicament.'

Sir Hugh de Grey took my hand. 'I shall continue my efforts, I assure you. Don't give up hope, Doctor Somers, don't ever give up hope.'

After they had left I held misery at bay with one joyful thought. Bess must be in France with the Fitzvaughans. She already knew me for a base, unfaithful wretch who was unworthy of her. By the time she returned, the possibility that I might cause her more unhappiness would have been removed forever. The thought was forlornly comforting.

269

Ten days after I had received my only visitors, the two gaolers entered the cell together and I could tell from their gleeful appearance that they had something to tell me I would not relish. I had asked them repeatedly what sentence had been passed on the Duchess but they shrugged off my question, denying any knowledge of such a lofty matter. Now, it seemed, something had changed.

'We're to give you news, Doctor Somers, just like you want,' the taller man said and he pulled me to my feet. 'Your mate, Bolingbroke's to be strung up in the morning and the Witch of Eye will burn soon after. He'll have his belly ripped open and his guts taken out while he still breathes and she'll shrivel in the fire as the devils escape from every opening in her body. As for Eleanor Cobham, she's done her first round of penance, like the foul slut she is.'

I resisted the instinct to protest at their vile words and concentrated on what was new to me. 'She's doing penance?'

'Three times she's to walk bareheaded through the City, carrying a taper, with the Mayor and all the sheriffs in attendance and the officers of the guilds following behind. This lucky bastard got to see her yesterday. Go on, mate, tell him how she looked.'

He pushed his colleague forward and the shorter man moistened his lips. They brought her by barge to Temple Steps,' he said. 'Then she walked by way of Temple Bar to St. Paul's where she offered her taper at the High Altar. Bloody great heavy thing it was but she carried it with a meek expression and never stumbled under the weight. I saw her go by on Ludgate Hill. A fine procession it was and she's still a lusty woman, worth any man's tumble in the hay.'

The other gaoler caught my wrist as I raised my fist. 'Steady now, Doctor Somers. We're only telling you what's what. Your turn's coming. You're to face the judges in two days' time. It's what you've asked for enough times. Before that you'll be able to hear all the excitement when Bolingbroke's done to death and the crone screams at the stake. Then you're to get a special treat, God knows why.' He clenched his mouth as if that was all he had to say.

'What do you mean?'

The other man chuckled. 'You're to be taken to see the whore do penance the second time, as she comes up Swan Steps. She's to walk by Gracechurch Street and Leadenhall to Christchurch at Aldgate, carrying her taper just like I saw. You'll be in chains so you can't run off but you'll see her large as life and twice as miserable. How are the mighty fallen, eh? Don't do to tangle with them in their glory, I always say. Never know when they'll drag you down in their disgrace. Then you're to be taken on to Westminster, to appear before the justices and hear the sentence they've in store for you.'

I could not disagree with the man's conclusion on the folly of tangling with great nobles. I saw myself as their helpless pawn. I had served their turn and was dispensable.

*****

During the hours which have passed since the gaolers came, listening to the sounds of Bolingbroke's pathetic end, I have attempted to fill my mind with coherent reflections but I've barely succeeded in holding terror at bay. His screams curdled my guts with their dreadful desperation and I shall hear them in nightmares throughout the time remaining to me. He was an evil man but it gives me no pleasure to know he died a despicable coward.

The ruin of my life is not wholly my fault but my most miserable transgression is mine alone and all the worse for being towards one I could have loved with true and pure devotion. For that perhaps I am deserving of my fate. I cannot explain why I am to be privileged to see the

271

Duchess in her shame and fear the prospect but there is relief in knowing my trial is imminent. I have no doubt whatever of the outcome.

Part III –November 1441

Chapter 25

Judged by the streaks of lighter grey, which dappled the glowering clouds in the east, it was early morning when my gaolers led me from the cell. Over the Thames plumes of thin mist curled and dissolved and the water fowl were silent, motionless in their night-time resting places, but I had no opportunity to study the coming dawn. The men who took charge of me at the river gate wore Beaufort livery and they handled me roughly, kicking my weaker leg so that I staggered and beating me with a cudgel when I stumbled. I offered no resistance but that seemed to annoy them and, under the archway at the top of the steps down to the small boat, after they had manacled my hands and feet, they set about me with vicious efficiency, battering my face and body with their blows.

'Devil's filthy scum,' they howled, bludgeoning my birthmark as if they could beat it from my skin. 'Was your mother a witch like the hell-hag we burned at the stake? Did you lie with the sorceress, you foul monster? Have you bred more demons from her belly? Let's squeeze out your juices so you'll get no more misshapen brats.'

I screamed with pain as they twisted my genitals while chuckling lewdly. When one man lowered his hose I feared I would be raped but the arrival of an officer of the royal guard halted their antics and, at his order, they flung me into the stern of the vessel where I was content to lie in a crumpled heap, trying to steady my breathing and resist the impulse to vomit. I had no mantle and my threadbare gown, worn throughout my imprisonment, was insufficient to prevent the paroxysm of shivering which seized me. I knew these were no random hardships I suffered; they were contrived to ensure I would appear as a miserable wretch before my judges, not a dedicated physician but a broken, heretical traitor.

I felt the movement as the boat swung away from the Tower and the rowers pulled against slack water for the short distance to Swan Steps. I wished the journey was longer so that the throbbing of my bruises might recede but I was dragged ashore and made to stand, propped by a wall, while we waited for the Duchess's barge to bring her downstream to Upper Thames Street. Along the road crowds had gathered to gawp and some sought immediate entertainment by hurling mouldy apples and rotting cabbages at my head until they were chased off by soldiers. Twice I slumped and nearly fell to the ground but the royal guardsmen lining the roadway were more considerate than the oafs at the Tower and one gave me a swig of rough but invigorating ale from his flask. I smiled my thanks with swollen lips and managed to lift my fettered wrists to dab a sleeve against the gore congealing on my chin.

I explored inside my mouth with a sore tongue and felt foolish relief that all my teeth were firmly set in their gums despite the mouthful of blood I spat on the ground from my bitten tongue. 'Guards out in force,' I said experimentally to the considerate soldier and was surprised I could speak clearly.

'Scared shitless they are that Gloucester'll mount an attack to rescue his wife. Small chance, I'd say, with a troop of armed men surrounding her every step.'

'What'll happen to the Duchess after her penance?'

'I've heard she's to be locked away for the rest of her life. She's been kept at Leeds Castle down in Kent and that's where she'll go again, at least to start with – if I know anything they'll move her around for fear she enchants her warders.'

So they dared not have her killed, I thought. Even the Cardinal was not powerful enough for that but he would be satisfied to damage Duke Humphrey by his wife's guilty association with heresy and treason. Whether it was Eleanor's pride and ambition which had brought this about, or simply her unthinking curiosity about the Black Arts, there was no doubt her credulity had been exploited by her husband's enemies and his influence at court would be shattered. How many others, like me, had become caught up in this deadly rivalry between the King's counsellors: months ago Lady Anne Wenham had died, a pawn in their lethal game; now I would.

My reveries were interrupted by movement on the steps and I glimpsed the gilded barge as it slipped towards the mooring place. Rows of bowmen stood on deck, behind the rowers, as the oars rose and fell with elegant symmetry, and soldiers with drawn swords jumped ashore to line the steps as their prisoner was brought from under her canopied seat. Her face was thinner than I remembered but as she came close I could see she was still beautiful and, in her plain shift, she moved with natural grace, forever the finest and fairest lady of the nobility. The Lord Mayor, in his furred robe and chain of office, stepped forward and, on bended knee, presented her with the great candle she was to carry, which she took from him as if it was a trivial matter to bear its weight. With dignity she acknowledged the perfunctory bows of the members of the Corporation and the representatives of the guilds, as if she was robed in cloth of gold rather than unadorned linen, with a kerchief, not a flowing headdress, covering her loose hair. She walked forward slowly, between the ranks of jeering onlookers, and then, seeing me, she stopped.

'Doctor Somers?' she said uncertainly and, weighted with emotion, I was unable to reply. 'May God have mercy on you as you come to trial.'

Suddenly there were sounds of a disturbance on the roadway ahead and the soldiers sprang to surround her, blocking her from my view. Then, as quickly as it had started, the shouting subsided and, at a signal from their

275

officer, the posse advanced again, with the Duchess in their midst. All eyes turned to follow her progress along the thoroughfare and, like other bystanders, I turned my head to watch the receding phalanx as it reached the corner of the street. I scarcely heard the scuffle behind me on the steps, unaware that anything was amiss until I was dragged from the wall and a gag bound tightly round my mouth. In a fleeting glance I saw the Duchess's barge had pulled off from the shore and a smaller boat was waiting, the one I had been brought in I assumed, but a sack was thrust over my head and I could see no more as I was bundled on board. The sack was large enough to cover me entirely, when I was forced to bend my knees, and it was tied fast below my feet, no doubt creating an anonymous if knobbly appearance.

As the rowers dipped their oars I realised the tide had now turned and we were moving smoothly upstream with the incoming current: not only that, but the rapidity and motion were quite different from the cumbersome boat that fetched me from the Tower. This was a fast skiff racing away from Swan Steps and, I gathered from the angry shouts at our back, incurring the disapproval of my erstwhile guards. A swish and splash alerted me to the force of that disapproval but these sounds were greeted with mockery by my captors, who urged the oarsmen to pull harder and cheered as succeeding arrows sploshed into the water at greater distance from us. A muffled voice that sounded vaguely familiar told me to keep down and not to worry about pursuit as no other boat on the river had our turn of speed. Nonetheless I had no idea whether I had been abducted by friends or foes – and friends seemed hardly likely as I was trussed so securely in the sack. If foes were intent on removing me from lawful process at my trial it could only be that they planned a less official form of execution, so the indications were not promising, but some stubborn recollection of that time when once before I had been shrouded in a sack filled me with a ridiculous sense of hope.

I tried to judge how far we had travelled, noting when the rowers turned to follow each curve of the bank, and listening to dim noises on the land. We reached a quieter stretch of river and it occurred to me that we might be near the Savoy Steps, where I had so nearly found a watery grave, but at that thought my hopefulness dissolved in fear that my demise in the embrace of the Thames had only been deferred.

We continued to glide upstream until, unmistakeably, we pulled towards the western shore and I wondered if I had become disorientated for, by my estimation, we were nearing the Palace of Westminster, the very place where I was due to stand trial. It seemed unlikely that this charade had been staged merely to frighten me but I could think of no reason why I had been brought in this strange manner to where I was expected. The boat was made fast quietly, without the usual shouts of the watermen, but I heard the grinding of the rope against the edge of the stone jetty, followed by the thud of boots landing beside me.

'What've you got there?' The question came from the shore.

'Sack of turnips, mate. For the kitchens.' I was heaved over someone's shoulder and we moved forward. 'Don't wriggle and try not to breathe too much, said Thomas Chope quietly. 'You're with friends.'

*****

My masquerade as a shipment of vegetables took some time while I was manhandled by a sturdy porter and carried down steps and ramps into the bowels of the palace. At last I was set down, none too gently, on a rough cobbled floor, and I heard a bolt snapped into place as my carrier departed without releasing me from the sack, let alone freeing the shackles which chafed my wrists and ankles. My short-lived optimism evaporated and alarm replaced it, for I began to fear my mind was playing tricks and I had imagined Thomas's voice. I dared not call out in case friends had indeed contrived an elaborate rescue, which required me to be hidden until the right moment, but I dreaded being left to starve in my gloomy container by foes intent on my permanent disposal. I was constrained to lie in a crouched position with little room to move, which intensified the pain of my bruises and added the agony of cramp to my discomfort. My ordeal seemed endless.

When at last the bolt was drawn back the grating noise roused me from exhausted drowsiness and I was scarcely in my full senses when the sacking was ripped apart and Thomas, kneeling at my side, offered me wine. He poured from a jug and held a goblet for me to drink while I looked round and realised I was in a windowless storeroom, probably underground. 'Don't try to speak yet,' he said. 'First the blacksmith will saw off your fetters and then the barber will give you a good shave. You've got to show a fair smooth cheek for the next part of your escape.'

Bewildered but intensely relieved, I yielded to their ministrations although I was puzzled by the emphasis on shaving. Even though I recognised that my untidy growth of beard was unsightly, its removal hardly seemed the highest priority, but later, as comprehension dawned, I allowed them to replace my shabby gown and tattered jerkin with a serving maid's kirtle and hooded cloak. 'Can you walk, sweet mistress?' Thomas asked after my transformation. 'We've stairs to climb and several lengths of corridor to cross. Cling to my arm and keep your eyes lowered as a modest maiden should. Try and stoop a bit so you don't look so tall.'

'This is Westminster? Am I not to go on trial here?'

'It's the place Beaufort would least think of looking for you. Clever, isn't it? The Earl of Suffolk arranged it but you're going to Lord Fitzvaughan's rooms for a day or two until they can get you away safely.'

I looked up sharply at his words and Thomas wagged his finger at me. 'I told you not to raise your eyes. Your chin may not be stubbly but it's pretty rough. Besides your lip is split and your right eyelid half-closed by swelling. Remember you're walking on my arm and I don't want a reputation as a wife-beater.'

With remarkable luck we made our way without incident to Lord Fitzvaughan's quarters where I was provided with clean water in which to wash and food to revive me. By then I knew that it was after nightfall and Thomas pointed out the pallet where I was to rest until morning He explained that I must continue to wear woman's clothes for the duration of my stay and I would remain out of sight in the same small room until it was time to depart. 'I'll see you again, Harry,' he promised as he left but I sensed something doleful in his words and I wondered where I might be taken and what was to become of me. My clandestine rescue gave little hope of living freely and practising openly as a physician again.

When I awoke the winter sun was threading a beam of light through the narrow window above my bed and it picked out the colours of the tapestry on the opposite wall. I recognised the wheel of fortune with princes and nobles attempting to cling to the spokes of the revolving disc, grinning with pleasure as they rose and grimacing with fear as they descended towards those who lay crushed beneath its weight. It seemed entirely apposite as a moral tale, given my volatile fortunes, but I almost wept with joy to see this symbol of cultured life after so many weeks of bare walls and spiritual deprivation. Remembering my condition, I smoothed my skirts and drew a wrap, which I found on a stool, across my too broad shoulders. I bathed my face and peered into a small hand-mirror to see the damage to my features, which were grossly unattractive but would heal, and the thought came to me that this mirror, even these clothes, might belong to Bess Barber. I stifled the sob which came to my throat as door opened.

'Not a pleasing sight.' Lord Walter Fitzvaughan lolled against the lintel, appraising me. 'Gaston advises me to have you flogged but there seems no need. Others have made a fairly good job of disfiguring you.'

'My lord!' The implication behind his words conflicted with his affable tone and I was tongue-tied in confusion. 'My lord, how can I thank...?'

'Gaston further suggests you should be castrated after the flogging.'

I was in no state to bandy words. 'Gaston has already tried to have me drowned.'

'Ah, you identified the culprit! I forgot your skill at divining guilt. I did not approve his action and sent him away for a while after your ducking. He did not accompany us to France but now I have forgiven his peccadillo and he has re-joined my household. I missed his lusty presence, as you no doubt missed my wife's.' Lord Walter strolled languidly to my side and struck me across the face. 'You have dishonoured me, physician, and I have every right to claim your life.'

I attempted not to show how much his blow aggravated the soreness of my wounds but the split in my lip reopened and I bowed my head. 'So I am to be spared trial by the Cardinal's men but must pay my forfeit to you?'

'That sounds reasonable, does it not?' He picked up a chicken leg from the plate which contained the remains of my supper and delicately stripped a piece of flesh from the bone. He dangled the sliver of meat in front of me. 'You did not finish your meal. These are leavings to which you are entitled. But my beloved wife is not, however she may represent herself. I am well aware that she is a whore but I will not have my chambers at court turned into a bawdy house. Do I make myself clear?' Without waiting for my answer he span on his heel and laughed. 'Fortunately for you, Doctor Somers, I am not a vindictive man and I accept entirely that the slut seduced you. Since our return to England she is banished to my lands in Norfolk for the winter and I trust will benefit from the chastening of her exile. Meanwhile it is necessary to provide for your future – as the Earl of Suffolk has decreed.'

My mouth was dry and I put out my hand to lean on the table as I staggered with relief, not just at my reprieve but because Bess would be with her mistress, far removed from my disgrace and ignominy.

'Sit,' he said, 'and listen carefully. For your own safety it is not possible for you to remain in this country. You are the last remaining recreant from the farce at Greenwich and you have uncovered the full story of the Cardinal's machinations. He understands well enough why you were a witness to the sorcery but he cannot countenance your release and he seeks your death. If you were to expose the truth about the spies Beaufort employed at Greenwich, Gloucester would use it to restore his position with the King and that the Cardinal will not allow. There is one chance for you to escape with your life. You must live unobtrusively across the Narrow Sea until the situation changes. There are many English merchants in Flanders and I don't doubt you'll be welcome to practice your craft among them.'

I had never contemplated exile but Fitzvaughan's logic was impeccable and, despite the hollowness in my stomach, I nodded.

He put his hand on my shoulder. 'I must say you are fortunate in your friends, Doctor Somers. Sir Hugh de Grey has procured you passage on a ship leaving for Sluys shortly and your man, Chope, has contrived a means to bring you to it secretly. Even dear Gaston has a part to play in the next instalment, to demonstrate that bygones are to be bygones. I will be leaving Westminster today and have King Henry's permission to join Lady Maud in Norfolk. What message shall I convey to her from you?'

'My dutiful respect,' I said and Lord Fitzvaughan gave a hoot of laughter.

'I thought you an honest man, physician, but I see you can dissemble with the craftiest of courtiers. Build up your strength for the journey while you rest here and may God be with you.' Then he gave me an ironic bow and left the room.

*****

Over the next two days I felt much revived and Thomas outlined the arrangements he had made to get me to St. Katharine's wharf where a trading vessel was waiting. He told me the Cardinal had summoned his minions from far and wide and had search parties scouring the river so it would be safer to travel through the City on horseback. Although there would be checkpoints to pass, the story he had concocted and the companions with whom I would ride would be fully convincing. I was lulled by his confidence but my mind kept straying to the prospect of my lonely exile and at length, as we sat over dinner in my small sanctuary, I broached the subject with him.

'Wouldn't you fancy the adventure of coming to Flanders with me? I'd be glad to have a friendly face beside me.'

Thomas stretched back in his chair and toyed with his knife, chasing fragments of broiled fish round the platter. 'I owe it to you,' he said, 'and any other time I'd gladly come.'

'You owe me nothing, you know that. We've looked out for each other and what you're doing now wipes out all debts.' I tried not to show the surprise and disappointment I felt at his obvious rejection of my offer.

'I reckoned you'd need someone with you so I've hired you a body servant,' he said brightly.

'No need for that. I've never had a servant before.' I must have sounded brusque.

Thomas stood up and tramped about the room before returning to his seat. 'It's Grizel, you see. I've got her with child and Dame Margery says we must marry. I've promised to go back to Greenwich as soon as you're at sea and go with Grizel to the church door.' He shrugged mournfully. 'It would be unkind to leave her so soon.'

'You villain!' I smiled and shook him by the hand. 'May the saints bless you both. Of course you can't come to Flanders. Why didn't you tell me before?'

'I thought you might suggest that I joined you – and I was tempted.'

'You mean you've only just made up your mind to stay with her?'

He gave a sheepish grin. 'Don't ever tell Grizel. My life wouldn't be worth living.'

*****

Next day as dusk was falling Thomas returned in company with Gaston de la Tour, whom I had not seen since I took up temporary residence in the Fitzvaughan chambers. He greeted me gruffly, wasting no time on apologies or recriminations, and told me we would be departing within the hour.

'You are to play the part of maid-servant to Lady Maud. The lady will ride pillion with me and you will share a saddle with your long-suffering friend here.'

I stared at him stupidly. 'I thought Lady Maud was in Norfolk.'

He gave me a pitying smirk. 'Lord Walter's wife is indeed secure on his demesne. It is another lady who will represent her. I hardly think it would be proper for Lady

283

Maud to involve herself in such an escapade, whatever other indiscretions she may commit.' I accepted the rebuke in silence and he continued. 'Lord Fitzvaughan's barge is at St. Katherine's wharf and we are escorting his wife there. That is our story. No one will question our departure from the palace for I am well known but, if we are interrogated as we near the City, I shall explain that we are conveying her ladyship to the barge for her return to Westminster. You will keep your hood forward and your head down and you will say nothing. Is that clear?'

'Perfectly,' I said. 'I am grateful.'

Gaston paused at the door before he left. 'You'd best make the acquaintance of the lady you serve, pretty maid. I'll send her in. Stay with them, Thomas, to make sure he doesn't ravish her.'

Thomas raised his eyebrows and tilted his head as if to encourage me to explain Gaston's parting gibe but I did not respond and soon afterwards the door opened once more.

She wore one of Lady Maud's dresses that I remembered from our days at Greenwich and she wore it regally, although it was a fraction short and showed a glimpse of her slim ankles. An enamelled brooch hung on her bodice and from her horned head-dress a long veil floated, which she held across her face. Only her eyes were visible but the merry light in those huge, brilliant irises could not be disguised and I caught my breath in amazement. Thomas shrank back against the far wall.

'Bess! Mistress Barber. I thought you were in Norfolk!'

'I was needed here.' She dropped her veil and looked me up and down. 'You are in a sad plight, Doctor Somers. Physician heal yourself is the appropriate phrase, I think.'

'I beg you not to put yourself in danger for my sake. I had no idea they had arranged to involve you in this business. I would never agree to it.'

'That's why you weren't told until we are ready to leave. You have no choice.' She took a step towards me and her voice softened. 'Besides I should never forgive myself if I failed to help you escape. For my own heart's ease, I need to know you are safe.'

I gasped at her poise and sincerity as she made this declaration. 'I don't deserve your attention. I have failed you miserably.'

She nodded briskly, shaking out the mantle she carried and Thomas stepped forward to spread it round her shoulders. 'I know,' she said, 'but we do not choose where our affections are engaged. Your name, by the way, will be Maria and you will obey my instructions instantly.'

I was aware of Thomas beaming at me in a tiresomely meaningful way but I ignored him. 'Yes, my lady,' I piped in as near an approximation of a falsetto as I could manage and I followed her from the room. My joy was so overwhelming that I would have flung myself into the river without hope of rescue if she had bidden me.

Chapter 26

As Gaston de la Tour had foretold, we passed through the gateway of the palace without challenge and were soon trotting along the well-trodden roadway towards the City, before striking across country to join the main thoroughfare from the west. We would enter London at Newgate, to make more credible our route to the Fitzvaughan barge at St. Katherine's wharf. At the beginning of our journey most other travellers were making in the opposite direction, anxious to reach the security of Westminster before nightfall, and Thomas and I were able to talk without being overheard while I sat sideways, clutching his waist awkwardly.

'Pull your mantle down, Maria. It's not seemly to display so much leg and, besides, your feet are too large to be believable. How did they find a lady's slipper to fit you?'

'They had to cut a pair and tie them on with ribbon – but it's not polite to refer to a maiden's attributes.' I dug him in the ribs and in retaliation he spurred the horse to go faster. 'Whoa! Go Slowly. I'll slide off.'

'Mind your manners then. You'll be able to dress as a man again when you're on board the *Fair Nell*. There's a chest in the cabin with shirts, a new black gown and hose; a fancy tunic too and a physician's cap to make you look the part. I rescued your instruments from Greenwich so you'll find them under the clothes with a purse of money from Gloucester to ease your passage.'

'The Duke? He knows about me?'

'Yes. Our Humphrey has retired to the Pleasance to lie doggo for a bit. He's got his foreign scholars and poets to amuse him and he won't miss sweet Eleanor as much as she'll miss him in her solitary prison. He's no friend of Suffolk's but he's content that we're working with the Earl to slip you across the sea. He gave Sir Hugh an audience to say so.'

Gaston and Bess were some way ahead of us and out of earshot as Thomas turned to glance at me with one of his annoying winks. 'He's a randy bastard, Sir Hugh. Soon as he met the winsome Mistress Barber he was after her.' He must have felt my grip tighten on his middle as I stiffened. 'It's all right; she told him where to go. You're a sneaky one, Doctor Somers, bedding the mistress and captivating the maid.'

I grunted and this time I was relieved that we quickened our pace. It was not simply embarrassment on my own account which I felt but because I had never told Thomas of Hugh de Grey's role in Alys's sad story. Fortunately he did not seem to have made the connection or he was sensible enough not to dwell on it. He reverted to the subject of the *Fair Nell,* which was to carry me over the Narrow Sea.

'I gather there's another fugitive being given carriage by her master so you'll be sharing the cabin. Best not to open your chest while he's around in case he's a cut-throat outlaw but the chances are he'll have fallen foul of the Cardinal so you'll have that in common.'

I opened my mouth to make a suitably sarcastic reply when we rounded a bend in the wall and the barrier of Newgate became visible, straddling the roadway. Our companions halted to wait for us, so we could approach the gate together, and we did so in silence.

The guards all wore the familiar Beaufort livery and were officious in their questioning but they responded courteously to Gaston's urbane explanations and treated Bess with proper respect. It looked hopeful that we would be permitted to enter the City without undue difficulty when the men's officer emerged from the lodge beside the gate and my heart quailed in terror.

'It's Sir Bertram Wenham,' I whispered to Thomas and, watching Bess pull the hood of her mantle forward, I realised with relief that she had also seen who it was. She had lived and served in the household at Dunmow for most

287

of her life and had been tiring maid to Sir Bertram's step-mother. Inevitably he must recognise her and then, if he peered at me as intently as he was regarding her, he must surely identify me. Bess gave no hint of the alarm she must feel but stared straight back into his enquiring eyes.

'My lady, have I had the honour of meeting you before?' he asked and I could not tell if his query was ironic.

'If you have been at court, sir, it is possible,' Bess said with admirable aplomb. 'My husband, Lord Fitzvaughan, has introduced me to many distinguished gentlemen but I fear I do not recollect them all.'

'Of course, apologies, my lady. I cannot place the circumstances.'

He sounded uncertain but he turned his attention away from her towards her servants and I drew my veil across my disfigured cheek as Thomas rode forward so the two horses stood flank to flank. I was acutely conscious of the fading yellow bruise round my right eye which I could not cover without rousing suspicion and Sir Bertram looked at me with curiosity. I lowered my gaze but he reached out a hand to lift my chin and as he did so Bess yelped.

'Oh! You useless fool, Maria! You have not fastened the pin of my brooch properly. It has come loose and jabbed my bosom.' Somehow the offending ornament was in her hand and, still holding it in her fist, she leaned over and boxed my ears with considerable force. I squeaked in not entirely assumed distress. 'I'll take the birch to you when we are home, you careless slut, and close your other eye.'

Whether it was the thought of Bess's pierced bosom or the exhibition of her violent fury, I will never know, but Sir Bertram stood back and waved us on our way. I heard one of the guards chuckle behind his hand as we passed. ''Best find a kinder mistress, lass, or your face'll be black and blue.'

We rode on in suppressed mirth until we were well along Cheapside when Gaston broke our silence. 'My lady, you were magnificent. I salute you.'

'How could he not have recognised you?'

Bess turned slightly towards me. 'I trusted he would see what he expected to see: a richly dressed noble lady, graciously supercilious to inferiors in positions of authority and vicious to her servants.'

'I am humbled by your wit and bravery,' I said and wished I could say more but Gaston and Thomas were listening intently and I did not wish to embarrass Bess in front of them. I was rewarded by a wistful smile as the horses drew apart once more and Gaston urged his mount ahead. Regardless of my impending departure, joy surged in my heart.

*****

We quickened our pace and swung round on the road behind the Tower, so lately my unhappy resting place, until St. Katherine's wharf lay in front of us and the masts of the *Fair Nell* were picked out by the moonlight against the blackness of the Thames. Despite the sadness of the parting I must endure, I felt a sudden burst of excitement. I had never been to sea but I remembered my father speaking of the motion of the waves and the awe of having water on every side, with the wind filling the sails and tossing the vessel on its way. Then I was brought back to earth when I realised there was another hurdle to be overcome before I could embark.

The soldiers guarding the jetty had been alerted to expect Lady Fitzvaughan, aware that her barge was waiting, alongside the *Fair Nell*, and there was no problem at all in permitting her party to board it; but the men had no power to allow a maid-servant of unproven identity onto the trading ship. 'She's about to sail,' the fellow in charge said, 'and passengers need to show their papers. For the last few days we've had special orders to be particular in enforcing the rules. Seems they're after some criminal who might flee the country. Can't make an exception, even for a gentlewoman.'

I shuddered at the thought that I might have to return to Westminster, with the almost certain prospect of capture and execution. Gaston was becoming impatient, obviously believing that he had fulfilled what his role in our drama required, and he signalled that Lady Fitzvaughan should enter the barge. We had dismounted and Bess came over and took my hands, as a lady might if she was comforting her trusted attendant. 'There must be some mistake,' she said. 'Thomas is to take the horses back by road. Perhaps you should stay with him until it is sorted out.'

We heard shouting on the ship and Thomas moved beside us. 'They'll miss the tide if they delay. Where the hell is that bloody brat?'

I had no idea what he was talking about but Gaston had taken Bess's arm to lead her away. 'If I am fortunate,' I said, 'I shall return. I hope in a year. I have no right to ask but perhaps...'

'I will wait.' Bess smiled radiantly. 'If you are not too long.' Then she kissed my cheek gently, as a lady might in parting from her trusted servant, and moved towards her barge.

I choked back tears while I heard movement on the ship's gangplank and, erupting down it ran a small and dishevelled urchin. 'Christ Almighty!' it shouted. 'I nearly missed you. That bloke on board were teaching me a trick or two with dice and I got hooked. Here, mate, this is me sister, Maria Tonks. Look, I've got her papers. We've off to join me Dad in Flanders. Quick now, or I'll get thrashed.' He thrust a document at the soldier and grabbed my hand.

'Rendell,' I piped. 'You naughty boy.'

The soldier glanced at the paper and indicated I could go aboard. I stepped onto the plank and Thomas held it steady for my dainty steps as I climbed. 'I told you I'd found a body servant for you,' he whispered.

*****

Rendell led me along the deck, past bundles of merchandise, heaps of canvas and coils of rope, threading our way between men hauling up the sails. He chattered incessantly although I was so distracted I hardly registered the meaning of his words.

'We're to call him Master Forrest. He says you'll get it. I never knew he were a dab hand at the gaming board. He's got loaded dice, the bugger. Here, down this ladder. That's the cabin.'

He threw open the door and I entered a small well-furnished room where a man stood with his back towards me, looking out of the high window towards the Surrey shore. There was a single lamp hanging on the wall but the man was in shadow although his crumpled soft bonnet was clear against the moonlight outside. It reminded me of something so painful that I caught my breath and the man turned.

'I'm so sorry, Harry,' said Geoffrey du Bois. 'I hated deceiving you but there seemed no other way. I was in great danger and I readily admit I was afraid.'

'But how...? What?' I stumbled over my questions.

'After Lady Anne died Beaufort's bully-boys visited me to persuade me to spy for him at the Pleasance. You remember I grew up in his household and loathed him. I refused but they came back with menaces against my life. It was just the time you wanted me to go with you to interview Bolingbroke and I didn't want to be involved. I couldn't explain. Then Bolingbroke accused me of being the Cardinal's informer and threatened violence unless I joined

291

his enterprise, as he called it. I met you outside his room just after our argument. My position was so intolerable I decided to stage my own disappearance, even though it meant trashing my treasured things, smashing the retorts, trampling the powders, spilling the potions, even pricking my finger to spill a little blood...' His voice tailed into silence.

I wanted to believe him but something did not fit and I forced myself to remember. 'There was a paper on your desk,' I said, 'it used words like those Lady Anne spoke when she was dying. It was the beginning of a prayer.'

'*Lord Jesus, think on me; By Care and Woe oppressed,*' Geoffrey recited. I'd taken it from John Home's room. I suspected he'd been recruited to spy for the Cardinal and I saw him copying the words in a letter he was writing. I knew enough of Beaufort's methods to work out that "woe" could stand for the Witch of Eye and I feared that "care" might refer to me so the message he was sending might result in my death. I thought I had destroyed the paper.'

'Not well enough. How did you get away without anyone knowing?'

'I didn't quite. Bolingbroke had set two men to watch my movements and when I reached the creek, where I'd hidden a rowing boat, I was attacked. I have some skill at wrestling and I think I broke the neck of one of them. He fell into the river. The other slashed my shoulder but I managed to wound him with my knife and I left him howling on the bank. I don't know how badly he was hurt.'

'He survived.' I understood now why Doctor Southwell had sewn the soldier's arm in such furtive circumstances; the wound was no accident. 'Oh, Geoffrey, I'm so pleased to find you safe. Where have you hidden since then?'

'My mother is kin to the Earl of Suffolk's wife. He gave me sanctuary and undertook to get me out of the country but then the sky fell in and you were all arrested. I asked to wait until we knew the outcome of your trial.'

'So now we can share our exile? I'm glad.'

'Here, this is all very well,' Rendell had been fidgeting by my side and he interrupted loudly,' but I've got these letters to deliver. Promised the chamberlain faithfully I would.' He produced a crumpled bundle from inside his tunic and held it out to me.

'Who are they from?'

'One's a commission from Gloucester to buy him some book.' The joy of having a task to carry out for Duke Humphrey was interrupted as Rendell continued. 'The others are from that Italian doctor.'

'Giovanni!'

'Yes. They're letters of introduction, he says, to his mates.'

'Mates? I didn't know Giovanni had mates in Flanders.'

'We ain't staying in Flanders. Not on your life! This is a proper adventure!'

'Quiet, Rendell,' Geoffrey said. Then he stretched out his arms and gave me a hug. 'You are very slow, master investigator. Isn't it obvious? It's what Giovanni always said you should do. We're going to Italy.'

HISTORICAL NOTE

Humphrey, Duke of Gloucester, his wife, Eleanor, the learned members of his immediate circle and the principal players in the plot which implicated the Duchess are all historical characters. The names of John Bolingbroke, Thomas Southwell, John Home, Mistress Jourdemayne, Gilbert Kymer, John Swanwych and Giovanni dei Signorelli are all to be found in the annals but there are few indications of their personalities. The interpretations given in the story are my own.

Harry Somers, his family, friends and closest supporters, together with the Wenhams and Fitzvaughans, are introduced for the first time in *The Devil's Stain*.

The author

Pamela Gordon read history at Oxford University, which she enjoyed, but, despite the more austere approaches of her learned tutors, she continued also to love the drama and romance of characters and plot in historical fiction. She tried her hand at such creative writing over the years but, due to the exigencies of her career, she mainly wrote committee reports, policy papers and occasional articles for publication. After working for the Greater London Council, she held the positions of Chief Executive of the London Borough of Hackney and then Chief Executive of the City of Sheffield. Later she held public appointments, including that of Electoral Commissioner when the Electoral Commission was established. Since 'retiring', she has been active in the voluntary sector and for three years chaired the national board of Relationships Scotland. Importantly, during the last few years, she has also been able to pursue her aim of writing historical fiction. *The Devil's Stain* is her first attempt at a story involving elements of a historical 'whodunnit'.

Pamela has published three short stories with historical backgrounds in anthologies published by the Borders Writers Forum (which she chaired for three years). She is currently President of the Melrose Literary Society and is also a member of the Melrose Historical and Archaeological Association.

The Devil's Stain is the first in a series featuring Harry Somers. *The Angel's Wing* will take his story to the next stage.

Other Mauve Square books:

For young readers:
Shadows from the Past series by Wendy Leighton-Porter. '*...Wendy has written a fantastic series of books (Shadows from the Past) filled with mystery, suspense, and adventure.*'
Firestorm Rising & ***Demons of the Dark*** by John Clewarth '*...Children learn that there are far more terrifying things in the universe than they ever learned at school, as a terrifying monster is awakened from a long hot sleep.*'

For young adults:
Golden Jaguar of the Sun (for young adults) by Oliver Eade. The first book of a trilogy by prize-winning author, Oliver Eade: a story of teenage love and its pitfalls and also a tale of adventure, fantasy and the merging of beliefs

For adults:
Crying Through the Wind by Iona Carroll. '*...Sensitively written novel of love, intrigue and hidden family secrets set in post-war Ireland... one of those books you can't put down from the very first paragraph...*'
Familiar Yet Far by Iona Carroll. Second novel in *The Story of Oisin Kelly* trilogy follows the young Irishman in *Crying Through the Wind* from Ireland and Edinburgh to Australia where the author was born and brought up.
The Manhattan Deception, The Minerva System, Seven Stars and ***Bomber Boys*** by Simon Leighton-Porter. '*...Fast paced thriller with a plot which twists and turns.*' 'I loved it...' 'As soon as I picked this book up I knew I wouldn't be able to put it down...'

Lightning Source UK Ltd.
Milton Keynes UK
UKOW06f1346030516

273484UK00001B/1/P